T0190936

RETROGRADE FLAW

BRIAN SHEA

RAQUEL BYRNES

SEVERN RIVER
PUBLISHING

Copyright © 2024 by Brian Shea and Raquel Byrnes.

All rights reserved.

No part of this book may be reproduced in any form or by any electronic or mechanical means, including information storage and retrieval systems, without written permission from the author, except for the use of brief quotations in a book review.

Severn River Publishing
www.SevernRiverBooks.com

This is a work of fiction. Names, characters, businesses, places, events and incidents are either the products of the author's imagination or used in a fictitious manner. Any resemblance to actual persons, living or dead, or actual events is purely coincidental.

ISBN: 978-1-64875-605-4 (Paperback)

ALSO BY THE AUTHORS

Memory Bank Thrillers
The Memory Bank
Retrograde Flaw
Aurora Fragment

BY BRIAN SHEA
Boston Crime Thrillers
The Nick Lawrence Series
Sterling Gray FBI Profiler Series
Lexi Mills Thrillers
Shepherd and Fox Thrillers
Booker Johnson Thrillers

To find out more, visit
severnriverbooks.com

For David. Always.

-R.B.

1

Seattle, Washington

The moon was a bright bulging eye staring down from a dark sky pocked with delivery drone lights. Bullet Black stood on the shore and shivered in the crystalline cold of the late February night. Waves, their white foam glowing in the moonlight, crashed softly in the distant dark of the beach. Icy mist hovered over the sand and made everything sticky. He checked his watch again and tried to ignore the worry squirming in his gut. His partner was late. He was never late. Bullet fiddled with his phone, thinking, then made a call. It went to voicemail, and he was leaving a message when head-lights slashed across the empty parking lot to his right. A car he hadn't seen before.

Bullet tensed. "Call me back," he whispered and ended the call. His hand slipped to the pistol at his waistband, but the car made a U-turn, pulling away. Shaking his head, he decided he needed to lay off the pot. It made him paranoid. Maybe just cut back a bit, he thought as his fingers searched the inner pocket of his vest for his emergency blunt. He sensed movement behind him and flinched. His partner stood much too close, the hood of his sweatshirt pulled down low over his forehead.

"Whoa!" Bullet reared back.

"Feeling jumpy?" The older man asked, amusement in his voice.

"I get right twitchy when my partner calls an emergency meet right before a big buy."

"I just want everything squared away." He circled around, shoved his hands in the pockets of the hoodie, and took a deep breath. "Can't be too careful."

"Hey, uh . . ." Bullet glanced at him sideways as he blew hot air into his hands. "What's with the beach? We always meet in town."

"I needed the wide-open space." He pulled something out of his pocket. A pair of telemetry specs from the kit. "And the dark. For research's sake."

"Research? We already put the heads-up display and the weapon through its paces. What's more to test? It's ready. When they see what it can do, they'll love it. Trust me." Bullet scanned the perimeter of the beach, his eyes going to the parking lot entrance, searching. He got that heaviness in the gut when something was off. "Is this what you wanted to talk about before the buy? Because you can relax, these guys are interested."

"One last test."

Bullet sighed. This guy's nerves were getting on *his* nerves. "I'm freezing my nuts off out here. I still gotta go and scope out the place—"

"Have you ever heard of the zombie ant fungus?"

Something in his voice made Bullet still. "Uh . . . what?"

"You've heard of this." He nodded, the corners of his eyes crinkling with mirth. "The Cordyceps fungi. There're hundreds of different varieties but they all do one thing. Be it to a beetle or an ant . . . they take over the will of the victim."

Bullet tried to seem chill, but his fingers found the dime dangling around his neck, a talisman to ward off evil. He forced a laugh. "You alright there, podna? You're talking a little crazy right now."

"Mmm, sounds crazy, but it's true. You see the spores take over the brain of the insect and direct it to do very specific things. Like bite onto a leaf and not let go while the fungus grows its spores inside it."

"Dude." Bullet looked at him, disgusted. "Where are you going with this shit?"

"Hang in there," he said and put a finger up in front of Bullet's face.

"The other thing it does is that it makes sure the insect dies *just* outside the ant colony. To draw in more victims."

"What are you talking about—" the words died on Bullets lips as he felt the knife slip into his chest. So fast. So sharp. It felt like a punch. His gaze lifted to his partner, who held the blade between them. He stared serenely into Bullet's eyes as if nothing were wrong. Bullet staggered back, shock and confusion blaring in his brain. "W-What are you doing, man? We had a deal!"

Hand to his gut, Bullet tried to stop the blood seeping from the stab wound as he stumbled backward. His partner lunged again, landing another blow, and Bullet fell to his knees on the sand, fear ripping through his mind as the pain hit. He coughed, blood splattering out of his lips. His legs went numb, and he hoped it was the cold. "But . . . Ça c'est bon. It's all good."

"Good for me. Not so much for you." He donned a thin metal and glass headset, and the surface of the lens lit up with a bright orange grid. Bullet gasped. He'd worn those same specs when they did a test run a week before at a quarry. The heads-up display had flashed on and hovered over the dark gravel as the program streamed readings for temperature, windspeed, rotation, light saturation, down the side of his vision. And when Bullet had slipped his finger to the trigger, his touch launched a targeting grid. Outlines in bright white encased slabs of rock, excavators, and mining equipment in rapid succession. Analyzing and discarding each one until it locked on their drone target. It didn't miss once. Bullet let out a desperate whine and scrambled on his hands and knees across the sand to one of the broken cement blocks. His partner followed and stood in the light of the street level lamps, watching as Bullet struggled to his feet. Fury roared through him as he screamed, "You wouldn't have been able to make this deal without me!"

"Plans change."

"Plans change?" Bullet repeated. "You don't make changes to plans with these people! Have you lost your mind? They'll kill us both."

He laughed. "I don't think you'll have to worry about them killing you, Bullet. Besides. I'm not the one changing anything. I never met them, remember? Everything goes through you. Those were your terms." He held up a phone and played a video recording. "And that's exactly what you did."

Bullet didn't understand what he was seeing, and his gaze shot to his partner's. "How did you do that?"

"No matter, it's all moot now. You have another job to do."

Bullet tried to laugh but it came out in a gurgle, and he spit blood onto the sand. "Job?"

The diagnostic graphic of the round flashed on the telemetry lens, making Bullet freeze. It was armed. He raised the weapon, pointed it at Bullet's forehead, and said, "Run."

Bullet hesitated for a split second, then turned and ran. He scrambled along the beach, trying to get away. His motorcycle boots sinking into the sand, belt chains clinking along the empty shore. Wheezing breaths buffeted out of him as he gasped.

"You can't do this!" Bullet stumbled, his knees giving a little with each step, until he was hunching along the rocks and cement like a goblin. His partner fired and Bullet flinched, diving to the sand, covering his head with hands warm with his own blood. Heart ramming painfully, he sobbed, "My son. I need to get back to my s-son!"

The round tore across the inky black of night, crackling through the air. It flew past Bullet, singeing his hair as the targeting laser's green flashes painted the terrain. He rose, quaking as the blinking lights disappeared in the mist beyond. He spun, ran toward the shore, and clawed his way over the cement blocks, trying to get to the water. He pulled his T-shirt collar over his mouth and nose and chanced a glance back. The growing glow of the round returning, its lights pulsing in the fog, sent terror spiking through him. Giving him strength. He trudged through the lapping waves trying to get deeper, hoping to evade the program's gait detection.

But it was already too late. As the high-pitched scream of the round tore a hole in the stillness of the night, dread coursed through Bullet's veins. He spun. His mouth opened wide, a scream choking inside his throat, a moment before he was blown apart.

2

Belltown, Downtown Seattle
6 a.m.

Detective Morgan Reed walked with a deliberate limp as he shuffled down the decrepit sidewalk past a liquor store with bars on the windows. When he passed the door to a smoke shop, he triggered a hologram of a lottery advertisement that spewed flickering dollar bills and scratch-off cards toward his face. They disappeared a moment after most people flinched. It started to loop again as Reed moved on. Belltown had undergone gentrification, but signs of its roots as a low-rent industrial district were everywhere. As a kid growing up there, he'd walk to the downtown touristy area in the summers and watch the tourists pose for pictures outside of the Pike Place Market sign or record the fish-throwing mongers as they tossed toddler-sized halibut back and forth.

Reed trudged through the trash and dead leaves that had flooded up from the clogged gutters. He saw a quarter lying in the center, picked it up, and dropped it in his pocket before moving on. Behind the strip mall, a small tent city emerged, with portable fire rings burning brightly against the dawning sky as the unhoused woke to scratch out a breakfast. Reed wove in and out of clusters of people talking and hugging themselves against the frigid wind that whipped their flimsy shelters. An air of wariness had settled on the camp over the past two days as news of another victim spread. Then an influx of people from a recently "relocated" camp a few streets brought many unfamiliar faces. The turmoil made his presence less noticeable as well as a killer's. Several days' worth of dirt and grime caked the dark, shaggy curls of Reed's full beard as he struggled to push the case forward. He smelled bad. That much he knew.

The earpiece hidden by his watch cap clicked and his partner's amused voice sounded in Reed's ear.

"You look like a Yeti in a trench coat," Nat chuckled.

"Detective De La Cruz, you are a stone-cold cheater." Reed grinned behind his dirty coat collar and glanced at the surveillance van a block down the street. "No way that coin toss was valid."

"Hey, you're the man with the plan."

Reed squinted at the sky. The rising sun brushed pale gold on the undersides of dark gray clouds. They warned of the coming snow. "We're short on time. If things get worse out here, they're all going to scatter, and he'll be gone with the wind. Some people are already packing. They're scared."

"Well, if you're right and he's one of them, I don't want him to start offing people at shelters, too."

"I'm right and he *is* hunting here. But he's not one of them. Remember what the Kramer sisters said about him." Reed shuffled past a pawn shop and nodded at the counterman.

He heard her typing in the background. A transfer from cybercrime, Nat's custom keyboard had a strange, muffled sound. "I know you've got a soft spot for those old ladies, but they're not exactly giving us a clear picture. 'Smells clean' and 'he had a hard chest' are pretty vague. And both of those old biddies wear glasses so thick they can start a fire if they stare at their feet too long."

Reed grinned at that. "I walked them through their encounter with the killer again last night. They heard their friend cry out, they hurried toward his space, and someone rushing away knocked both of them to the ground as he ran past. They're solid. Besides, they were both schoolteachers back in the day. Watching that many kids all at once, you learn to notice things in the midst of chaos."

"I know, but apart from just sniff testing everyone for soap . . ."

"Karina clarified it was a 'chemical' scent. They said he smelled like he worked with solvents or cleaners. She said it was a very distinct odor. Sharp."

"And the hard chest? I need more than that."

"A fit guy would likely be young, right?" Reed asked. "Or new to the streets. Because life out here doesn't keep the body strong. Oh, and Anna said he had, 'impeccable skin.'"

"So ugly people can't be killers?" Nat snapped her gum as she worked, and it made Reed's eye twitch.

"Out here in this wind my skin is chapped. Cracked. Even sunburnt. And it's only been days."

"Hmm, good point," Nat said. "What else? I need more input to work your theory."

"You don't buy it, yet?"

"Meh," Nat said with a hint of her father's Bronx accent. "You're good, but data delivers in court. Juries get charts. Your creepily accurate gut . . . not so much."

"Gotcha." Reed rounded the corner and strolled into the alley, his gaze drifting from person to person as he shuffled along. It was drizzling and grayed out figures moved through the misty underpass like lonely ghosts caught between the living and the dead. A group of people stood crowded around a white RV that had parked along the curb. It had a red cross painted on the side that looked hand drawn and no other identification. So far, he'd seen churches bring sandwiches, another group brought blankets and early Valentine's candy. All of them showed up in civilian busses and vans.

Nat snapped her gum again. "I'm just saying it could also be some rando walking into these camps. They're out in the open."

"I haven't seen even a thread of that weird rope the killer uses. Nothing around here even comes close. Also, he leaves no fingerprints. No physical evidence at all. And no one hears anything?"

"I mean it's winter. Who doesn't have gloves on right now?"

Reed glanced at the bare hands of those around him. "You'd be surprised. They're a hot commodity out here. Worth a lot for trades."

"Okay, I'll feed the Kramer twins' interview wording into Cybercrime's language model and see what it spits out, but off the top of my head I'm thinking what . . . metal shop, a fabrication place, maybe a hospital janitor because that stuff they used to disinfect the morgue is so astringent. Every time I go in there—"

Reed stopped walking midstride and turned back toward the group of people. He'd only been on the streets for four days. Not long enough to see patterns. "What services are supposed to be out here? They have to clear it with the city, right?"

"Give me a minute," Nat's keyboard clicked in the background. She said something to one of her cybercrime techs in the van with her and then came back. "Okay, we've got the dental van due this week and I've got a local public kitchen delivering soup and bread tomorrow."

"Who's parked out front right now?" Reed worked his way through the crowd, his eyes on the guy in front with a clipboard. Blue scrubs, a bandana tied over his hair pirate style, no identifying credentials on a lanyard. He was asking for social security numbers.

"No one's supposed to be there officially but there's no law against being charitable."

"There's a guy taking down information and then just handing out water bottles here," Reed said as he pushed through the front of the crowd. "He's giving off strange vibes."

"Weird how? Describe him." She snapped her fingers at someone, and her voice got muffled, then was back. "We're tasking some cameras to get a visual."

"Young. Strong." The orderly turned and locked eyes with Reed. He wore surgical gloves. "Leaves no trace." Reed pulled his badge out of his ratty shirt by the chain, hand slipping to his hip holster. A plastic badge on the orderly's scrubs read, Gary. Reed called out, "Gary, you got a second?"

The orderly tensed, his gaze dropping to the shiny badge. A snarl curled up on the guy's face before he shoved a mom and her kid into Reed's path before taking off in a dead sprint.

"He's rabbiting," Reed shouted. He chased him down the sidewalk dodging carts and sleeping bodies, throwing off the dirty layers of clothes as he went. Trench. Army coat. Reaching for his weapon. "He's heading for the rec center."

Nat and three other tech cops poured out of the surveillance van, attempting to head off the runner. Reed pushed himself, catching up fast, tackling Gary before he ran into the crowded center. They hit a brochure stand and the pamphlets when flying as they fought on the ground. Nat came in with backup and they wrestled the swearing orderly into cuffs. Nat searched his pockets.

"Well look at this." She held up a length of coiled orange rope. "How much you wanna bet this matches the fiber we found on one of the victims?"

"Remember Fred?" Reed asked, getting into Gary's face. "The last person you strangled?"

Gary glared at him but couldn't help the sliver of a smirk that curled his lip. "I don't know what you're talking about."

"Fred had hair tangled between his fingers. Did he reach back for you while you pulled the rope tighter. Maybe in the heat of the moment you didn't feel the sting of a dozen hairs with intact roots getting ripped out of your skull?" Reed snapped, and the anger in Gary's eyes flashed to worry. Reed yanked the pirate bandana off Gary's head and shook it between them. "He wasn't as helpless a target as you thought."

"Lawyer!" Gary screamed as two of the cybercrime cops walked him out to the squad car. "This is entrapment. I want a lawyer!"

"That's number four if you're counting cases," Nat said, watching them go. All five feet five inches of her was bundled in the largest black puffy coat Reed had ever seen. Her long dark hair was pulled back in a soft bun and her heart shaped face had a blush of color from the frosty air. "Closing a murder case on your last day of probation is cause for celebration. How about I do the paperwork and you go and take a shower."

Reed sniffed his armpit. "Do I offend?"

"My eyes are watering," she said. "I think you went a little too method on this one."

The detective next to Nat nodded in agreement.

Reed put his hands up in surrender and grinned. "Fine. Let's meet at Rampart in an hour. And you're both buying me a steak for that one."

"Its six in the morning, Reed."

"A stack of pancakes then," he said over his shoulder as he walked away. "Extra bacon."

Twenty minutes later, Reed was showered and dressed and rooting around in his gym bag for his car keys when one of those hot, sharp pains stabbed through his shoulder. He sucked in his breath and sank to the bench between the lockers, rubbing at the scar underneath his collar bone. A weaponized drone in a previous case had shot him through the back and the round had gone right through his collar bone. Surgery to repair the damage was nearly healed but the weeks of physical therapy hadn't stopped it from aching when it was cold. At least the scar over his eye was faring better. A gift from a drugged-out teen, the hair-thin line ran from just above his left eyebrow to just below his eye. Nat said it was barely visible, but Reed thought it made him look like he'd once had a cyborg eye.

A clang in the shower room pulled his gaze. Reed stilled. Steam from his shower still lingered, drifting over the white tiles of the floor like fog. A memory of rain flashed behind his eyes. Not his memory, but the panic surged through Reed's chest just the same and then he was sinking into the waters of the ravine, his head throbbing. The water crept toward him sideways, from the wall, until it had filled the room and pooled up around his face, almost to his lips. And then he was floating on his back staring at the pipes when the ceiling of the locker room blew apart like smoke. A vast, onyx sky bore down on him. There had been a storm that day and lightning streaked across the sky. The temperature plummeted and then he was Firash, dying in the water. Bubbles screaming out of his throat as Reed looked up at himself through the surface of the rushing river—

He jerked out of the foreign memory, coughing out nonexistent water, the bitter taste of adrenaline in his mouth. He shot to his feet, panting. Back in the station, surrounded by concrete and steel. Dry. Alive. Himself.

"I'm okay. I'm okay." His voice barely a whisper as he worked to slow his breath, pushing back the intrusive memories he'd injected months ago from a dying man. They were still unpredictable. Overtaking him without notice. Nat would figure out how bad it was soon. His phone trilled in his locker, and he pulled it out. It had been days since he left it there and the missed calls and messages had piled up. A tomorrow problem, Reed decided. He went to toss his phone in his bag, but a name caught his eye. A familiar one. From another life ago. A chapter he'd rather rip out and burn to ashes. He played the message, and his gut pulled into knots as he listened.

"Hey, Morgan. Uh, it's me, Dontae. I know we haven't spoken in years, but umm, I did something that's gonna . . . it's gonna be bad. I'm sorry." Dontae sniffed once, his voice cracking. *"Look, it was the only move I had, but things are taking a turn, Morgan. I never meant for you or anyone else to get involved and I know I don't deserve it, but I got no one else to call. I need your help, man. Something bad is going down. I can feel it. I need to talk to you, and I mean as soon as possible. So please. For old times' sake, call me back."*

Reed did, but it went straight to voicemail. He checked the date of the message. Yesterday. Reed called Dontae five more times and sent a text before he sat staring at his phone. What kind of trouble makes you reach out from the past after decades of silence? To a cop no less. The worst kind of scum in Dontae's eyes.

His phone buzzed in his palm and Nat's number came up.

"I'm on my way to Rampart," Reed answered. He headed for the door.

"That's on hold," Nat said. "We got pulled into another case."

Reed stopped walking. The weight of exhaustion crept through his bones. "You've got to be kidding. I just got off a four-day undercover—"

"A body dropped, and the detective here thinks you know either the victim or the killer," Nat cut across him. "You didn't pick up, so they called me."

"What? Why do they think that?"

"Because someone left you a message with the desk sergeant. They said there was something you needed to take care of at Matthew's Beach."

"Did they leave a name?"

"They did. On the wall near the body, they found at Matthew's Beach."

"What?" Reed strode out into the misty, gray morning.

"Someone wrote your name in the victim's blood."

3

Matthew's Beach Park, Lake Washington

Brown, frosty grass covered the hilly knolls that ran from the parking lot of the public lake shore to the water. Usually green and peppered with picnicking families, Matthew's Beach Park was a favorite among locals who shied away from the larger touristy spots. Reed had come here often as a kid. They had lifeguards in the summer, boats, and little food shops were open and cheap. He'd learned to draw while sitting next to his mother on the grass where a play structure now stood. It looked just like it had back then, only winter had taken its toll. Graying out the vibrant colors of trees and shrubs. Even the play structure looked muted. An earthly odor of decay and mud—lake stink, they used to call it—drifted to him from across calm waters.

Some sort of event was in full swing. Winter themed tablecloths and streamers decorated the eating area. A small crowd gathered around a grill. Their laughter floated along the breeze bringing with it the scent of sausage links and pancakes. Reed's stomach growled. At nearly eight thirty, it was a melancholy morning. Heavy with mist. The rising sun mottled behind thick, brooding clouds.

"Okay two things happened," Nat said as she sipped coffee from a disposable cup while they walked. She'd brought him one and it tasted like consciousness. "One, someone left a message for you last night around midnight with the desk sergeant. A phone call that said that you had 'something to take care of' at Matthew's Beach Park. No name. Didn't seem urgent and you were still under, so as per protocol, it wasn't relayed until we'd closed the sting."

Okay," Reed prompted. Dontae's call had been yesterday as well, and he wondered if it was from him. "And the second thing?"

"Patrol found a body with your name above it." She nodded to the crowd making breakfast. "This polar bear ice water thing needed additional patrol because last year the majority of the 'swimmers' were drunk by seven thirty a.m. They had a couple of probies walking the sand and checking the area for celebrants who might need medical care. One of the new guys found the body and called it in. To their credit they didn't set the whole winter festival crowd into a panic. The last thing we need is looky-loos tangled up in this. That's therapy they don't need to pay for."

"This park isn't popular. It's not even in most travel guides," Reed said, and his words came out with puffs of vapor as they cut across the lawn and headed for a side road. Stands of towering pines encroached on the beach. "I haven't been here in decades."

"I gotta get out more." Nat shook her head. "You know, I've been in Seattle since before college, and I have never been here."

"Locals like it that way."

"If the killer chose this place. You think he could be a local?"

"Maybe."

"And it's convenient." She checked her watch. "It's maybe twenty-five minutes from the city center."

"A peaceful place. Quiet." Reed checked his phone for messages. None.

"Yeah, unless a bunch of lunatics throw a mid-winter swim party." She nodded toward a row of food trucks and groups of people erecting tents just off the parking lot area. Bright orange cones cordoned off a portion of the sidewalk. "Apparently the Polar Break Festival goes till noon."

"Right. They moved it from New Years because of that ice storm." Generators hummed in the background and standing heaters dotted the gray morning with brilliant orange light. They passed a group of people dressed head to toe in long fleece jackets as they wrestled to get a banner up on the dais. "It's tradition. To stave off the winter cabin fever."

"You see the ambulances? They know running into that icy lake can literally stop their heart and yet . . ."

Reed grinned at her irritation. "But you get free donuts and a T-shirt."

Nat rolled her eyes. "We've got a few patrol guys out there taking statements, but the event goers were all too busy cheering on their fellow man to brave hypothermia to see anything."

"I want to talk with them myself," Reed said. "When we're done."

A copse of looming cedars butted up against the shore cutting off the road from the crime scene and light from the halogens flickered between the branches as he followed Nat through. A group of people stood on the other side of a large piece of broken cement partially buried on the shore. Part of an erosion repair project, it looked like the city had broken apart old sidewalks and dumped them on the sand. The ME, Jake Sanders, and his technician set up the LiDAR robot for the 360-degree scan of the scene. Another detective, familiar in a distant sort of way, stood off to the side, tapping on a digital tablet. He looked over when Reed passed, sized him up, and went back to his work without a word.

That was interesting, Reed thought. Could be rumors of his suspension for "health reasons," could be something else. He'd had weird responses to the fallout from the Neurogen case. Reed kept the guy in his peripheral as he followed Nat.

"Man, I hope you don't know this victim," Nat said as they ducked under the crime tape fastened to one of the rebars sticking out of the cement chunk. A camera drone zipped around her for another angle to photograph the body and she batted at it with her palm. "He's mangled."

Reed rounded the tip of the cement piece, and the scene came into view. A body, a man in his mid-thirties, was lashed to one of the pieces of sidewalk with chains that crisscrossed his chest. Nat offered Reed disposable gloves and he pulled them on as he eyed the body. The victim was lying on his side partly buried in the sand of the lake shore. He drifted with the subtle wave breaks, bumping against the concrete behind him. His face was in the water and dark hair obscured his features. Reed moved closer and shone his mini flashlight on the body. A leather vest with patches and insignias hung off the man's chest, part of it ripped and dangling into the water. Reed moved it with the light. "He has a motorcycle cut. And prison ink."

"I'll run them," Nat said, snapping pictures of the vest and tattoos with her phone.

A jagged chunk was missing from the torso as if bitten off and the enormous wound glistened in the artificial light. Reed shook his head in disbelief. "Is that a shark bite?"

"It got me at first, too," Sanders said with a chuckle. "It certainly looks like one, but no." Dr. Sanders was a runner, generous with his time, and a good friend of Reed's. He kept his dark natural hair trimmed tight to the scalp. Sanders held a pen out to the wound. "This tissue is ruptured. And there are burns all the way through the dermal layers."

Reed stepped back. "Are we talking explosion?"

"We're seeing the kind of blunt force injury we'd get from tremendous pressure," Sanders nodded to the victim's awkwardly bent arm. "He's practically a rag doll."

"Pressure." Reed considered the corpse. There were no burns on the extremities. The clothing was ragged and had char, but only near the wound. "If he was near the explosion, we'd see more overall damage, right? Shrapnel distributed evenly outward?"

Sanders nodded. "Yes. If he was next to the explosion."

"What about in it?" Nat asked. "Like a car bomb."

"We'd see almost no body past the torso and there's usually extensive fire damage," Sanders said. "This looks—" He shook his head.

"What?" Reed asked. "However nuts you think it is."

"It's almost like he *swallowed* the bomb," Sanders said.

Reed looked at him for a moment. "Close damage. Precision damage."

Sanders shrugged. "I won't know until I get him on my table, but yes. Looking at him, the damage pattern is rather odd."

Reed nodded. He slapped his friend lightly on the shoulder as he moved away. "Not nuts. But scary if it's true." He left them by the body and strode a few feet away keeping his gaze on the edge of the sand. "If he'd been killed down here, we'd see evidence, wouldn't we? A blast radius, melted sand, shrapnel, something related to the manner of death."

"Except, we're not finding anything like that." Nat gestured down the beach at the patrol cops walking a grid. "No sign of any components, switches, not even a singed rock. We can get divers. Maybe he was killed on a boat and floated to shore."

Sanders shook his head. "He was in the water long enough to obscure time of death, but not enough for the lake to have helped with decay. And with all the activity up the way, you'd think someone would've seen something. Explosions are pretty noticeable."

"Let's get a canine up here to sweep the whole area for residue." Reed walked to the retaining wall between the beach and the public restrooms. The ice plant and dirt leading up to the street looked undisturbed. "And send someone to take a good look up there by the bathroom building and along the street, just to be sure. Let's also get a canine to walk the water's edge."

He started back down the stretch of sand and Nat followed him. "A sniffer dog. You're thinking he ran into the water? He'd know he'd freeze to death."

"The physiology of survival is a wild thing," Reed said. "And for the record. I have no idea what happened yet. But I do know there's not enough blood over there." Something about the chains bothered Reed. Like a bad dream you couldn't remember but still felt. "With that kind of wound, the sand would be saturated if he was killed here. There are no waves to speak of. No rising tide. If he hasn't been here that long . . . where is all the blood? Where's the rest of him, as a matter of fact? Did someone take off with all that tissue?"

Almost thirty yards down Reed picked up dark sand in the morning light. He crouched down and picked some up, moving it between his gloved fingers. Still wet, a tinge of pink stained his disposable gloves. "I think the victim died here and was dragged to the grouping of cement blocks back there." Reed stood, looked back at the crime scene. Faint ruts in the wet sand could be drag marks. "We need to cordon this area off."

"This is familiar." Nat snapped her fingers as they were walking back. "The guy's liver is gone, right? He's chained to a rock. Didn't a Greek god die like that or something?"

"A Titan," Reed muttered, distracted as he approached the scene. It echoed something long forgotten from his own past. "Prometheus. He was punished for giving technology to man."

"I wonder what *this* guy did. This doesn't feel like a gang hit to me."

Reed reached for the victim's head, tilted it out of the water, and bile rose up in his throat at the familiar face. *Dontae.* Reed stared at his old friend and the fear and anger of that night came blazing back. Blood washing from his palms in the rain. The gnash of teeth. The clang of a chain against a metal canoe. He dropped the head, backing up.

"Hey," Nat glanced at him a moment before he slammed a blank expression down. "Something wrong?"

Reed avoided her gaze. "Did we get an ID?"

She shook her head. "No phone either but look at this." Nat showed him close up photos on her phone and then pinched to zoom in even further until shards of pointed metal came into focus. They were buried deep in the flesh. "See those shiny bits?"

"Shrapnel." Reed tilted his head to look. "Are those wires?"

"We don't know yet—" Sanders tried.

"They're wires," Nat said over him, her eyes lighting up. "But the scale, Reed. Astronomically small compared to most explosives."

Reed spotted the dime with a hole dangling from a string around Dontae's neck. A dark feeling knotted his gut, and Reed took another step back from the body, scanning the concrete. "And my name?"

"There," Nat pointed to the side retaining wall about ten feet away.

In Memory of Detective Morgan Reed, was emblazoned with blood on the smooth cement surface. It had dripped with the moist air and the "R" in his name ran down to the sand like a horror movie title. Situated at an angle to the victim, Reed had no choice but to view Dontae's body if he wanted to see the name. It was a deliberate choice. A taunting one. Designed to cause the most distress. This guy knew him. Somehow knew of his past with Dontae. The thought sent a sliver of dread through Reed's chest. No one could possibly know what happened.

"Not exactly your name in lights," Nat said as she walked over. "And 'in memory' is a definite threat. You say that about dead people."

"He's . . . melodramatic," Reed muttered taking a closer look at the writing. It was thick. Like it had been done with a rag and Reed searched the ground. He found a matted bandana and motioned for one of Sander's techs. He photographed it before Reed picked it up and it unfolded. White stars on a black background.

The detective with the tablet looked up. "That's Kindred colors."

Reed nodded and shoved it in the baggie the tech offered. "Run the DNA. On both the wall and the bandana. And look for prints. Maybe the killer left one while he was writing."

"Yeah." Nat nodded, already on her tablet.

The other detective slipped into Reed's peripheral.

"How well did you know the victim?" He asked as he walked over. Hands in his pockets, he stared Reed down as he approached. "Or is it the killer you're buddies with? I can never keep them straight."

Reed remembered where he knew Parker from. He relaxed his stance, feigning ignorance. "We have a problem?"

"We do," Parker said. "I don't like the company you keep. They get people hurt."

He ignored the aggression. "You look familiar. White Collar, right?"

"Organized Crime," Parker looked insulted. "I worked a sting with you in Narcotics."

Reed smiled. "Doesn't ring a bell, but thanks for your help, man."

"What the hell are you talking about?"

Parker wore his red hair in a regulation cut, had a voice like a cigar-smoking card shark, and he used his middle finger to point. Reed found him ridiculous in a cartoonish kind of way. He took in the tension, the way Parker rolled his shoulder forward subconsciously, the change in his breathing.

Reed gave Parker his back, crouching down to view Dontae's body. There was a slit, cleaned with the lake water, in his upper abdomen. Another further down. He'd been stabbed as well. Reed sat back on his haunches and met his friend's empty gaze. "You don't have to worry about who I count as friends, Parker."

"Clearly you've worked together," Nat said, eyeing them both. "So, let's just do that."

Parker gestured at Reed's chest. "I got pulled to work on one of his cases—"

"Let me guess, things went south?" She clicked her tongue and smirked. "You gotta ride it out. Like you're on a broken rollercoaster that's on fire."

"We made the collar," Reed said evenly. His gaze went to the growing crowd near the Polar Break dais as families arrived for the games and food.

"By executing the most unhinged version of a sting possible,' Parker spat.

"I read your complaint, thanks."

Parker gasped. "Screw you! You *do* remember me!"

Reed shrugged. "Why are you here, anyway?"

"He thinks it's gang related." Nat made a speak up motion with her hand. "Tell him."

Parker frowned at Reed but started talking. "We've been seeing more of those southern motorcycle gangs encroaching on Portland and Seattle. They're moving drugs, people, and weapons. We just busted a pretty sophisticated racket out of Bellevue last month." Parker pointed to the chains crisscrossing Dontae's body. "This, lashing of the victim and the writing in the blood is new, but not out of the realm of what they'd do."

"Don't they usually just shoot each other?" Nat asked.

"Oh, they're getting creative," Parker said. "Especially with this territory issue over in Belltown."

"There's creative and there's psychotic," Nat muttered, eyeing the body.

Reed shook his head, bothered. "This isn't our precinct, Nat. So why dump him here? If someone wanted me specifically, why choose a place a half-hour out of my jurisdiction?"

"Not unless the place itself is significant." She looked up at him. "Is it? Significant, I mean?"

"I can't think of anything. I came here as a kid, but so did most of SPD if they grew up local." Reed scratched at the scar over his brow. "I made my first arrest here."

"That's weird," Nat said, but flashing lights in the distance pulled her gaze.

Their boss, Lieutenant Montigliano, pulled into the parking lot. Reed had called him "Tig" back when they were partners. They'd butted heads in an earlier case and things were still icy. Seeing Reed's name over a corpse wasn't going to help matters.

"You didn't answer my question, Detective Reed," Parker said. His gaze was intense. Hostile. "Do you know the victim? Yes, or no?"

Reed could feel Nat's eyes on him, and he glanced at his name on the cement. It looked even darker red as the sun began to burn the morning fog away. Dontae's terrified shout echoed in Reed's head from long ago.

Morgan, stop him!

Reed shook his head. "No. I don't know him."

4

Tig arrived at the scene and talked with Parker first, since he practically ran to meet him. Then Tig pulled Reed aside and grilled him about why he thought a lunatic might write his name in blood and then call the station. Reed answered truthfully. He told Tig that he had no idea who would do that to someone or why. His former partner turned boss shoved his hands in his pockets and stared out at the lake.

"You can't land a normal murder? You have to have this dramatic shit happening again?" He'd let his gray hair grow out a bit from the high and tight cut, but his eyes still held that East Coast irritation that Reed found amusing. "What's going on with you?"

"We don't even know if the caller and the killer are the same person. I have to check the time of death with the ME," Reed said as they walked together to the parking lot. "I'll see when the call was. Nat said she's going to pull the number."

"You're on the level?" Tig asked, watching Reed. "You don't know what's going on?"

"I know someone wanted to send me a message. I just don't know what it means yet."

"The optics, the writing in blood," Tig pulled off his glasses and rubbed his eyes with the back of his hand. "It's going to be a circus when this gets out so tie this one off fast, will you?"

"I will. If I ever get to leave the scene." Reed nodded to Detective Parker who stood off to the side watching the forensics team. "That guy's going to be a problem."

"He definitely has a problem with *you*."

"That was in the past. Plus, it's a completely irrational reaction."

"Not to him. He ended up on medical leave and needed physical therapy."

"For getting shot in the ass?" Reed looked at him askance.

"There was muscle and stuff involved," Tig said. He held up his hand at Reed's argument. "It's his jurisdiction. He wants in. You're working with him. I'll clear it with his lieutenant."

Reed let his head fall back and he stared at the dark clouds. "Who's in charge?"

"You for now. You're the ranking detective." Tig held up a gnarled finger. "For now."

Tig went off to talk with Parker whose body language and glance at Reed said it all. Nobody was happy but that's what was happening.

Twenty minutes later, Reed sat in his unmarked car and sketched the crime scene from memory into his leatherbound notebook. He ran the tip of his pen over and over the large links of the chains, the rough edges of the cement, and thought about Dontae. What would he have said in that call had Reed been able to take it? What trouble did he pull Reed into? A knock at his window made him jerk and he looked up to see Nat jiggling the handle. He unlocked it and she slipped into his passenger seat.

"So, Parker just announced he's heading over to ask homeowners in the nearby development to check their doorbell and house cameras for any cars." She shrugged. "What is with that guy?"

"I irritate him to no end," Reed said and grinned at her. "Sound familiar?"

"Extremely," she said, smiling faintly. She caught Reed checking the rearview. "Are you still being followed by Danzig's guys?"

Reed hesitated for a moment but nodded. "I see them when I'm out jogging. Way behind but there. There are cars that drive by slowly at night or early morning. The crunch of their tires on the street outside my window wakes me up."

"You have to tell the lieutenant. I know he told you to steer clear of Danzig because of his connections, but this guy is not letting up."

"Can't prove it's him. The cars have no plates."

"Oh, come on. Danzig all but threatened you. You blew a trillion-dollar deal for him. He's probably got a dartboard with your face on it."

Reed rubbed his sore shoulder. Rain was coming, he thought. "I've got too much on my plate right now to worry about what some billionaire thinks he's doing."

"Everett Danzig isn't just rich, he's feared. For good reason. Ask Congresswoman Joshi if you should be concerned. Oh wait, you can't."

The stress in her voice made him look away. He hated that she was tangled up with Danzig at all. He nodded. "I get it. I'll be careful."

Nat waited for a beat and then, "Hey, I thought you wanted to talk to the Polar Break people yourself?"

"I'm just writing down my thoughts first." Reed closed his notebook and turned in his seat. Nat had only been his partner since November when she'd transferred from Cybercrime. She was younger than him, green. But not a newbie. And because of what those short months had put them through, she knew him. And she sensed something was up. "You're stalking me now? I thought you wanted to go with the body and Sanders to the morgue. Don't you have cyber bits to inspect?"

"Yeah . . ." She tapped on her tablet. Tiny drops of mist had settled on her lashes. "I saw your reaction to the body."

"What reaction? It was a grotesque scene."

"Please. You're a Homicide Detective First Grade, but you get squeamish at a bloodless crime scene?" She made a *pffft* noise with her lips. "I know what's going on."

Alarm blared through him. "Listen, you can't get—"

"It's the memories, isn't it? They're still getting on top of you. Hitting you without warning?" Worry furrowed her brows.

"I—yes." Reed sank back into the seat, relieved. "You're right. One caught me off guard when I was in the gym. It was Firash's death memory." Nat was one of only two people in his life who knew about what the MER-C system did to him. No one else would believe he'd had to experience the dying memories of one killer to stop another one. Not without proof and the only bit of that was in Reed's head. "I've been trying meditation. I'm sure I can learn to trigger specific ones. There's more about Danzig and his plan here. I just have to figure out how to stop them from coming on unbidden."

"I thought when you injected the memories, they would fade. Especially because both donations were from dying men—" Nat stared at her blank tablet screen. "You have to see someone about this."

"If I explained what's wrong with my brain to anyone, they'd lock me up and you know it, Nat. No one would believe it."

"Just . . . give it some thought, okay?" She pushed out of the car, a forced smile on her face. "I'm not breaking in a new senior partner."

He smiled back, though both of them knew none of it was real, and then she left. Their first case together, her first case as a detective, had nearly gotten them killed. Reed wondered just how truthful Nat was when she told him she was fine. And then he thought of Dontae, and his chained and tortured body splayed out on a rock, and he started the car. He had to stop all of this before things got worse. Starting with a visit to a life he ran far away from.

He placed a call, dialing from memory. A low southern drawl came back at him through the phone.

"Morgan Reed, what makes you think I want to hear from your troublesome ass again?" Coyote asked.

"Dontae's dead."

Silence, then, "How?"

"That's what I'm trying to find out. I need his last known if you have it."

"We all parted ways for our own good back then, you know that. Why would I know where he's at?"

"Because you keep tabs on everyone." Reed clicked his pen and held it over his notebook. "I need to talk to whomever he was with before someone else does."

Coyote sighed and then. "Pick me up. I'm coming with you."

"This official business."

"That you're hiding from your fellow cops," Coyote countered. "Because you can look up Dontae on your own. Besides, it probably won't matter if I'm there 'cause they'll likely shoot you on sight."

———

North of downtown Seattle, Belltown, a once densely populated, crime-ridden area had been gentrified within an inch of its life. It was Reed's old haunt, but his childhood apartment building, packed to the gills with families, had been demolished a few years back to make way for a hotel. It was a gorgeous Georgian revival building that looked over the streets he used to run in with his friends. The boxing gym he'd found solace in as a kid was long gone as well. But the soul remained. Belltown's vibe held a promise of danger with its urban street art galleries, occult shops, and a punk rock vinyl studio that offered open mic nights. The streets were crowded. Belltown drew visitors with its dramatic views of Elliot Bay, beach access, and famous sculpture garden. But behind every white granite façade glowing in the moonlight there was a dark alley where the old ghouls of desperation still crept.

Dontae's apartment was in a waterfront building near Pier 66. A place not graced with money. Flanked on both sides by construction sites, the noise alone would've driven Reed nuts. A layer of dust covered everything from the meters on the street to the security screen on the door. The lock itself was busted so Reed and Coyote let themselves in.

"I heard his kin moved up here from their parish when Dontae got busted for some interstate deal. He got himself federal time," Coyote said. "The prison's not too far from here."

"Family follows trouble," Reed murmured. "They do the time with you."

"Yeah, you know, people from back home hear about someone they know doing well out here and they wanna try their luck. They move in with family in these tiny places and try to make it work." Coyote flicked his unstyled mohawk with a snap of his neck. He wore a black and gray flannel, black cargo pants, and Doc Martens boots. A chain hung from his beltloop and the leather and spike strap around his wrist picked up the stark artificial lights overhead as he fiddled with an unlit cigarette. He looked regretful. "I hadn't checked in on folks in a while. I haven't been back to New

Orleans since I don't know when. Hell, I didn't even know Dontae was out on parole until you called. I heard he's working part time at a mechanic shop."

"Chopping cars again?"

"One does tend to return to the familiar during hard times," Coyote mused. "He's only been out about ten months."

Reed shook his head. "It's an act for his parole officer. He's still with The Kindred." They walked down a dark corridor with water stains on the ceiling. It was cold and dank, and the contractors had apparently gotten a discount on prison gray paint because they'd used it on every possible surface. The hallways were empty save for a single trash bot that rattled in the opposite direction down the hall. It was graffitied and trailed strings and soda cans like it had just gotten married. A skinny kid in a purple sweatshirt booked it around the corner as soon as he saw them. Other than that, there were no running kids or brooding teenagers like he usually found in buildings like this. Just like his own had been growing up. The emptiness bothered him. "He was wearing their cut. I just saw it on what was left of his body."

"Well dang, Morgan, be sure not to lead with that image when we get in there."

They stopped in front of a dented door at the end of the hallway and tapped the lock screen. The security program that came with the door sounded an internal tone within the apartment. No one answered. Reed could swear he smelled cooking from behind the door. Real cooking. A spicy stew, maybe some dirty rice. Someone was home. According to Dontae's information, Fleur Benoît had rented the place one year prior. It was listed as his residence on his parole release paperwork.

Would you like to leave a message? The cracked digital screen prompted.

Reed ignored it and knocked. "Ms. Benoît. My name is Detective Morgan Reed. I'm here about Dontae Black." Wood scraped against the floor just inside the apartment and the neighbor's door opened a crack. He pulled back his suit jacket and flashed his badge. The neighbor's door shut. "I need to speak to his next of kin."

Several locks disengaged before a teary eye appeared in the opening.

Fleur Benoît stared back at Reed and his summers in Louisiana as a kid flashed behind his eyes. "Did you say *Morgan* Reed?"

"The very same. And Coyote Doucet is with me."

"My stars, is that you?" Her gaze flit to Coyote as the door widened. "And aren't you Camile's wayward brother?"

Coyote smiled, "In the flesh."

Reed stepped forward, crowding the door. Most of the neighbors were friends or kin, he suspected. Calls that she had a visitor were going out as they stood in the hallway. "My apologies, Ms. Benoît." He let the lilt from his summers in the south creep into his words. "May we come in?"

"Is it true then? He's really gone?" She asked as she stepped aside. Fleur was a few years younger than Reed. She'd gotten to high school just as he stopped going down to Louisiana. Still, he remembered her jet-black hair and light blue eyes from back then. They were still sad. Like they'd never known peace. She was heavily pregnant and when she led them into the apartment, two women sitting on the couch looked over at him with suspicion. They were older, dressed in black, and clearly in mourning. They'd been cooking. Which meant they expected company. Reed didn't want to be there when the rest of Dontae's family showed up.

"Looks like I'm not the only one with early knowledge of today's events," Coyote muttered. Reed glanced down the hall and then at Coyote. He nodded, then, "Ms. Benoît, may I use your washroom?"

"Down the hall," she gestured easily, and Coyote slipped away.

"You mind me asking how you heard about Dontae so quickly?" Reed asked softly.

"Do y'all want somethin' to eat?" She walked over to the stove and pulled up the lid of the bubbling pot. The heady scent of crawfish étouffée filled the kitchen. She scooped him a bowl of the stew onto some rice and topped it with a piece of torn baguette. When she handed it to him, her gaze briefly settled on the partially obscured holster beneath Reed's suit jacket, and she smiled softly. "I heard you became a cop. I remember thinking, The Terror of Belltown on the right side of the law? That's gotta be some story."

"I'll have to share it sometime," Reed said and settled onto a barstool pushed up against the counter. He pulled out the other stool and she sat next to him like they were old friends sharing a drink. Reed took a spoonful of the stew and it beat the cold of the day back. Coyote returned, and leaned against the fridge, his eye on the door. He shook his head at the offer of a bowl for himself. "Now this may be the best stew I've had in a long while, Ms. Benoît, but you still didn't answer my question. How did you know what happened to Dontae so fast?"

"I don't want to get anyone in trouble."

"I hear you and to be honest, I don't really care *how* you know about Dontae so much as *what* you know. I'm trying to find out who hurt him, and I need all the help you can give."

She sniffled into a paper napkin and glanced at the old women. They shot disapproving looks Reed's way. Fleur leaned in, whispering. "Family. They don't want me to talk to you."

He moved to block their line of sight from Fleur. "Alright, how about this? Tell me what you know, and I'll fill in the gaps for you." She nodded, and Reed got her started. "You know we found his body? You know where?"

She blinked. As if surprised for a moment but nodded. "Yes. Some lake."

"What was he doing all the way out there?"

Her face pinched, turning red as more tears started. She shook her head. "I don't know. We don't ever go out that way."

"Was it for work?"

"Not likely, he works with my brother. Marcel has a garage and Dontae's been putting in some real long hours." She patted her tummy and a sad wisp of a smile flashed across her pale features. "He was out of the life. He promised. We were going back home."

"Still in Terrebonne Parish?" Coyote asked. "Your auntie still have those seafood boils on Sundays after service?"

"She does," Fleur said, she held up her left hand. A diamond chip in a simple, thin gold band encircled her swollen finger. "We got us a place on Dulac not ten minutes down the bayou from his momma. That's why Dontae is . . . *was*, working overtime, saving up. He said he was going to be a proper daddy. With a straight job and . . . retirement and all. That was my condition for following him up here. And when he got out. He kept his word."

Reed's heart sank. He'd heard those same empty promises from his own father back in the day. "Walk me through the last twenty-four hours. When did you know something was wrong?"

"I didn't. Dontae spent the night at home with me. I think I heard his phone, but he left the room and told me to go back to sleep. I shouldn't have, but I was so tired." She wiped her eyes with the napkin and left a streak of mascara on it. "In the morning, I think it was nearly two when I got up to use the bathroom, I noticed he was still gone. His phone must've been off or something because it went straight to voicemail. When he wasn't back by breakfast, I called around. I don't usually keep tabs, but things were going so well. We're going back home before the baby is born. We're gonna raise him with family."

Reed considered her for a moment and then leaned forward, holding her gaze. "When I saw him just now, he was wearing a talisman. A dime with a drilled hole. He wore it on a string around his neck. Everything wasn't fine, Fleur. Dontae thought evil was on him."

Fleur's face flushed. "I don't know what you're talking about."

"Tell me what he was he afraid of."

"It was stress. He was having nightmares—"

"Heads-up," Coyote cut across her. "Company."

Loud footfalls just outside the door cut Reed's question short. He left the stool and walked over by the sink as several men pushed through the apartment door. The largest, ugliest one, was Marcel Benoît, her brother. Reed recognized him immediately. He had vitiligo and exactly half of his beard was dead white, the other black as a witch's heart. He walked in carrying bags of groceries and a case of beer but stopped in his tracks when he saw Reed. The other two men with him, Reed didn't know. But they all had on mechanic's overalls, and they smelled like shop grease.

Marcel dropped the groceries on the floor. "You better be here to tell us you've killed whoever did that to Dontae."

Reed leaned a hip against the counter. "How do you know what happened already? I'm just now making the notification."

"How do I know?" Marcel chuckled and turned to his buddies who did the same. "We got people down that way. They saw the lights and went to take a look. Someone took a video with his phone and recognized him."

"Care to share that video?"

"With a pig? No," he sneered at Reed. "Not unless you promise to do right by Dontae. Bring the killer to us if you can find him. We'll take care of him."

"I don't do things that way anymore. *When* I catch who did this, he belongs to the law."

Marcel shook his head and stepped up to him. He jabbed Reed with his finger. "Stop pretending you're anything different than what we all know you were, Morgan."

Reed moved blindingly fast, grabbing Marcel's wrist, twisting it behind him, and slamming him against the fridge. The crockpot lid on top fell and hit the counter, shattering. Fleur let out a startled squeal. And the two men lunged toward them. Coyote stopped them with a peek at his revolver.

"Oh, I'm still here," Reed whispered to Marcel, pulling up on his arm and straining the man's shoulder. Marcel hissed in pain. "So, you best stay out of my way."

Reed let him go, stepping back. Marcel whirled on him but one of the old ladies yelled his name and he froze. She walked over from the living room, her silver bun and stiff black dress reminded Reed of a pilgrim. Her cobalt eyes were rheumy with age, but he could see the resemblance. She looked like an older, world-weary version of Fleur. He remembered her standing on her porch with a shotgun threatening the cops when they came for her son one summer.

Setting a gentle hand on her daughter, the old woman's gaze bore into Reed. "I don't care how it's done, you understand? But my grandson *will* be safe from whoever did this to his daddy."

"Blood for blood," Marcel growled. "You know that's what's called for."

"He'll be made to account. You have my word," Reed said to Fleur's mother, ignoring Marcel. "But your son steps one toe in my way and he's going down with him. Are we clear?"

She nodded and they both looked at Marcel.

"You're bound by the law. They've got a yolk around your neck. Nothing you can do to make things right." Marcel yanked his overalls straight and wiped his nose with the back of his hand. A smear of blood marred the white of his beard. He grinned at Reed. An unhinged, menacing grimace. "No promises, turncoat."

"I guess it's whoever gets to him first, then," Fleurs mom said and the hardness around her eyes told Reed she was telling the truth.

"I make a better ally than enemy," Reed said to him.

Marcel chuckled, holding his arms out at his sides. "I got all the friends I need. Dontae's brothers are going to take care of whoever did this. Our way. And if you don't like it . . . maybe we take care of you too."

"Enemy, then." Reed nodded, his face calm. He shouldered past Marcel and let his hand slip to his hip as he passed. Marcel's gaze flit to the holster there as he backed up. "Just know, you chose this."

As they walked out to the car, Reed noticed the purple sweatshirt kid on a bike had been circling the apartment parking area since they left the building. He would glance at the car, then up at the windows of the building, then back. Reed sat in the driver's seat watching him.

Coyote looked up from his phone. "Are we going? I really don't want to wait around to see if Marcel decides to have another go at you."

"Hold on a second." Reed pushed out of the car and jogged toward the kid who motioned with a nod to the alley where they kept the dumpsters. The kid couldn't be more than ten or eleven. Blonde with freckles, skinny, he had the hyper awareness of someone who grew up around dangerous adults. Reed shoved his hands in his trench pockets and tilted his head. "You got something to tell me?"

The kid sat on his bike facing Reed and scraped at the rubber of his handlebars with his thumbnail. He wouldn't look at him. "Dontae was good people. He treated me nice even though I'm not his kid."

Reed nodded. "He once helped me beat up this guy who kept stealing my shoes from the gym locker room."

The kid let out a snorting laugh and looked up at him with wet eyes. "*Étiez-vous amis?*"

"Yes, we were friends. When I was a little older than you. I'd go down to the bayou in the summers, and we'd take his dog for a ride on the pontoon boat. Catch us some dinner. What's your name?"

"Remy."

"Remy what?"

"Remy that's all you're gonna get," the kid said, but he smiled. "Dontae bought me kicks or uh . . . shoes for school. Nice ones like the rich kids wear. Even though I was gonna grow out of them in a few months anyway."

Reed nodded. "He knew what it felt like to have nothing."

Remy narrowed his gaze at Reed. "You too, I suspect. You got some hardness to your smile." When Reed didn't balk or explain, Remy continued. "I thought you all should know that last week past, there was this big fais do-do. Lots of music and food. You know?"

"Yes, a family party. Were you there?"

Remy nodded. "All the uncles were sitting outside, you know, smokin' and drinking." His Cajun accent lilted over the words. "Dontae was talking about a partner. Complaining really. He called him a couyon."

Reed hadn't expected to hear that. "Have you ever laid eyes on this man?"

"Nah," Remy nodded at the building. "Dontae's not supposed to have business outside of Marcel's."

"Did you heard Fleur and him talking?"

"More like yelling about it."

"What was Dontae saying?" Reed asked. "The complaints?"

"Well, I heard he met this guy at a restaurant once, well in the kitchen. Dontae said the guy had weird tastes. Something about row?"

Reed made a rowing motion with his hands at his sides, "Like that kind? On a boat?"

"I don't know."

"Was the place near the water?"

Remy shrugged. "Maybe. Anyways, I thought you should know." His brows furrowed. "Can you keep it to yourself? That I talked to you? Folks around here—"

"Never met you," Reed said.

The kid took off and he returned to the car. Coyote had been smoking and Reed rolled down the windows and stared out the windshield, thinking.

"Nice code switching back there, Morgan. I hadn't heard your accent that smooth since you were courting my sister." He tossed the cigarette butt out the window. "Did the kid know anything?"

"He said Dontae had a partner. Called him a 'couyon'." Reed scribbled the kid's name and what he'd said in his notebook. "That's French, right? A fool."

"In Cajun it's an insult. Means crazy man." Coyote turned in his seat to look at Reed. "I know you think you can stay on that razor's edge you walk between who you are and what you were, but this—they will kill you if you betray them, Morgan. You will just disappear."

Reed rubbed his face with both palms as if washing away the nightmare this case was becoming. "I know they hid me when my father came looking—"

"And later when the cops did. They stuck their neck out for you when you were down."

"I haven't forgotten," Reed said. "But this isn't the same thing."

"It is in their eyes."

Reed shook his head. "I know what I'm doing."

"I don't even think you know who you're doing it with," Coyote said. "Marcel told us that he and Dontae's 'brothers' would take care of things. As in the motorcycle club. Marcel is Kindred. I'd stake my mohawk on it."

"I'm not delivering up a man to be murdered," Reed said.

"That's where you're wrong, *mon ami*. You will either way. You just have to decide if it's going to be your life or the killer's."

5

The Northwest Precinct Station was in downtown Seattle where Reed saw a healthy dose of both banal and bizarre crimes. The Queen Anne District's exclusive neighborhoods with private social lounges, expensive hotels, and arts centers were bordered by the edgier Belltown to the south, and the increasingly high-tech Lake Union to the east.

Reed dropped Coyote off at his speakeasy and headed to the station hoping to get some preliminary findings on Dontae from Sanders. It was later in the afternoon, and the traffic on the return trip was horrible. Tig called just as Reed was pulling into the station parking lot.

"The brass put a priority on your case with the MEs office this morning. You should be getting a call soon." Tig sounded like he was eating potato chips.

"I guess having a detective's name written in blood at the scene will do that."

Tig snorted and crunched some more. "Those damn news streamers were camping outside my office an hour after we found him, the vultures. They don't even have to be accurate, just first to post."

"He had family who has to see that crap everywhere they look."

"Well, likes are likes, right? Gotta get those click dollars," Tig said. "Look, I know it's just the opening volley of the case, but do you have anything? Something I can hang my hat on when I talk to the bosses at CompStat?"

Reed thought for a second, staring at himself in the sun visor mirror. "So far it appears to be a deal gone wrong. Though no drugs or money were found at the scene. Maybe an attempted robbery by one of the parties ended badly."

"He was affiliated, right?" Tig's keyboard clicked in the background. "Motorcycle gang."

"Yes, the Kindred. I'm hoping Parker can get me more information through his connections with organized crime."

"Yeah, utilize him. Maybe he'll stop trying to make appointments with my office."

"It's early but we're gaining traction. I've got a couple leads."

"The sooner the better. The guy looked half eaten for Pete's sake," Tig said with another bite of chips. "That's gold for the newsies. Did you see they have video? Some idiot flew a consumer drone over the crime scene before they got the tent up. Online sources keep playing the flyby in slow motion."

"That tracks," Reed muttered.

They signed off and Reed headed for the homicide floor to look for Nat when he spotted her getting onto the elevator. She bounced on the balls of her feet when she saw him, motioning him to hurry. Once aboard, she handed Reed her tablet, told the elevator to take them to the basement morgue, and hit him with a huge grin.

"What'd you do?" He asked.

"Okay, so I was over at the Technology Building with Imani from Cybercrime, and we were doing a data scrape of the Matthew's Beach area for devices active during the murder." She gave him a look. "Where were you? I didn't see you with the food trucks when I left."

"We got a warrant, right?" Reed hedged. Nat's days as an ethical hacker in Cybercrime made her scarily efficient at getting what she needed. He just didn't understand her methods enough to know if he should worry.

"Oh, totally." Nat reached over and tapped on the tablet in his hands, calling up the data. "There was a little more activity than usual for that area. But we know that all the Polar Break people were there pretty early so we're in the process of pinpointing where their devices were exactly. Sometimes we can get down to yards, which would help. Then we can start eliminating them as possible suspects."

"Did you find the victim's phone?" Reed wondered if she could trace it back to calls made to him by Dontae the day before.

"Not yet." Nat pulled up a grainy still. It was dark, almost black and white. A man ran down the beach, his hand to his middle. He was looking over his shoulder with his face obscured by something. "I found a weird data burst in the signal tower that services that area. The repeaters keep a cache to prevent lag and there was a huge packet of information sent from one device to another right on the beach during the time frame the ME says the victim died. The data from the towers is anonymized, but now that we have a specific signal, we can get more from the communications company."

"Is this video?" Reed's gut knotted. Dontae had locked eyes with the camera, a look of terror etched on his face. "This angle would make it what . . . a drone?"

"No, no. This wasn't anything like that," Nat took the tablet back as the elevator stopped and they walked down the white tiled hallway. "It was a *huge* amount of data. Way more than a drone recording would be. When Imani and I took the file apart, the information turned out to be telemetry."

They were almost to the double doors of the morgue when Reed stopped. "You found instrument readings? For what?"

"I mean, distance barrier, altitude, speed, acceleration . . ." Nat scrunched her nose at Reed. "You'll get the picture when Sanders shows you what we found."

They pushed into the morgue, which had been rebuilt after vandalism destroyed most of the equipment a few months back during a prior case. Sanders stood next to an intake table as the overhead scanner mapped Dontae's body with a red beam of light. Next to him, a service robot attached to the specimen counter filled specimen trays with samples. Reed passed it just as its metal arm sliced another section of someone's heart with a water scalpel. Sanders waved them over, stirring a mug of coffee with a pen.

"Did she tell you about my new toy?" He nodded to a cube set up on a corner table. The size of a donut box, it was made of black metal with lights flitting between seems in the surface. "I've got my own virtual depot."

Nat was already there, fiddling with the controls on the digital screen next to it. She scooped up a pair of goggles and handed one to Reed. "You've used the whole-room virtual reality program over in the Technology Tower. We upgraded Dr. Sanders's lab with a portable hub from the field for use when talking with investigators."

Reed donned the VR glasses with her and Sanders. Pinpoints of light appeared and blinked out, calibrating to his view. He raised his hands and virtual ones popped up in front of him. Dontae's body appeared without warning, floating in the deep black of the virtual world. He was situated vertically as if standing, his genitals covered with a modesty cloth, eyes closed. His arms hung at his sides. Reed reared back involuntarily and bumped into a surgical tray.

"You okay?" Nat's avatar asked. "I know you hate technology, especially VR."

"I forget how vivid it can be," Reed managed. In truth, he preferred the paper and paint of his studio to the cold efficiency of technology.

Sanders's digital-self appeared. He stepped forward and a green laser pointer light emanated from his finger as he indicated the damage to the side of Dontae's body. He made a gesture and the area of the missing flesh expanded to the size of a pizza. Sanders touched the pieces of metal in the wound, and they flew out from the body and spun in front of Reed. Sharp, long, slivers of metal rotated while Sander's explained.

"Contrary to what it appears to be, the victim's wound was not a bite," Sanders explained. "It was the result of a focused explosion from within his body. I took scans of the individual pieces of shrapnel I found in the victim's wounds and Detective De La Cruz ran them through a puzzle program."

Nat's avatar made an exaggerated insulted face. "It's more like a reverse explosion algorithm. They use it at MIT. Anyways, it helped us figure out the original shape of the projectile given the telemetry information we pieced together, the shape of the shrapnel in the victim, the condition of the wound it caused, and damage from the concussive wave. We zeroed in on this . . ."

A white schematic form appeared before Reed. A projectile.

Nat's avatar feathered at the edges slightly as she manipulated the schematic for him. "We took the telemetry data and ran it through some paces. We determined it was a missile-based system, but the measurements are way weird." She waved her hand and an office marker appeared in the palm of her hand. She then grabbed the schematic from mid-air, and it shrunk as she positioned it next to the pen. The projectile was roughly the same length and thickness. "It's tiny. A micro missile.'"

"We're running the clothes for residue. Maybe we'll get a hit on the kind of explosive used," Sanders said. "The canines didn't alert conclusively at the scene. Not near the bathroom or the cement chunks. They were agitated near the shore, but it wasn't a solid hit."

"Makes sense," Nat said. "Given the size of the slug, there wouldn't be much."

"A smart bullet," Reed murmured. "This is a weapon of war, not consumer grade."

"You've heard of it?" Sanders asked. He flared out his fingers as if flicking off water and the schematic enlarged revealing details of the design. "This is the telemeter. It's seated in the missile shroud along with where the explosive should go. Sanders zoomed in on the modular system and indicator labels glowed alight over each of the components. "It has everything a full-sized missile would have on a vastly reduced scale. I've never seen anything like it. In fact, I feel like I need a lawyer just looking at the guts of this thing."

"It's called a Kraken Round," Nat said, "Because of what it does after it hits its target. Check this out."

Reed heard her tapping on the control panel and the black virtual space morphed into a blue sky with wispy clouds. The schematic of the round filled out to a solid state and the VR program simulated flight through the air. It raced toward a circle target on a fake hay bale in the distance, the view following close. Data scrolled down the left side of Reed's vision. Distance to target, heat signature, altitude. When it hit, the round went through the target, and shredded into a spinning projectile, its sides flaring out in jagged pieces like the arms of an octopus. A moment later, the round detonated a second time, and the simulation tracked the damage radius at ten to fifteen feet."

Nat made a disgusted face. "It stops itself from exiting the body."

"That's . . . awful," Reed muttered, and his gaze flit to the still suspended body of his friend. "I thought rounds like this were still a way off. Mere concepts in tech circles."

"There was a consumer grade version floating around about fifteen years ago. It wasn't a smart round, but it did expand upon impact. It was banned." Nat called up some concept art and the drawings peeled away as she went through them like real paper. They floated to Reed as if on the wind and hovered in front of him. "I mean, look at what goes into tech like this. No reputable weapons manufacturer would touch this because it's likely to never get off the ground. Even if a team did get funding, it's not really cost effective. At least not for the average consumer. A round like this would arguably be tens of thousands of dollars apiece. There's got to be cheaper ways to kill people."

"Unless the weapon of choice was the point," Reed said. "Some sort of clue we're supposed to figure out."

"It's a hell of a choice as far as weapons go," Sanders said. "It's a ramjet cruise missile, air breathing, in that it draws oxygen during hypersonic speed for propulsion directly from the atmosphere."

"Low altitude launches for the oxygen, but it has a longer range," Reed murmured.

"Yeah," Sanders made a face. "Have you come across these before?"

"Not in the states and not that size," Reed said.

Nat's avatar nodded. "This is next generation stuff. The speed and scale make it virtually undetectable until it's too late."

"Like a sniper bullet." Reed manipulated the projectile, peering at the schematic. "What's it's flight time?"

"Sixty seconds, maybe less," Nat said.

Reed shook his head. "That's an eternity."

"It gets worse," she said and disappeared from the program. Reed took his headset off too, and Nat pointed to the smart screen on the wall. "It wasn't just sending standard telemetry. It was also sending facial recognition, gait, and voice signature data to someone. This thing was programmed to take out *this* man specifically."

"And you can time when to detonate the second explosion," Sanders added, pulling off his own headset. "If the first hit doesn't kill you, the second will blow you in half."

"And the feedback is real-time," Nat said. "I hit the forums while you were gone and heard that some concepts had a heads-up display for the shooter. So, it's possible you could manually target and launch this thing using the onboard camera."

"He was watching," Reed remembered Dontae's desperate eyes in the still. "Can we track the receiving device?"

"We could track the signal if it was live back to the shooter, maybe, but the thing is, other designs have the micro missile operating autonomously. As in once you're target-locked, it's not stopping."

Reed set his headset on a nearby metal table and rubbed his eyes. "What the hell?"

"The weird thing is, the victim doesn't seem like he'd even have access to something like this," Nat said. She called up a file on the smart wall and Dontae's mug shot slid into view along with a list of his priors. "Dontae 'Bullet' Black is a known member of the Kindred Motorcycle Gang out of Louisiana. Served time up here on a weapons charge. He was on parole. The club is known for moving drugs, people, wire fraud, and weapons so it's possible, but doesn't a micro missile seem sort of highbrow for his customers?"

"I don't even know how he'd get ahold of a weapon like that," Reed said. He thought for a moment, and then, "This kind of tech. It takes money, right? Lots of it? You'd need a manufacturing facility, specialized materials, and trained staff. Maybe the metal itself is specialized enough to narrow the list."

"Yeah . . ." Nat narrowed her gaze, watching Reed. "What are you thinking?"

"I'm thinking it would be hard to keep this a secret."

Nat gestured with her tablet at him. "That might mean that it wasn't funded by venture capital or other outside sources. It would have to be in-house all the way. From research to fabrication."

"We need to find out what companies might be able to pull that off."

"I'm sending a sample upstairs to the materials lab," Sanders said. "They'll find something."

Reed nodded to Sanders and headed to the hallway. "I'll talk to my contact in the technology finance arena and see what he thinks."

"Hold on," Nat said, following behind. She snagged the back of his coat sleeve, stopping him. "What's up with you lately?"

"Pardon?"

"You definitely had a weird reaction to seeing the body this time. I thought at the beach, you were just, you know . . . twitchy from the memories, but now, not so much." She folded her arms. "You're hiding something."

Reed looked down at her and then motioned for her to follow him into the stairwell. He leaned against the wall trying to look casual. "What are you talking about?"

Nat glanced down the stairwell and up, listening for a second. Then her brows furrowed as she turned her sharp gaze on him and pointed at his chest with a red-tipped fingernail. "You know the victim. I saw you react at the beach, but you told me it was some stupid memory and I believed you."

"I did have an episode in the gym—"

She waved his explanation away. "Bullshit. Maybe you did have a flashback or whatever, but that's not why you're acting all sketchy, is it? Admit it. You know this Dontae guy."

Reed regarded her for a moment. She'd had his back through stranger times. "Fine. I know him—"

"Ha! I knew it." She narrowed her gaze. "How? Was he a CI or something?"

"Not exactly." Reed's phone trilled in his pocket, and he pulled it out. She shook her head, but he pointed at the screen as it sounded again. "It's the desk sergeant."

She frowned and leaned back on the rail with her arms. She was angry he kept things from her. Reed answered his phone.

"I got a guy calling for you," the desk sergeant said. "He says he wants to talk to you about Matthew's Beach."

Reed stilled. Someone had left a message for him earlier and he'd ended up at his friend's crime scene. "Is it a reporter?"

In the background, someone with a drunken slur was cursing at the desk sergeant who, responding in kind, told him to take a seat before returning his attention to the call. "I didn't ask, and he didn't volunteer."

"Is it from a number that left a message for me earlier?"

"There's no note from the previous shift on that," the sergeant said and patched the call through before Reed could argue.

"Detective Morgan Reed?" A soft, masculine tone, spoke. The caller's voice was digitally altered, Reed thought. Not an AI generated one. He could hear background noises. The city. Wind buffeting along the mouthpiece. "You found your friend, yes?"

"My friend?" Reed tapped Nat on the shoulder, pointed to his phone, and mouthed, "Trace?" She nodded, looked around for her tablet, and then ran out of the stairwell toward the morgue. "Yes, on the shore."

"I'm sorry for your loss," the caller said though they sounded slightly amused. "I was surprised to find an officer with such a motley crew of friends. Is he the first you've lost to the violence of his occupation?"

Reed gripped his phone so tight the case creaked, but he kept the calm in his voice. "How did you know about the murder?"

The caller laughed softly. A strange, almost muffled sound. "That's very diplomatic of you, Detective. You didn't accuse me outright of being the killer."

Nat slipped back into the stairwell and gave him a thumbs up.

"Are you?" Reed asked. "Did you murder him?"

"Haven't you noticed the men lurking in the shadows around you, Detective? The slip of a hard face past your peripheral when you're out and about, maybe?"

Something cold settled in Reed's gut. "Who is this?"

"A friend. An ally against a common enemy. You can call me Visage."

The smooth modulation of the voice snagged something in Reed's brain, but he couldn't quite place it. "I have a lot of enemies."

"Not like this one," Visage said. "None are like this enemy."

"You mean Danzig." Reed caught the startled look on Nat's face.

"We can help each other. I have information that can hurt him. Take him down completely."

Visage's diction, his cadence felt east coast to Reed. Elevated. "Why don't *you* use it then?"

"One man can't bring down a titan like Danzig. He's too fortified, too careful. But *we* can."

Nat made a keep going gesture with her index finger.

"Who's *we*?"

"There are quite a few people Danzig has razed for his own gain that wish to hurt him back. One of which is a federal judge, eager to get out from underneath Danzig's thumb. He'll talk to you."

"A compromised judge and a man too afraid to reveal himself," Reed deliberately poked at the caller's ego. "Not exactly a dream team. You could just as well be the killer."

"I couldn't prevent your friend's death. Only tell you of it. I hoped you'd take the body as proof that I know more than you think. I know about what you did for him."

Dread and anger surged through Reed. "What the hell do you want?"

"I want you to live long enough to do what needs to be done. Meet with the judge. His name is Leone. He has quite a story to tell but you must move quickly. Danzig is always ten steps ahead."

"I'm not your errand boy. You talk to him."

"He'll only speak with you. What you did to Danzig's plans is well known," Visage said. "Conversely, *because* of what you did, you're running out of time. Danzig has a vendetta against you and everyone who helps you. Dontae is proof of that."

"It's proof of jack shit," Reed snapped. "You could be setting me up."

Nat looked up from her tablet, her face tense. "More time."

"Talk to Leone, today" Visage said. "Before Danzig uses what he found out about you and your friends and what you all covered up that summer."

Reed opened his mouth to argue, but the call ended.

"Was that the caller from before?" Nat dusted off her pants as she stood.

Reed didn't answer. He couldn't. All he could hear was the blood pounding in his head and the scream of his friend right before a muzzle flash lit up the dark. If what happened that night, so many years ago, ever got out, Reed would not just lose his job, he'd lose his freedom. That is, if the Kindred didn't kill him first.

6

Parker

Detective Benjamin Parker strode down the central hallway of the NW Precinct station. He'd come to regroup with Reed and De La Cruz but had been told they already came and left. No messages for him. It was already almost four thirty in the afternoon on the first day of investigation and he had seen neither De La Cruz nor Reed all day. He dialed the number and waited impatiently as the digital ringtone resonated in his ear.

"They're shutting me out already," he hissed into his phone. "And something is up between them. They had a moment at the lake in the car." Parker opened the door for an elderly woman, smiling and nodding while she took an ungodly amount of time to actually walk out of the lobby. He stepped back inside near the stairs and cupped his mouth to the phone. "They looked like they were arguing."

"Arguing about what?" the caller asked. "Did you hear anything?"

"No, the windows were up. But he left suddenly and was gone for hours."

"You think he knows more than he's letting on?"

"Reed always does," Parker chewed on his inner cheek. "I have to stay close. He'll slip up."

"Be careful," the caller said and was gone.

Parker stood at the window, steaming. He'd decided to head to his car to call his lieutenant when he spotted the woman detective in the break room. He sidled over, pretended to contemplate the coffee flavor choices on the dispensing machine, and then cleared his throat when she didn't notice him there. She glanced over and he took the opening.

"De La Cruz," Parker said with a friendly smile. "I'm glad I caught you. Where's your partner?"

"It's Nat," she said and held a pink donut with pink frosting and chocolate sprinkles in front of her chest. She picked off a piece of the frosting and tossed it in her mouth. "He went to make a call. Did anything pop on the door or house cameras from the neighborhood?"

"Not yet," Parker said and hooked a thumb over his shoulder. "I just came from the ME."

"Crazy, right? What would a low-level gang member need with a micro missile like that when you can just walk up behind someone in a dark alley and stab them?" She made a jabbing motion at his throat with her donut. "Doesn't make sense."

"That's, uh, a good point." Parker tried to get that image out of his head. "You think the weapon is the key?"

"Reed does."

He thought he caught a whiff of irritation there and decided to use it. "And what he thinks is always right?"

Her eyes met his and she seemed to size him up. "We just met, so I'm going to overlook that condescending comment. I may be new, but I don't follow his lead like a puppy."

"I didn't say you did."

"You insinuated it."

"I just wanted to know if you had any theories of your own."

"You mean instead of the one Reed tells me are mine?"

"That's not what I meant."

She sighed heavily and shot him a look. "It's almost the end of shift. Why did you have to go and say that?" She dropped her donut in the metal trashcan by the door and gave him a scathing look on her way out.

That touched a nerve, Parker thought.

He followed her out of the breakroom, a chagrined look on his face. "Let's start over."

Nat stopped walking in the middle of the hallway, her brow raised. "So, talk."

"Okay, look, you made detective after helping to take out a multi-state child trafficking sting, right? All I'm saying is, you have a bright future."

She smirked. "Should I be wearing shades?"

"You should be wearing a bullet proof vest," Parker intoned. "Because anyone who spends too much time at Reed's side eventually gets hurt."

"You know, I went and read up about what happened during that sting. There're are contradicting accounts."

"Yeah, mine and all of Reed's buddies. He's been cited for recklessness, misconduct toward authorities, noble cause corruption—as in the ends justify the means. . ." Parker counted them off on his fingers. "He was reprimanded for violence while in Narcotics. He had to go to rehab to kick a habit he got while undercover. . . I mean the list goes on."

Nat's gaze traveled his face, her body going tense. "How do you know all of this? That kind of information is supposed to be confidential."

"Don't tell me you haven't heard the rumors."

Nat shrugged again. "What's your angle?"

"I don't have an angle," Parker said with a little edge to his voice. "And you've been a detective for what, six months? You have it all figured out?"

"I'm not the one predicting calamity, Nostradamus." Nat shook her head. "What are you doing here? Just stirring up crap for no reason? Or do you have a point?"

"I'm saying that Reed is on thin ice. And when it breaks you don't want to be anywhere near him. If you don't think the brass is aching for a way to get rid of him then you're more naïve than you let on."

"Naïve?" She rolled her eyes. "Forgive me if I don't take the word of a guy I just met."

"I'm ranking detective, De La Cruz. And watch your mouth." Parker crossed his arms. "I read your file. Smart, probably smarter than me, just a whole lot greener. Something is going on with Reed. He's off. Maybe you're blind to it, or he's blinded you, but it's there. And deep down you know it.

Whether or not you apply that big brain of yours to figure out why, might be the saving grace for your future within this department."

The smug look on her face wavered and he pushed it. Softening his approach. "You aren't getting out of this partnership without a stain on your record. I guarantee it."

She considered him for a moment. Her dark eyes, almost black, incredibly piercing. Intelligent. He could see why Reed looked at her like he did.

"Why are you telling me this?" she asked.

"I'm just trying to warn you."

"Why?"

"What?"

"What do you care about my career? You don't know me from Adam."

"Because—" He stumbled over what to say. "I just think you should watch your step."

"Well, that sounds threatening."

"It's a warning."

"Which is . . . a threat."

Parker sighed heavily. "I'm just trying to help you, De La Cruz."

"Mhmm. Whatever." Nat's gaze narrowed. "And it's Nat."

She turned to leave but Parker stepped in her space, leaning over her. His temper flaring at being dismissed by a subordinate. "Why are you so loyal so quickly?"

She didn't back off. Instead, she slid her hands to her hips, the ruffles of her bright blue blouse flaring out as she scowled at him. "You seem to know an awful lot about what the 'brass' is planning. How is that? Are you spying on us? Gathering dirt for them? Are you with the rat squad, Parker? Is that what this is?"

"What? No." Parker took a step back. Why did she suddenly sound like a New York gangster? His gaze slid to those passing and working around them and anger burned up his neck, flaring his face hot at the sheer insubordination. "I think I can explain the fierce defense of a man you met only three months ago. Maybe Officer Caitlyn isn't the only fellow cop Reed got close to?"

"And there it is." Nat smirked. Her eyes bore into him. "Let me tell you something, Detective Parker. Much scarier men than you have tried to bully me, and they all learn one thing. I am *not* the one. You got that?"

She turned without waiting for him to answer. Parker watched her leave, wondering if he'd just made a mistake or uncovered something useful.

7

Reed didn't see Nat for the rest of the shift after they talked at the ME's office the day before. Apparently, she'd left right after. He had thought she might be running down the phone call he'd gotten from Visage but when he called cybercrime, they said she wasn't there. He'd seen Parker wandering the halls but managed to slip away via the stairwell to avoid dealing with him. He'd ended the day at the gym. Reed worked a speed bag for a while, did some sparring, and finished with the jump rope until his arms felt like lead. His shoulder was aching, but strong, and Reed decided that was progress.

The following morning Reed dropped by the materials lab at the station to see if they'd narrowed down anything on the metallurgy of the Kraken. He hoped the material would be specialized enough that he'd have a direction to go in. They didn't have anything yet, other than some components seemed to be made of a proprietary material. Not really shocking news. They said they'd call if anything changed. Nat wasn't on the Homicide floor, so he made some phone calls, worked on the report for the homeless encampment sting for a few hours. Nearing lunch and still no Nat, Reed went to go look for her at cybercrime. She wasn't there, but he knew where she might be hiding out.

The Technology Tower was Seattle Police Department's crowning glory.

A white stone and glass ivory tower of technology in the center of down-town that shone in the morning sun like a citadel of justice. Reed had sketched the building when he'd first visited and later decided the angular lines made it look more like a villain's lair. It was actually just bureaucratic offices and support staff, but the façade inspired confidence. The building housed the more advanced labs and forensic departments, the Intelligence Office, the Office of Police Conduct, and the Virtual Depot were all ensconced inside the glossy, highly secure walls of the five-year-old building.

Reed passed the reception center, fiddling with his phone, as he tried to reply to Nat's strange message. Usually full of text-speak, emojis, and excla-mations, her recent text simply said she was in an Omni-Flex virtual reality room on the premises. Weirdly succinct for her. The lack of communica-tion was odd. She'd texted him a picture of a huge bug on the street earlier in the week just so he'd have to "witness its grossness himself." No word from her until the morning was odd.

He walked past the reception counter, through a hologram of an officer helping an old lady onto a curb, and then cut across the polished floor toward the secure elevator. He swiped the security fob Nat had given him and rode it to the Virtual Depot floor. The hallway was softly lit with thick security doors along both sides of a narrow corridor. One of the doors had an overhead readout that showed the room was in session with the name De La Cruz underneath. Reed kicked off his boots, walked in, and paused to let his eyes adjust to the darkness. He didn't see Nat, so he grabbed a pair of VR glasses and some haptic gloves from the counter and slipped them on.

Sunken like an arena, a wraparound virtual display wall lined the space. Behind the walls, ambient lights, an array of cameras and projectors, and surround sound speakers created an almost too immersive experience, in Reed's opinion. He stepped into a rustic coffee shop complete with baris-tas, percolating liquid sounds, and the crackle of a roaring fire. Reed knew there were options like this, but he'd only ever been in these rooms with Nat who preferred the clinical settings or the black abyss of neutral space. Something was up. He glanced out the windows in the far corner of the café. Fluffy snowflakes drifted onto pristine, billowy mounds along a picturesque village street. The café rendered around him was modeled after something you might find in a sleepy mountain town. Artificially generated people sat stiffly at tables murmuring quietly with each other over steaming mugs they never drank from. In fact, if you listened hard enough it was actual non-word mumbling. Blue noise, the programmers called it, for authenticity without distraction. It was bustling, but quiet, and it gave Reed the creeps.

Virtual screens floated over the wood floor of the café streaming the surveillance video Parker had gathered from the area of the crime scene. Joggers, cyclists, the approaching food trucks all ran at two times the speed with no sound. Text cascaded down from the top of the screen with the data scrape information on the devices in the area.

A river rock fireplace glowed with a roaring fire in the center of the café for no reason and Nat's digital self stood to the side of it, putting something on the wall of the café. She was moving her hands like she was tacking up paper and virtual sheets hovered around her in space.

"Hey, where'd you go yesterday? I came back from making a call and you disappeared."

"I had stuff to do," Nat said without looking up.

Reed regarded her silently as he pulled his trench off and dropped it on the control desk. Something was up. "What're you working on?"

She gestured at the floating screens. "Finishing up the surveillance we got from the houses. Nothing popped, though I'm not done yet. I still have the parking lot camera pointed near the entrance. The parks and rec department got it to me this morning."

They sat in silence for a few seconds, then Reed asked, "I just talked to Tig. He wants us moving fast on this, which is understandable."

"Okay."

What was going on? Reed moved toward her, but he wasn't on a tread-mill, so his surroundings were off, and it left him feeling thrown, like he was drunk. "Why is it weird in here?"

"It's calibrated to my height. Welcome to Lilliput," Nat said, but there was no mirth in her voice. She made a gesture with her hand and the café evaporated around them, replaced with the program's grid overlay against the black of virtual nothingness.

"I didn't mind that," Reed said and walked over to where she stood. "Do you want to come with me to talk to the victim's parole officer or are you on to something? I want to try to catch him at the office."

She shrugged, not looking at him. Her avatar's hair rustled as if by a breeze. "Dontae's parole officer left us a message. He can meet us whenever. We just have to give him a heads up first."

"You called him, thanks."

She put up another sheet. "The victim's juvenile record is sealed, but I'm working on it."

Reed's gut tightened at that. "You really think his distant past has anything to do with what happened to him?"

"I think the past rears its ugly head more often than we like."

Reed hesitated, then let it go. Squinting at the papers before realizing he could just make them bigger with a pinch of his fingers. "You're researching Judge Leone."

"Despite what your mystery caller implied, he's clean so far," Nat said and slid another virtual computer screen in his direction. "That's like the third award this year alone. He's got humanitarian, community appreciation, even environmental awards. This guy is popular for all the right reasons. I don't see any connection between the judge and Danzig either."

"You've been careful poking around?" Reed didn't know a lot about infotech, but he knew enough not to trust that someone wasn't watching.

"This guy isn't an operative. He still uses a laptop."

The virtual screen drifted in front of Reed, and he scrolled through several posts and articles. The judge's full name was Rudolpho Leone. He went to an Ivy. Played lacrosse. Professional head shots of Leone showed a distinguished if not well-nourished man in his late fifties. White hair and brows over a deep-set, probing gaze gave Leone that air of judicial integrity you really only saw in movies. A golfer, Reed thought, given the tan and sedentary body type. Reed read the articles, fluff pieces, suggesting big things to come for Leone and extolling his immigrant parent origins. Refugees from a war in Europe. It smacked of a campaign press release. Each piece seemed to commemorate Leone's selfless service. His time in the coast guard came up as well. There were a few mentions of a daughter's acceptance into his prestigious alma mater.

"How does a guy like this end up under Danzig's thumb?" Reed shook his head and swiped the screen away. "There has to be something that makes him vulnerable to Danzig."

"I dated a prosecutor last year," Nat said. "I can ask him if he's heard anything juicy."

Reed grinned. "A lawyer, really? This casts your dating life in a whole other light."

"Check this out," she said, ignoring his remark. She waved her hands and Dontae's mug shot dropped down from the ceiling. It was flat and spun like a trading card, throwing off papers and files, photos and reports. Every item landed and slid together into stacks of digital pages that fanned out and touched other groups to form connections until Dontae's photo was surrounded by the records of his life like the center of a vast and complicated mosaic. Nat had done the same for Judge Leone's information as well. Reed considered the entire collection for a moment. The one thing that jumped out was that no paper, no point of data, nothing connected Dontae's pile of information to the judge's.

"No nexus at all?" Reed ran his gaze along the hovering groups. "Not one appearance before Leone? Not one community program that the judge was a part of?"

"Nada. This Visage either knows something buried so deep we can't access it, or he's lying. I did learn something interesting." Nat closed the program.

Reed removed the VR glasses as the wall lights glowed on softly. "What?"

Nat looked at him and pulled her gloves off. "Dontae's father was in the Kindred too. At least before he dropped off the grid. That makes Dontae a legacy member. And something else. I checked his prison visitation records. A Fleur Benoît was a regular visitor of his. One of only two. I'm guessing girlfriend because she also added funds to Dontae's commissary account."

"And the other?"

"Has to be family, maybe brother, because he has the same last name and is only a few years older than her. Do you know what Marcel Benoît's records show? He has suspected ties to, you guessed it, the Kindred Motorcycle Club. You know what else I found?" Her gaze locked on him, holding his. "They're all from Louisiana. Terrebonne Parish, specifically. Just like Coyote. Just like you."

"I'm not from there. I visited with Coyote and his family during the summers," Reed said evenly. "I told you that. Our mothers knew each other from the neighborhood, and my mother thought it might keep me out of trouble while she worked."

"That turned out swimmingly," Nat muttered as she tossed her gloves and VR glasses at the desk.

Reed stilled, watching her quietly. She muttered to herself, her head moving subtly as she jabbed at the dashboard control screen.

"You're upset," he said and moved into her line of sight. "Tell me why."

"Why?" She laughed ruefully and swiped her hand like a conductor. The wall screens winked off and the room glowed bright with overhead lights. "Either you're my partner, my fully invested partner, or you're some dude I drive around that keeps secrets."

"Those are my only choices?" Reed tried for humor, but she stared at him with narrowed eyes.

"Tell me what's going on with you."

Reed took a troubled breath. "Nat, I'm not sure how believable all of this is."

"You know what I know, right?" Nat said. "All the crap we saw with our first case that no one would believe. Why don't you trust that I'll have your back this time too? Why're you hiding stuff again?"

"I'm not—"

"You didn't interview the food truck people," she cut across him, her bangs swishing as she shook her head vehemently. "So don't even. You signed out of service for almost two hours."

"How did you check that?"

She gestured vaguely around the technologically advanced space. "You really need me to answer that?"

"Alright. You know how I told you that this Visage said he called to warn me about Dontae's murder?"

"Yeah, you told me he said the judge was under Danzig's thumb. Which is why I did all this research. To find out how to approach the judge before we go talk to him," Nat said.

"Yes, well, that may be easier than you thought. Visage also might have said that Judge Leone wants to speak with me. Actually, Visage said the judge would talk *only* to me."

Her arms dropped to her sides, and she stared at him with a blank face. "You just forgot that part earlier, right?"

"I was considering whether or not to do it first." Reed shrugged, at a loss. "Leone apparently wants to talk with me about taking Danzig down. According to Visage, the judge isn't the only one willing to join forces against him."

"Why would you need to think about it before telling me?"

"Because Visage also said that Danzig ordered the hit on Dontae as payback for us blowing up the Ghanzi deal for him. So, diving into this conspiracy with an anonymous phone caller with questionable motives might put you—us in the crossfire again."

She looked at him askance. "That's literally my job."

"Not like this." His gaze slipped to the minute fading scars on her throat. Shrapnel that had nearly killed her. "If I take a meeting with this judge, who knows what we're walking into."

"Or who this Visage is or how he knows that you know the victim. . ." Nat froze, realization on her face. "You knew this Dontae Black well, didn't you? I mean, otherwise why go through all that trouble to position a body if seeing it wouldn't really hit home? If the person was a CI or an old collar, you'd be surprised, but not shook. You knew the victim personally, closely." She planted her hands on her hips. "Tell me I'm wrong."

Reed stared at her for a moment. She really was a singular woman, as he'd heard someone say. And she'd been there, through the chaos of every-thing. Pulling him back from the abyss of an endless nightmare when no one else could. And she'd kept his secret about having the MER-C system hidden. Reed took a long breath through his nose and then nodded. "If I tell you this, you're in it. As in, 'able to be subpoenaed,' in it."

Nat sat back on the control desk and folded her arms. "Tell me."

Reed took off the gloves, dropping them on the control desk. He glanced around the space, aware of the cameras and microphones. "Not here."

8

The pachinko parlor on ninth avenue downtown was a favorite spot for Reed to meet with confidential informants. It was the sheer noise and activity that made the place impossibly loud and way too crowded to eavesdrop on anyone effectively. The first thing that hit them was the smoke. Outlawed in most areas, pachinko parlors somehow always had a cloud of smoke hovering near the ceiling. Warbly, incoherent music blared over the clang and alarms of the pachinko machines. Cartoon voices and flashing lights announced winners with artificial cheers sounding from the speakers around the parlor. Metal bearings clanged as they bounced around the inside of consoles that resembled squat pinball machines before spilling out into a waiting tray. Coins clattered every few seconds, mobile service bots rolled from stool to stool offering haggard gamblers free drinks in both Japanese and English, and security guards at the back entrance drank from something wrapped in a brown bag. Perfect.

They walked over a carpet littered with discarded machine receipts and sat in a far booth near the snack bar. Reed called up the menu on the table kiosk and ordered a Pachi Plate, which was really just a bunch of stuff coated in tempura and then deep fried. He waited for the service bot to slide their hot lemon waters onto the table before speaking.

"I went down to the bayou with Coyote's family nearly every summer from the time I was ten. My mother was an ER nurse and her shifts left me alone a lot so when school let out, she'd packed me up and send me off."

"To play with alligators?"

Reed smiled a little. "It was good for years. Coyote and I would take his pontoon boat and explore the waterways. We'd sneak into rated-R movies. Play ball. Just. . . kids, you know?"

"And then what?" Nat played with the lid of the little metal teapot, making it go up and down like a puppet mouth, not looking at him. "You said it *was* good. What happened?"

The memory, long cast aside, drifted to mind and the heat and humidity of that night sent a shard of dread through Reed.

"We were seventeen. Coyote and I had started hanging out with Dontae more that year because his dad was a bad ass and we thought we could be too." He poured the bright green tea into the porcelain cup as he tried to find the words. "The Kindred were seen more like Robin Hood than outlaws back then. They gave back to the parish here and there. They paid to rebuild a youth center that had been torn down in a storm and gave a wad of cash to the food bank. We thought they were cool."

"Never mind the drugs and guns?"

"The poor see displays of wealth differently, I think. I know I did." The entrance pinged with new customers and Reed glanced back at the door. When he turned back, he met Nat's concerned gaze. "My father was a career criminal. He was kicked out of the army and did odd jobs. Mostly he was a thief and a gambler."

"I didn't know that," Nat said. "I just heard he'd died when you were young."

"When I was fourteen, he wrapped his truck around a tree running from the sheriff over a speeding ticket. Stupid." Reed shook his head. "On the other hand, Dontae's dad was important. He gave back. He was somehow respected."

"You admired him."

"Until we got to know Dontae better. He'd show up with bruises, busted lips, twisted elbows. We knew his dad was a drunk. We knew he hit them but. . ." Reed leaned forward on his elbows, head in his hands. "We didn't know how bad until it was too late."

Reed sat back in the booth, telling her about that night. The memory of it flooded his mind. The whirl of the evening sky as he looked up at it through the tree branches. Stolen beer sloshing in his belly and making him chuckle at the way Coyote was cawing to the wind. Dontae couldn't stop laughing at the squeaky sound of his own voice. They stumbled together, shushing each other, knowing they were out too late. Purple light hugged the horizon as the sun set late into the evening. They stumbled across the field, hopped the fence at the edge of Dontae's property, and crept along the side of the house toward the back yard. Then they heard the screams.

"We ran toward the shouting. I remember seeing Dontae's father standing over Dontae's mom as she cowered on the ground against the back fence, sobbing hysterically. I'd never seen anyone hurt like that before." Reed rubbed his eyes with his fingers, trying to forget her swimming eyes. The sad confusion on her face. "I'd been in fights at school. I boxed. My dad wasn't a saint either."

Nat nodded, trying to hide the shock, but her eyes never lied to him.

"I'd seen enough fights to know the difference between a scuffle and a beating. And her face—" Reed pushed against the table, looked away at the frantic anime cartoon playing in the center of one of the pachinko machines. "She looked like she'd been in a car wreck or something. So, swollen. So misshapen. I just froze."

"You were a kid."

Reed shook his head. "I should've moved faster. I should've . . ."

He closed his eyes, and he was transported back to that moment. But unlike the immersive, fever dream state caused by the MER-C device, Reed knew without a doubt these memories were real. They were his and the impact of that pivotal moment flooded his senses. Each breath he now drew carried the thick, pungent scent of the Bayou.

Dontae had seen what was happening as soon as they were through the gate. He grabbed a piece of lumber lying near the fence and ran for his dad. Screaming for him to leave his mother alone. Reed and Coyote ran after him. Dontae's father, Mack, was big and fat and mean. He batted the scrawny Dontae away like he was nothing and kicked his wife in the thigh. She screamed and the sound ground through Reed, pushing him faster.

He and Coyote ran at Mack, and it took both of them to move him. They knocked him off-kilter, making him stagger sideways. Dontae shouted something and ran at his dad again with the two by four, but Mack was faster than he looked. He ducked and yanked it from Dontae, slamming it into his back. Reed swung, landed a blow to the chin, and then Mack hit him back. Reed's world went tilt. He stumbled into a partially finished flower bed and the bricks tore into his back. He couldn't breathe, the wind knocked out of him, and he gasped at the sky, tears heating a path past his temples. The moon poked through the ragged clouds, lighting the yard in the pall of death.

"We kept running at him, but he just tossed us around like we were rag dolls," Reed muttered. "And then Dontae landed a blow with the board. I don't know how he got it back. And Mack almost went down. Then pulled a gun from his waistband."

"Oh, man," Nat whispered, leaning forward. "He pulled a gun on kids?"

"On his own son." Reed shook his head. "On his wife."

Mack had screamed at Dontae's mother. Incoherent, drunken words filled with hate and accusations. And then he raised his gun and pointed it at her face and Reed saw the piece of pipe on the ground. He dove for it, came up with a swing he'd learned during PE, and hit Mack in the arm. Reed felt a crunch. Mack shouted with pain, his body twisting toward Reed, the gun coming around, and then the night exploded with light. With a blast that tore past Reed and slammed into Mack, throwing him back. He lay sprawled in the patchy grass. Crimson seeped across his middle, saturating the filthy t-shirt. His wide eyes held Reed's for an aching moment before they went empty. Panting with panic, Reed turned to see Dontae with a shotgun. A rivulet of smoke drifted up in the pale glow of the moon.

"It was self-defense," Reed said quietly. "That's what we told ourselves."

"Is that what is in Dontae's sealed record?" Nat asked, her face a mask of calm. "A conviction for killing is father?"

"The most you'd get is that we were all questioned days later just as a matter of routine, but," Reed shook his head. "We never told anyone."

Nat made an incredulous guffaw. "What'd you guys do, hide the body? Clean up the hysterical mother?"

He held her gaze until her face fell and she shook her head slowly.

"How?"

"Coyote kept his head. And we talked about calling the cops, but they weren't who we were afraid of. We'd just killed a member of a vicious motorcycle gang. In his own home. With his own gun. This was—"

A service bot ambled over on rickety wheels. The screen that served as its face lit up with a friendly line drawing smile as it told them their food was almost ready. Nat waved it away, her gaze resting everywhere but on Reed's.

He continued. "Dontae had priors for fighting. So, we talked with his mom who was barely there. And we all decided to just... make it go away."

"Go away?" Nat sank back on the bench, her brows furrowed. "What did you do?"

"I did what I had to. And if I could go back in time, I'd do it all over again."

"You didn't answer my question," Nat pushed.

"Dontae took his mom to the hospital. He told them his father had attacked her and he had fired his dad's shotgun into the air to break them apart. This was in case anyone heard the blast or tested Dontae's hands for gunpowder residue. He also said his dad drove off on his bike afterward. The mom corroborated everything. The prior calls for domestic violence gave Dontae credence. Not to mention the way his mom looked during the interview. Coyote knew bikes so he took the motorcycle to another gang's territory and left it. He made it look like it had broken down. I think he walked it the whole way. He was so afraid to be caught riding it. And I, uh, I was bigger than both of them." Reed shrugged, his throat in a vice. "I took care of Mack."

As Reed spoke, the pachinko parlor shifted. He was no longer in the booth. Instead, the hard wooden plank of the boat seat was beneath him and the slow-moving waters of the bayou drifted past the pontoon. Reed rowed steadily, the smell of churned up rot surrounding him as he paddled down the waterway. It was quiet, almost still. The only sounds were the occasional scrape of the cinderblocks against the metal hull of the boat and the night creatures that accused him with every slow, creak. Every plaintive whine of a bird. Reed refused to look at Mack. He'd found a chain in the garage, and it slid against Reed's leg. When he looked down, the water at the bottom of the boat, darkened by the blood, looked black. It rose up on his sneakers, staining them. And then he heard it. The low, rumbling growl of a bull alligator. It was close. And all Reed had to do was push.

"They never found him. We think the gut shot helped him stay down."

Nat's eyes got wide. "Oh crap! The sidewalk chunks at Matthew's Beach, the way Dontae was chained to the cement."

"He knows." Reed nodded. "The killer knows exactly what I did."

A moment passed, then another, without words. The frenetic chaos of the pachinko parlor drowning out everything until Nat spoke.

"Every time I think I understand you, I find out I don't even know you," Nat murmured as her gaze traveled his face. Unreadable to him for once. She stood suddenly, shrugging on her coat. "I gotta go."

"We drove together—"

"I'll call a ride share."

"Nat," Reed reached for her arm, but she slipped away. He let her go and hoped he hadn't just lost someone else to the secret of that night.

9

Reed left shortly after Nat did with a takeout box of the tempura plate they never had a chance to have. By the time he got home it was dinner time and he ate it while watching a racing movie on mute and then fell into a fitful sleep. His dreams were filled with snapping jaws, black clouds over a sliver moon, and pachinko balls raining down on the dark bayou waters like hail. A strange bird call wailed through the dark. Staccato, insistent, more like an alarm. He startled awake just as his phone stopped ringing. The call indicator had a city number. Reed called the number back, thinking it might be Nat calling from somewhere in the technology building, but he got a man's voice.

"Detective Reed?"

"I just missed you," Reed said, recognizing the caller. He only knew Steuben Fernandez in passing but heard he was a decent parole officer. He was a good guy. Fair.

"Sorry to get back to you so late in the day but I thought I'd try to knock this last thing off my list tonight. Some things broke loose in my schedule for this weekend and I'm trying to keep my promise to take the family out for some fun."

"No problem." Reed checked his watch. It was nearly eight at night.

"Good, good." Papers rustled in the background and then Steuben said,

"Your partner called about Mr. Dontae Black, aka Bullet Black?" Steuben's voice was gruff, but kind. Like he'd been a drill instructor or a coach and was trying to do penance.

"Yes, we were checking up on a claim made by his girlfriend, a Fleur Benoît. She said Dontae met with a lawyer to clear the way for him to move to Louisiana in the next few months."

"That's the first I've heard of it," Steuben said. "Black was almost through year one of a three-year parole. I don't see how that's possible. Hold on." There was typing in the background and then Steuben came back. "Yeah, I mean sometimes, based on performance and risk factors, if a parolee demonstrates a vital need to relocate for job or family or health. But we'd have to get approval from the state he's moving to as well."

"Courtesy Supervision, right?"

"Yes, and then he'd go through a whole vetting process, it winds through different departments. It's a whole rigmarole."

"But it's possible?" Reed drew circles around Fleur's words in his notebook.

"Possible, but not unless you go through the proper channels, which it seems Mr. Black had not."

"For some reason he seemed to think it was happening. I was told he already secured an apartment in Louisiana."

"Mr. Black would've needed to go through me for all of that and like I said, this is the first I've heard of it. With these guys, sometimes they believe wishful thinking is the same as permission."

"Huh." Reed thanked Steuben, ended the call, and then typed up a text with the gist of the conversation and sent it to Nat. He stared at the phone for a few minutes, but she didn't text back.

He tried to go back to sleep but by midnight, he was tired of trying and getting sore. Reed forced himself to get up, throw on some sweats, and wandered through the chaos he'd created in his own bedroom. Books on memories and head injuries, neurological articles, and medical journals sat piled in stacks on a trunk at the end of the bed and on the floor underneath his window. He had little specimen bottles with different scents he'd collected over the past months lined along the sill. Smells he'd gathered to trigger a memory like smoke, jet fuel, and gun oil. His research led him to try scent, sound, even motion exercises to elicit a memory and none of it worked reliably. Reed reached for his notebook, flipped to the sketch of the beach scene, and stared at the haunting profile he'd drawn of Dontae's body. How would Danzig know Dontae? Where would they have possibly crossed paths? Why come after Reed now, after months of truce?

The book on meditations sat open on his coffee table and Reed stared at the breathing chart on the glossy pages. He got up, grabbed one of the bottles from his room, and then sat on the living room couch. He closed his eyes and concentrated on one of the memories he'd taken from Slater. An image of the metal halo on the dying man's head as the MER-C system ripped the memories from his mind flashed behind Reed's eyes.

When he'd injected the serum with the enhanced memories, they'd been powerful, overwhelming, and Reed had been trapped inside the terrifying moments of Slater's life until Nat had shocked him out of it with a blast of a fire extinguisher. Those memories were too dangerous. The aftereffects too harsh. But retrieving a "viewed" memory, one already in his head, by himself was different.

They were shorter, disjointed, random moments that were hard to hold on to before they faded. But they were there, and Reed needed them. He pulled the cork on the little bottle and breathed in the sharp scent of jet fuel. He set the bottle aside and sank into his breathing, blocked out the sounds of the room, the street outside, the tick of the heater's hot metal. He tried to see what Slater had seen. To imagine the hangar where Danzig had ordered the death of Reed's girlfriend. He reached for the memory. The room darkened around him, and metal walls flickered into view across a vast polished floor. Slater's thoughts furled at the corners of Reed's mind, but like vapor, they vanished into nothing.

Reed's eyes snapped open. His fingers dug into the couch cushion, his breath ragged with the effort. The room was stuffy, and he walked out onto his front porch and stood in the cold taking in a deep breath of the brisk winter air. It was frostier than the night before, the car he'd spotted driving by his house before sat a block down right underneath the streetlight. So that he could see them watching. Reed thought about walking out to confront them, but that last time he'd tried it, they sped off before he could get close enough to see their faces.

A stiff wind swept across the grounds chilling Reed. Ice crystals made fractals in the flash coming from the streetlight across the condo's small grounds. It was broken, had been for a few days, and it blinked slowly, lazily, the warm yellow drawing Reed in . . .

Slater's memory exploded before his eyes and Reed was no longer himself. He was lost in the foreign memories of a killer. Cold determination settled into his gut and a *knowing* flit across Reed's consciousness. Knowledge of the yacht's floorplan, the coordinates of his inflatable craft, the resistance of the sea to his flippers. The synaptic connection with the mercenary blurred Reed's reality until there was no separation between him and Slater. Flashes of that night flared before his eyes.

The hull of a ship through a diving mask, the fog hovering low over the water, a sliver of light glowing just beneath the horizon. Cold seeping into his bones from the frigid water despite the cold suit. Reed had been here before. Viewed this memory through Slater's eyes, but it was different somehow. The edges of his vision blurred, the sound muted, equipment on the deck faded in and out of existence as if the memory itself were degrading. Reed focused on the moment, willing himself to stay in the memory. A man's voice, loud and slurred, echoed out from the deck. The ting of ice in a crystal tumbler sounded. Clear as a bell out on the black of the sea. The drift of the water rocked the yacht and made the older man stagger. He caught himself against a sun chair and giggled drunkenly to himself. Slater had used the noise of the mistress's shore boat to mask his own arrival. Eisen Danzig was nothing if not consistent. His wife was due back in the afternoon. He'd be alone all morning on the boat.

The old man froze when he saw Slater. A look of terror flashed across his face for a moment but was gone. Reed felt the triumph that had washed over Slater in that moment. When the tyrant saw his end.

"I wondered if he would send you. That evil little bastard couldn't even do it himself." Eisen sneered at Slater, taking a final slug of his drink.

He's stalling. Slater's thought flared brightly through Reed's mind. He had a weapon. The old man moved suddenly and then everything sped up. Like a movie on fast forward, Slater lunged with the knife, slamming the knob of the handle down onto the top of the old man's head. He fell to his knees and Slater stood over him. Panting with adrenaline, watching the blood seep into the teak deck. Reed tried to look away, but he was locked in time with Slater, with what he'd done and thought and felt.

The old man moved, and time slowed back down. He groaned and tried to push himself up with his bony hands but slumped back down to the deck. He craned his neck, staring up at Slater, a ragged sheet of thin, liver-spotted skin dangled from the wound to his scalp. Blood oozed between his eyes as he let out a wheezing cackle. "She'll fight him for it. She'll make him p-pay—"

Slater hit him once more and then stared at the still body of one of the most powerful men in the world. A man who'd ordered the destruction of empires, the ruining of lives, the deaths of many. He looked so frail, so fragile now. Slater picked Eisen up, leaned with him over the side of the boat, and tossed him into the ocean like garbage. Then he bent down, swiped a gloved hand through Eisen's blood, and smeared it on a nearby bracket poking out of the bulkhead. He put a little more on a bolt on the outside hull, so it looked like Eisen hit on the way down as well. Reed stared through Slater's eyes down at the water. Blood-red, it lapped at the hull.

Sunlight erupted from the horizon. Bright, orange, and blinding. Reed turned his face to it, seeking warmth but it was cold. Empty. Alarm pulled at the periphery of Reed's mind. Something wasn't right. The floor shifted underneath his feet and Reed stumbled. Was he not in his condo? He gasped, yanking himself from the memory's hold. Confused.

He was outside. In the real world. Frigid, salt air assaulted his senses. The boat he now stood on listed in the water of a harbor. The memory faded, its dark shroud lingering as he realized he wasn't looking at the sun, it was a flashlight beam that slashed back toward him and then blinked out. Reed shook his head, trying to get his bearings and then a figure in the dark lunged. Reed moved, not fast enough, and the punch threw him sideways. He stumbled on the deck of a yacht, blinking, hand to his throbbing jaw. Two men flanked him, silhouetted by the rising sun behind them. Dressed in sweatsuits and ski masks, they had on gloves, no weapons. One taller than the other.

"What the hell?" Reed shivered in the cold. His arms had a layer of frost clinging to his skin and his legs ached to the bone.

"Did you hear what I said?" The taller one shouted. He shoved Reed against the railing, nearly toppling him over. "Back off the judge!"

The blow to his back nearly took his breath. This was definitely real. He just didn't know how. He couldn't remember how he'd gotten to the marina. Reed's fingers were stiff from the cold. His head fuzzy. "Who are you?"

"You know who we are," the other one said. "You know who sent us."

"This is your last warning," the tall one said, and he grabbed Reed by the sweatshirt, his shoulder coiled back. "Or next time you won't walk away—"

Reed kneed him in the groin, caught the man by the back of his shirt as he staggered forward, slammed him into the railing, and then overboard. The other man was already moving, and Reed used the momentum in the narrow passageway to his advantage. He ran straight at him, slid at the guy like he was stealing home plate, and cracked his knee sideways. The guy flew into the bulkhead and then crumpled onto the deck. He reached for his hoodie pocket and Reed slammed his fist into the guy's kidneys, another uppercut to his ribs. The metal of a blade sliced past Reed's neck, barely missing. Reed stepped back, kicked the attacker full in the chest, and sent him flying backward into a stack of boogie boards. Reed strode over him and stood above the writhing man. He kicked the knife overboard then he leaned over and pulled up the attacker's mask. The guy was young. Maybe mid-twenties. He clutched his side, a groan of pain tearing out of him, a look of utter panic on his young face as he tried to breathe. Reed crouched down and smacked the guy's cheek.

"Hey," he snapped, holding the guy's chin with his hand. "Look at me."

The guy gasped, pulling in a desperate breath. "I think you broke my ribs."

"Tell Danzig this was the wrong move," Reed said. "You got that?"

The kid nodded, eyes red with exertion.

Reed stepped over him and walked off the boat. "Now it's my turn."

Reed called 911 from an emergency kiosk at the entrance of the marina and reported a break in and possible injured party before hanging up when they asked his name. He was at the Bell Harbor Marina near his condo and so Reed opted to jog home. It took him under twenty minutes, and it warmed him up but the entire trip he was still unable to remember how he'd gotten to the marina in the first place. He had no business there. He owned no boat. He'd never even been inside the grounds until that night.

His clothes and shoes were soaked with frost or sweat, and he was shivering uncontrollably when he got home. His door was open, like he'd just stepped out of it, and he pushed through silently, listening. Nothing. It was empty and freezing inside. He grabbed his phone from the coffee table. The clock read four thirty in the morning. Reed rushed to his room and stared at the clock on the dresser with disbelief. He'd lost more than four hours. In a daze, he ambled back to the living room and sank onto the couch. He pulled the blanket around his shoulders, trying to warm up. His service weapon sat in his holster on the mantle and his gut knotted. What if he had fired his weapon during those hours? What if he had driven? Had the men he fought even been real? Reed pulled up the leg of his sweatpants, exposing his knee. An angry red bruise covered the joint. Scrapes marred his knuckles. He'd hit something. Whether or not it was a person was anyone's guess. He ran his hands through his thick hair and took in a ragged breath. He was losing control.

His phone beeped next to him, and Reed looked over. He had five missed calls. No voice mail messages. No texts. He didn't recognize the number, but it was local. The calls had started an hour ago, at five a.m. He picked it up and returned the call. It rang once and then Visage's voice came through.

"Detective Reed, what are you doing?" He sounded agitated, angry. No longer the helpful informant.

Reed hit the record call widget Nat had installed on his phone. "You're going to need to be more specific. I pissed off a few of people today."

"You've put everyone in danger. My sources say that Danzig found out you've been researching Judge Leone."

"You told me to."

"I told you to *meet* him, and quickly. Now you've possibly exposed an asset, not to mention drawn a target on your own back. I hear there's a price on your head."

Reed rubbed his jaw. "Not the first."

"Please don't. You're more than a thug. That much has been made clear to me."

"By whom?" Reed snapped. "How do you know Danzig?"

"Meet with Leone. You'll like what he has to say."

"I have no legitimate reason to corner a judge and interrogate him. Nothing in his past even hints at impropriety. And your 'information' is always a day late and dollar short."

There was a pause and then, "Someone came after you," Visage said. "I knew it."

Reed ground his jaw. The night had gotten on top of him, and he revealed more than he meant to. "It was a warning."

"So, Danzig knows already," Visage muttered. "Do you see how fast he's moving, detective? You must make contact with Leone tomorrow."

"I want to see your face first."

"What?"

Even with the digital altering, Reed recognized the uncertainty in Visage's voice. "Yeah, I think before I do anything on your word, I want to meet face to face."

Visage was quiet for a long time before he spoke. "It baffles me how hard it is to get you to do something about your girlfriend's murder."

The pain, the sleeplessness, the confusion boiled up on Reed and he shot to his feet, he growled into the phone. "Say her name again, and Danzig won't be the one you have to worry about."

"He's laughing at you. He had her killed, an officer at that, and still you've done nothing."

"Go to hell. If you know so much, you take him out. Though I doubt you have any actual means of hurting Danzig. Otherwise, you wouldn't be hiding behind a fake name and a goofy voice. You probably haven't even met the guy. Maybe you're just some wackadoo in his mother's basement stroking some imagined vendetta against Danzig because he discontinued your favorite hunting rifle."

"Memory Containment Pod number three-three-seven."

Reed froze. "What did you say?"

"From the MER-C system you stole from Gerald Price. You have it, yes? Hidden somewhere safe, I'd imagine."

A cold sweat slid down Reed's spine. "Who are you, really?"

"Find it. View the memory," Visage said, his voice edged with anger. "And then do what you're told."

Reed sank back down onto the couch, his mind churning. "How do you know all of this?"

"Because I am who I say I am," Visage nearly whispered it, his voice steady once more. "The question is, *who am I talking to*? Hmm? The law dog or the outlaw? The good detective or the kid who clawed himself out of the Belltown gutter by sheer will? Because only one will survive what's next."

10

Nat showed up at his place at five thirty in the morning. The security screen in his room flashed her face at his door. She held up a bag of donuts and a coffee. He buzzed her in. She was-wandering around in his kitchen in her giant puffer jacket opening and closing cabinets when he stumbled out of his room. She busied herself with choosing a donut and wouldn't look at him. When he walked over, she opened her mouth to speak, closed it, and then slid his coffee toward him.

"Apology accepted," Reed said and took a sip from his disposable cup. The coffee was gloriously hot, dark, and bitter. Perfect.

She shook her head, leaned into his fridge, pulled out the milk, and sniffed it. As she poured it into her to go cup, she said, "It's just . . . you're like an onion, but the layers are made of effed-up surprises and danger."

"Understandable." Reed tried to smile at the strange analogy, but his jaw ached and the scab at the corner of his mouth stung. "If you want a different partner, no hard feelings."

"That attached to me, huh?"

"No, I meant—"

"I know what you meant." She looked over with a smirk but as soon as she saw his face, she frowned. "Please tell me you were in a bar fight."

"That would be better?"

"Probably." She waved her hand at his face. "Spill."

"Danzig's men attacked me last night."

Her gaze flitted around his front room. "Here?"

"On a yacht, actually."

"What?"

The confusion of last night roiled in his chest and he cleared his throat before answering. "Let me show you something."

He led her to his bedroom and showed her the research, the articles, the bottles of specimens, and piles of books.

"What is this?" Nat wandered the space, her gaze flitting from sketches he'd made of previous crime scenes to the scribbled-on notepads on the dresser. She picked up articles he'd clipped and stood in front of his far wall to study the glossy photos of Danzig and Slater and everyone else tied to what happened at Neurogen. Statements and bank records lay fanned out on a foldable table in the corner of the room, and she picked them up, read them. Nat ran her index finger down the rows of numbers, muttering to herself.

"You've been digging into Danzig's financial ties."

"Just what Coyote could get me."

"Find anything?" Her eyes watched him. Like he'd seen her observe suspects.

"I followed a few financial threads as far as I could but I'm not a forensic accountant."

"SPD has those guys to spare."

"I didn't want to bring SPD into it. Not yet"

Nat's shot him a hurt look. "Or me, apparently."

Reed's shoulders slumped, but he nodded. "Or you. Not until I had something."

Nat waved a hand at the board of information. "You realize you're only like a few lengths of yarn shy of this being a serial killer wall, right? I mean, what are you doing? You were told to stay away. Everett Danzig is not someone you stalk."

"I haven't talked to him for months. Just that one time in person."

"And that went spectacularly well," Nat shook her head. "I thought you were meditating. Sitting on a pillow and contemplating your breathing. Are things this bad? Are they getting worse?"

"I lost time last night."

Her startled gaze snapped to his. "How long?"

"Four hours, give or take?"

"You don't know for sure?" She turned her back to the wall and leaned a hip on his desk, arms folded. "You just walked around in a fugue state for who knows how long?"

Reed shrugged. "Yes? I guess. I don't know. I was standing at that door looking out at the grass one second and fighting a stranger on a boat the next."

"I'm sorry, did you just say it's the guys who'd been watching you? They were on the boat too?"

"I think they followed me." Reed caught her gaze flit to the scabs on his knuckles and he slipped his hands to his hoodie's front pocket. "They warned me to back off of the judge."

Nat frowned. "How would they know we're looking into him?"

"That was my question," Reed said. "Is there any way you could've left uh, cookies, or something?"

She smirked. "Not cookies. Not footprints. I tripped no digital security wires. I was careful."

"You're sure?" She arched a brow at him, and he put his hands up. "Okay, you're sure."

"Speaking of the judge, Leone's clerk won't give me a straight answer on when we can meet. I can't get any information from his office, but friend in the DA's office said Leone cleared his docket and took a personal day, maybe two, it's unclear."

"So, he's at home?"

"No, I had patrol do a drive by, maybe see him puttering around in his garden or whatever. No one's been home for a couple of days. They sat on it for a while and the neighbor came over after the mailman, an old lady from next door, and took his letters."

"He's having someone collect his mail." Reed shook his head. "He's in the wind?"

"I mean, he could've gone somewhere warm for the long weekend. Don't we have a Federal Holiday coming up?"

"President's Day. Keep digging. I want to be sure he's not running."

She was silent for a moment, and then, "Reed, how did you get to the marina? And why there? What was significant about it?"

"I think I might have walked." He told her about that evening. Trying meditation. Viewing Slater assassinate Danzig's father again. Which had occurred on a yacht, just not the one he'd been on last night. All of it.

When he was done, she tilted her head. A weird look on her face. "What else? There's more, I can tell."

"Visage called again."

She sat up straighter. "Shut. Up. What did he want?"

"He also knew about us looking into the judge. He was pissed. And pushy. Not like the helpful whistle blower he first presented himself to be." Reed repeated the conversation high points for her.

"That sounds threatening," she said. "And it was the same guy?"

"Yes, same cadence. He said I'd exposed an asset." Something flitted at the edges of Reed's consciousness. "He insisted I meet with the judge again."

"What did you say?"

"I told him to kick rocks. That I didn't know who he was or what his agenda was, and why should I listen? I tried to rile him up, but he wouldn't engage. Then he mentioned the MER-C system. He told me to 'view' a containment pod if I didn't believe him. He even gave me a specific number."

"Holy crap!" Nat's eyes went wide. "How does this guy know all of this?"

"I don't know. He's connected. Somewhere in Danzig's proximity. Privy to police info."

"What are you going to do?"

Reed hesitated. "Listen, the injected memories are fading, but not like normal ones. Not like my own. These are different. There's something about reliving them that's, I don't know, degrading them. Altering them to something worse. Like nightmares in technicolor. I can't stop them. I can't sleep." Reed paced the area near the kitchen. "And now I'm blanking out."

"I think it's smart you're not going to inject any more. . ." She pushed up from the desk. "Right?"

"Maybe I actually need fresh memories to mine for information. Maybe you can only revisit or relive them a few times before they corrupt?"

Nat regarded him for a moment, chewing on her inner lip, and then, "Okay, I need to tell you something."

"I already don't like where this is going."

"I've been using the cybercrime AI, Ada, to help me research memory therapies and drugs from not just here, but globally. Hold on." Nat strode out of his room, went to her purse by the door, and pulled out a digital tablet. She flipped to what she wanted and handed it to Reed when he caught up. She'd brought up a few research papers.

"What am I looking at?"

"What is the most commonly known symptom of PTSD?" She didn't wait for his answer. "Flashbacks, right?"

"Right . . ."

"It's what you're experiencing, essentially. Real memories of real horrors perpetrated by Slater and you're reliving these events not like a bystander, but with your heart and soul. You feel the anger, right? The shock of the moment? If there's blood, you feel it. If there're screams, they echo in your ears. You get real adrenaline rushes, I know. I've seen your hands shake—"

"That about sums it up," Reed cut her off, not wanting her to go on. She'd been paying more attention than he realized, and a vice tightened around his chest.

"Neurogen created the MER-C system first as a memory augmentation for Alzheimer patients. Then later, as an interrogation weapon. That first injection of the serum acts like a primer. It's like a jolt of adrenaline to the brain, right? It lights up the memory trail like a Christmas tree with chemicals and hormones and the electrical current of the mind. So, you're not just watching memories of an event. You're feeling, seeing, and *knowing* everything at an intensity that is off the charts. They're more intense than any memory you could manifest on your own. That was the point of the drug and the system. To enhance them enough to be retrieved and relived by someone else."

Reed flashed on the sense of incredible speed and scope at the first onslaught of the chemical on his mind. "What are you getting at?"

She tapped the tablet. "This is a paper on PTSD. Specifically new studies on memory and how it affects treatment outcomes."

"Wait a second," Reed put his hand up.

"Just bear with me for a little bit," She talked over him, her eyes locking with his. "Studies show that when you relive a memory, the act of doing that changes the memory itself. That's why eye-witness accounts can change, why we could swear we remember something one way and then we see a picture or a recording and realize we remembered it wrong. But that's not what happened. It wasn't remembered wrong in the first place. It's the recalling of the memory *after* the fact that degrades it. Morphs it. Imagine what a chemically altered memory would do?"

"You're saying I'm remembering the memories wrong?" Reed shook his head. "I can't believe that's a sentence I'd ever need to say."

"I'm saying the kind of memories you are triggering are not just Slater at the beach or Slater driving on the freeway. It's him killing people with his bare hands. Him dying, literally. These may not have been your original memories, but these are traumatic experiences all the same because you're not observing these events on a television screen. You're experiencing them in the same way as if you'd lived them."

"Not seeing how this helps."

"Dammit Reed," She slapped her thigh, her brows knit. "It's not help. It's a warning. You need to treat these episodes as if you were having actual flashbacks from actual events you lived through." Nat's eyes slid from his. "And, there's something more."

"Awesome." Reed looked where she pointed to on the tablet.

"I had a guy I went to school with take a peek at what they were doing at Neurogen. It's bad. Even the consumer grade treatments were skating the edge of acceptable risk. The therapies included augmentation via drugs, electrical stimulation, hormone therapy, et cetera. What my guy found was that the memories formed while under these intense chemical, electrical, and hormonal drugs make the memories corrupt more easily for lack of a better explanation. Quicker too, than standard Alzheimer drug would cause."

"That's just great," Reed rubbed his face with both hands.

"Look, this tech is new. Most aren't even in human trials yet. That's what put Neurogen so far ahead of the competition."

"And made their discovery able to be weaponized."

"Unfortunately." Nat hugged herself, watching him.

Reed leaned against the wall and folded his arms across his chest. "You're telling me that these memories are not only finite, but they also get more dangerous the more I try to access them?"

"Yes." She rifled through the stack of research. "It's called a retrograde flaw. Not like the amnesia one where you can't access memories or information from before an injury. This paper is about current memory augmentation therapies like the ones they were using at Neurogen. Drugs that restore, repair, and enhance existing memories are lifesaving for people with Alzheimer's trying to hold on to basic needs, but the memories themselves, the altered, super-charged memories have a shelf life. Those memory paths, however brightly blazed across a person's mind, will eventually degrade away without continued therapies."

"So now I'm like that mouse in the book that they made smarter and then he died?"

Nat rolled her eyes. "Well, you didn't get smarter. I can vouch for that. But you do have artificially boosted memories floating in your brain. And those augmentations, when they burn through or change, will likely alter tissue around it."

"Tissue that makes me who I am."

She nodded silently and handed him a stack of papers stapled together. "I know how you like printouts. I compiled all the studies and stuff together, but that's the gist."

"Did they know this would happen?" Reed flipped through the papers, skimming the dire news. "How is this legal?"

"Reed, treatments like these, they're a Hail Mary for most patients. Think of the warnings associated with experimental cancer trials and yet people are willing to try it because it's probably their last chance. These patients are in the same boat. Their mind is fading faster than other drugs can stop it. It's a last-ditch effort for them not to slip into oblivion. And unfortunately, like most human trials, there can be unintended outcomes."

He sank onto the couch again. The hallucinations, the aggression, his false memories about himself. Slater had warned him. "Can I stop it?"

Nat sat down next to him. "I think if you can stop the memories that come on without warning, you can slow if not arrest the damage."

Reed sighed heavily. "Well, shit."

"Do you see why I don't think you should inject more memories? Screw what Visage wants you to see. You have no idea what's on that memory containment pod or what it'll do to you."

"Danzig had Dontae killed. He had Caitlyn Killed. He had his thug throw an innocent teenager off a university roof to cover up his crimes." Reed said, frustration burning through him. "He kills or takes whatever he wants and thinks no one can stop him. He's a criminal, Nat."

"Then catch him how you caught everyone else so far," She reached up and tapped his temple. "By hunting them. Like you were trained."

Reed shoved his hands in his hoodie pocket. "Solve Dontae's murder to take down Danzig."

"Hey, works both ways, right? They got to you through Dontae. You run them down for killing him. It's the natural order of things." She forced a smile. "And it doesn't require you to poach your own brain for answers."

He stared out at the bleak sky, at the dark gnarled branches of the bare trees, and the brown of decayed grass. It was starkly beautiful, the scene. Like the melancholy of a poem, you couldn't quite shake. Nat made sense. He'd been spinning his wheels chasing after wisps of rumors regarding Danzig. Dontae's body was real. His murder was solvable.

"You're right. Dontae is the weak leak for Danzig. He doesn't fit. Not with the weapon or the money amounts that would be involved, not even how he was killed."

"You mean as revenge? To piss you off?"

"More like pull me in." Reed shook his head. "To what end though? I've studied his business decisions, who his allies are abroad, and the way he approaches vast projects. Just the hierarchy alone of High Rock Holdings screams discipline. Danzig thinks like a general. Deliberate, measured, strategic. He wouldn't have done this without a bigger plan. Something other than just hurting my feelings. There's a goal here I can't see."

"Well, I guess we just have to figure out how your friend, who by all counts was a small-time crook," she put her hand up. "No offense. Crossed paths with one of the world's biggest ones."

"Tens of thousands of dollars a round," Reed murmured. That was the key. Something occurred to him, and he looked over his shoulder. "When you were upset in the Virtual Depot earlier, was this retrograde flaw thing the reason why?"

She let out a soft snort through her nose. "No. That was Parker."

He turned to face her. "What did he do?"

"He's watching you. Both of us, more likely. Whatever." She got up and put her disposable cup in the compost bin. Her big coat swished all the way. "He pulled me aside to warn me about associating with you and the peril it will inevitably wreak on my career."

"That's fair," Reed said and was relieved when Nat smiled back, though weakly.

"He told me about your addiction and treatment." Her dark eyes held his. "Your reprimand for violence while undercover."

"You already know all of that." After their first case and the fallout from it, Reed had told Nat about the intervention by Tig, his partner at the time, and his stay at a facility that specialized in treating LEOs. And he walked her through the bar fight while undercover that got a complaint from an overzealous DEA agent on the same task force. He'd told her everything he could that wouldn't endanger her life.

"Yeah, but Parker shouldn't know those things. They're confidential." She pointed angrily out the window. "He's snooping in our records. *My* records. How does that look for a rookie detective to have a senior one questioning cases? He cornered me and warned me that you're toxic to my career. He hinted that the brass was watching our every move, maybe even looking to get rid of you. Oh, and he knew you took off from Matthew's Beach without talking to the food trucks—" She stopped mid-sentence, her eyes narrowing at him. "You went somewhere, didn't you? To talk to Dontae's friends or was it family?"

"I was going to talk to them again with you today, but yeah." Reed grimaced. "Sorry, Nat. I didn't know what was what yet and I was trying to tie off what I thought was an artery of crap coming our way over Dontae's body."

"Well good job heading that off," Nat said, but the edges of her mouth turned up and the vice loosened from Reed's chest. "Who'd you talk to?"

"His girlfriend, Fleur." Reed bobbed his head side to side, debating. "Coyote went with me."

That pissed her off. "What?"

"He knows them and insisted on being backup."

She waved the comment away with an irritated flick of her wrist. "Whatever. Was she helpful?"

"Not really. She's under the impression Dontae left the gang life and was taking her to raise their baby in Louisiana after a few months."

"Survey says that was untrue," Nat said. "What else?"

"That's it. I checked out her story with the parole officer, and it was a lie. Dontae wasn't taking her anywhere but down with him. My mother believed those kinds of stories for years. Not one of them true."

"I got your text." She stood, hands on her hips, small figure lost in that ridiculous coat, but it was her deep gaze that rooted him to the floor. "Reed, I know you were trying to keep me out of this, but that's not how this is going to work. I'm safer knowing what might be coming."

Reed hesitated and she sighed, turning from him. "No, you're right. You're in. One hundred percent."

She crossed her arms and looked at him askance. "Okay, then tell me what happened with Parker."

"He thinks I got him shot."

"Did you?"

"Not if he'd listened," Reed said. "He's just being vindictive. Trying to drive a wedge to cause trouble because we're on his turf."

"I don't think that's it." Nat chewed on her lower lip.

"What are you thinking?"

"He's got to be from professional conduct, right? The rat squad? At least that's what I called him."

"You didn't."

"I'm surprised I didn't get written-up right then. He's up to something though. Gathering info for someone."

"Slater did say that Danzig had a mole high up in the department."

Nat made a so-so gesture with her hand. "He's not that high-up."

"We need to handle him." Reed was relieved to concentrate on something other than his damaged brain. "Keep him chasing his tail."

"I'll put in a few queries into your past cases and make sure to do it via the general conduit and not the one in cybercrime. If he looks into what I've been doing. He'll see it." She grabbed her tablet from the couch and started tapping. "Let's see if this makes him think I'm having doubts. Maybe he'll try talking to me again. Although I was sort of harsh, to be honest."

Reed studied her. The downturn of her lower lip as she typed. The faint wrinkle between her brows. Nat had lost her family in a fire while she was still in high school. She was the daughter of a cop in San Diego. She was tough, but Danzig was a whole other tier of trouble. "Are you? Having doubts? You worked your ass off to get to where you are. It wouldn't be a dumb move to consider a new partner."

"No, but it'd be a boring one." Nat stopped working and looked at him. "I decide what's good for me and what's not, alright? Not some opportunistic weasel who thinks he knows what I want and then threatens it. He wants to play games, we'll play games."

Reed put his hands up in surrender. "You're impressively conniving. Mean, even."

Nat smiled then. A genuine one. "Stop buttering me up."

11

Reed and Nat decided to hit Marcel's garage early in the morning before things got busy and his buddies arrived. Reed wanted to talk to him about Dontae, the imaginary lawyer, and where Dontae thought he was going to get enough money to leave the state. If they were in the Kindred together then Marcel knew more about what was going on than he admitted. Especially if it was club business. They pulled some relevant information on both Marcel and the business and were on the road by six.

Reed played the recording of Visage's call from the night before while Nat drove. When it was over, she gave him a concerned look.

"He sounds desperate," she said and honked at the car in front of them. They'd waited a millisecond too long after the green. "What happened to the moral citizen just helping out law enforcement?"

"He's angry. I'm not following his script."

"Do you even know how this little game of his is going to end?"

"Hopefully with Danzig in jail."

Nat peered out of the driver's side window. "Aren't we going to get there too early?"

"I had patrol cruise through. There's a loft space over the garage. The light was on, so my guess is that Marcel's home. The place is listed as his address as well."

They talked about Reed's conversation with Steuben at the parole office. And what that meant about Fleur's account of what happened.

"I don't think she was making it up," Reed said and braced himself against the door as Nat took a turn wide. "She said he was out of the game, and I think she believed him. At least she was clinging to that hope enough not to question much."

"What I want to know is what he was planning on telling her in a few months when it became obvious going home wasn't happening."

"I don't think he planned on doing it officially."

"And just not tell her?"

"Lies lead to lies lead to lies," Reed said and shrugged.

"How did Dontae get the nickname, Bullet, anyway?" Nat looked over with a grin. "Was that from his dad or do you get a free one with gang membership?"

"No, he was fast," Reed glanced out the window. The buildings got older, more run down as they moved further into the heart of Belltown. "He was a running back. Best in the area. Everyone believed he'd make it out."

"What happened?"

"Family. Fate. Who knows?"

Marcel's garage was on Western Avenue sandwiched between a night-club and a parking lot. The sign said it was Travis's Fabrication Station, but Reed doubted Travis was around anymore. Records showed Marcel had bought the place ten years prior. Nat pulled into the gravel parking lot, and they watched the front door and windows for a minute while they put in their earbuds before getting out.

Nat made a clicking sound in his hear and he nodded. Check.

The metal corrugated building was like every other auto shop Reed had been to, save for the rusted work bots and automated appendages stacked onto shelving just inside the rolling hangar door. The air tasted of grease and dirt and the wan light of the morning sun cast a weak light on the rusted siding. They stopped at the threshold and Reed leaned in. It looked empty. An air compressor droned in the way back and a rickety metal ceiling fan rattled overhead.

"It's Reed and De La Cruz with the SPD, Marcel," Reed called out. "I have an update on Dontae's case." A clang in the upper loft pulled Reed's gaze and he stepped inside, Nat right behind him. He motioned for her to take the opposite end of the same and then he took a turn along the storage area eyeing the machines. A plastic tarp covered a bumpy pile behind a stand holding pipes. Reed bent down to take a better look and spotted a city sticker on a piece of equipment. "Marcel? That you? I just want to talk."

Reed passed a few unfinished fabrication projects that looked legitimate. Enough to give the impression of respectability if you didn't look too closely. Another noise from the upper loft, this time the sound of something falling onto the floor made them move. They joined at the foot of the stairs.

"Mr. Benoît, this is the police. Are you home?" Nat called as she slid her hand to her waist.

Reed led the way, Nat following close. They eased up the steps, the floor of the next level visible as they rose. A groan sounded and Reed drew his weapon. Nat did as well, and they crouch walked up the last few steps. A beat-up pool table dominated the loft space and on it, Marcel lay with his head hanging over the edge, an empty bottle of whisky in one hand, the tip of a pool cue in the other. An eight-ball sat on the stained carpet beneath. Reed figured that's what they'd heard fall. Marcel snored again, a gurgling noise that sounded like he was trying to swallow his tongue. His ample gut rose and fell beneath a torn heavy metal band t-shirt. One boot was missing from his feet. Tarnished neon signs flickered behind a padded leather wet bar. Reed scanned the loft. Crushed beer cans, beach balls, and a pair of hot pink stiletto heels were strewn on the floor.

He put his finger to his lips, holstered his weapon, and gingerly pulled the pool cue from Marcel's fingers. Nat walked over, her weapon on the sleeping behemoth. Reed held the cue just over Marcel's neck like a barbell and then nodded to her.

She leaned forward and yelled into Marcel's ear. "Looks like I missed a good one!"

Marcel's eyes snapped open, and he lunged for her with a grunt, but Reed held him down with the cue.

His hands went up when he saw Nat's gun. "What the hell?"

"Relax, podna," Reed drawled. "We're here as friends."

Marcel's eyes swam for moment, but he looked up, saw Reed, and batted the stick away with a snarl. He pushed himself off the table. He favored his booted foot, his other clearly hurt. "Don't you need a warrant or something, *pig*."

"That's getting old," Reed said and whacked Marcel's gut with the pool cue. Hard. "And a little hypocritical, don't you think?" In the corner of Reed's eye, Nat stiffened. He stepped back from Marcel, his hands out at his sides, and smiled.

Marcel steadied himself on the edge of the table. "What is it you want, Morgan?"

"I need to clear some things up about Dontae. That's it."

Marcel glanced at Nat, frowned, and then looked at Reed. "I don't know jack about what that dumbass was doing."

Reed grinned and nodded to Nat. "Did you know my partner is a cyber genius? She's a reformed hacker. At least that's what we tell ourselves."

Marcel glanced at her suspiciously. "And?"

"And she found a whole bunch of information about you before we came. Like the city program you joined to qualify for the loan to get this place. Remember that? The taxpayers secure your loan if you promise to hire ex-cons for gainful employment. Ring a bell?"

"Yeah, so?" Marcel squared his shoulders, his hungover brain finally catching up to the situation.

"So those programs have a lot of rules. Sometimes they even perform audits. All it takes is a tip from a concerned citizen."

"I'm legit," Marcel snapped, but his gaze slid from Reed's. Nervous. "If answer your question, will you get the hell out of here?"

"Dontae told your sister he was taking her home," Reed said. "They had a place in Terrebonne all lined up. Out on Dulac by her momma."

"Probably a lie," Marcel scoffed. "You know all about those, don't you Morgan?"

Reed ignored the dig and walked along the wall, making Marcel turn on his unsteady legs to stay facing him. "He told her he had gone legit, that he was working overtime here with you to make enough money to go. Did you know any of that?"

"He worked at the shop and went home for all I know. I didn't get in his business."

"Now *that* is a lie," Reed said. "Because he was Kindred. Which is exactly your business."

"No, he wasn't."

Reed pointed to Nat. "She has access to the most amazing personal details on that digital tablet. Things like property taxes. Which you have not paid in three years."

Marcel licked his lips. "That's a fine at most."

Reed walked to the stairs and motioned for Marcel to follow him to the first floor. "Dontae was wearing a cut. He didn't have rank, but he was in."

Marcel shook his head. "I'm not following you anywhere, man. I heard the stories."

"Those are mostly made up, Marcel," Reed said with a drawl that felt foreign after so many years. He put his hand on his holster. "Come on, now. I want to show you something and don't want to drag you down these dangerous looking steps by your ankles."

Nat moved in and Marcel hesitated for a moment, sizing her up, and then walked toward Reed. She followed behind and they all walked back to the stack of equipment covered with the tarp. Reed pulled the corner of the material, and it slipped all the way off the pile revealing at least seven, maybe eight city work bots.

"That's a municipal trash collection unit," Reed pointed as he walked past them. "Parking lot attendant buggy, security quadruped," he paused and looked at Marcel. "Those are expensive."

"They're decommissioned. I got them cheap at auction," Marcel snapped, his eyes going to the door.

"This was serviced eight days ago." Reed pointed to a sticker with the toe of his boot. He clicked his tongue. "You've been pinching city robots, Marcel."

"And this . . . this is definitely not up to code," Nat said. She tapped the flaps of plastic sheeting at the entrance to a paint shed next to her. "There's no filter system. Just a nozzle and some garbage bags for walls? This'll shut you down."

"You're running a chop shop. With ex-cons. How many employees do you think you'll have after today if we dust those stolen machines for prints?"

Marcel scoffed. "You didn't have a warrant to search. That's inadmissible."

"I don't care about your little side hustle, Marcel. I care about this." Reed pulled a stack of pictures from his trench jacket. He held up a full color, glossy, autopsy photo of Dontae's mangled body.

"What the hell, man?" Marcel cringed, and the color drained from his face. "A little warning?"

"Why? You won't have one when this guy comes for you." Reed dropped the photo on the cement floor in front of Marcel and pulled another. It was a close-up of the wound made with the Kraken. Ragged and burnt. The flesh butchered like meat. "He lured Dontae out to the lake in the middle of the night and then blew him in half." Reed tossed the photo at Marcel. "You think he won't come for anyone associated with whatever this mess is?"

"I don't know anything about anything," Marcel snapped. He backed up from the images like they were the surf coming for his feet.

Reed held up a photo of the stab wounds to Dontae's chest, another of his cloudy, lifeless eyes. Marcel slapped them out of his hand. Reed balled his fists at his sides, rolling his shoulder forward as he got in Marcel's face. "Yes, you do know. All those guys who work for you are Kindred or want to be. *Nothing* happens out of your shop without you knowing. That's how it works, if I remember. Not one bruise, not one bone is broken without permission, right?"

"I don't talk to cops without a lawyer," Marcel said and tried to turn and leave, but Reed stepped in his way, gave him a shove backward.

"Reed," Nat said, her gaze on Marcel's reddening face. "He wants a lawyer."

"Then just listen." Reed put his hands up but didn't move out of the way. "Dontae called me the night he died. He told me he was in trouble. Something bad was coming."

Marcel hesitated and Reed saw an opening. He pointed to the pictures on the floor.

"He wanted out. Just like Fleur. They were hopeful. They were trying to be a family. Your sister said they put money down on a place, man. She said it was ten minutes from your momma." Marcel shook his head, but it was disbelief on his face. And worry. Reed pushed. "But something went wrong.

The guy turned on him or something, but it went wrong, and he killed Dontae."

"I said I don't know what he was into."

"But he was into something, right? One last job?"

A car pulled into the gravel lot. Nat peered out and then tapped the side of her head. Her voice whispered in his earpiece. "We got some serious looking dudes heading this way, four of them."

Reed pulled his notebook from his jacket, slipped out the printed still he'd made of the drone telemetry, the one showing Dontae's terrified look as he stared at the Kraken camera when it soared past him. He held it up for Marcel. "When the guy killed Dontae, he was watching."

Marcel turned away, he paced, limping on his injured foot and then slammed his fist down on one of the partially stripped robots. "I told him to stay away from that freak."

Reed nodded to Nat, who met the guys at the door with her badge. "One second guys."

"Who was Dontae doing the job with?"

"I don't know. It wasn't club business."

"But it was a job, right? With whom?" Reed bent down, picked up the photo of Dontae's ragged wound. "*This* is what he did to your sister's fiancé. Your soon-to-be nephew's father. A 'brother,' isn't that what you said earlier? Don't you want whoever did this to pay?"

"Marcel, you alright, man?" One of the men in coveralls yelled over Nat's head.

"Stop, Morgan!" Marcel snapped, limping on his hurt foot. He called out past Nat. "Give me a second."

"All I need is a name. A place to start. Was it an old associate? Another gang, maybe? Was he trying to branch out?"

"No, no," Marcel rubbed his hands over his two-toned beard. "It was some weird posh guy."

"A couyon."

"Yeah, he was crazy. Dontae told me one time they were always meeting in weird ass places like the guy thought he was in a spy movie. Anyways, they were at a bus station and some homeless woman started bugging them or something. Dontae said this guy just punched her out cold without a word. One swing. Must've broken her nose because Dontae said the guy pulled out a handkerchief and wiped the blood from his collar like it was nothing."

"Reed?" Nat called.

The group of men, four deep, stood just in front of Nat who had her hand on her weapon and a try-me look on her face.

"Tell them to back off or we finish this conversation in the alley behind your shop."

Marcel rolled his eyes but waved them off.

"You said this guy was posh, like in groomed or clean cut? In what way? Military high and tight, businessman, model, what?"

"I never saw him."

"Any idea how he knew Dontae?"

"I don't know, man. Dontae was all hush-hush about it. He didn't want Fleur to worry, so he kept what he was doing to himself."

"But he told you about the incident."

"When he was toasted, Dontae didn't know how to shut up." Marcel kicked at the pictures with his good foot. The look on his face almost hurt. "That was messed up. You got problems."

"I need a name. Something other than a well-groomed psychopath." When Marcel balked, Reed pointed up at the loft. "Am I going to find narcotics up there? Maybe something for the foot? You still keep a stash in the left corner pocket?"

"Really, man?"

Reed nodded. "A name, Marcel."

"Alright, look. Dontae mentioned going to Mookie for advice. Something about Serbia?" Marcel said as he walked back toward the stairs. "Didn't you talk to him yet?"

"Who the hell is Mookie?" Reed asked.

"Guess you aren't always the smartest guy in the room," Marcel said. "Why don't you do some actual police work and find out for yourself?"

Back in the car, Nat sat staring out of the windshield. "You switched on the bad cop real quick back there."

"That's the only thing Marcel understands. He grew up hard. Been a criminal his whole life."

"I'm just worried about how fluent you seem to be in that language," Nat said. "After all these years, I mean."

Reed stopped writing in his leather notebook and looked at her. "What language?"

"Violence," she said, and her eyes were sadder than he'd ever seen them. "You're gifted in it."

12

Nat wanted Reed to drop her off at the Virtual Depot to check out Marcel's assertion that the mysterious "Mookie" was somehow connected to Dontae Black.

"I'll start with known associates, though I don't remember seeing the name in the file. Then we'll widen the search. Once I get an actual name, I'm going to start feeding everyone we've come across into Ada," Nat said as they pulled into the parking structure.

"Please don't name the AI." Reed looked at her in all seriousness. "That's a bad idea. If you treat them like they're real, they'll start to think they are."

"I'll have you know that Ada Lovelace is considered the world's first female programmer," Nat said with a bit of a superior air.

He grinned. "I didn't say it was a bad name. I said it was bad to name it."

"Oh, for Pete's sake. I'm not going to say the 'Cybercrime Neural Network AI every time we talk, okay?" Nat rolled her eyes as she gathered her gear. "As I was saying, *Ada* is testing a new net-matrix program and I think it can help with this case." She held up her tablet. "If I get anything, I'll shoot you a packet."

Reed drummed the steering wheel with his thumbs and then said, "This guy Marcel described, Dontae's partner, he sounds like a psychopath.

Cold cocking an innocent lady, an indigent one?" He shook his head. "Coyote should know about him."

"Can it wait an hour or so?"

"No." He gave her an apologetic look, and she sighed.

"You don't want me to come."

"I don't want you on the stand if this all goes sideways."

Nat nodded once, stepped back, and tapped the hood. "Try not to get each other arrested."

Twenty minutes later, Reed walked into Automatica, a completely unstaffed lunch counter near the station. The sequence of automated arms and kitchen appliances whirred behind a protective glass barrier as the robot chef churned out the only six meals the café offered. Three breakfasts, three lunches, all of them sandwiches. Reed had eaten there quite a bit before Nat was his partner because he liked the quiet and that most orders were for pick-up. Done in bright red and chrome, it resembled a movie diner from the nineteen fifties. An entire wall of small square vending windows lined one side of the café. Reed waved his phone over the reader, bought the lunch special of the day, and walked to the glass door that swung open. The turkey sandwich meal came with a brownie he liked and Reed grabbed his food and the accompanying drink and looked around.

Coyote was sitting with his back to the wall at the last table. Though there were standing customers, no one approached him despite his clear lack of purchases. Reed didn't blame them given the styled mohawk, skull T-shirt, and spiked leather jacket. Reed's black trench coat, suit, and tie seemed downright welcoming. Coyote waved Reed over.

"Well, your ears must have been ringing, Morgan, because you are the talk of the town this afternoon."

Reed slid onto the chair opposite and took out a triangle of turkey sandwich. He put it on a napkin and pushed it toward Coyote. "Sounds like Marcel speed dialed the entire parish as soon as I left."

"It's called a message blast now, but essentially," Coyote said. "And yeah, he complained."

Reed took a bite of his sandwich. "I barely touched him."

"You know Marcel was there when his old man got mangled in that machine. Their metal shop was covered in blood, not to mention the carnage of the man's arm and chest. He barely survived."

"I know." Reed dropped his sandwich, no longer hungry.

"Marcel couldn't stop shaking when he was telling us, remember? He looked like he was going to pass out."

"I do. And he tried to stop the bleeding with his bare hands. I know." Reed rubbed his face with his palm.

"And I *know* you remember his mamma saying he used to wake up in a cold sweat, trying to wipe the blood from his hands all over again." Coyote leaned forward, his expression pained. "You are supposed to be the better of us, you asshole. Try acting like it."

Reed's gaze snapped up. "Best of us? That's not what you all want from me as long as I'm pointed in someone else's direction. Marcel wants results, Fleur needs them, and her mother threatened to get to the killer first if I don't. So, I needed a name." He jabbed his finger on the surface of the table. "Yes, I used a horrible knowledge I had of Marcel against him. I *could have* used a metal pipe."

"Simmer down, Morgan," Coyote said as he scanned the café.

"Danzig displayed Dontae's body, man. Even if it wasn't him personally, he ordered it. He watched Dontae die via camera, and I don't think he's done hurting people who are associated with me." Reed shook his head, his temples throbbing. "And then there's the caller. This Visage who claims he wants to take out Danzig, but then threatens me with exposure. I have to find out how Visage is connected with Danzig before I lose—before more people die."

Coyote considered him for a second, then grabbed the chips, and leaned back in the chair. "What did you want to meet about?"

"That's it?"

He shrugged. "You made a decent point."

Reed pulled out his notebook and showed Coyote the sketch of the crime scene. "This caller, this Visage, he knows everything about that night at Dontae's house. Everything."

Coyote's face went more white than usual. "How?"

"I think whoever it is got it straight from Dontae himself." Reed held up a finger at Coyote's questioning look, pulled out his phone, and played Dontae's voicemail from the day he died.

"*It was the only move I had. I never meant for you or anyone else to get involved.*" Coyote repeated Dontae's words. He rubbed his bottom lip with his finger, his gaze settling on Reed. "I believe Dontae sold us out, brother."

"Sounds like it, but to whom? Danzig or Visage?" Reed pointed at Coyote with his last bite of brownie. "You know what I've been asking myself? If Dontae told one of them, then how does the caller know? Who else did Dontae tell for that matter?"

"Honestly, this just ain't sitting right at all." Coyote shook his head. "Dontae kept what happened that night a secret for almost twenty years. Hell, we all did. Why would he start squealing now?"

"It's not the when, it's the who. Think about it." Reed leaned forward across the table. "He was trying to do what his father couldn't or wouldn't. He was getting his son and his wife far away from the Kindred, the danger of Belltown, everything. It's what he'd been trying to do his whole life, first with football, then with this. But this time, he wasn't just trying to save himself. He was trying to save his family."

Coyote stared out the window for a few moments before turning to Reed. "If Dontae did squeal to someone about that night, to what end? What purpose would that serve giving someone leverage over you like that?"

"I don't know. A way to establish a kind of trust? Danzig has made people 'unavailable' before. He could have promised Dontae a deal for information on my past. Maybe this partner, this couyon is working for Danzig?" Reed moved to gather the lunch trash but stilled when something occurred to him. "That's why I need to figure out who this Visage really is. To see what he could have offered Dontae for the same thing."

"What's his angle?"

"Destroying Danzig is what he claims, but I don't think so. Or at least that's not all of it."

"You're going to have to walk me through that maze of a mind. What are you talking about?"

"I've been thinking about the players in this scenario." Reed counted them off on his fingers. "A mogul, a killer, a snitch, and a thief."

"And a cop," Coyote said.

"And a cop." Something below the surface was going on, Reed thought. The mechanical whir of the automatic food doors opening and closing pulled his gaze. Trap doors, hidden contents, tucked away from view. "There's another layer I can't see. That's the only thing that makes sense. Something triggered all of this. Danzig has a reason for doing this. I just have to find out what it is."

Coyote pulled the fresh cigarette from behind his ear and tapped it on the table. "The list of enemies for a man like that is mighty long. Everett Danzig is a bona fide bastard. Likely the reason he's a billionaire, but also the reason for which he is despised. Are you looking for anything specific?"

"I want to know about the people who actually fought back."

"If he's gunning for you, he'll have tripwires on anything important. Killing Dontae was supposed to set you off, yes? That is your theory?"

"Yes," Reed frowned. "What're you getting at?"

"You say Danzig had his goons following you for months, but they didn't do anything."

"Well, they *tried* to be intimidating."

Coyote's gaze went to the bruises on Reed's face. "Okay, and that's after torturing you with Dontae's death and a gruesome display with your name written in blood. But you didn't do anything?"

Reed shook his head. "Visage says he's after revenge."

"Yeah, man, but why now?" Coyote bothered the silver ring pierced through his bottom lip with his top teeth. "What's the impetus?"

"I don't know. Last time he was protecting a high value target, Congress-woman Joshi, could be a similar situation. Maybe I'm getting close to him somehow?" Reed fought for a thread of probability in that and found none. He'd gotten no closer to Danzig's inner organization than he'd been when he started no matter what he'd told himself.

"Doesn't matter his reason, he knows you'll come after him."

"I have no way to prove he's connected to Dontae's murder." Reed thought for a moment and then. "I think I'm going to end up seeing this judge whether I want to or not."

"You could be walking into a trap."

"Probably." Reed finished his drink.

"A most dangerous game, my friend." Coyote looked at Reed, his head shaking slowly. "What do you need?"

Reed didn't answer. He stared at his turkey sandwich, panic prickling under his skin. "I ate mayo."

Coyote looked at the sandwich. "So?"

"So I'm allergic. Deathly allergic." Reed tapped his coat pockets looking for his epi pen.

"No, you're not. You inhaled my momma's potato salad every summer."

"Yes, I am," Reed said, but faltered. Wasn't he?

"You don't have any food allergies," Coyote gave him a worried look. "What are you going on about?"

Reed sat back in the booth, breathing hard. That wasn't his memory. He'd never carried an epi pen. Looking down at his hands, Reed felt a stirring of dread. The false memories were slowly blurring the lines of who he was.

Shaking his head, Reed looked at his friend. "Sorry."

"You good?" Coyote raised a brow at him. "What's your favorite color?"

"Do you even know that about me?"

"I just assumed it was black, man. That's all you wear."

Reed smiled. "Listen. Nat and I can follow the public records, lawsuits, things like that, but I need an insider. You have your financial friends in the emerging market and your network of informants. That's something I can't access."

"Oh, so now it's *not* insider trading. It's vital information," Coyote said with a grin.

Reed knew his friend's association with financial bros and their bad habits had made him a ton of money, which he'd poured into local real estate. He had staff all over the city, maids, cooks, even pediatricians, who informed for him on the goings on of key tech and financial people. Not surprising given what he paid.

Coyote smiled. "I can dig up dirt on anyone."

Reed leaned forward, the cool of the metal table on his forearms. "Who did he screw over recently? Disgruntled employees, deals that fell through, people burned by Danzig's ruthless practices. Unless someone sues, those things stay in the background, but there's something. With men like Danzig, there's always something."

"You want his enemies."

"This Visage found Danzig's enemies. Like Judge Leone, possibly others. I need to do that too. There's truth buried somewhere in there."

Coyote pointed the unlit cigarette at Reed. "Hold on, you aren't seriously considering takin' him up on his challenge, are you?"

"I don't know yet." Reed got up, threw his container in the recycler. "I need to find this Mookie character Marcel told me about. Have you heard the name before?"

"No, but I will consult the ether," Coyote said. "And the brilliant Detective De La Cruz? Isn't she able to do this for you?"

"I don't want her anywhere near this until I know what I'm looking for. The more I learn about this partner of Dontae, the more the guy sounds like a lunatic. You might want to watch your own back."

"I'm covered. Does Nat know you're sharing case information with me?"

"She understands you might be in danger too."

"Is that so?" A wicked grin spread across Coyote's face as he slid the cigarette back behind his ear. "I would be happy to give her a call and allay her fears. Is she worried about me?"

Reed chuckled and headed for the door. "You're not that lucky."

On his way out to his car, something Danzig had said to him earlier gnawed at the corner of Reed's mind.

"Assets or enemies," Reed muttered, wondering which one he was to Danzig in this game.

13

When Reed got back to the station, he went up to the Homicide floor to find Nat. He looked for her by the digital wall in the center of the bullpen. She'd definitely been there. All their case notes were up. The smart screens displayed a floor to ceiling view of the Matthew's Beach crime scene. Aerial drone footage of the cement blocks, the canines searching the bathrooms, and Dontae's chained body in situ played on the screens. Updates scrolled along the edge of the display from various departments next to notes from Nat's tablet, and Parker's scrawled messages on digital sticky notes. Tig's office took up the far side of the homicide floor where a big picture window allowed him to look out onto the bullpen. His blinds were closed, which was never a good thing. His former partner was an even keeled guy, unless he was yelling at you.

Reed sidled over to the snack table, contemplating what to do when Nat's unique tone trilled in his phone and a data packet appeared on his screen. He opened the file at the snack table, throwing brownie bites into his mouth as he read what she'd found. He hated to admit it, but Marcel was right. Reed definitely needed to talk to Mookie. Her tone sounded again. This time a text message.

Don't go up to Homicide. I'm hiding in cybercrime. Parker tattled. Tig is on a tear. Watch out. Also . . . I sent a packet of information to your phone.

Reed was just about to turn and leave when Tig yanked open the door, locked eyes with him, and pointed. "You!"

"Boss?"

"In my office. Now."

Reed squeezed his eyes shut. "Crap."

Parker exited Tig's office just as Reed walked in. He avoided Reed's gaze as he passed.

"I need you to stop stonewalling Parker, you got that?" Tig snapped without preamble.

"I'm not. He was working on the neighborhood surveillance, doorbell cameras, lawn drones, like that."

Tig's index finger came up between them. "That was two days ago. He is an excellent detective and you're sending him on errands."

"I didn't send him anywhere. He *told* us what he was going to do and then left." Reed held up his phone, shaking it. "This works. If Parker really wanted to get ahold of me, he would have. Instead, he comes in here—"

"You're giving him the run around and you know it."

"He's up to something."

"Here we go." Tig shook his head, hands on his hips, then, "Work with him or I make you."

Reed shoved his hands in his suit pant pockets, a slight grin on his face. "Make me?"

"New protocol from on high says homicide cases need two detectives working a case and Intelligence has been bugging me to lend Nat to them for their taskforce . . ." Tig shrugged. "Your choice."

"I only work well with one person," Reed said, and meant it. "And you're going to ruin that because of Parker's whining? Turf or not, that crime scene literally had my name on it."

"Exactly," Tig snapped. "Do you not get that you're on thin ice? That suspension, that fiasco you called an investigation into Neurogen, blew up in our faces."

Reed jabbed his finger at the doorway. "I broke that case wide open!"

"Your career barely survived. Hell, you barely did." They stared at each other, years of working together quelling their arguments to a scowl and a shaken head. Tig looked at him with tired eyes. "Reed, people are watching you despite the clearance the shrink gave you. Be smart. Keep a low profile, and don't crap in the company pool. Play nice with Parker or you're riding a desk, and *he* solves this with De La Cruz. We clear?"

He ground his jaw but nodded. "Crystal."

Reed strode out toward the parking lot to look for his unmarked car when Nat called. She was munching on something, probably popcorn, as she spoke.

"Did you get busted down to meter maid?"

"They have bots for that now," Reed muttered. "We have to work with Parker or Tig is going to ship you out to Intelligence."

"I mean, I would rock it over there," Nat said and the amusement in her voice made some of the dark clouds in Reed's head dissipate. "But you can't get along without me. It would be a fiasco for you."

He grinned. "Well, for my sake, I'm taking Parker to talk to this Mookie character Marcel mentioned. He's downtown right now according to your notes."

"You read the data packet, good." Nat said something to someone in the background and was back. "I'm moving through the victim's financials, but it's sparse. I was hoping to find this lawyer you said he mentioned, but I see no payments going out to a law firm. Not even one of those legal sites where you download forms and fill them out yourself. Also, no PO Boxes popped either in case there wasn't an office."

"Mobile sharks, that's nice," Reed said.

"Oh, that reminds me. I talked to that one prosecutor I dated, and he said Leone just got named to the state supreme court."

"Wait, how?" Reed slowed his pace. "Washington elects their supreme court judges."

"Unless one dies. Then the governor appoints an interim judge."

"And that's Leone?" Reed sped up his pace, an inkling of a lead sparking alight. "Who died? And how?"

"I'll check," Nat said. "And I don't like where your mind is going."

"Me either."

"Back to Dontae, we can't locate any kind of cell phone or device under his name, so he must've used a burner to leave you that message." Nat crunched some more. "Which is moot because the killer probably took it."

"You might want to switch gears with Dontae's financials. He wouldn't go near a bank."

"You're telling me Dontae was cash only?"

"Or cryptocurrency. The whole motorcycle club operates that way. Anonymity is a contraband runner's best friend." Reed thought for a second. "Though, Dontae never trusted anything digital when it came to his money. He'd use cash."

"I can check wire services. See if he's been sending and receiving money. If his girlfriend is on the account, she can let you take a peek if you can convince her. Other than that, I'll need a reason for a warrant."

"Where does Fleur's money come from and is it enough to move states and hire a lawyer?" Reed asked.

"I believe her mom was somehow getting cash to her."

"What makes you think that?"

"I talked to the building manager earlier. He told me that Fleur handed him cash every month. She doesn't make enough to cover rent at her job. She works at a grocery distribution warehouse downtown stuffing bags into delivery drones. She makes squat," Nat said. "I checked wire transfers to her. Nada. But . . ."

Reed smiled. "What'd you wheedle out of the manager?"

"Two things. Fleur gets a box delivered every month from a place called the Spicy Griller. It's too big for their assigned mail slot so the package is left at the office until she picks it up. He just happened to read the label. They're a small business out of Terrebonne that sells seasonings and rubs. They have a PO Box and murky ownership."

"Probably someone's grandma selling out of her kitchen."

"Right, but how much does Fleur grill that she needs a twenty-ounce shaker of Bayou Jerk every month?" Nat clicked her tongue. "I think this is a cash delivery."

Reed stopped walking "That's just paranoid enough to be true. Without using banks, digital transfers, or crypto you're left with cash. And since you can't hand it off yourself, the next best thing is mail. But you'd be worried about sending that without at least trying to hide it was money. The problem is, we don't know what it was for. Rent, a lawyer, moving?"

"I might have a way to check," Nat said. "Although Fleur pays in cash every month, she did have to give the manager a checking account number to rent it in the first place. It's her mother's account at a bank in, you guessed it, Louisiana. And get this. The packages stopped a couple months ago. Right when the manager said Fleur's mom came to live with them. She could be there to help with the move. Especially if it's in a couple of months when Fleur will either be ready to pop or taking care of herself and a newborn. Either way there's movement."

"Okay, we're not doing this right. We're not going to get anything out of Fleur or her family. Her brother Marcel and her mom won't cooperate. I'm thinking a call down to Terrebonne to any place for rent near Dontae's momma would be more productive. Fleur said they had a place near her already. If that's true, she'd be preparing the place for them and probably knows quite a bit. I'll bet it was cash or promise. Friends and family will rent to you on your word that you'll pay them back when you find a job." Reed rubbed his scar over his eye and sighed. "I'll make the call. She won't talk to you."

"Oh, you know what? Give me the number for Dontae's mom. There are some things I can do to clear the picture, if you know what I mean."

Reed lowered his voice. "I don't, and I'm really glad about that."

Her throaty chuckle floated to him and then, "Any other fallout from your conversation with Tig?"

"Nothing except for him making it crystal clear we can't keep Parker so far out of the loop."

"That could be dangerous given the whole teenage killers thing you've got in your closet."

"No kidding." Almost to the car, Reed nodded at Parker who sat waiting in the passenger seat. "I'll keep you posted if we get anything from this Mookie guy."

"Okay, I'm going to dig into the Spicy Griller business, see what I can find. I'll also talk with the forensic accountants, maybe they can see something I can't." She paused and then, "There's something else. Someone gave an interview about you."

"What?"

"Yeah, a private news blog posted an article about you and this case. It's a small site, but it's gone viral before. This thing could grow legs. I spoke with the author. She said an anonymous poster sent them an audio file, it was mostly questions about you. Like had she thought to look into your past. Did she know she could request information about you from the SPD, stuff like that. The blogger said the file was uploaded via the site's anonymized tip line. No way to tell who sent it. I'm sending you the blog. The writer sort of hints at the Neurogen case, it mentions you and hints at a fight between you and a wealthy captain of industry. But it's vague. It does quote an unnamed source that described you as having a questionable past. Needless to say, Tig is not happy. I think the only reason he hasn't blown a gasket is the blog's reach is small."

"How did you find out about it?"

"I had web crawlers trolling for your name. If the big news streamers push this, it could be a problem."

Reed rubbed his scarred eye. A headache was forming behind it. "That's Visage putting pressure on me to meet with Leone. He still hasn't contacted me to meet."

Nat was silent for a moment, and then, "You think this guy might go after Coyote? I mean, he was there that night too."

"It would be a mistake if he did." Reed leaned over to peer into the car at Parker. Held up a finger and gestured to the phone pressed against his ear. "My good friend Parker is waiting. I'll call you when we're done."

They disconnected, and Reed climbed into the driver's seat. He intended on driving in complete silence, but Parker's angry huffs told him that wasn't going to happen.

After a few miles and the fourth sigh, Reed gave in. "What is your problem, Parker?".

"You. You're my problem," Parker muttered, his gaze out the side window. "You shouldn't even be on this case."

"How do you figure that one?"

"I may not like you, but I know how you work. You tear apart everyone and everything until you find who you're hunting. This. . ." Parker gestured generally at Reed. "What even is this that you're doing?"

"What the hell are you talking about?"

"You're pussyfooting around the people and the information surrounding this investigation like you have a stake in the outcome."

Reed looked at him askance. Parker was sharper than he looked, and that was going to be a problem. "You done?"

"I am if you are."

"We're going to go talk to the guy our victim was arrested with. His name is Momčilo 'Mookie' Balian. He and the victim served time together at the Federal Detention Center, SeaTac. He might know who Dontae was talking to about this mysterious last job that got him killed."

"That info must be on the data packet that I *just now* got from De La Cruz." Parker poked his middle finger on his tablet not looking up. "I'll need a minute to catch up."

Reed took in the slumped shoulders, the pressed lips, and the red of Parker's face. The color extended up his pale forehead to his flaming hair like a lit match. Pressed suit, stiff white shirt, bland tie. Everything about him was ship-shape except for one thing. Reed's gaze slipped to Parker's socks peeking out from underneath his pants hem. They were bright purple with green dinosaurs. They were the kind of socks he saw on fellow cops the day after Father's Day or Christmas. Reed frowned. Did Parker have kids?

They drove toward the Denny Technology Triangle over by Westlake where one of the computer gurus kept his giant glass spheres you could each lunch in, and other digital geniuses set up shop. Formally a hilly area, a massive project in the early twentieth century transformed it into a flat, amorphous district with undefined borders. It was thought to encompass Belltown and stretched north from the business district all the way up to either Mercer or Stewart Street, depending on who you talked to. High rises with upscale restaurants, bohemian eateries, and trendy clubs all catered to the affluent high-tech workers that lived in astronomically expensive condos.

"We don't have much yet," Reed said. "Dontae was arrested with Mookie for trying to move a case of grenades up through the Canadian border. Mookie rolled on Dontae for a lighter sentence, but he got in a few fights while in prison. That added to his time, and so he ended up getting out the same month as the victim."

"Sounds like a stellar decision maker." Parker scrolled through the packet. "How did you get the name?"

"I spoke with Marcel Benoît, the brother of Fleur, the victim's girlfriend, earlier this morning. He mentioned Mookie. Nat did the rest."

"Parker held up his tablet when Reed stopped at a light. A grainy video of a man pumping gas at a station played across the screen. "After I looked at the neighborhood cameras, I hit all the gas stations and mini marts on the road to Matthew's beach, both ways. I was hoping to catch something on their surveillance. Mr. Black bought cigarettes and gas for his motorcycle about a mile from Fleur Benoît's, apartment."

"That's good. Supports the theory he was meeting someone," Reed said.

Parker craned his neck to peer up at the glossy skyscrapers. "What's a career criminal like this Mookie doing among the ivory towers of tech?"

"Prison training program." Reed took them toward Westlake Station, veered past Pine Avenue, and stopped at a construction site. The beginnings of a huge building butted up against the sky between a rental car lot and a medical building. "He qualified for work furlough and job training. His file says he learned to operate heavy equipment."

They parked just outside the chain link safety fence and Reed located a guy in a hardhat and asked for the project manager. After donning com earpieces, they checked reception with each other, then stood in silence watching the construction work as they waited. It was cold for the early afternoon, and Reed tilted his head to follow the line of the building up to the tenth floor. Self-rising scaffolding latched onto the structure's exposed sides. It moved people and lines up with it as it climbed. Air freight platforms hovered on massive fans as they moved netted supplies up and down the façade. The sun streamed through the breaks in the walls with a strange pattern. It shone onto the dirt that swirled at his feet in the afternoon breeze.

A pudgy guy in a light blue polo shirt and khaki pants fast-walked toward them. He shielded his concerned face with a clipboard as he approached. "Can I help you gentlemen?"

Reed and Parker flashed their badges and introduced themselves. The project manager's name was Lee, and he had the stiff bearing of a man who never had enough time.

Reed held up his phone with a photo of Mookie. "We're looking for Momčilo Balian."

"Oh, Mookie, yeah," Lee motioned to them as he turned, striding back the way he'd come with Reed and Parker rushing to keep up. He gestured at the building as he spoke, dodging an auto delivery cart carrying a pile of unused hardhats. He grabbed two as it passed and handed them to Reed and Parker "Your guy is working up on the ninth floor with the welding arms."

One of the finished sides of the building was deeply corrugated, and the pattern on the siding seemed more than aesthetic. Incredibly dark, Reed realized that what he'd thought were gaps in the walls were panels painted with the deepest black he had ever seen. The sunlight simply disappeared into the undulating surface as if it were pouring inside.

"What's this place going to be?" Reed asked as they climbed a flight of temporary stairs to the second floor. Long tube lights in hoods lined the walkway, their faint glow almost purple. "There are no windows."

"Very good, detective. It's going to be one of the first all vertical farm buildings on the West Coast." Lee smiled proudly. "Once completely online, this one building can grow the equivalent number of vegetables as five standard farms. With almost no water."

"No water?" Parker asked.

"We use a constant vapor stream filled with nutrients. Just saturate the roots. No bugs either." Lee nodded to a suspiciously skeletal looking elevator. "Here we are."

"You want to get on that?" Reed wasn't convinced it was even completely assembled, but the project manager got on anyway followed by Parker. The lift started with a jerk and Reed's hands shot out to the walls.

Lee chuckled. "Not a fan of heights?"

"Does this elevator seem rickety?" Parker teased as he bounced on the balls of his feet.

Reed shot him a look but didn't answer. He was too busy listening to the creak of the metal as it climbed ever higher. Parker's amused side eye made the torture worse.

"Can you tell me what this is about?" Lee asked. "Mookie is one of my best operators. I'd hate to lose him."

"We just need to ask him about one of his associates," Reed said.

The cage door of the elevator eased aside, and they stepped onto the unfinished level. The smell of hot metal and drywall dust floated on the wind. The complete lack of walls and the chill air of the ninth floor made the sweat on Reed's brow ice cold. Welding arms attached to overhead tracks worked under the direction of a task hub situated at the edge of the room. A control bank flashed as the automated welding appendages moved blindingly fast, shoring up the support welds with a shower of bright sparks. Iron workers walked easily along beams as if they were immune to gravity, the safety wires hooked to their belts dangled listlessly from the ceiling struts.

"Stay behind the railing and you'll be fine." Lee said over the sound of the welding arms as Reed and Parker followed him to the far wall and tapped his palm on the waist-high bar that ran along the perimeter of the floor. It sat a good four feet from the open wall with caution signs every-where. Lee pointed across the vast open floor at a man moving crates off a freight platform. "That's him."

Mookie was young, willowy, and sweating through his work uniform as he maneuvered a box marked five times his weight. He was strapped into an exo-lift suit and the outer skeleton of metal and hydraulics whirred with each power assist. Three other workers in similar suits stomped around the edge of the platform, and the vibration from their footfalls rattled up Reed's legs.

He signaled to Parker, who circled left, flanking the still unaware Mookie. Reed pulled the flap of his suit jacket aside, exposing his badge, hand resting on his holster as he approached.

"Momčilo Balian?"

Mookie looked over. "Who wants to know?"

He had an Eastern European accent and it struck something in Reed's consciousness.

"Detective Reed. I need to talk to you."

"Did you say Reed?" Mookie squinted at Reed as he approached, seemed to twist away, and then he snapped back around as he flung a crate in their direction. Silver tubing flew out of the box as it hit the platform. The clang of metal echoed through the bare floor as dozens of pipes scat-tered at their feet. Parker did a flailing dance before going down. Reed scrambled back, his hand finding the railing, steadying himself.

Reed pressed his finger to the earpiece. "Go left, go left!" He snapped at Parker and took off down the walkway.

Mookie flailed with the harness as he tried to run away. He stomped down the walkway, his gaze on the emergency chute ten yards ahead of him. He glanced back, saw Reed catching up and heaved a barrel of trash at him.

"Watch out!" Parker shouted in his ear.

Reed leapt over a gap in the flooring to avoid the barrel, but a welding arm swung at his head, pinging off his hardhat. Sparks flew at his face, burning as he navigated the cords and fallen debris. Mookie was almost to the chute. Another few yards. Reed caught Parker closing in out of the corner of his eye, and sprung at Mookie, taking the entire suit to the ground in a cacophony of clattering metal. They rolled, trapping Reed beneath the heavy equipment. His breath crushed out of him. Mookie wiggled out of the harness, elbowed Reed in the nose, and tried to crawl away.

"Grab him!" Reed heaved the suit off his legs. The metal support rods scraped the skin off his shins as he yanked his legs free.

Parker's gaze snapped to the edge of the building and then back at Reed. "But the railing—"

Reed sprang to his feet and jumped over a pile of equipment, running to intercept. He was almost to him when Mookie stumbled, went down in a full sprawl like he was on ice, and then came up swinging with a piece of rebar. Reed skidded to a stop, his gun coming out.

"I just want to talk to you, Mookie!" Reed shouted. He held his weapon down at his thigh.

"Nuh-uh," Mookie swung the rod, backing up. "I will not go anywhere with you!"

Reed could feel Parker's gaze on him. "Drop it!"

Mookie shook his head. "I want immunity."

"From what? I just want to ask you about Dontae Black."

Mookie let out a crazed laugh. "What's to talk about? He is dead."

"And I'm investigating why." Reed stepped closer, hand out in front in a calm down gesture. "All I want to do is find out who did this."

Mookie shook, the rod lowering to rest on his shoulder as he panted, blood from the fall dribbling down into one eye. "I have nothing to do with nothing."

"No one is saying you did." Reed watched from the corner of his eye as Parker closed in from the other side.

Mookie backed up some more, almost to the chute. Reed slid along the edge of the floor. The wind from below flapped his suit and tie upward. "Tell me what Dontae was into. Who was his mystery partner?"

Shaking his head, he gaped at Reed. "You are blind to what's really going on! All of this is so much bigger than you realize."

"Then explain it to me."

Mookie started to pant, to hyperventilate, his eyes darting from the edge of the building to Reed. "I am not going back."

"I have a bead on him," Parker whispered in Reed's earpiece.

Reed glanced to his side, Parker closed in, gun drawn.

Reed shook his head. Negative.

"Dontae was playing with fire. I warned him!" Mookie shouted.

"I can get him," Parker hissed. He was moving too fast, too aggressive to remain unnoticed.

Reed opened his mouth to stop him, but Parker was already in motion, propelling himself at Mookie who turned at the last moment. They tangled, veering toward the open wall. Mookie twisted toward the ledge, Parker in his grasp.

"Don't—" Reed grabbed the safety line dangling from the ceiling track, slammed the hook onto Parker's belt with one hand, and shoved Mookie away with the other. Flailing, Mookie caught Reed's sleeve for a second, his eyes going wide, before he tumbled off the side of the building, screaming with terror.

"Oh, my god!" Parker shouted, his hands on either side of his head. He was on the floor, a hairsbreadth from the edge.

The project manager stood clutching his clipboard to his chest, white as a ghost. Everyone on the floor stared in disbelief.

Reed edged closer and forced himself to peer over the side. Mookie stumbled around on the safety net protruding from the building two stories below, shouting what Reed was sure were obscenities in another language.

Parker staggered to Reed, the color drained from his face as he stared down at Mookie. "You knew that was there, right?"

Reed stepped back from the edge, his face a mask of calm despite his shaking hands. "Do you think I would throw someone off a building if I didn't?"

Parker stared at him for a moment, uncertainty flitting across his face, then, "What now?"

"Now we find out why Mookie was willing to die rather than tell us what Dontae was up to."

14

Reed called it in on the way down in the elevator. He radioed for an ambulance, which Mookie kept saying he didn't need, and wouldn't get into. Since he had used robot strength to throw metal at them and then tried to leap off the building with Parker, Reed placed Mookie under arrest. He cuffed him and read him his rights as soon as the manager ordered some ironworkers reel him up from the net.

"You need to get checked out. You can't even put weight on your knee," Reed said as he helped him hobble to an empty conference room they were told they could use while they waited.

"Do you know how many people die in ambulances?" Mookie shook his head, his accent thicker with pain. "I am not adding to that number. No way."

"Okay, but people in ambulances are probably at a higher risk of dying simply by virtue of *needing* an ambulance," Reed argued.

Mookie frowned. "I don't talk to cops."

They were on the first floor, which was finished and had walls, to Reed's great relief. The portly manager led them to a room decorated with botanical sculptures and botany sketches. A conference table sat in the center surrounded by cushy chairs. Reed dropped Mookie in the closest one and then swung his arm, trying to work the spasm from his healing shoulder.

He realized his earpiece was missing. They'd been given a couple of chemical ice packs and an ace bandage that Reed used to pack Mookie's injured knee. Then Lee disappeared, presumably to contact lawyers.

Parker finished his call. He nodded at Mookie. "You don't have to go, but once they're dispatched, they can't clear the call until on scene and you sign the refusal waiver."

"Whatever." Mookie sat cross armed and glared at Reed from the opposite side of the conference table.

"Mookie," Reed said. "You and I need to talk."

"No. Way." Mookie tried to swivel away but Reed stopped the chair with his boot.

"Okay, settle down." Parker stepped between them.

"You two nearly killed me." Mookie wiggled his finger at them. "That is attempted murder. I'm gonna sue your asses all the way off."

"For what?" Parker leaned over Mookie, getting in his face. "Detective Reed stopped you from taking me with you over the edge. Now *that's* attempted murder. Of a detective, no less. A parolee pulling that kind of crime is looking at life."

That took Reed by surprise. He wondered how Parker would land on what had just happened. Reed pulled out his notebook, flipped to the sketch of Dontae, and slid it in front of Mookie.

"Pfft! It is a good thing you are a cop. This is terrible," Mookie said and pushed it away, but the fear was there.

"Dontae was stabbed twice, made to run for his life, and then blown apart."

"Why are you telling me this? I have no dealings with him."

"Not since you were busted together, you mean," Parker chimed in.

"Yeah, so. We weren't even in the same cell block," Mookie snapped.

"But you were friends. You knew what he was up to. You know how I know?" Reed asked and sank into the chair opposite him. He leaned in, catching Mookie's gaze. "You said you tried to warn him. That he was playing with fire. What made you think that?"

"Man, I don't know," Mookie snapped, but his leg started bouncing under the table.

"You knew he was pulling a job." Reed turned the page of the notebook where he'd tucked the autopsy photos he'd shown Marcel. He flipped them over in front of Mookie, one by one. "His partner betrayed him. Then he did this." Reed showed the panorama view of Dontae chained to a block of cement, blue skin, ragged wound, eyes staring at nothing. Reed tapped the photo with his finger. "Who is this monster?"

"I don't know!" Mookie lifted an already mangled thumbnail to his lips and started gnawing. "The guy, he was paranoid, okay? So much that even Dontae, who could not keep a secret if he locked it in a safe, would not say his name. He was *that* scared. That was not easy to do to Dontae. Not how he was brought up. Which is why I should not be talking to you."

"He had reason to be afraid." Reed leaned in. "And so do you. This guy was violent. I heard he knocked out a homeless woman for just walking by."

Mookie nodded. "Yes, Dontae said they were at the train station and this man got into argument at the, uh, ticket computer."

"The kiosk," Parker offered. "What'd he do?"

"He beat the man up," Mookie said. "Dontae said he got blood on his expensive jacket."

Reed put his hand up. "Wait, back up. Was it a train or a bus station? You need to be accurate."

"What does it matter?"

"It matters," Reed said. "Be sure."

"Train, okay?" Mookie waved his hand in the general direction of east. "He said he ate at that burger place that serves the different colored buns and then walked over."

"Did Dontae ever mention any other meeting place?" Reed asked. "Think carefully."

Mookie started to shake his head but then stopped. "Pike Place Market. They met at a bookstore on the underground floor."

Parker answered his phone and then nodded at Mookie. "The bus just pulled up. I'm going to lead them back here."

"Yeah," Reed said, his mind already churning as Parker left them alone. Marcel had said something similar. All those places. Bus and train stations, the tourist rich Pike Place, and a dark beach in the middle of winter. They were all strategic. He'd have chosen them himself if he was setting up a meeting, Reed thought. Multiple close egress points. Minimal police presence. There would be ample crowds to melt into. A lot of noise and movement. Or places regularly deserted at that hour. This killer was trained. "'Like in a spy movie,'" Reed muttered, repeating Marcel's words.

The analog clock on the wall ticked quietly over Mookie's head. Tap. Tap. Tap. The staccato snaps bored into Reed's head. A familiar smell assaulted his senses. Burning. Slater's memory unfurled in Reed's mind without warning. He was in a room standing over a dentist's chair. The man tied to the chair cried out in pain. A loose, bloody gag dangled around his neck, his face bruised and bleeding. When Slater looked down at the pair of pliers in his hand, the man's swollen finger in his other, Reed tried to pull out of the moment. Horror and dread at what he had done poured out of the festering memory.

Slater's words forced themselves out of Reed's lips. "What do you know about Aurora?"

The man in the chair squeezed his eyes shut. He shook his head vehemently. "They'll stop you."

"Who?" Slater grabbed the man's face, made him look into his eyes, Reed's eyes. "Who would dare?"

"Go to hell," he shouted and tried to curl his finger away from Slater's grip.

Danzig walked out from the shadowed corner of the room. Light gray suit, pristine, despite the filth around them. Not one strand of his salt-and-pepper hair out of place. He turned to Reed, to Slater in that moment, and nodded. *Break it.* Bile rose in Reed's throat, and he tried to stop it, to yell for Slater to let go. "No—"

Mookie's voice cut through the scene. "Are you having a stroke or something?"

"What?" Reed broke free from the memory. The dark room. The chair. They burned away like paper and Reed was back in the construction site conference room. His pulse pounded and he shook his head to clear it.

"I said, before your partner returns, we should talk deal."

The echoing shouts of pain faded and Reed focused on what Mookie was saying. "Meaning?"

"Meaning I know what you all did for Dontae. And nice as it was, it was most definitely murder." Mookie clicked his tongue. "No statute of limitations, yes? I love the American justice system."

"You really don't want to threaten me." Adrenaline from Slater's memory burned through Reed's chest, his legs, muffling his thoughts.

"I am negotiating. I want no attempted murder. No resisting arrest. No jail. And maybe I will forget what Dontae said about his father and his friends one summer night, a long time ago." Mookie shrugged. A smug smile on his stubbly lips. "If not, I tell them what you did. You are not dealing with a street thug. I survived a civil war in my country. I know how the police really work."

"Civil war, huh?" Reed rose slowly. He scanned the room for cameras and flicked the window frost switch on the window. It blanked out. Then he walked around to Mookie's side and kicked the chair out from under him. Mookie yelped as he tumbled onto the floor and tried to crawl away, but Reed was already on him. He flipped him onto his gut and shoved his knee between Mookie's shoulder blades. Mookie's wrists, still cuffed, had ended up behind him and Reed grabbed Mookie's ring finger and bent it back. Mookie yowled and Reed let go of the pressure, just a little. "Is that where the grenades came from?"

"What are you doing?" Mookie shouted. "You're going to break it!"

"You know, it's not the bone you have to worry about. That will heal. It's the nerves.

They get damaged with all the swelling and they just. . . die." Reed leaned forward so that Mookie could see him from the floor. "How're you going to operate that fancy robot with dead fingers, huh, Mookie?"

"That is messed up. This is my livelihood," Mookie panted, eyes wild with fear.

"Well, this is mine and you're screwing with it. I know you and Dontae were busted for moving weapons. Is that why he came to you? Because he thought you could help him?"

"No!" Mookie snapped. Reed put more pressure on the finger, and he changed his tune. "Yes! Yes, that's why he came to me. But I couldn't help him."

"Mookie, my friend, as you so usefully pointed out, was killed by a weapon that isn't even supposed to exist. So, I don't really believe that you have no idea what Dontae was up to." When Mookie didn't answer, Reed pulled back until Mookie yelped. "You said you've heard the stories about me. Tell me what I want to know or you're going to find out the reality is a whole lot worse."

"Okay, I will tell you! Let go!"

Reed backed off Mookie. He yanked him up with his good arm and plopped him back on the chair.

Mookie regarded Reed with a genuine look of hurt feelings on his face. "This man who killed Dontae, if he is the same as the partner then I will lose my life it he learns I talked to you about him. I want protection."

"As far as I'm concerned, you were too mad to speak to me and kept your mouth shut the entire time Detective Parker was gone." Reed checked his phone clock. "Which is about to end."

"Ok. Dontae said to me that he needed a seller for high grade smart rounds. I have family in Serbia. Men who fought in the war. They joined, what do you call it, the uprising? Dontae thought maybe they would be interested in the weapon. To end the war." Mookie winced. "There is no price too great for the people's victory."

"Okay, so, you hooked him up with a buyer." Reed made a keep going gesture with this index finger. "Why did Dontae break with his partner?"

"This partner. He was driving Dontae crazy. He kept changing the time to meet. He did not like the meeting locations. Dontae said he thought he was stalling, you know? Waiting for something. It made Dontae very nervous. I see he lost weight. Two days before he died, he came to me and said if his partner canceled again or messed up the deal in any way, he wanted to make the sale without him. Dontae was worried that whoever his partner had stolen the rounds from would send people after them. He wanted to get rid of the Kraken weapon fast. So, I set up another meeting. One last time, I tell him. I reach out, to my connection in Serbia. They sent representatives."

"Who'd they send?"

"I don't know. They don't give me a file on who they are sending."

"Alright so some guys came for a meeting with Dontae and his partner. And?" Reed checked the time again.

"And nothing. Someone killed Dontae hours before the meeting and so the buyers went home."

"Do you think Dontae's partner found out he was planning to cut him out?"

Mookie looked genuinely confused. "I don't know what happened. But the way the man talked, he knows weapons."

Reed sat up straight. "Wait, you've seen him?"

"No, I was on a call with Dontae. But he was just repeating what he was being told. I heard someone in the room telling him what to say to me for the buyers. Specs and technical jargon I know Dontae could not know. He knew weapons, yes, but only the kind you can buy. This thing he was selling was," Mookie looked around the room as if the right words would be there. He gave up and turned back to Reed. "This thing, it has a timer to explode."

Reed nodded. "Yes, a secondary detonation after it hits the target."

"Makes you wonder what would happen if someone got shot with it and the timer was set to wait until they ran for cover."

Reed sat back, his stomach dropping. "You'd be an unintentional bomber yourself."

"You run for help and then kill the help. Sounds like it is for war, no? This man, this partner told Dontae how to sell it to them. How to use it best. And he promised more."

"More?" Reed saw the seriousness in the man's eyes as he answered with a single nod. He considered the implications for a moment before continuing. "Tell me this. If the partner is the one who brought the weapon to the table. Knew how to sell it. How to use it. What did he need Dontae for?"

Mookie cocked his head. "I thought about this. I think it was for his connections. Weapons buyers, Dontae knew. He was a good schmoozer. You know this word? Dontae brought the buyers to the table through his connection to me. Also, the Kindred smuggling routes to move the product. That is what your friend offered."

"Did Dontae ever say how he met him?"

Mookie stilled, his eyes going sharp. "He did not want to talk about it. He said that he didn't want to put his payment in danger."

"What's that supposed to mean?"

"I did not ask."

Reed tapped his leather notebook on the table, his mind churning. "How did this partner know Dontae could hook him up with the kind of sophisticated buyer they'd needed for a sale like this? One with deep enough pockets. He couldn't even get twenty surplus grenades across a Canadian checkpoint, but this partner trusts him to broker a deal worth millions?"

"The limes *did* trick the dogs!" Mookie spat, insulted. "It was some by-the-book rookie who decided to hand-check the crate. We would have made it otherwise."

Reed waved away the comment. "You're telling me this partner, one savvy enough to possess a secret high-tech weapon, *needed* Dontae? What would make him believe Dontae would have connections to do that? Nothing in his arrest record would bear that out."

"Like I said, me," Mookie said, confusion on his face.

"Yeah, but you're not exactly a lord of war, are you?" Something occurred to Reed. "How did this partner know about Dontae's relationship with you at all? Do you know this guy?"

Mookie was silent for a moment at the thought. "No, I don't think so. Dontae asked me to come have a beer with him one day."

"And you just went? You rolled on him for a better sentence."

"What can I say? He said no hard feelings, that he just needed to do this one job, and he was going to walk away from everything. He did not care about such things anymore. I know him," Mookie nodded solemnly. "He was not lying. So, I said, why not?"

There was something in the *knowing*, Reed thought. The partner knew of Dontae's connection to Mookie and that was the hanging thread. That connection was going to unravel everything hiding the truth.

"Yes, but how would this partner know about you?"

"I don't know. . ." his voice trailed off as the color left his face. "Maybe I should not be talking to you."

"We can protect you," Reed said. "Protective—"

"Do you know what that thing can do? It will hunt through a crowd and hit only you." Mookie's gaze shifted to the door. "No one is safe."

"You've seen it in action?" Reed leaned in. "The partner must have been there then. It's too expensive to waste rounds."

"No more talking." Mookie's eyes slid away from Reed. "Lawyer."

Reed shook his head. "He'll come for you next. If you can connect him to Dontae and these weapons, you're on his list, maybe at the top of it."

"I think I will take my chances with the DA," Mookie said and jutted his chin at Reed. "I have a bigger fish to leverage."

Reed moved so fast Mookie gasped when he grabbed him by the shirt collar, hauling him out of the chair. "Are you sure about that? Because you just admitted to trying to sell a weapon of war to armed insurgents. How much you want to bet that I can dig up enough evidence to nail you for that before you can find anything on a murder from my past you can't prove even happened."

"It happened," Mookie hissed. "I can see it in your eyes. Dontae did not lie about that."

"I'd keep that in mind, then." Reed swung Mookie against the wall, lifting him up on his toes by the shirt. "Answer my question. There is no way you didn't run a demonstration of the Kraken first. Maybe even a test run? Was Dontae's partner there or not!"

"No. Dontae was going to demonstrate to them that night!" Mookie flinched in Reed's grip. "I swear!"

The door swung open, and Parker pushed through followed by two paramedics. He took one look at the disheveled and wincing Mookie and his gaze shot to Reed. "What's going on here?"

"Nothing," Reed said and stepped back.

Parker's gaze shot to Mookie. "That true?"

Mookie cleared his throat, glaring at Reed. "I fell. He was helping me up."

"Okay, well," The paramedic said as he moved past Parker to treat Mookie. "I'm going need his cuffs off."

"I got it," Parker said and moved to unlock the cuffs when he froze. He squinted at Mookie's hand. "What happened to your finger?"

"I hurt it in the fall," Mookie said.

Parker turned to Reed "Is that what happened?"

Reed shrugged. "Are you calling him a liar?"

"No, I –"

Reed pushed off from the wall and headed for the door. "I need to make a call."

He didn't wait for Parker to answer, rushing for the bathroom as soon as he cleared the room. Stumbling into a stall, Reed dry heaved and then washed his face with cold water. He stared at himself in the mirror. Not recognizing the hate and fury still burning behind his eyes. Reed held up his shaking hands. He'd been an enforcer in his dark days, sure, but a torturer? A well-placed punch here and there, some harsh words to encourage repayment of a loan, but nothing like that.

Reed forced air into his tight chest. Slater had snapped that man's finger without hesitation. The pleas and cries of pain falling through him like he was made of nothing but dark power and vengeance. Reed fought to slow his breath, to quiet his blaring mind, but he could only hear one thought. Over and over. Slater was changing him from within. He could feel it. And what sent dread tearing through Reed the most was he didn't think he was capable of stopping it.

15

Parker

He barely spoke to Reed as the paramedics wrapped up Mookie's knee. It took some effort, but they convinced him to get it scanned given the swelling and loaded him into the ambulance. They spent the next couple of hours with the Critical Incident Supervisor who talked with Reed first and then, as always, Parker to confirm. Parker told him the truth. He had no idea if the man going off the roof was an accident or on purpose. Perhaps Mr. Balian *had* intended to jump and take Parker with him. Maybe he'd just wanted to get past him, away from Reed. All he knew was that Reed might have saved his life, but he had to do so because once again, Reed had pushed past *literal* safety boundaries during the investigation. How much risk to others was the great mind of Detective Reed worth?

And then there was the aftermath. Reed seemed cold. Too steady for what had just happened to them. Meanwhile, the near-death adrenaline whirled in Parker's head and made his hands shake. And when he'd walked back into the conference room, Mookie had been scared.

Parker had offered to go with Mookie to the hospital and take his statement as soon as the doctors let him if Reed went back to the station to write the incident report. Reed agreed. When Parker was done questioning Mookie, he strode to a quiet part of the building, the chapel/meditation room provided for the families of patients and checked for people. It was empty. He went to the front, sank into a pew, and made a call. It was picked up on the first ring.

"Did something happen?" The caller asked.

"I have to wrap this up soon. Reed is too dangerous to stay on the job. He nearly," Parker cleared his throat. "He has to go."

"What happened?"

"Reed threw someone off a building," Parker started, then he relayed the highlights of the entire chaotic arrest.

The caller gasped. "Holy shit!"

Parker glanced around the chapel guiltily over the cursing but continued. "I told you Reed was unhinged. And I have reason to believe that he roughed up our suspect when I was out of the room."

"That could be what we're looking for. What did the victim say?"

"That he fell." Parker ran a shaking hand through his hair. "I have nothing, don't I?"

"Well, he saved your life, possibly, but also threw a suspect off a building."

"Actually, it happened so fast that h-he may have fallen." Parker stood and paced the lush carpet. "I don't know."

"Unless there was video of Reed doing something illegal, then you don't have anything yet."

"It was an unfinished building. No cameras."

"Was anyone with you?"

"No, it was just me and him. His partner wasn't there."

After a few moments the caller said, "You're going to have to do it. I know you said you didn't want to but—"

"You're right." Parker leaned against the wall and stared at the wood carving of a swooping dove tacked over the podium. It looked like it was flying in the shifting candlelight. "I'll wear a camera."

They talked about strategy and evidence for a few more minutes, then Parker ended the call. He drifted for a moment, wondering if he was doing the right thing, hating that Reed was always a hairsbreadth from getting caught. His phone pinged and another data packet from Detective De La Cruz appeared on the screen.

He'd been told of Nat's case searches after he talked to her the first time. Was that evidence of doubt or possible complacency? He thought about her reaction, and it occurred to him she might have been trying to cover her own butt. Maybe, Parker mused, Nat was being defensive not protective.

He needed to talk to her. Parker took in a centering breath and then straightened his suit blazer with a yank to the hem. He'd give her one last chance to swim free before she got swept up in his net.

16

Reed stood at the threshold of the decrepit warehouse. It had started raining on the way over and the cement walls dribbled with sheets of dirty water coming from the corroded metal roof. Icy wind blew through the vast, open space. It howled through cracks in the remaining window glass. A low, mournful sound, Reed thought beautiful in its own haunting way. He buried his chin in the collar of his coat, his breath wafting away in the waning light of the late winter afternoon. The place hadn't changed much in the three months since he'd last been there.

The light was fading, and it cast the gray tones of coming night upon every shape and shadow. He stopped in the center of the floor and took in the scent of rain and rust and what he hoped was cat pee. Cracked paint peeled away from the walls like decaying tree bark and fetid water pooled in the crumbling corners of the workshop. Spray cans left over from the graffitied walls and old welding detritus littered the floor. Abandoned years ago, the industrial space showed signs of recent squatters. Their empty meal packs from the shelters got caught in the steady wind that moved through the vast space and swirled in lazy circles along the ground. Once a metal and welding shop, the far wall now had a hole where the door used to be. Beyond the gaping maw, rainwater flowed in a thin rivulet down the center of the concrete ravine where Reed had nearly drowned a few months ago.

The MER-C System's case was hidden beneath a loosened grate in a small alcove near the rear of the shop. A wire from a splice Reed had made in the line feeding the overhead fluorescents snaked down into the hole. Reed knelt next to it, reached through the grates for the lock he'd placed there, and used his thumb print to disengage it. It fell open and Reed dragged back the grate, reached into the dark drainage hole, and pulled out the metal security suitcase he'd concealed there. He disconnected it from the makeshift power supply and walked it over to some built-in counters still attached to the far wall.

When he lifted the case, a puff of vapor escaped. Reed picked up the metal halo that went around the victims' heads. It thrummed softly in his grasp. The MER-C system, a device that ripped memories straight out of victim's minds, sat nestled in the foam interior of the suitcase. Also inside sat the activation serum, the injector pen to deliver the memory right into a user's mind, and the memory containment pods. Reed set down the halo and picked one of the pods up. Gold metal discs like fat chocolate coins held stored memories stolen by one of Danzig's Spector mercenaries, Slater. The coin flashed in the overhead lights and Reed's gaze found the inscribed number on the side. Pod #337. Reed took the injector in his hand, dread twisting his gut. He raised it to his neck, the needle pressing against his throat. And froze at the familiar cadence of footsteps behind him.

Pulse pounding in his head, Reed turned to face Nat. "How did you find me? I didn't take my car. I searched my clothes for trackers. I turned my phone off."

She snapped her gum and shrugged in her giant coat. "I'd say it's because I'm a detective, but really your self-torture is predictable. Of course, you'd store it here."

"Yes, but how did you know I'd be here *today*?"

"Because Parker told me what happened with Mookie during your interrogation and knew you'd go straight for more memories. Despite what you know might happen."

Reed shut the case and leaned against the counter with folded arms. "A memory hit me while I was with Mookie, yes. And then I may have taken some intimidation too far."

She gestured at him. "You're not skirting the line anymore. You're so far beyond you can't even see it."

"Mookie threatened me. He threatened Coyote. He wanted to get off with no charges after trying to take Parker off the side of the building with him." Reed shoved his hands in his pants pockets. "And yes, I nearly broke the finger of a man already cuffed. I'm not proud of that."

Nat shook her head slowly. "Slater's changing you."

His gut dropped and he wandered away from her, stopping to stare out the gaping hole of the missing door. "I don't know what to say to that."

"Say you won't make it worse." When he didn't answer, she strode over to him. "Tell me you won't give that murderous, ruthless, mercenary more power over who you are, Reed!"

Reed steadied himself but the fear in her eyes cut right through him. "What other choice do I have? I've exhausted the memories I took from Slater and Firash. Danzig is still out there, untouchable despite Caitlyn and Dontae and everyone else he's left in his wake. You know there is likely evidence in these pods I can use to find a way to take him down once and for all. We can stop looking over our shoulders for his thugs. I can stop worrying about everyone around me being used as game pieces."

Nat looked up at him, her brow furrowed. "Have you forgotten that those foreign memories don't fade? They don't leave. They twist and turn into dark versions of the original. What's to say that won't happen with the rest? And don't forget the physical effects of viewing the memories. The fever. The pain—"

"Nat, I don't know what's going on," Reed cut across her, his chest tight. "Danzig is coming for me after months of silence and he did it in a very personal, vindictive way. Which doesn't make sense. Then there's this mystery caller who claims he's friendly but threatens me if I don't meet a corrupt judge that he says wants to help me take down Danzig. Why? Clearly, he's an enemy of Danzig, but that doesn't necessarily mean he isn't mine as well. And forget Dontae. I have no idea how he fits in and *he's* the only real thread that ties me to any of this."

"Don't meet with this judge. I mean it." She shook her head. "We're not there yet."

"Nat—"

"Okay, then *I'll* view the memory." She strode to the case and picked up the injection pen and pod. "I just suck out the memory and plunge this into my carotid, right? The needle is automatic?"

"Wait," Reed caught up and grabbed her wrist. "Stop."

"Oh, okay. So, if it was me, you'd try *anything* else first, right?"

"Come on, Nat," Reed whispered. His hand slid up her wrist, taking the pen gently from her grasp. "Don't . . . do that."

"Then we find another way for you too, okay?" She smacked his stomach with the back of her hand. "What's your gut telling you this is all *really* about? You may not have facts yet, but you *know*. Tell me."

"What do I know?" Reed placed the injector back in the case and closed it. "I know that Danzig is a chess player. Methodical. Controlled. He cultivated doubt about my accusations against him and his company. High Rock stock didn't even dip. He played up my suspension and threw Slater under the bus. No one believes he had anything to do with any of those deaths." Reed looked down at her and shrugged. "Why would he come after me now? This whole thing. Dontae, the judge, getting followed and assaulted . . . it's more than just about me. It has to be."

"So, your theory is he'd have to have another, very pressing reason to do this to you."

"He thinks like a general. With strategy. Going after me now after months is a deviation in his behavior. I've studied him. He's not rash. He isn't impulsive."

"Did you stalk this guy?" Nat asked and did a little loop back to her original place next to him. "What are you saying?"

"What about this?" Reed spread his hands out. "If you walked in on this case cold to everything but the evidence in front of you. What would you think?"

"That I should probably check out the detective whose name was written in blood."

"Right, so it would immediately go to me. My past cases. My relationships in and out of work. You'd land on Caitlyn, right? So now two murders of people I know. Then you'd figure out I've had no contact with the first victim, Dontae, for years. Why would this man's name come up now? You think, maybe our connection must be from my past. Boom, the sealed juvenile records come up."

"Where are you going with this?"

"Indulge me," Reed leaned on the cold cement wall. "If you didn't know me. What would you do next?"

"I'd check into your work record. Look for something in your old cases."

Reed nodded. "What else?"

"I mean, I'd try to get the records unsealed. I'd look into the reason you guys were detained and find out that the victim, Dontae, had a father in the Kindred who disappeared." She tried a reassuring smile, but her heart wasn't in it. "It's a dead end. There's no body, no evidence, Dontae can't talk, and Coyote won't. Nothing here would hold up in court."

"I don't think any of this intended to," Reed said.

"Then what would be the point?"

"To create a narrative." Reed pulled out his leather notebook. He flipped it open to his sketch of the crime scene. "If Danzig wanted to screw me over, he'd have made it look like *I'd* killed Dontae to keep him from revealing our secret past." Reed tapped his finger on his drawing of Dontae. "This is something else. A bloody tableau that's part of a much bigger set piece. Something big is coming." Reed ground his jaw, thinking. "Danzig had people killed to cover up the MER-C system. He doesn't play by any version of the rules. And like I said, he'd have a concrete reason to do this to me, not an emotional one. So, what does Danzig really get out of it? Am I a distraction for something he's doing? A convenient patsy for some scheme I can't see?"

Nat rubbed her forehead with her palm. "The sealed juvenile records is the thing. That's not easy. I checked with the technical response unit down in Terrebonne. There *was* a breach of records down in Louisiana, but it was months ago. They still don't know how. Or what was looked at."

"Months. That's planning." Reed scratched his sideburn. "Long enough for this partner of Dontae's to gain his trust."

"This sounds way more convoluted than it first looked." Nat flapped her arms at her side. "What the hell is going on?"

"All I know, is I don't believe Dontae was killed for revenge." Reed pulled out his notebook from his trench. "That reminds me. The way people have been describing Dontae's partner is gnawing at me. Marcel said, 'posh.' The guy had a handkerchief. He wiped blood off his collar with it. Mookie said something like, 'expensive suit.' And the kid at Fleur's apartment, Remy," he nodded to her tablet. "I sent you the notes on that. He said that Dontae complained his partner had weird tastes. Something about the sea and row."

"Like a rowboat?"

"That's what I thought at first but now I think he used the word 'tastes' for a reason. The kid said Dontae had met the partner at a restaurant so, I think he meant R-O-E as in fish eggs, like the kind they put on sushi."

"You mean caviar?"

"Dontae would've said that. No, I think it's something even more gourmand. Sea urchin roe, the creature's eggs, are a delicacy. Expensive restaurants will buy them fresh, break open the spiny shell, and serve the egg sac, the roe."

"Why are rich people like this?"

"Right?" Reed agreed. "And how many normal people go around with handkerchiefs in their pockets?"

"I mean Dontae had one, right? It had stars, I think?"

"That's a bandanna. People know the difference. Certainly Marcel, who wears those same colors, would." Reed tapped his temple with his index finger. "And now Mookie says this partner of Dontae's, was the brains. He brought the tech, and he knew how to sell it. Mookie heard him. But he kept stalling the sale for some reason."

Nat's gaze narrowed. "Mookie said that?"

Reed nodded, "You know what I think? I think this partner never wanted a sale. I think he wanted Dontae and being that he was a weapons smuggler, the Kraken was the quickest way for the killer to establish trust."

"But why? You just said you don't think it was just to torture you."

"I don't think that's what the crime scene was about. I think the Kraken, the sale to the Serbians, Dontae's body with my name over it, the idea of revenge for what I did . . . all of it was to pull me, Danzig, and Dontae's name together publicly."

Nat shook her head. "I don't understand why that would serve Danzig at all."

"It wouldn't." Reed paced. "But it would serve someone trying to take him down."

"Visage?"

"I think Dontae's partner, his killer, and this Visage are the same, Nat. The diction on the phone, the choice of words, the references are all lining up with what people are saying about this partner. I'm getting refined, elevated, vibes when I talk to him." Reed shook his head, trying to imagine the face that would go with a man like Visage. "He's in Danzig's realm and he's playing us against each other."

"If this guy knows Danzig, then he knows doing this is deadly. What's the angle?"

"I think I am being set up. I just can't see how. My past, this leak of me at the scene, the mystery blogger being fed information and prompted to bring up my past. Whoever Visage is, he's connected in a way that's close to Danzig somehow. A rival or a former colleague. Someone who is doing all this on the downlow because Danzig would know who he is."

"I can dig into people in Danzig's social circle, those close to him. See if there's any litigiously bad blood. I have a friend at the SEC that might be able to help."

Reed raised a brow. "SEC?"

"I interned in her office when I thought I might go white collar."

"I need to get back with Coyote. I had him look some things up for me." Reed patted his pockets and then gave her an embarrassed grin. "Can I get a ride?"

On the way back, Nat drove while Reed set up a meeting with Coyote.

"He's meeting me at my condo," Reed said as he ended the call. "He said he found something interesting."

"Hand delivery," Nat mused as she swerved onto his street. "Old school. What did you ask him for anyway?"

Reed moved to answer but, his words died on his lips as they pulled into his driveway.

"Heads up," he said, and Nat's gaze snapped to his condo.

"Tell me you left your door open like that," Nat said as she turned off the engine. "Want me to call it in?"

"Not yet." Reed climbed out of the car, his hand on his holster. He approached his door and could see something beyond it, in his living room.

Reed pushed open the door with his knuckles and peered inside, Nat at his six. Dozens of eight by ten photos were nailed to his wall. They were on the floor, standing up against his vinyl collection, splayed across the kitchen counter. Spray paint scrawled across his wall read, DO WHAT YOU ARE TOLD.

"Holy crap," Nat whispered, her eyes wide.

Reed took a turn in his home. "Nothing stolen. Nothing destroyed. Just a clear message. 'I can get to you whenever I want.'"

"Bullshit. The coward did this when you weren't home." She walked into the kitchen and picked one off the fridge. "These are all of Judge Leone. Is that Danzig?"

Reed nodded, peered out into the yard to see if his watchers were still there. They weren't. He shut the door, already dialing Coyote when his gaze landed on the photo that had been nailed to the inside of the front door. He yanked it off the nail, adrenaline spiking through his chest. It was a photo of him and Nat sitting outside next to a food cart near the station, drinking coffee. She was looking up at him, laughing at something he said, her hand halfway to smacking his arm. Someone had drawn a target over her chest. A message in red ink across the bottom of the photo stopped him cold.

She's his next target. ~V

Reed folded the photo, slipping it into his coat, and made a call.

Coyote picked up on the first ring. "I'm one minute out."

"Keep your head on a swivel," Reed muttered, his gaze slipping to Nat as he stepped back outside. "We've got a problem."

"How bad?"

"Worst nightmare," Reed said.

Coyote was silent for a few seconds and then, "Are you gonna tell her?"

Through the front window, he could see her in his kitchen. Nat fished a box of cereal out of his pantry, grabbed a palm full, and tossed it in her mouth. She turned to him, her cheeks puffy as she crunched.

"What?" she asked.

Reed pointed to his phone and mouthed Coyote's name. Stepping off his front walk, he eased out of her line of sight. "Please tell me you found something on Danzig."

"I might have, but, Morgan," Coyote said. "You have to tell her. She can handle it. She's tougher than nails."

"Yes, but she's not bulletproof," Reed's breath came out in staccato puffs. "Knowing Danzig is gunning for her won't scare Nat, it'll piss her off. She'll push harder." Birds hopped around the frost damaged grass looking for worms. The building breeze rushed through the tree that canopied the corner of the sidewalk. Its bare and gnarled branches quivered in the wind. "I need her to be scared. It's the only way she'll survive this."

"A storm's coming?"

"I can feel it in my bones, brother," Reed said as Coyote's motorcycle rounded the corner. "A bad one."

17

Coyote and Nat stayed to help Reed clean up the mess left by Visage. Reed didn't want an investigation given the assertion by more than one person that Danzig had ears in the SPD. Still, Nat had grabbed a few photos and nails saying she wanted to walk them through the fingerprinting station herself as soon as she could. She said she wanted to put them in as "test evidence" in the automated system to keep things confidential. The label was used for calibration and shouldn't raise any flags. Reed wasn't hopeful she'd find anything, but she seemed to want to do it anyway.

He spent the rest of the night pacing his kitchen and pouring through Coyote's notes. More and more, Reed believed that Visage and Dontae's partner, were the same man. A helpful informant bent on taking Danzig down and a killer rolled into one. Reed had trouble wrapping his mind around the kind of person that dichotomy could exist in. Then again, Marcel had thought the guy was a spy. Cold and calculating yet socially adept enough to manipulate a detective and possibly Danzig himself.

Reed kept wondering what the end game looked like. Danzig down at Reed's own hand? Did Judge Leone have damning evidence? Why the desperation, the stubbornness to make the meet happen? Did Visage even know the judge had already taken leave? Why not have Leone simply pass on the information and if Reed finds it credible, then meet? Questions gave way to more, not answers. Reed had survived way too many close calls because of his gut and this time it was telling him that something was about to blow up in his face.

Reed had just fallen asleep on the couch when Nat called him at five the following morning.

"Meet me at the breakfast place. I've got chisme," she said simply, and hung up.

Reed tried to remember if chisme was Spanish for gossip or not as he pulled on his coat. Either way, he hoped it was good.

Twenty minutes later, while driving to meet Nat, Reed clocked two guys on motorcycles following him when he left his street. Far back, too far to make them out, but the black leather vests were unmistakable. Kindred. They were restless. He'd hear from them soon.

The Pioneer Square Café was busy despite the early hour. Reed stood behind three nurses grabbing a coffee for the drive home. He placed his order and sat in a booth by the window and stared out at the senior walking troupe as they moved as one track-suited mass along the sidewalk. If one could imagine the most bland, brown, and nondescript café in America, it would be Tomeo's. A nowhere place that looked like every other café you'd ever been to while on the road. Cream-colored counters with stools faced the kitchen. Booths lined one wall, which was decorated with random framed pictures of the town in its heyday. The faded wallpaper somehow seemed nostalgic, but Reed couldn't quite decide why. Music too low to be recognizable droned on underneath the steady conversation and laughter. Tomeo's was always busy because he made the best breakfast burritos Reed had ever tasted. He wasn't alone, given the crowd.

He glanced at his watch and went back to scribbling notes in his leather notepad. The door jingled as it opened once more, and Reed looked up and saw movement as Nat jostled through the crowd waiting in the front. She wiggled out of her jacket as she walked over and blew some wayward strands of wispy curls out of her eyes as she plopped down opposite him.

He'd ordered and she smiled at her coffee and donut. "You're forgiven."

Reed raised a brow. "For?"

"For this." She reached into her coat pocket and pulled out the photo of her that Visage had left at Reed's place. Nat worked the sides of the picture back and forth like she was opening and closing a book. "It's folded. You folded this and hid it, didn't you?"

"Five minutes tops," He held his hand up as if swearing. "I gave it to you as soon as Coyote got to my condo."

Nat shook the photo at him. "Better. But not great."

"Noted." Reed grinned but she saw through it.

"I'm fine," Nat said. "I mean it was inevitable the killer would expand his grid. He knows a lot about you. And people he can use against you. I hope you told Coyote to watch his back."

"I want to keep someone outside your house until we know what's happening."

"I only agreed to last night."

"It's a credible threat." Reed took in the stubborn jut of her chin and knew she wasn't having it. "Come on, Nat."

She leaned forward, her brow furrowed. "Who's sitting on Tig's house?"

After a few seconds, Reed conceded. "No one." He leaned back his hands up in surrender. "I get it. Doesn't mean the danger isn't real."

"Hey, I can run and gun with the best of them. I passed the tests. Even saved your butt a few times. I understand we're not dealing with something I trained for. I get the gravitas of the situation. I really do. I just," she looked away, her jaw working. "I refuse to be bullied. I decided that a long time ago."

"Ok," Reed said. "But I'm sending a car anyway. Coyote already offered."

"Knock yourself out." She shrugged, her expression nonchalant and Reed hoped it was a front.

He considered her for a moment, she was buzzing with energy. "You said you had chisme? That's gossip, right?"

"Yeah, I'm getting some interesting results on our query into Danzig's inner circle."

He drank his coffee, while Nat told him about what she had found with her search. Several pending lawsuits over trademark infringement, a dispute over one of Danzig's subsidiaries, and some sort of arbitration with a country club. When she was done, he read her a section from Coyote's files. "A name keeps popping up in reports from various sources. Sylvia Plaques. Do you have anything on her?"

"Lemme check." As she swiped through her tablet, her lips pulled into a frown.

"What is it?"

"That photo of me, that threat, strikes me as weak. Visage is trying to pressure you into doing his bidding while he sits in the shadows safe from Danzig." Nat dunked her donut angrily in her coffee. "You're expendable to him, keep that in mind."

"I always do," Reed murmured, finishing off his coffee. He turned the page, read a few lines, and then sat up straighter. "Listen to this. According to Coyote's snitch, the old man left his empire to Danzig and his sister who is estranged from the family and living in Europe. But there's something here that says she might be back in the states. Did you find anything on that in your public records search?"

"The old man?" Nat looked at him askance. "Danzig's father?"

"Yes," Reed hesitated, realizing the notes read, "Eisen Danzig." It was Slater who had called Eisen that. Or at least he'd thought it as he killed him. Dragging up the lingering trace of Slater's memory sent a chill down his spine.

"Reed, look at me." She leaned forward, her gaze scanning his face. "Did you sleep last night? Like at all?"

"I'm good," Reed shook his head. He tapped the paper with his finger. "This thing with the sister could be something."

"You might be right. I put in some queries out on the family last night after I left your house. The AI is scraping for the names of Danzig's immediate family, siblings, rivals with litigation, complaints to the SEC, the whole shebang. Deep web. Behind paywalls kind of stuff." She slid the tablet in front of Reed. "I just got something on her this morning. She has current litigation against High Rock Holdings regarding a board seat. She claims it was part of her inheritance. High Rock says it's honorary not a full seat or something to that effect. I'll send you the packet. They're coming in piecemeal because I'm hiding the queries in these SQL injections—"

"Squealy, what?"

"They're query commands you can put in certain search bars to retrieve information that is supposed to be hidden. Basically, you can use them to tell the search bar to start making lists of stuff and see if you can modify the query enough to trick it into giving away more than it should. It's what hackers do to fish for any information people thought was secure but isn't."

Reed tilted his head. "Which sites did you do this to, exactly?"

She smiled. "All you need to know is that the queries don't trace back to us. The problem is, I have way more data than I need. So far there are at least two hundred people from the first tier of connection. That's a lot of angry people to vet."

"Danzig's sister is on both lists," Reed said.

"Yeah, but Coyote's is made up of paid informants and rumor."

"He once told me that a hairdresser on his roster called him to say that a CEO of a major satellite company had ordered a full spa at his office in the middle of the night."

"That doesn't sound sketchy at all," Nat snarked and poured a steady stream of sugar into her coffee. "Is she a professional kind of lady?"

"No, this is legitimate, spa-level home visits. The kind celebrities order for appearances and awards shows. Expensive. On demand. The beautician said that he had his entire face and head done. A barber was there. Everything was done right in his office with four of his lawyers in an adjacent room arguing about something. She called and told Coyote. He dumped the stock in the portfolio he manages as soon as he could. Later that morning, the guy holds a press conference, they're earnings are in the toilet and he's getting indicted."

"Gotta have that glam makeover before all the cameras show up," Nat said. "Okay, I'll concede Coyote can be useful."

"The sister is one person on both your list of official information and Coyote's, which *is* rumor and innuendo, but usually has some kernel of truth. I say if someone is on both lists, we go and talk to them."

"Okay. Who else you got?"

He ran his finger down the paper, looking for a name. They vetted former low-level employees with harassment or promotion complaints, worked through a list of vendors High Rock allegedly stiffed for tens of thousands, and struggled through various other minor beefs from Danzig's professional life. Reed came across a name for the fourth time in Coyote's notes and stopped. "I keep seeing this Sylvia Plaques woman. Anything of value?"

"Uh, let me see." Nat tore her donut, dipped it into her coffee, and popped it into her mouth. She pulled the tablet back to her while she chewed, swiping around in cyberspace. "Here we go. It looks like Danzig or High Rock Holdings, rather has sued her plenty. There's a case winding through tort law right now. For libel. Get this, she used to work for him."

"And left under hostile circumstances according to Coyote's notes. She hates Danzig. She accused him of insider trading and illegal arms deals at a museum benefit last year. His lawyers hit her with a suit two days later. Doesn't seem to faze her. She keeps beating the cases. There's even talk of sabotage."

"Oh yeah, she should definitely go on the enemies list." Nat read the info on her screen with a grin. "She actually tried to help his workers unionize at one of his factories in California against him, *allegedly*. Power to the people, Sylvia."

"Agreed. She's on the list."

"What about his family?"

"Not much. They're notoriously private to the point of being almost reclusive. I talked to a news streamer friend of mine, and it's well known that Danzig uses his influence to control narratives about him and his company."

Nat frowned. "Yeah, look how he smeared you from here to Canada with total lies. No one even checked before posting."

"No doubt that extends to his family." Reed leafed through a few photo-copied pictures looking for the right one. He pulled a family Christmas photo that had been on one of High Rock Holding's websites. Danzig stood flanked by two couples next to a giant, professionally decorated tree. Reed pointed to the woman in the couple on the left. "Danzig has a daughter, Aria, that's her." She was pale with icy blue eyes like her father. "The man on the other side of Danzig is his son, Kaspar. Both of Danzig's children work for him but I *heard* they barely speak."

"To each other?"

"Yes, according to a spa aesthetician, they can't stand to be in the same room." Reed shrugged. "Do with that what you will."

Nat made a face. "Did Kaspar look like his mother?"

Reed nodded. "She was a dancer. I think." Kasper looked frail next to his father's robust stature. He was a brunette with hazel eyes, not quite brown, yet not quite blue.

Nat tapped the photo. "Who's the blonde?"

"Son-in-law. His name is Nicholas. He's an executive of some kind at a hedge fund company. He doesn't work for Danzig."

"Bet he makes enough to keep Danzig's princess in diamonds, though," Nat said.

"The juicy gossip from Coyote's sources is the wife." Reed pointed to a raven-haired woman much younger than her husband in the photo. "Apparently, Kaspar met his wife while he was house hunting. Her name's Veronica, she's a realtor. Someone who works at his golf club said he complains about how his family treats his wife all the time to his friends. Says he'll tell anyone who listens about how mean his sister is. Last year, Aria, tried to block the wife from membership."

"That's cold. Your brother's wife?" Nat shook her head. "Nothing legal or official between them but that could definitely cause bad blood if Danzig sided with one over the other."

"All of this is thin, but worth a look. Does anyone else in the family look good for this?"

"I'm still waiting on those files. I had to be super careful digging around that close to Danzig. I didn't come across any kind of official disagreement, other than the suit Danzig's sister, Helene, brought against High Rock, but that was a couple of years ago." Nat scrolled through documents. "I need to get some legal minds on this. I don't know what I'm reading here."

"I don't think any of Danzig's family will speak to us even if we did find something to question them about. It's a fishing expedition right now. I'd like to get some bait on the hook before we try to reel them in." Reed sat back. The coffee had helped. He pushed his plate toward Nat, and she finished off his donut. "What do you say we pay Sylvia a visit?"

18

Sylvia Plaques had a building on Sixth Avenue just past the towering Westbrook Telecommunications hub and the other glossy high rises on Tech Row, as the locals called it. Beautiful, streamlined buildings that rose to the firmament like pillars of digital wisdom. The city's green infrastructure laws called for flood-friendly landscaping, walls of trees, and rainwater harvesting ponds. The overall feel was supposed to be that of a futuristic utopia. A sponge city that could withstand the worsening weather with finesse. But to Reed, the peaceful fountains and climate-friendly gardens were ruined by the spiky, anti-homeless benches and armed security trolling around in golf carts.

"What do you think she's trying to say here?" Nat asked, nodding up at the ten-story building. Low hanging fog spread a blanket of mist at the tree line and tiny drops clung to her eyelashes. "Not exactly rolling out the welcome wagon."

The stark, angular lines and black stone exterior of Sylvia's Interface Solutions company reminded Reed of a fortress.

"I think that's the point," Reed said as they walked into the glass vestibule of the entrance. The inner doors had no handles and didn't open. "What the—"

"Flash," Nat said and closed her eyes.

A bright light flared inside the vestibule once on Reed then on Nat. Reed rubbed his eyes, blinking to see again. "What the hell was that?"

"My guess, rapid facial rec." Nat scanned the ceiling and then held her badge up. "Detectives De La Cruz and Reed, we need to speak to Sylvia Plaques."

The inner doors drifted open and the security guard on the other side of the glass nodded when they showed him their badges.

Read leaned in and whispered to Nat, "Explain again what Sylvia does, exactly?"

"She was the Chief Technology Officer for one of Danzig's cybersecurity holdings."

"One moment, please," the guard said and kept his gaze on a bank of screens on the control desk in front of him. He was fit, looked military, and wore a sidearm. No nametag. He nodded stiffly at Reed. "You'll be escorted up in a few minutes." Then he gestured like a game show host toward a bank of leather couches and went back to his monitors.

Reed and Nat wandered to the seating area but neither sat. The lobby was tiled with black marble. It boasted high tinted windows, espresso colored leather furniture, and more chrome than Reed had ever seen. Floor to ceiling display walls played scenes of crowds milling around Times Square, another of a football stadium full of fans. Digital indicators rose and fell next to people. Identification lines showed possible match statistics, estimations of height and weight, and little skeletal lines that tracked gait as they wove through the crowd.

"Talk about Big Brother is always watching," Reed muttered.

"More like Big Sister," Nat said.

"That's very good, detective," a woman said from behind them. Her heels clicked on the tiles as she strode from nowhere that Reed could see. "I'll have to run that past my marketing team."

Sylvia Plaques had dimples when she smiled. Blonde, maybe early forties, tall, and incredibly beautiful, she had the intense gaze of someone who liked to fight. Her soft, muted makeup and stark white dress was offset by black leather pumps with metal stiletto heels. Her silver choker necklace was in a sunburst pattern that splayed sharp points across her chest. Unapproachable. Maybe even dangerous. Reed wondered if she cultivated the look or if she was naturally a predator. He guessed the latter.

"Gus told me I had visitors, so I thought I'd meet you myself," she shook both their hands, but kept her gaze on Reed. "Please understand, the nature of my work makes it impossible for me to speak with law enforcement without my lawyer. About anything official, anyway."

"What is it you do, exactly?" Reed asked.

"We collect and store interface metrics for industry clients."

"That was a whole lot of nothing," Nat said with a smirk. "Biometrics, I'm guessing?"

Sylvia looked at her curiously and then smiled. "You're right. This is right up your alley if my sources are correct."

"You should give them a raise." Nat hooked a thumb on the glass vestibule. "I better not find any of my 'metrics' in the ether, Ms. Plaques."

"Not to worry. Just a weapons and facial check." Sylvia splayed her hands out in an open gesture. "To answer your question, Detective Reed, Interface Solutions is pioneering quite a few projects, we have many irons in the fire, so to speak, but our bread and butter is, as your partner surmised, biometrics."

"She's a data broker," Nat said to Reed as her eyes wandered the lobby. "A good one, apparently."

"Do you have someplace private we can talk?" Reed asked.

"Of course, detectives," Sylvia gestured for them to follow her into a secure elevator ensconced behind a barrier wall. It was small, with glass walls, and no floor buttons. In close quarters, Reed caught the scent of her perfume. It was sweet and thick. Jasmine. She tapped the wall screen and they moved. "What can I do for you?"

Reed ignored the idea of dying in a glass elevator accident, shredded to ribbons like some kind of ill-fated horror movie character, and focused on how to approach Sylvia. She was a fighter. No nonsense. Had tussled with Danzig and was still walking around. Reed decided not to bullshit her. "We're looking to talk with Everett Danzig's enemies."

Sylvia tilted her head and considered Reed for a moment and then a smirk spread across her face. "He's after you, isn't he?"

"Yes." The elevators opened and Reed followed Sylvia. "He's taken an interest."

"What is it you think I can do about it?"

"From what I hear, you're one of his most formidable foes."

"Oh, you're smoother than the rough exterior suggests," Sylvia said with a click of her tongue as she pushed through a dark mahogany door into her vast office. "You're more than meets the eye, aren't you, detective?"

"You have no idea," Reed muttered.

The tenth floor offered a spectacular view of the technology district's most remarkable buildings. The morning sun hadn't quite burned off the low hovering clouds and the monuments to scientific wonder pierced the dark mist like giant metal fingers clawing out of the earth. The inside of Sylvia's office was done in white leather and steel. Yet her wall décor struck Reed as sentimental, maudlin even. There were watercolor paintings, originals, Reed guessed, of glass garden cloches belled over the sinewy, decaying plants. Another of a wilting bouquet on a weathered wood table, jewel-colored insects peeking out from between dried and broken stems. He glanced at Sylvia, there was something soft there underneath all that armor.

"This is your work, isn't it?" Reed pointed to the watercolor of a shack by the sea. Battered by squalls, the brooding sky raked waves against its weathered side. Purple stones littered the sand around it. Ground down by the sea's continual, pounding force. "It's forlorn, but it's also familiar, some-how. Why is that?"

"Familiar?" Sylvia glanced at the piece and a sad smile flitted across her face. "Well, that's quite interesting."

She didn't elaborate and Nat shot Reed a bemused face.

"So, you want to talk about Danzig?" Sylvia's massive leather desk chair resembled a throne. She motioned to the clear resin chairs facing her desk and sat down, looking at them over crossed arms. "Did he send you?"

"No one sends us. We're the police," Nat said.

"That makes no difference. Everyone has a price," Sylvia said with a shrug. "At least that's what Everett said all the time."

Reed slid into the chair hoping it was stronger than it looked. "You used to work for him. In what capacity?"

"He recruited me straight out of university." Sylvia flicked the executive toy on her desk and the glass bird bobbed at her. "Before long I was head of projects and then Technology Officer of the research and development branch of High Rock Holdings."

"Why aren't you now?" Reed asked. "What happened?"

"I believed him when he said my hard work, my killing myself with seventy-hour weeks, would be rewarded," Sylvia shrugged, and her hair cascaded over her shoulder. She looked like both a screen siren and a stone-cold killer. She caught Reed staring and smiled wickedly. "You just can't trust anyone these days."

Nat stepped between them to get to her chair. "So, I heard you were promised a seat at the table and despite everything you did, he left you out in the cold."

Sylvia's smile wavered. "I built his R&D department from the ground up. I deserved a seat on the board. He'd promised me."

"In writing?" Reed asked. "Or was it whispered, this promise?"

"I didn't sleep with him," Sylvia said, amused. "But points for subtlety. He was more of a mentor. He didn't treat me like a raving lunatic when I spouted on about the evils of biometrics and the use of our own personal data against us."

Nat looked at her, confused. She waved her hand around the office. "Then help us make sense of this."

"How better to steer the boat than to be at the helm?"

"Doesn't hurt that you now can afford a boat off of other people's information, right?"

Sylvia swiveled in her chair to face Nat. "You're a scrappy one, aren't you, Detective De La Cruz? I could afford a boat at birth. But that was my father's money. This is mine."

"Gotcha," Nat said. "Silver spoon."

"We should have lunch," Sylvia said with a grin. "I'll bet you have a lot of exquisitely dark secrets."

Nat sat back, and then shrugged. "Ok. Time and place. I'll end up walking away with more than you meant to give."

"Oh, we are definitely going to be friends," Sylvia said. To Reed, she asked, "I have a meeting in ten minutes, detective. Use it wisely."

"Ok, does your company make weapons?" Reed asked. Sylvia's gaze snapped to his, but she didn't answer. She stilled. A technique he'd seen before to force more information. She was good. Reed sat with an expectant face until she answered.

"Have you come across any information that says we do?"

"That's a yes," Reed said. "What about a man named Dontae Black, Bullet, as a nickname."

"No, I don't know the name." Sylvia cantered her chin, looking at Reed sideways. "What does he have to do with Danzig?"

"I was hoping you could tell me," Reed said. "Seems like you're the type of person who loves to poke the tiger."

"Hah, tiger," Sylvia smirked, but the anger underneath it burned through. "Alright, clearly there is animosity between me and Danzig. That's likely why you came to speak with me, but I don't know anything about him personally anymore. I've been fighting him for five years so the invitations to his garden parties have obviously dropped off."

"Sabotage, union forming, industrial espionage," Nat ticked off the offenses. "You must really hate him."

"He's an evil bastard," Sylvia said with the sweetest face. "I hope he dies in a fiery plane crash."

"Wow, okay," Nat chuckled.

Reed pulled his notepad from his trench pocket. "We ask because our investigation of Danzig involves a weapon that isn't supposed to exist."

"Uh, Reed," Nat shook her head. "That's need to know."

"Well now you *have* to tell me," Sylvia said, perking up. "What kind of weapon?"

Reed gave her a general description of the Kraken and then rose from his chair and walked around to hers. He leaned down, opening his notebook to several pen and ink sketches he'd done of the Kraken. They were of different angles and the one demonstrating an explosive charge flying outward caught her eye. A weird look crossed her face, but it was gone in an instant. She ran the pad of her finger over the ink and then looked up at Reed through her long lashes. "You're very aggressive. Deep, almost angry strokes."

"You can hit on my partner *after* the interview, Ms. Plaques," Nat said, clearly enjoying Reed's discomfort. "For now, can you answer the questions?"

Sylvia chuckled a little. "I'm just teasing."

"Ms. Plaques," Reed said. "This weapon is not consumer grade. As I said, it's an incredibly advanced micro missile and I think it came from Danzig's arsenal. You know about that, don't you? Weapons would have been your purview at R&D."

"It's Sylvia, and I *knew* all about Danzig's nasty little toys. I got fired, remember?"

"Well, one of them killed this man, Dontae Black, recently out at Matthews Beach. Are you sure you've never heard the name before?"

"I haven't. Did you say, Matthew's Beach? This is the body found chained to a rock?"

"Sidewalk. What about Danzig and anyone involved in motorcycle gangs or smuggling?"

Sylvia chuckled. "He wouldn't deign to work with blue collar criminals. It's senators and diplomats all the way. They're easier to threaten and keep in line."

"I need something that connects them." Reed shook his head. "Anything but me."

Sylvia's expression softened. "You knew this victim?"

"He was an old friend and Danzig killed him." Reed caught Nat's surprised expression. Telling Sylvia about a personal connection to Dontae was risky, but warranted, Reed decided. "Your old boss had him run down like prey."

"My sympathies," Sylvia said, but the news didn't faze her at all. She tapped a pointy nail on the paper, then tilted her head and peered at the side of the notebook. She pulled out the autopsy photos Reed had deliberately made stick out from between the pages. "May I?"

"If you can stomach it," Reed said and sat on the edge of her desk, getting in her space.

Sylvia shook her head slightly as she perused them, no other expression. Controlled, Reed thought.

"Have you seen enough?" He asked.

She pushed the notebook and the photos against his thigh and looked away, but not before Reed caught a flash of worry. "This is indeed a weapon that should not have been made a reality."

Reed slipped off her desk and gathered the photos.

"And you've never heard of the Kraken or anything like it?" Nat asked.

Sylvia smiled. "There's a handful of companies that could fund something like this, but I doubt you'll get much cooperation. Research and development are a tech company's greatest expense, and we guard our secrets with vigor."

"Yeah, we vetted the other companies, at least what they made public," Nat said. "You're capable."

"Just because I'm capable of something doesn't mean I actually did it," Sylvia said with a little heat.

Nat smiled. "You were neck deep in Danzig's R&D and you've never heard of it? The concept for the Kraken isn't new, it's just never been attempted."

"What can I say? Boys and their toys. We deal in data here, detective," Sylvia said, standing up. She smoothed her dress. "I think we're done here."

"It had telemetry," Nat said, not getting up from the chair. "Everything a missile would have but with added information. Gait, facial recognition, voice print, all that is right up your alley, isn't it? That's your biometric bread and butter."

"I don't think it's Danzig's," Sylvia said. "He isn't interested in weaponry for destruction's sake. He wouldn't find one death worth the effort. Especially at what must be an astronomical price per missile. Besides, Danzig is more concerned with intelligence."

"Like the MER-C system?" Reed watched her struggle to hide the surprise. "Yeah, I have firsthand knowledge of that one. Did you know about that?"

"After my time." Sylvia sat back down, recognition brightening her face. "You're the one who blew up the Ghanzi deal, aren't you?"

"Maybe," Reed shrugged. "And you're welcome, by the way. Because I plan to take him all the way down, Ms. Plaques. He's killed too many people for me to let him walk free."

"Stay away from Danzig, detective. He's destroyed more than one brilliant mind over the years. Yours won't be the exception."

"Then help me. Point me in the right direction. Someone is attempting to use me to get to Danzig. Who would have the audacity do that to him?"

"Who would go after Danzig using a cop?" Sylvia laughed. "A lunatic or a genius."

"Anyone come to mind?"

Sylvia hesitated, and then, "You're aware that Everett Danzig swims with sharks. His own family is in constant combat with each other."

Reed glanced at Nat.

"You mean his sister?" Nat asked. "We know about her."

"I wouldn't worry about Helena. I heard she's just as likely to drop the suit and live her life out in Europe with a young lover," Sylvia said and flicked her wrist. "Can you blame her?"

"Who else?" Reed pushed. "His kids?"

"Oh, yes," Sylvia nodded. "The daughter, Aria, runs the art acquisitions branch. She also owns a gallery. I see her at benefits and galas. She's quite charming in a cold, snow queen sort of way. She hates her brother's wife."

"We heard," Nat said. "Does she have good reason to?"

"Only if you think being elitist counts as one." Sylvia turned in her chair, crossing her legs so that Reed would have to take a step back from the side of her desk. Push and pull. Sweet and sour. "Aria thinks Kaspar's wife is trash for some reason. But Kaspar and Aria always fought. Even as teenagers."

"How do you know that?" Nat asked.

"We travel in the same circles socially, even as kids. So, you see, we must be cordial to one another, even if there are clashes in the boardroom."

"Does she have reason to go against her father?" Reed asked.

"Ambition. She inherited both the brains and brutality of her father." A tone sounded from Sylvia's desk, and she tapped the glass surface, then swiped the message away. "Time's running out."

"What about Aria's husband?" Nat asked.

"He's not usually mentioned in their frays. And he didn't grow up in Washington. I believe Aria met him in college. I'm not sure what he does. I think he might be some sort of advisor?"

"And Danzig's son, Kaspar?" Reed asked, leaning over to catch Sylvia's eye. "Have you had any dealings with him?"

Sylvia twisted her chair back and forth, chewing on her inner cheek, and then she said, "I guess I should disclose that Kaspar came to me last year with a plan to unseat his father."

"What?" Nat leaned forward. "A coup?"

"A baby one, anyway," Sylvia said. "He's angry about not being on the board himself. He believes he does more than he actually does. The arrogance of privilege."

"Are you saying your birthday ponies weren't the best ones?" Nat asked with a smirk.

"You're such a pill, Detective De La Cruz. I'm serious. If you ever want to come play with the big girls of tech, let me know. I'll hire you on the spot." She turned to Reed. "I meant more in the audacity to believe your name guarantees brains. His plan was clumsy and mostly wishful thinking. He hasn't risen in his father's company because he hasn't earned it."

"Do you think Kaspar could pull off a coup against Danzig?"

"Who knows," Sylvia said wistfully. "They might be fated to."

"What do you mean?" Reed asked.

"Danzig took out his own father to take control of the company. Eisen's death was no accident. He was killed."

"That's not what the autopsy report said," Nat flipped through her tablet notes. "It's listed as a boat accident."

"Well, there are accidents, and there are accidents that are *extremely* convenient. I heard Eisen was about to push Everett out. I swear their family history reads like Shakespeare. Fratricide seems to be a tradition with them. Figuratively, I mean." Sylvia's gaze landed on Reed, and he wondered if he hid what her words did to him. Reed knew for a fact that Eisen Danzig had been murdered. He had the memories to prove it. "Something wrong, detective?"

"Very," Reed buried his hands in his pockets and stepped forward, leaning into Sylvia's space again. "You're holding back. I didn't think Danzig could intimidate you, but you're clearly afraid to say something solid. Either that, or you're involved somehow and dodging our questions."

Sylvia rose from her chair, her heels making her nearly the same height as Reed. A foot apart, she squared off subtly, with a smile that was pure aggression. "Are you trying goad me into something, detective?"

"I'm trying to stop Danzig from killing anyone else." Sylvia's sudden laughter threw him off. "You find that funny?"

She patted her palm on his chest and then pushed past him, walking to her door. It opened automatically. "I find it small minded."

"Still too afraid to go up against him head-to-head?" Reed asked, following her.

"Head-to-head?" Sylvia looked at him as if he were a dumb child. "You're still thinking too small. What I know about Danzig would give you nightmares."

Reed stopped in front of her, maybe a little too close. "You clawed your way to the top of a male dominated industry despite one of its titans gunning for you. What do you know, Sylvia? Show me how to fight him."

Sylvia stepped back and leaned against the door. She tapped her nails softly on the wood behind her, then, "This isn't about tech or even that deal you ruined for him. That's not worthy of his attention. Danzig works on a global level with entire countries at stake."

"What would make him move, then? You know him. If this were a chess game. If you could see all his moves so far, what does your gut say?" Reed raised his palm to the door near her shoulder. "What's he doing?"

"He's patient. He gets what he needs in place and then he pulls the trigger. No one rushes him, but. . ." Sylvia locked eyes with him, the guile falling away to show fear. Confusion. "He's gathering strength. Aligning allies. Whatever it is, it's close."

"Strength and allies for what? Anything you have, would help."

"I don't know, why." Sylvia's confusion seemed genuine. "But I heard he's been moving favorable judges into important seats. That's all I know."

"Judges, huh?" Reed caught Nat's gaze. She'd heard it too. "All set?" he asked her.

Nat nodded. "Good to go."

They thanked her and left. Reed thought he saw Sylvia whisper something to Nat as she passed.

"Detective Reed," Sylvia called when they were down the hall.

Reed turned and she looked so small in the huge doorway, dwarfed by the stronghold she'd built. "I am truly sorry about your friend."

Before he could answer, she stepped back inside, and the door shut.

"That was a hell of a dance you just did in there," Nat said as they headed back to the car. "That judge comment, are you thinking Leone?"

"I think I can't avoid at least speaking to him at this point. Just not on Visage's terms."

"I was afraid you'd say that." Nat glanced at the building. "Do you think anything she said was true?"

"She probably told us enough to get us to leave her office satisfied but not enough to get her name thrown into the fray."

"Maybe you should meet with her again." Nat smiled as she walked beside him. "You guys can chat about pen strokes. Maybe she'll open up this time."

"I think she's said everything she's going to say," Reed said.

"I don't know. She clearly liked you."

"She likes me like a cat likes those toy mice. It's all fun and games until she rips my guts out for kicks. Besides, I think there was a reason she got so close." Reed patted his chest, there was a lump, and he pulled out a strange glass circle. The size of a poker chip, it was etched with minute markings. "I felt her plant this."

"Shut. Up." Nat took it from his hand and held it up to the meager sun. Her breath clouded as she laughed. "That woman is a piece of work. This is a data lens."

"In English, please."

"It means she may have given us something real on Danzig. These are files, data lenses are used to hold massive amounts of compressed information." Nat looked at him, puzzled. "Why'd she hide that she gave it to you from me?"

"Not you," Reed said. "I think she was worried she was being watched."

"From within her own company?" Nat tucked the data lens into her tablet cover.

"It would cross my mind. Especially if I was a thorn in Danzig's side." Reed glanced back at the dark windows of the building. He wondered if Sylvia was watching them. "Hey, what did she whisper to you back there?"

"A number. Starting salary."

"And?"

"Let's just say the dark side has cookies." Nat slid into the driver's seat and faced Reed. "Did you catch that look when she was going through the Kraken drawings?"

"Yes, it was weird."

"Wasn't weird. It was how my friend looks at her kid."

Reed stared at Nat for a beat. "The Kraken is Sylvia's creation?"

"Explains her hesitance to help us." Nat said as she fought to get her arms out of her coat. "She definitely has the know-how, the capital, and frankly, the audacity to build something like that. Arms dealing is lucrative, but dangerous."

"I'm pretty sure both of those ideas appeal to a woman like Sylvia." Reed shook his head. "There was nothing in the research about a weapon. Not even back chatter from Coyote."

"She wouldn't be the only tech mogul secretly dipping their toes into something shady. But there's no way I can legally get into her system without cause, and I definitely wouldn't try to get in illegally. She'd be expecting it and from what I've learned of her, she will absolutely prosecute threat actors. At least we know she's probably linked to the Krakens, which connects Dontae's murder to all of this."

"Let's take a look at what she gave us. Kaspar was moving against his father and possibly using Dontae to do it. Tig will give us surveillance based on that. Coyote can do it on the down low." Reed pointed to the data lens. "And we need to figure out what to do with that. Do you know how to, you know, turn it on?"

"I have a reader, yes," Nat said with a grin, but it wavered. "Listen, I don't think I want to take this data lens back to Cybercrime. Everybody seems to know more than we do. And you're right, if Danzig's reach is what we've been told. He definitely can't know we have this. It'll put Sylvia in danger."

"What do you want to do?"

"There's an off-book place I know. It's completely walled off, security wise, and there's someone there who I think can help us."

"What, exactly, does 'off-book' mean?"

Nat started the car and then grimaced. "It means I'll have to blindfold you."

He started to chuckle but stopped when he saw her face. "Are you serious?"

"I'll have to make arrangements first, make sure we have what we need, but yes. It's sort of a secret hideout."

"For what? Pirates?"

Nat pulled out into the street. "In a way. They ride the unchartered waves of information out there in the dark net. As such, there is a certain amount of secrecy needed."

Reed braced himself as she stopped for a light. "And these people are friends of yours?"

Nat looked at him with a raised brow. "And how is, Coyote?"

"Touché," Reed muttered. "Set it up."

19

After leaving Sylvia's building, they stopped for giant pretzels at a vendor's cart down the street. Reed grabbed two bottled sodas as well and they walked over to some benches overlooking a little park. Nat pulled her tablet from somewhere in her big coat and traded him for the pretzel in his hand.

"So, I kept digging into Leone and how he got the federal seat. Like I said, he was appointed when a sitting judge died." Nat nodded at the photo on the tablet. "The honorable, Sarah Westerbrook, sixty-nine years young. She died in a single car accident. Went right off a bridge near her home into a river. Died instantly."

"That's convenient," Reed said, swiping through her information. "For Danzig."

"Yeah, especially since she'd given up her license when she turned sixty-five due to a cataracts issue. She rarely drove, according to her daughter. She used a car service."

"And somehow Danzig maneuvered Leone into her position."

"I mean, it's interim, but yeah." Nat bit off a piece of the soft pretzel. "The accident was investigated and ruled just that, an accident. The judge lost control of her car during a foggy night and went over. End of story. The thing is, my friend in the DA's office told me there was drama with the clerks."

"Westerbrook's or Leone's?"

"Both," Nat said and sat up straight like she was sharing gossip. "So normally, in an instance of losing a judge, the clerk would stay on to help the new judge's incoming staff."

"But this didn't happen."

"Correct," Nat said. "Apparently Westerbrook's clerk was transferred almost immediately. Like the next day. And get this, Leone's own clerk, Tamlin Prior, was reassigned that day as well. A new federal clerk, a guy by the name of Ezra Tan, was assigned to Leone."

"By whom?"

"I'm still digging on that. But Leone's original clerk filed a complaint saying Leone had told her she was staying on with him. She made a big stink, and you don't do that. It's a career killing move."

"But she did." Reed twisted open the soda, let some of the fizz dribble down into the grass and took a swig. "You know, in the hospital, the ER, in particular, you don't mess with the people who make the gears go."

"You're talking about your mom. The nurses," Nat said. "You're saying the clerks in this instance, are the grease that gets stuff done at the courthouse."

"Yes, and you don't mess with the system, not unless you want headaches. There's a reason that staffing the courts is an ordered, fair process."

"Which means, what, someone did this outside of that hierarchy?"

Reed took a long drink, thinking. "Where did Tamlin end up?"

Nat looked up her details via the SPD program on her tablet. "She doesn't work for the court system anymore." She tapped around in her tablet, then, "Her social media bios say she's a yoga instructor downtown."

Reed grinned, "Seriously?"

"Yeah, what is this, LA? Who quits the law and goes full granola?"

"Someone who is mighty pissed. And angry people love to tell you why." Reed crumpled up the pretzel bag and tossed it into the green waste can a few yards off. "Let's go see her."

Tamlin Prior worked out of a posh studio near Jefferson Park on Beacon Avenue. Asana Hot Yoga sat sandwiched between a raw juice bar and a doggy daycare and within spitting distance of a chiropractor's office. Reed wondered if anyone found that ironic. They'd called ahead and Tamlin had agreed to meet with them. They waited for her behind the studio in the alley where she could take her smoke break while they talked. Reed, who had been a smoker stood as close as politely possible to catch a whiff, Nat stood upwind.

"I'm totally happier now," Tamlin said as she took a puff and blew it out the side of her mouth." She caught Reed's look and held up the cigarette. "I'm still working on some bad habits." She had a pixie haircut dyed purple and a pierced eyebrow. Tamlin stood cross armed, in a pink oversized fluffy sweater and yoga gear. The wind tunneled down the alley, frigid with a bit of frost and she shivered. "Walking away from the law changed my life. I'm vegan, I get a full night's sleep. I don't have ulcers eating holes through my stomach . . . better."

"But you were angry then," Reed said. "You filed a complaint."

"Oh, that," she shifted on her feet. "The last agonal thrashes of someone else. I don't know why I fought so hard to keep my job with Leone. I mean, he was a great jurist, I learned a lot, but he wasn't a mentor or anything. Turns out he was kind of a doormat. Or a liar. But he definitely told me I was staying on as his clerk. My mom was so excited for me. And pissed when it all went down. I thought she was going to protest on the court-house steps or something."

"Any idea what happened?"

"No, I don't. I was told I could go with Leone. I moved closer to the federal courthouse, sold my car, the whole shebang and then nothing. So, come Monday, when I show up at work there's this new clerk who meets me at the door and says that things have changed. Just like that. I'm out. They offered me something in family court." Tamlin let out a rueful laugh. "That's like twelve steps down from where I was at. Besides, I make more money now than I did as a clerk."

"Stay at home moms paying top dollar, are they?" Nat asked.

"Yeah, for their kids." Tamlin rolled her eyes. "Stressed out little pipsqueaks need to learn how to relax, and their parents certainly don't know how. These kids go to competitive private schools, play sports, take language lessons, you name it. I'll bet none of them ever get to just lay on the grass and stare at the clouds, you know? I can totally relate to that."

"Back to Leone," Nat said. "His new clerk was Ezra Tan, right?"

Tamlin nodded. "Yes."

To Reed, Nat said, "I don't know who Leon's clerk is right now. They haven't seemed to assign anyone."

"Well, the guy that took my position first, was Ezra Tan." Tamlin flicked ash on the asphalt. "Yeah, he basically gave me the brush off when I asked to speak with the judge. He headed me off and handed me my things from my desk that he'd already put in a box. And tossed me a gift card for some chocolates. I'm allergic." She rolled her eyes again. "Like that was it. Never heard from Leone."

Nat typed furiously on her phone in Reed's peripheral.

"Do you know anything about Mr. Tan?" Reed asked Tamlin. "Had you known him before or heard anything that might explain why he was slipped into that position instead of you?"

"No," Sarah checked her watch and then dropped the butt in a nearby bottle filled with dubious liquid. "Honestly, he came out of nowhere. The poor kid must have had great connections because he was definitely green."

Her word choices bugged him. "You said he took your job *first*. And I know that he's not listed as Leone's clerk anymore. Why isn't he still working for him? Did he piss off the judge, somehow?"

Tamlin shook her head, hugging herself. "He ran afoul of karma. Ezra Tan died a few months ago. October, I think. Froze to death in that early storm."

Back in the car ten minutes later, Nat said, "If no one replaced Ezra, who is answering Leone's phone?"

"Maybe it's—"

Nat's phone bleeped and she checked her messages. "Ah, a secretary. Apparently, there was a clerk and a secretary for that office. I've been getting the run around from Leone's secretary. Newly assigned. No prior connection."

Reed thought that smacked of isolation, something Danzig might to do insulate Leone and keep him under his thumb. "We need to go and talk to Ezra's family."

Nat looked up Ezra's next of kin. His only surviving relative was his mother who lived about an hour away.

Reed checked his watch. "It's two thirty right now. I say we run over there and speak to her."

"I'll give her a call." Nat was already bringing up the route on her tablet.

Reed peered out the windshield, thinking about Sylvia. If the Kraken system was hers, how did Visage or Dontae for that matter get their hands on it?

Ezra Tan's mother lived in a nice home in the residential neighborhood of Hillman City. It was an older development with sturdy cedar siding houses on big lawns. Their claim to fame was an arts collective that ran a festival every spring and a bohemian pub on the main strip. Tan's house was white with gray-blue scrollwork trim that made it look like a doll house. When Nat had called earlier, Mrs. Tan was surprised, but curious enough to talk. She smiled at them cordially from her porch, but it didn't reach her eyes. Tan was pretty, a soft sixty, and yet her beige sweater set, and khaki pants washed her out. That or the grief. The effect was that she seemed to be fading as if sorrow were erasing her from existence.

She let them in and answered Nat's question about Ezra's living arrangements as they followed her to the kitchen. She had a pocket folder on the counter with a naval emblem and hand lettering done in marker that said, "Ezra Tan Docs."

"I went over his papers after you called, trying to remember details. It hasn't been that long and yet I couldn't remember the name of his apartment complex. He lived at the Weston Village in First Hill over by The Museum of Museums. A nice little studio that was only twenty minutes from the courthouse." She smiled. "He said he had a BBQ with his neighbors on the rooftop lounge."

"Sounds lovely," Nat said.

"I'm not sure why you're here," Mrs. Tan said as she poked around in a cabinet. She pulled out three mugs and a tin of shortbread cookies. "Ezra died in a skiing accident."

Nat showed her some sort of form on her tablet, and explained, "We're just following up on some background for the judge's new position. We have to vet everyone like, in triplicate."

Mrs. Tan nodded. "Sounds like the legal system."

"We understand your son landed quite a coup with the position as Judge Leone's law clerk. How did that come about?" Reed asked as he opened his leather notebook.

"My Ezra was a good boy, hard worker, just like his father." Her gaze went to the China hutch behind Reed, and he looked. A few model ships lined a shelf that held a photo of an older, Asian man. A young boy stood next to him, and they held one of the model ships up together for the picture. "That he was given this opportunity right out of law school . . ." She smiled sadly, set the paper cups of cookies on a little gilded plate, and slid it toward them. "He was going far, my Ezra."

Reed took a cookie, and they followed her to a little white café table by a bay window. It overlooked a fallow garden, the bare lattice still tangled with last year's vines. "Mrs. Tan, can you tell me about that offer? To be frank, most clerkships are for graduates at the top of their class. Ezra was in the top ten percent, which is great—"

"The judge must have seen something special in him. Ezra was so smart. And funny," Mrs. Tan said with a frown. She wore her salt and pepper hair in a modern bob and a sheath of it fell into her eyes as she set the plate of cookies down. "He was up to it."

"But it was a surprise, yes?" Nat asked. "We're not saying he didn't deserve it. It just seemed all of a sudden to the other clerk."

"Oh." Mrs. Tan pursed her lips. "Yes, she filed a complaint."

"Can you tell me what happened the weekend he passed?" Reed asked. "We looked up his social media, and I didn't see any ski trips at all until this past year."

"Ezra said the trip was a big deal. A bonus for his hard work. It was the first time he was ever going to ski." Mrs. Tan shook her head. "Our family mostly hiked. Some camping here and there, but always in warm weather. Ezra had no experience with snow or skiing. Apparently, he got disoriented and went down a closed trail or something. He took a wrong turn and ended up on a treacherous route. They said he hit a tree." She looked away, blinking. "A head injury made worse by the sun setting and another storm rolling in. He had been missing for hours by the time the local sheriff called me. The sheriff explained it but, you know, I don't think I heard much on that phone call. Just that he was lost."

"Did they recover him?" Nat asked.

"Yes. A couple of days later because the weather had made them call off the search effort. After the storm, they went out again and found him. I buried Ezra next to his father."

"I'm so sorry, Mrs. Tan," Reed murmured. "It sounds like he was a dedicated servant of the law."

"That's what the card Leone's office sent said." She ground her jaw. Reed could see the movement beneath her skin. "That's the least he could have done given how hard he was on Ezra."

Reed leaned on his elbows on the table, looking up at her as she struggled with something. "Tell me about that."

She dabbed at her eyes with the edge of her long sleeve. "I know you have to pay your dues, but Judge Leone had my son running all over the place at night, during holidays, early morning. He was at the judge's beck and call."

"He took advantage," Reed said with a nod, urging her on. "For example?"

"The judge had no family close by. His daughter is at college, his wife is gone. He worked late every day, even weekends, which meant Ezra did too."

"Did the hours cause tension between them?" Nat asked.

"Oh, no. Ezra loved it. He thought Leone was a great man." A flash of anger crossed her features, but she turned away. "He didn't mind the grind. He knew it was paving the way for his future."

"But you didn't." Reed leaned into her line of sight. "You thought it was excessive, didn't you?"

Mrs. Tan nodded, dabbing at her eyes with the sleeve of her sweater. "Last Easter, we were all sitting down to eat, and Ezra's phone rang. He answers it, and of course, it's the judge. Leone wanted him to bring some files for a case scheduled for the next week. As if it couldn't wait for one day."

I begged him to stay, but he left. Didn't get back until early morning." Mrs. Tan touched her fingertips to the edge of the plate, thinking. "He made Ezra drive him around. Like a chauffeur. To official events at first, but then he'd have to go to all the judge's engagements. Even the ones out of town or out of state. Ezra once spent all day on a fishing boat while the judge met with some old law school friends. He got so seasick." She shook her head. "Then he had to drive the judge back down from the lake at night, two hours, while trying not to vomit."

Reed stopped writing in his leather notebook. "What lake?"

"I don't know. Apparently, the house up there is part of a family trust belonging to Leone's wife. Her family bought property there decades ago. The house is really his daughter's now, but it's maintained by the trust executor, which is Leone."

"So, it's available to him," Nat looked at Reed. "That's why it didn't pop in our property search. He doesn't own it."

Mrs. Tan smiled sadly. "Ezra tried to explain it to me. He loved the law. He said the place was beautiful and that you could see the observatory site off the back deck. Just across the water."

Reed shot Nat a look and she nodded. "Thank you, Mrs. Tan," Reed said and snapped his notebook shut.

Walking back to the car, Nat said, "You think Judge Leone is hiding out at his daughter's lake house?"

"I do," Reed said, climbing into the driver's seat. "We need to find that house before anyone else does."

"Yeah, but who is he hiding from? Danzig or Visage?"

Reed started the engine, gazing to the street behind through the mirror. He looked for familiar cars. "I guess that's something we'll have to ask when we find him."

20

They left Mrs. Tan's and sat in the car a block down the road, talking. Nat was flicking her data about, looking for something. Reed thought about Tig and how he should loop him in as soon as possible. He set the phone to speaker mode and dialed. Tig answered on the first ring.

"So, you *are* still alive," Tig said. "Are you with Parker?"

"No, I haven't heard from him." Reed caught Nat's gaze. She shook her head. "We're going to talk to a witness, and we might have a possible lead, still a bit sketchy. Also, I left a message for Parker asking him to start checking out his sources in organized crime. I know he's working on The Kindred members right now, but I need to know as much as I can about their smuggling routes. How far do they go and what happens after that. I want to know the reach. A witness said Dontae's connection to the killer may have been his ability to move product."

"By the way, that Mookie character you tossed off the building? He's threatening to sue," Tig said, and papers shuffled in the background.

"I can talk to him," Reed said.

"Don't make things worse," Tig warned. "Where does the Kindred route go?"

"North, to Canada."

"Crap, we've got that whole pipeline mess going on right now. There's tension, polite tension, but still. A smuggling issue definitely won't improve relations," Tig sighed. "Sounds like the case is gaining traction though?"

"Finally catching a break. We think our victim may have been connected to a judge. I'm running that down with De La Cruz as we speak."

"A judge?" Tig didn't sound happy.

"Dontae said to more than one witness that he was definitely getting out of Seattle soon. His parole officer says no. If I can confirm Dontae or his girlfriend put money down out there that's something. He'd have to get some sort of approval. I believe this is the payment Dontae mentioned to Mookie."

"And you think this judge may have done this for Dontae, why?"

"That's what I want to ask him. No names yet. I don't want anything official if the man is clean." Reed waited through Tig's hesitation. They'd kept things close to the vest when they were partners. Tig knew the precinct had ears, even if he wouldn't admit it outright. "We've got a lot of delicate plates spinning right now. I need a lock on information. Your eyes only."

After a few moments, Tig said, "You call me as soon as you have something solid. And that blogger who dropped the story about you just called wanting a quote about your disciplinary record. She used my private number. Who is this asshole?"

Reed looked at Nat. "We'll find them."

"Keep me posted," Tig said and was gone.

"Don't worry, that blogger is toast. They think they're slick, but I'm watching them. In the meantime," Nat said and held up her tablet. A picture of Judge Leone with his college-aged daughter at her high school graduation was on the screen. "I asked Imani in cybercrime to try and pull the property records and any trust documents attached to Leone's daughter. The thing is you can name a trust anything. And we have to go through the mother's accounts, because it was her side of the family who set it up. That's either probate or if they've cleared that, we'd need warrants for Leone's and his daughter's accounts, which would definitely raise alarms, so it's a little murky. Might take a bit."

"What about Ezra's phone? He'll have location data, right?"

"It would take days to get that information even with a warrant. Which we don't have. His mom can't give permission. The phone plan has been dead for months. I don't even know if they keep data from closed accounts." Nat grinned at him. "Something to ask Sylvia if you get a chance. Maybe during an impromptu lunch chat after you 'accidentally' run into her?"

"Yes, because we probably eat at the same hot dog stands." Reed chuckled.

"Kidding aside," Nat mused as she pulled a sliver of peeling silicone from the tablet cover, her lips turned down. "I can't think of a reason not to go see Leone at this point. We have to know how he knows Dontae."

"And Danzig." Reed pointed to her tablet. "Let's use a map. We have distance and time. Ezra's mother said he drove the judge back from the lake and it only took two hours. We know where Leone lives. That's our starting point."

"I mean if you want to go old school. It'd be great to have something more specific than a pretty lake house somewhere in Seattle." Nat opened up a map program and enlarged it on Washington State. "We're literally surrounded by waterways, lakes, the Sound, the ocean . . ."

"Yes, but how many give you a view of an observatory?" Reed thought for a second. "How many do we have in the area?"

Nat searched for observatories in the state. "Apparently there are four, but they're either too close, like forty minutes away, or much further than two hours. The other results are planetariums or museums. You think she lied?"

Reed shook his head. "When you talk about going somewhere you say the building, right? The library, the movies, the observatory. Mrs. Tan said that Ezra used the words, 'the observatory *site*.' That's for things no longer there usually. The crash site. Like that. Try looking up decommissioned observatories or historical ones."

Nat didn't find any by a lake, but she did find one near a protected water reserve. Tolmie State Park sat on the western edge of the Nisqually Aquatic Reserve. Above it, residential houses, and across the water, was Wilkes Observatory Trail.

"That's a military installation," Reed tapped her screen. "Ezra's folder had a similar emblem. And there were models of naval ships on the shelves of his mother's home. He'd know what he was talking about."

"According to this, they weren't looking at stars, they were mapping the lower Puget Sound," Nat said reading off her tablet. "It fits. A fan of history would recognize the site."

"Getting closer. The house has to be around here."

They fiddled with the area and landed on the town of Puget Washington. The town was two hours and four minutes from the judge's apartment, two-nineteen with traffic. It fit.

"Ezra told his mother that he could stand on the deck and see the observatory site across the water," Reed said. He reached over and tilted the map, adjusting the view to 3D. "If Leone's house is on this shore, with a deck in back to look *across* the water, that would put the house on the west side looking southeast at the observatory."

She pinched to zoom, and they used the street-view mode to look at properties on that side.

"There." Reed pointed at the map to a series of inlets around Anderson and McNeil Island just north of interstate five in Pierce County. "This area is in the right orientation to view the observatory."

"Hold on." Nat eliminated homes in the small, unincorporated town that were too far inland, didn't have a back deck, and were facing the wrong way.

"What do you think?" Reed said as he zeroed in on a property. "I can see why he'd feel safe. It's secluded, one road in. Back from the other houses by at least a mile on a private drive."

"Hold on, let me try a real estate site. They list approximate value, size, and ages of homes whether or not the property is for sale." She looked up the address she got from the street view. "Yeah, according to this, that house is thirty years older than the others further down."

"Mrs. Tan said the trust was set up decades ago." Reed called county records and got back information they already knew. It was not Leone's, it was part of a trust, and was listed as vacation property for tax purposes. "The utilities are current."

"Is it being used as a rental property?"

"Doesn't appear so," Reed scrolled the site.

"So, he could be there." Nat zoomed in on the property. "The timeline fits. This has to be the house."

Reed started the car. "Only one way to know for sure."

They took I-5 south down through the International District, past all of Beacon hill, and SeaTac airport. Veering west near Milton, they continued south around the Nisqually waterways and then hooked north up through South Bay where they passed multiple massive distribution centers. Snow appeared on the side of the road as they went, then up on the hills. Light, but getting heavier. Small thickets of trees and housing developments gave way to winding roads shrouded by towering pines too dense and dark to see through. By the time they passed the State Park, they'd seen multiple marinas and boat dealerships. Just beyond the reserve, they hit Puget. An unincorporated community, it had one of everything. One main road with one gas station, one market, a bait and tack shop, and a diner that looked sixty years old.

They stopped at the gas station. Nat needed to use the bathroom, so he dropped her off around the back side of the building and went inside the mini mart to fight with the cashless kiosk for something warm to drink. After, Reed gassed the car, glad for the SPD hybrids because the tiny town still hadn't installed charging stations despite the government incentives. Reed wondered if it was laziness or to keep out visitors. Once down the main drag there was only forest and gaps in it. Reed had studied the map of the area, but the only sign of the vast homes located there were the iron gates barring entrance to artfully hidden private roads.

Leone's address was five miles past the main road down an unfinished path that was mostly dirt with large swaths of crumpling asphalt. And then the house came into view. White with pale yellow trim, it was a large rustic contemporary home with river rock retaining walls and tall pines dusted with snow. Reed pulled into the driveway and an automatic floodlight flashed on sending yellow light along the top of the snow drifts piled around the house, the driveway, the bushes. Somewhere in the home an alert tone sounded.

"What do you think? Does it look empty?" Nat asked.

Reed shut the car off and pushed out of his door. "Hard to tell from here. I'll go take a look."

The snow was fluffy, pristine, and it muffled the sounds of the forest. It crunched under his boots as they walked to the door. He checked out the roofline, the eaves, looking for cameras, there were none. Leone had no security at all save for the lock on the original door. Up at the house, Nat gave the bell a few tries, but no one answered. Reed walked around the property looking in windows where the curtains weren't pulled. There was a utility shed in the distance, a large tank, maybe propane off the south wall, and a couple of snow shovels leaning against the fence. A six-foot solid wood gate barred the entrance to the back property. A cord of wood covered with a tarp sat against the house.

Reed came back around, stomped the snow from his boots, and said, "Definitely not vacant. There's bread and some bananas on the counter. Bread isn't moldy. Bananas aren't brown. Someone stocked this place recently."

"So where are they?" Nat did a three-sixty turn. "There's literally nothing out here but trees and water."

Reed checked his watch. Nearly four thirty in the afternoon, the light was going. He was debating whether to wait or go find a place to eat when the soft crunch of snow behind him made him turn. A pudgy man, older, with a fishing cap, winter coat, flannel shirt, and jeans ambled down the road toward them. His white brows and beard obscured the lower half of his face, but the eyes were unmistakable. Probing, intelligent. It was the judge.

Leone stopped, his body tense as his gaze flitted around looking for a place to run. "How did you find me?"

Reed stepped forward, confused. "Sir, we just want to talk to you—"

"Get away from me!" Leone went for his waistband, reaching for a pistol from underneath the flannel.

"Gun!" Reed dove for the judge, taking him to the ground. They wrestled for the weapon. Leone was much stronger than he looked and spitting mad.

"Whoa, whoa, whoa!" Nat shouted, her gun coming out.

"I should shoot you in the face right now, you, lunatic," Leone shouted, writhing in Reed's grip. "Killing me isn't going to be as easy as you think!"

"What the hell are you talking about?" Nat screamed. "What's going on?"

Reed subdued the judge, wrestling the weapon from him. He stood and left Leone on the ground, panting with exertion. Reed stepped back. "You think I came here to kill you?"

"You said you would," Leone shouted. He glared at Reed, pure hate in his eyes.

"What? I thought you wanted to talk to him?" Nat pointed at Reed. "Visage said you would only talk to Reed in person."

"Who the hell is Visage?" The judge shook his head and pointed an arthritic finger at Reed. "I don't want to speak to him. I was trying to hide from him."

"Wait, you *aren't* working with a man named Visage?" Reed asked, confusion scrambling his thoughts.

"Don't try to act stupid. You know what you did. You threatened to kill me!"

"When? We've been trying to get ahold of you for days," Reed snapped back. "We just managed to find you two hours ago."

"Last night." The judge looked at Reed like he was insane. "You threatened to kill me just last night."

21

Reed scanned the darkening horizon. "We should get inside."

"What's going on?" Nat asked.

"It's just getting cold," Reed helped the judge up, started moving him toward the door. He shot her a look. Heads up.

"I demand to know what is going on!" Leone shouted as Reed forced him into the lake house. "Explain yourself!"

"Inside," Reed said as he locked the door and urged them further into the house. He moved them away from the road, facing the lake. Reed took in the wood-carved ducks on the bookcase shelf, the umbrella stand with fishing rods, and the chintz flower pillows and felt like he'd walked right back into the nineteen-eighties. Leading the judge to one of the wingchairs by the fireplace, he eased him into it. "Your Honor, I need to see what Visage sent you as me. How did I contact you?"

"Stop acting like it wasn't you," Leone spat.

"You want me to prove the harassment didn't come from me, or not?" Reed asked.

"You better."

"Then answer my questions."

Leone crossed his arms, but answered, "Mostly by phone. A hidden number every time."

Nat stood to the side of the window overlooking the lake, poking at her phone. "What about your computer. Any emails?"

"Just one. It was a picture of my daughter. From a fake email. I tried to trace it with one of those reverse look up programs online, but the name is just a bunch of numbers."

"It would be a throwaway account, nothing there." Nat dropped her phone into her pocket. "There's no signal. How do you access the internet out here?"

"It's supposed to be a place to retreat. There's no internet."

"Try again," Reed said. "Mrs. Tan said you worked her son twelve-hour days, including weekends, even up here. There is no way you completely unplugged from life." Reed walked around the room, stopping at the desk. "Am I going to find a laptop or a tablet in there?"

Leone looked away and Nat walked over to the little roll-top desk facing out of a picture window. Pulling off her coat, she sat on a wooden office chair, and pulled out a tablet from the middle drawer. "It's charged. If I can sign into his accounts from here, we can look at what Visage sent him."

"How do you access a signal?" Reed asked. When Leone didn't answer, Reed said, "You can cooperate, or you can stay in the dark on this."

Reluctantly, Leone pointed to his bag, a leather satchel, sitting on the floor near Nat's foot. "I have a data hotspot. The device is in the briefcase."

Nat went to work setting up the tablet with the hotspot.

Reed walked to the front window and pulled back the lace curtains. The lake waves, choppy with wind, slapped whitecaps against a floating dock, and the setting sun cast orange rivulets of light on the turbulent water. Reed asked Leone, "What does Danzig have on you?"

Leone glared at him. "I don't know what you're talking about."

"You scurried off to hide at your daughter's house," Reed said. "You know something."

"The only thing I knew before ten minutes ago, was that you were threatening to kill me and then tracked me down to do it." Worry lined Leone's features. "I was hiding from you."

"No, you weren't. Visage has been playing all of us against each other. Danzig, you, me . . ."

"Do you hear yourself? You sound insane," Leone said. "Who's playing whom? What game are you talking about?"

"Betrayal. Someone is moving on Danzig. You're a pawn. *We're* pawns." Reed sat down next to Leone, in the other wingchair by the fireplace. "Have you ever had dealings with Danzig's son, Kaspar?"

"No, I have no business dealings with any of them. Why are you asking me these questions?"

"A friend of mine was killed, and a man named Visage contacted me and told me Danzig was behind it. Which made sense at the time given how I made him lose trillions of dollars recently. This caller also said that Danzig had hurt a lot of people and that they were fighting back. Starting with you. Visage told me that you wanted to speak. Only to me, about what you knew about Danzig."

"Why would Danzig kill a friend of yours?" Leone laughed ruefully. "Why would he even know who you are?"

There was pride there, like a chosen minion, flaunting that he knew the boss. Reed considered the judge for a moment. Maybe he wasn't a complete victim here. There had been dozens of images of Leone and Danzig left at Reed's place and it occurred to him they were all recent. He wondered if the judge would lie about knowing him. "You do know Everett Danzig, then?"

"Yes, I know him, of course," Leone said. "He's an internationally respected entrepreneur and philanthropist."

"And a bona fide psycho murderer," Nat said. "You forgot that part."

"But it was recent, your knowing him, right?" Reed studied the judge as he asked. "You weren't important enough until you rose to the federal bench."

Leone frowned at him. "We'd run into each other from time to time via the causes we champion. The charity circuit, if you will. Golf tournaments, regattas, and such."

Reed clicked his tongue, feigning disappointment. "Then you knew him incidentally, not personally."

"No, I knew him more than that. He went to my alma mater, for Pete's sake." Leone raised his hand stopping any argument. "And before you ask, no, I never heard or saw Danzig being anything but a model student. Nothing diabolical like you suppose. The most dangerous thing we did was steal the goat mascot from a rival fraternity. He wouldn't murder that Kindred gang member and chain him to a sidewalk. That's what you're referring to, correct? That victim was your friend?" Leone asked with a condescending look. "Why would a man like Danzig bother to even come after a city cop like you for revenge? He could simply have you shot in some dark alley, according to you. Evil mastermind that you claim him to be."

"Danzig isn't walking on water over here," Nat snapped. "Everyone knows that he's vicious to his rivals."

The judge raised his brow at her. "That's a far cry from murder. Why would Danzig risk being tied to that kind of crime, perpetrated against Detective Reed here, a man who has accused him publicly of harming others? That would give your claims credence, would it not? Danzig wouldn't fall victim to short sighted anger. He's brilliant. Measured. This kind of approach, the ham-fisted intimidation, the overt threats, doesn't sound at all like the man I know. He's an innovator, his advances on renewable energy alone should garner him a humanitarian award."

Leone was trying to spin his relationship with Danzig even now, Reed thought.

"I said Visage *told* me it was Danzig, not that I believed it was. Not anymore. I know Danzig didn't kill Dontae, not after spending all that time and money discrediting me. Someone close to him is doing this. I just don't know who or for what reason. Or what I have to do with all of it. I only know it was imperative to Visage that I meet with you in person." Reed shook his head. "Now it turns out, you never wanted to talk. In fact, you've been told, probably by Visage posing as me, that I want to kill you."

"He sounded like you do now," Leone said. "I had no frame of reference before, but now that I do, it was your voice on the phone. I'd swear it."

Reed caught the look on Nat's face. Worry.

"Was it all phone calls?" she asked. "Or did you hear his voice in person. Did someone confront you in real life?"

"No, it was mostly calls," the judge said, his face growing more uncertain. "And no, no one ever came up to me."

"First time I heard of you was a few days ago. And I'm not interested in prison time. I would not come after a sitting judge. Period." Reed rose from the chair, looking down at the older man. "Now, Your Honor, how long have you been receiving threats and harassment?"

Leone pursed his lips, blew out a long breath, then answered. "A month, maybe more."

"Any other means of communication?" Nat asked. "Text, tele-conference, courier pigeon . . . what?"

Leone sat up, remembering something. "Someone came to my house. About a week before all this started. They walked around looking into windows. I have it on my security system."

Reed turned to Nat. "Is that possible?"

"Very." she said quietly. "Your voice is cloneable with what's already out there on the internet. Security cameras are crappy, low light messes them up further, and they're rarely encrypted from user to offsite storage. Throw in a guy your height, messy hair, with a trench that obscures a large part of your face. . .yeah, they could fake you well enough to pass. Especially if it's to fool someone who's never interacted with you before, like Judge Leone."

Something scratched at the edges of Reed's mind, but he couldn't quite reach it. To Nat, "Can you get into his security system remotely?"

"Most systems have a client dashboard or an app interface." She walked over and leaned a hip on the fireplace mantle next to the judge. "Any chance you got a letter or something we can fingerprint?"

"He left notes on my car," Leone said. "Threats that he knew things about me. Would expose me."

"Will you let us fingerprint those notes?" Reed asked.

Leone shook his head. "I left everything at my house. My phone, my files, all of it in case. . ."

"I found you," Reed finished.

"Your Honor," Nat asked, "we can go and get them—"

"I'll turn them in myself when I get back. I'm not just handing them over to you two." Leone glared at Reed. "I could see him following me wherever I went. I'd go to a dinner meeting, and you'd pass by the window. You wouldn't let up—"

"Not Detective Reed," Nat said as she went back to the desk. "Looked like him. Wasn't him."

The judge's lips pressed into a thin line. "*Whoever it was* wouldn't let up.

Every time I tried to walk to them, they'd take off. Just constant harassment."

"And the caller gave you my name when he called you?"

Leone nodded. "You... he gloated that I'd never see it coming."

Behind Reed, Nat muttered to herself while making the tablet mad. It beeped and she swore. Then she walked over and smiled.

"Hotspot worked." She took Leone's information for his security camera program and went back to work.

Reed sat back in the chair, thinking. "Your Honor, you don't strike me as a man who puts up with the kind of treatment you described. So, why did you? Why not report me?"

Leone's face flushed red, and he balled his hands into fists. "I told you someone emailed me a photo of my daughter, right? Well, a few weeks ago, around the time the harassment started, someone left that same photo on my car. It was a candid or surveillance shot of her at school with her friends. Only this time, someone had drawn a target on her chest. A typed message along the bottom said that she would disappear if I didn't do what I was told."

"Do what you are told," Reed repeated. The vandalism on Reed's kitchen wall above all the photos had used the same phrasing. "And this was from me?"

"You called and told me to look on my car. I was at home at the time and found an envelope shoved under the windshield wiper."

"Okay, well Detective Reed received a similar message, virtually word-for-word. 'Do what you are told,'" Nat said and showed him a picture of it on her phone. "So again, Reed's not doing this harassing."

"Well, I didn't know that," Leone said. "And I assumed it was the man who called himself Reed."

"Aside from the threats, what exactly did I say to you?"

"Just, threats—"

"Your Honor, stop evading. It would take something significant for a man like you, one used to wielding power, not to defend himself. In my experience with this caller, let's just call him Visage, is very specific with his threats. It's how he shows authenticity. Details no one should know." Reed leaned in. "He's not bluffing. He will blow up your life."

"I'm screwed either way," Leone said, his face falling. "The caller, this imposter, told me that he knew that I had done... something for my daughter. Something I shouldn't have."

"What did you cover up?" Reed asked. "Are you talking about squashing a DUI or did you help her bury a murder victim? Give me a scale here."

"She hit someone's car and panicked. She drove off. Unfortunately, the passenger of the other car had a heart condition, and he had a heart attack due to the crash."

"A guy died?" Nat said, incredulously.

"It was an accident! She was only nineteen and . . ." Leone shook his head. "I thought that he wanted money, but all the caller wanted was for me to tell him when Danzig made a move."

"What does that mean?" Nat asked, she leveled her gaze at the judge. "Has Everett Danzig asked you for a favor, Your Honor?"

"No, but I think he may be planning to," Leone said.

"Because it was Danzig who got you the federal position, wasn't it?" Reed asked.

"I have no proof it was Danzig, really." Leone threw his hands up in confusion. "I received a letter, it was on my desk one morning, congratulating me on my new appointment. I didn't know what it was. That's not how things are done. I called my clerk, Tamlin, and she had no idea what it was about. But then the governor called me at my office to wish me luck and tell me he was confident in his decision. He said a good friend of ours recommended me to him as a replacement for Judge Sarah Westerbrook, who passed in an accident."

Out of the corner of his eye, Reed caught Nat tense as she looked at the tablet in her hand.

Leone continued. "The governor alluded to the name, Maiko. It's the name of a charity tournament I do annually for troubled youth. They build the little regatta boats and race them. Then there's a silent auction for funds to send them to technology camp. Danzig is on the board with me. In name only. He has never attended a single meeting. The other members are a retired thoracic surgeon, a restauranteur, and a charter member who is older than dirt. I realized then, that 'our friend' could only be Danzig. He's the only one I can think of who knows the governor and myself. He's the only one who could even conceivably influence federal judicial appointments. There are rumors that Danzig has taken the governor on some extravagant excursions. Private yachts, exotic locales, he even took him diving with sharks, I've been told. The governor is in Danzig's pocket."

Reed pulled out a photo of Dontae from his leather notebook and held it up for the judge. "Do you recognize this person?"

Without hesitation, Leone shrugged. "No."

Nat sighed deeply, her bad news frown creasing her forehead. Not good. She walked over, pulled her phone from her jacket, and started fiddling.

Reed asked Leone, "Sir, if you knew something was wrong with your appointment. Why didn't you say anything?"

"Refuse a federal appointment?" Leone looked at him like he was insane. "Unheard of. That would be egg on the governor's face if I rejected his offer. Especially since I'm not part of his political party. It would look like a snub from the opposing side. No, to say no would have ended my career. And, if I was right about Danzig being behind it, no one refuses Danzig."

"During your time on the bench, what's it been, months? Has anyone ever contacted you about wanting anything? A favor? Doesn't have to be Danzig himself. He would likely send and intermediary."

"No. Nothing," Leone took in a deep breath. "I have not heard from the governor or his staff or Danzig at all. Just that one call. I started to believe I was just seeing the fruits of my efforts. But I knew, deep down, it was as if I've been placed there for some future purpose."

"Kinda like a landmine waiting for someone to step on it," Nat said. She walked over to them and showed Reed the tablet. "You have to see this. The likeness is uncanny. If not for the weird gait, I couldn't tell this guy wasn't you."

Reed watched a few seconds of a guy that could easily be his brother amble around the outside of a very nice home. "If this guy has a weird gait, we can use that to find him. If he's in the system it'd be mentioned—"

"No, *you* have the weird gait." Nat tapped the screen. "This guy walks normal."

"Wait, what?" Reed asked, now wondering about his walk. He played a few more seconds of the recording. "What is going on?"

A tone sounded by the desk, and they all looked over. Nat rushed to her phone. Her cheeks paled and Reed shot to his feet. "What is it?"

She held up her phone. "I have an app that periodically scans for things like those trackers. You know, the kind creeps put on their girlfriend's car to stalk them. I made all of my friends get them because, you know, for safety. I just got a notification. One is transmitting right now, within a hundred yards of me. It must've just connected with the hotspot."

"Someone is tracking us, here? How?" He'd known it. Felt the danger close by but didn't see it.

Nat looked out the window. "The patrol car maybe? I don't know."

"Dammit, I led him straight to the judge."

"Who?" Leone asked, his eyes wide. "Who's coming?"

Reed ignored him. To Nat, "How long do we have?"

"They're right down the private road. Five minutes tops." She held up the map on her phone containing the tracking signal. "What's the plan?"

Leone jumped to his feet. "Somebody tell me what is going on or I'm leaving!"

Reed turned on him, his face set in stone. "Your Honor, you are going to sit down and shut up, so I can think. If you don't, I will duct tape you to that chair and save a piece for your mouth. You understand me, sir?" Leone glared at Reed but sat down.

"Visage set us up." Reed paced the woven carpet in the den. It was getting dark. And cold. With no other structures close by, there was only one place they'd shelter. Someone watching them would know that. They have no communications, no supplies, and an old man who couldn't run. Reed's gut knotted. Everything, the staging of Dontae, the insistence on Reed and the judge meeting face to face, the taunts, and threats to get him next to the judge, all of it designed for this moment. "This is bad."

"I'm starting to freak out a little here," Nat hissed. "Tell me something."

"Think about it. Danzig placed the judge. It's well known that I hate Danzig, so to get back at my arch nemesis, I ruin yet another one of his plans by—"

"Killing the judge," Nat gasped.

"He knew me," Reed shook his head. "Visage knew what I'd do. He set a trap, and I ran right into it."

Nat lifted the judge's tablet, stress lines under her eyes. "Reed, he's left a trail of evidence to nail you."

"That's a problem for later. Right now, we've got to move." Reed turned to Leone. "Your Honor, I believe your life is in danger. We need another way out of here."

"There's just the road," Leone said, starting to hyperventilate. "Or the water."

"We'd be exposed on the water," Nat said.

Reed agreed. "I say we do the woods. Circle around the back of the property to the main road." To Leone, "Do you have an ATV, one of those four-wheel buggies?"

He shook his head. "You think they're coming here to kill me and frame you? Can't you call for back up?"

Nat held up her phone. "The signal is gone again." She checked the judge's tablet. "I think they're using a dampener."

"Where were they the last time you checked?"

"They hadn't moved," Nat said. "What does that mean?"

"It means we stay here."

"What are you talking about?" Leone shot back to his feet and strode toward the front door. "We need to get out of here!"

"The house gives us cover. A place to defend and rooms to fall back to. There're multiple egress points." Reed stripped off his coat and walked around the judge's house. He rummaged in the utility closet and looked in a blanket chest by the couch. He turned to Leone. "Do you have a weapon?"

"In the bedroom. I have a shotgun." Leone walked past them to go and get it.

"Okay, no backup and no real way out of here," Nat said, her face set. She peeked out the front window toward the road. "You have a plan or what?"

"Chicken," Reed said as he walked around the room closing curtains. "We're going to see who flinches first."

The back screen door slammed.

"Leone!" Reed ran back through the house, Nat at his side. The judge scrambled out across the seagrass and sand to the dock. "Stop!"

Nat ran after him, but a crackling sound burned through the air and

Reed froze. He scanned the horizon toward the road. The telltale cone-shaped vapor of the shock wave streaked low across the sky followed by a distinct pop, the sound barrier breaking as the Kraken soared through the air.

Reed's gaze snapped to his partner, she was nearly to the judge. "Nat!"

He sprinted toward them, his gaze sweeping the sky, pulse racing in his ears. It makes a first pass, he knew that from the telemetry data. The image of Dontae running wasn't a head-on shot. The camera had been passing him when he looked over at it. Which meant it doubled back. There was time.

"Get down!" Reed yelled, waving his arms at Nat and Leone as he ran.

They turned in unison, the judge a few feet ahead of her, already on the dock. The wind whipped his white hair up in a solid chunk and he undulated with the lake waters beneath. Green flashes flickered as the micro missile soared between them. Gridlines marked the terrain, the target, mapping facial sectors in the blink of an eye. Reed was almost to them when Nat hit the ground, but Leone froze. His eyes locked on Reed as the Kraken banked, impossibly fast it arched midair, whining as it slammed into the judge's back, thrusting him forward. Leone gasped, eyes bulging, his arms reaching for Nat.

"Don't touch him!" Reed grabbed at the collar of her sweater, his fingers just brushing the material, missing as she scrambled to her feet.

"Your Honor!" She stepped onto the dock and clutched his hand.

Leone's face filled with terror. "Help me—"

Reed dove for Nat as Leone's chest exploded. Blood and bone tore through his clothes, pelting them as the force of the blast blew them off the dock. Then everything went black.

22

Reed hit the ground hard, Nat clutching to his chest. He nearly blacked out from the concussive force, but she flailed in his grasp pulling him back from the dark. He let her go and she rolled, coughing sand from her mouth and gasping for the breath knocked out of her. Crimson dotted the snow around them and when she sat up, it clung to her shoulder. Reed brushed it away.

"You're okay." Reed whispered already helping her to her feet. He moved them back toward the house.

"Where's the judge?" Her entire body trembled, and she jerked at a bird call. The adrenaline was getting on top of her. "Where's his body?"

"In the water." Reed pulled her by the sleeve, scanned the sky, and forced her into a run. "We have to get inside, now!"

"We need to call it in."

"Cover first," Reed said as they scrambled through the snow toward the house.

"What about the men in the car down the road?" Nat's hand went to her waist holster. "They could be coming to finish us off—"

A brilliant flash burned hot and bright as the propane tank exploded next to them. The blast twisted Reed through the air, the shock of it stealing his breath. He landed in the bushes by the house. The pain hit him in a crushing wave, and he coughed, hacking as he staggered to his feet.

"Nat?" He glanced around, his vision blurry, cold of the snow seeping into his sweater. The explosion had set the house on fire. Black smoke billowed from the roof and side room. He shook his head, trying to clear it. "Nat?"

Then he saw her, crumpled in the snow next to the back porch.

"No, no, no, no," Reed murmured as he stumbled to her, falling to his knees at her side, mouth agape. She wasn't moving. A ragged wound seeped blood down her forehead to the ground and her lips were blue at the edges. He touched her and the band around his chest let go at the flutter of a pulse beneath his fingertips. Tires screeched in the distance and his gaze shot to the road. A plume of dirt rose up into the sky. They couldn't stay there. He leaned in, his lips at her ear. "Please, Nat—"

She gasped awake, sitting up with shock, eyes wide with fear. "I blew up! I blew up!" She yelled, patting her body with her hands, checking for damage. Her eyes locked with his and she pulled at his shirt, moved his chin to the side to look at his ears. "You're okay?"

"We're okay," Reed said, stopping her hands with his own. "Take a breath."

She winced. "I can't breathe."

"Can you move?"

"Are they coming?" Her hair was plastered to her face with melting slow and mud like she'd been dragged behind a dog sled, but the look in her eyes wasn't fear. It was anger. "Tell me they're dumb enough."

"Simmer down there, Calamity Jane." Reed slipped his arm around her back, lifting her with him as he stood. He set her down on the snow and shook his head again. His ears rang. "I don't think they're coming."

"How can you be sure?"

"Check your smart watch. See if the dampener is gone."

She did and looked at him with confusion. "Why would they just leave like that?"

Reed's gaze went to the dock, where crimson snow soaked into the wet sand of the lake shore. Blood and bone. Flesh and fire. He could see the battle map now with startling clarity. Reed was neither a pawn nor a player. He was the weapon. "They left because they accomplished their mission."

Nat stayed outside to check the car for the tracker while Reed ran into the house to grab their coats and equipment. The fire from the explosion ate up the kitchen and back room, but Reed found their things and ran back out the front before the smoke got him. Nat stood at the rear of the car and held up a small device. It must've been attached sometime during the day when they were out talking to people. On the lawn, Reed dialed Visage.

The call went to voicemail but instead of a spoken message, the recording blasted old timey military brass band music with screaming fire-cracker rocket noises and canned cheers in the background. A glitching cartoon voice said over and over, "Thank you for your service. Th-Thank you for your service. Thank you for y-your service."

"You bastard," Reed said when the tone sounded for him to leave a message. "I'm coming for you."

A little over two hours later, Reed stood with Nat at the rear entrance of the knock-off sword and horse show dinner theater waiting to be let in. The manure smell was not that bad after a few minutes. It reminded Reed of a field trip he'd taken in grade school to a dairy farm. Nat leaned on Reed's arm for support. She'd been limping since their trek back to the car. Left ankle, he thought. Though she wouldn't admit that the blast caused any real harm, she agreed for one of Coyote's guys to take a look at her. Quiet for the entire ride back to Seattle, he was relieved when started talking again. They were somewhere in Capitol Hill at an arena that used to be an indoor racetrack for RC cars. The building had been converted a few years ago to an historically accurate arena for the sword fights and horse tricks performed during a dinner show that ran three nights a week.

"It's hard for me to wrap my head around just walking away from a crime scene," she hissed. Pressure had mostly stopped the bleeding, but a little blood from her head wound still oozed up around her hairline. "I mean, what're we doing? I don't feel like a cop. More like a criminal."

"We're being hunted, Nat. Set up for who knows what." He patted Nat's hand in the crook of his elbow. "We're using the time it takes to figure out he's dead to our advantage."

"I meant like, existentially." Nat picked at something on her sweater, held up a piece of sticky debris, and looked at him with horror. "D-Do you think this is a piece of the judge?"

Reed grimaced. "If it makes you feel any better, let's go with, no."

"I'm going to vomit." She pulled off her sweater in disgust, handed it to Reed, and yanked her T-shirt straight.

The large wooden door opened to Coyote standing there with a grin. "Well, don't you two look like hell warmed over? What happened? Did the roadrunner get away again?"

"Nice." Nat rolled her eyes. "I'm all blown up, and you're making cartoon jokes."

"Come on, it was kinda funny," Reed murmured with a tired smile.

They followed Coyote into the stable, and he led them down a sawdust covered pathway past box stalls filled with horses and riding equipment. The Viking-themed show was set in an arena where visitors cheered on their "clan" while eating grilled meats with their fingers. They passed an opening to the arena and Reed caught a flash of guys in T-shirts and sweatpants practicing an ax and sword battle. They couldn't be more than nineteen.

"I didn't know how bad the explosion was, so I opted for more equipment rather than the comforts of a hotel," Coyote said. "I believe this place is better able to accommodate your type of wounds."

"I appreciate it, man," Reed said. Nat stumbled and he caught her elbow. "She refused to go the hospital."

Nat gestured at her face. "How am I going to explain this to an ER doc?"

"I can have someone crash your car if you're worried about appearances. Plenty of people hit trees driving on these icy roads." Coyote winked at her as he pulled open a metal door at the end of the hall. "I won't even charge ya."

The veterinary clinic within the stables was small, but well equipped. In fact, it had an inordinate amount of machines Reed knew were *only* for humans. Apparently, Coyote's little vet/doctor arrangement ran a brisk business. He led them to an office in back where a young man stood from his desk chair when they entered. If Reed had run into the blonde, ruddy skinned young man on the street, he'd assume he was a farmer's kid. Sun burnt, freckled, with a backward snapback cap, he nodded with the stiffness of a former soldier when they entered his office.

Coyote gestured to him. "This is our newly minted Doctor Cole. He's going to take a look at you."

Nat took a step back. "What is he, twelve?"

"I'm twenty-five, ma'am," Cole said.

"He was trained as a medic for the marines, detective," Coyote said and gestured for her to sit on the examination table. "A scholarship to med school did the rest."

"Your doing?" Reed asked.

Coyote shrugged and gestured to Nat. "You're in good hands, De La Cruz."

She got on the table and as Dr. Cole worked on her head wound, Reed wandered back toward the horses and pulled Coyote aside. "Has your man seen anyone watching her place?"

"Nope, not a one." He crossed his arms and leaned against the wood slat wall. "What happened?"

He told Coyoted and as he did, something occurred to Reed. "The round that hit Leone wasn't loud. It could've been a balloon popping. The second one missed us, at least I thought it did. But now that I think about it, everyone in that dinky little town heard or saw the propane tank blast."

"And you believe that was the point of the second Kraken." Coyote bothered the zipper on his leather jacket. "To call attention to the judge's body?"

Reed scratched the scar over his eye with his thumb knuckle, thinking. "We were a mile from anyone else on a private road. The blast threw him into the water, which the killer would've seen on telemetry. Leone had cleared his docket and wasn't expected back in the near future. And he was hiding out in a cabin no one knew about. It could've been weeks before he was reported missing. If they only wanted him dead, why call attention?"

"Maybe to explain the wounds? If I understood you correctly, his body looks like it was in an explosion, and he was thrown."

"I don't think so." Reed paced the hallway, his mind churning. "You know that trap you warned me about?" He stopped and looked at Coyote. "I think I just set it off."

23

By ten at night Reed had dropped Nat off at her house and headed back to his condo. He showered, ate, and tried to sleep. Tossing and turning, he thought about Dontae and the judge and the way they both died near the water. He wondered about Danzig and who Visage was to him. But mostly he thought of Nat and her words. She *was* drifting from true north, and it was because of him. Reed slipped into a fitful slumber full of thoughts that ended in tragedy.

When he did dream, he drifted back in time. To that summer night on the bayou once more. Strange birds shrieked across the glowing sky. Reed kept his eye on them, dread blossoming in his chest. They dove at him, and he threw himself to the bottom of his boat as they slammed into the thin metal hull. A whirring, grinding noise underneath the boat made his skin crawl. They were drilling through, letting the blood red water rise to his ankles and slosh around the pontoon. The sound must have called the gators because he could see the craggy skin, the bulging sockets, of four, maybe five of them just beneath the surface. And when the birds had bored through the hull. They flew at his face, their feathers flaring out like the spikes of the Kraken round. Reed dove for the water, he had no choice. Ragged mouths opened, ready to embrace him, the stench of death on their breath heating his face as he fell...

Reed startled awake at the sound of his phone and the panic of the dream slipped away, letting him breathe. His phone rang again. He checked the time. Almost midnight. Private number.

He answered it. "Hello?"

"Detective Reed," A sultry, feminine, voice floated to him, and he sat up, curious.

"Ms. Plaques?"

"Please, it's Sylvia if I call you late at night." She sounded tired and maybe a little bit drunk. "I just knew you'd be a night owl. All that black you wear. I wanted to ask you something."

He yawned, scratching his head. "Shoot."

"A cop with a philosophy degree. That must help you to unravel the criminal mind."

"In my experience they unravel themselves."

"Clever," Sylvia said with a chuckle. "I learned a lot of surprising things about Detective Morgan Reed from the dossier we have on you. Like your checkered youth. Excessive violence." Papers rustled in the background. "Yet you have a minor in art. What a strange build your brain must be."

Reed smiled at her engineering vernacular. "Admitting you're a cyber stalker is a confession, not a question."

"Alright, here's what I want to know. You said there was something familiar about my work. My paintings. What did you mean by that?"

Reed stood and wandered around his room. It was cold and he settled by the window wondering what Sylvia was doing. She was smart. She wouldn't call without reason. If playing her game got him answers, then so be it.

"They were evocative of something." Reed rubbed his eyes, thinking. "Sorrow masked as strength."

"Well, that's an interesting interpretation of a scene about survival." She was quiet for a few seconds. "You can really see that?"

"Maybe I've just been there before. Fighting the waves. But knowing, deep down, you can't take the hits forever."

"What does your partner think of this? How close you dance along the ragged edge?"

"I've never asked."

"Why not? And don't lie to me, I'll know."

"Because her knowing would make it true," Reed said, and a flash of Nat's dark gaze pierced his mind.

"I knew it," Sylvia slurred, she sounded hurt. "It's subtle, but there. I watched you two. In my office and outside. She never leaves your line of sight. I come on to you and where's your gaze? Watching her. You aren't uncomfortable with a woman's advances. I mean, look at you. You were bothered because it was in front of your partner. She's more than that, to you at least."

"Whatever you think you saw—"

"Deny it all you want, but she is the weakness that Danzig will exploit."

Her sudden shift from flirtatious to dire threw him. "What are you doing, Sylvia? Why did you call?"

"Have you found my gift?"

"We did," Reed peered out of the curtains. The streetlights poured warm orange light on the freshly fallen snow covering the grass and street. Soft, pale shapes muted the bushes and cars beneath the pale moon. Reed shifted on his feet, not liking the fear in her voice. "Why does it feel like you gave us Pandora's box?"

"Because I did." Sylvia took a shaky breath. "I thought that more boots on the ground on my side would be good, but once you know, you know. There's no going back. You deserve the choice."

"What's that supposed to mean?"

"I like you, detective. You seem like someone I could really enjoy if the circumstances were different. So, I called to warn you to back off Danzig. What you're doing isn't even an official investigation, is it? You're going to get yourself or someone close to you killed."

"What do you mean?" All Reed could hear was her ragged breath. "Sylvia, talk to me."

"There's a silent war coming. A bloody one. I don't want you to get caught in the crossfire."

"Who is Danzig fighting? His son? A rival?"

"I told you this already. Stop thinking so small!" Sylvia shouted. "This isn't about some pointless family drama or a corporate coup!"

"Then tell me." Reed realized Sylvia was clearly more drunk than he thought. He wondered if she'd remember their conversation. "My partner thinks the Kraken is your baby, not Danzig's. She thinks you're more involved in this mess than you care to admit."

"Those eyes of hers," Sylvia said. "They do catch everything, don't they?"

"Was she right?" Reed challenged. "Maybe through Kaspar? Did you take him up on that deal to overthrow Danzig? Is that who Visage is?"

She laughed ruefully. "You're so behind the power curve."

"What did you do, Sylvia?"

"I will do everything in my power to take Danzig down," Sylvia snapped. "If that means getting my hands a little dirty, then I will."

"Dirty how?" Reed pushed.

"He knows you came to see me."

"Who?"

"Does it matter? They're all twisted with their lust for power."

"Are you working with Visage? If you are, I can get you into protective custody if you testify."

"Only the DA can do that." She laughed, an angry, helpless sound. "Even if you could protect me, which, you can't. Not from them. Why do I have to lose everything I've fought for?"

"Danzig has left bodies in his wake. Don't you want him brought to justice?"

She laughed softly. "It's so quaint of you to think I still believe there's such a thing."

"Listen to me—"

"No! You listen to me, Detective Reed. I have already given you everything you need, but that is as far as I go. None of it traces back to me, and I will deny giving you anything if I'm ever subpoenaed. But . . ." Sylvia sniffled, voice softening. "I really wish you would drop this. I really don't want anything to happen to you."

"Sylvia—"

"I have to go."

"What could possibly scare you like this?" Reed whispered, confused. "You've fought him for years. What's happened to change that?"

"There are worse things than Danzig to be afraid of," Sylvia murmured and ended the call.

He tried to call her back, but it went straight to an anonymous voicemail. Like a burner phone. Reed thought about calling Nat, but she was dragging after seeing Dr. Cole and in a lot of pain though she tried to hide it. Reed decided to wait until morning. She at least deserved some sleep after what had happened with the judge. He went back to bed and tried to force his mind to stop racing. He needed to talk to Sylvia again. When she was sober. Maybe he could go and see her the next day and get more out of her about why she was suddenly so afraid.

By four in the morning, Reed gave up on going back to sleep. He wandered around in his kitchen drinking chocolate milk from the carton. Then he sank onto his couch, grabbed one of the files nestled there, and settled into the patrol officer's notes from the initial crime scene. Reed read through the interviews from the neighborhood canvass, polar ice people, and the food truck staff. No one had seen anything. They were busy setting up, starting the grills, or plunging into the icy lake.

He was about to get ready for work when he came across the Indian Fusion chef's comments. He was the only one who'd seen anyone. A jogger. No description save for a comment where the chef had said that the jogger had "smiled funny" as he ran past. Reed reread the interview, stopping on the statement that the jogger had "ran past" the chef. If he remembered the position of the trucks correctly, that would mean the jogger had come from the beach. Or was going toward the crime scene. Either way, he could've seen something.

Reed jotted down the name of the patrol officer, Edwin Chard, then checked his watch. It was seven in the morning. He dialed Nat. She picked up on the first ring. Her hello sounded caffeinated.

"I want to go and reinterview this food truck chef," Reed said, grabbing a protein bar from the pantry.

"Oh, I'm fine, thank you," she said with some snark. "I'm a little sore from the whole flying through the air thing and the crippling nightmares, but I'm good."

Reed felt like an ass. "Sorry. I've been up for a while. Sylvia called this morning."

"Oh yeah? What'd she want?"

"I'm not sure. She sounded drunk. She warned me to back off Danzig."

"Really? I didn't expect that."

"Me either," Reed said. "She sounded scared."

"I don't think it's a good sign if the woman who loves to instigate Danzig is telling us to back off. Do you think someone got to her?"

Reed scratched the stubble on his chin. "Anything is possible in this case. Look what happened to the judge. We should see if she'll talk to us again. Maybe away from her digital fortress."

"Worth a try," Nat said. "Oh, speaking of the judge, I've been scanning for news. Something dropped in the Puget Cryer. The local paper said the lake house fire was possibly a propane tank leak that led to an explosion."

"But no mention of a body?"

"No. They said more details to come." Nat sighed. "I hate this so much."

"We're alright for now. The current might have taken Leone's body."

"What are we going to do?"

"We keep driving the investigation forward until something breaks. Hopefully before Leon's body is discovered. For starters, I want to go talk to this food truck guy. He said something I want to clarify. And yes, I know I should have talked to him that day." Reed pulled a white dress shirt and a charcoal, almost black suit from his closet. His black tie from the day before sat on his dresser and he grabbed that too. "If you're up to it I can pick you up in twenty."

"Yeah, no. I can't go with you. I looked in the mirror this morning and no one would buy I was just in a fender bender. It looks like I went through the windshield with theses stitches."

"Are you sure you're alright?" Reed asked, alarmed. "Let me drive you to the hospital—"

"No, no. It's just bruising. You can't even see the stitches if I wear a knit beanie, but I think I've got the beginnings of a black eye and so I'm gonna call in sick and take the time to dive into Sylvia's data lens."

Reed hesitated, then, "Nat, she said it was Pandora's box. Maybe you should think twice about going forward. This isn't cop stuff anymore. This is . . . I don't know what this is but it's way above your pay grade."

"Can you initialize the lens and extract the data without corrupting it?"

"Uh—"

"Do you even know what I just said?"

"Nat, I'm trying to give you a choice."

"I made that decision after our first case." Nat sighed on the phone. "Listen. This Visage guy has been yanking our chain from day one. Torturing you with your past, threatening us both. Hell, I've never even spoken with this guy, and he tried to blow me up. I take great offense to that."

"Alright, alright," Reed said not sure if he was relieved or more on edge. "Keep in touch."

"Actually, I'll be at the place we talked about, so you won't be able to get a hold of me. I can't take my phone."

"The hacker's lair?" Reed said with a grin. "Do they know you're a cop?"

"No. So don't come looking for me. I'll reach out when I know something."

"Really?" Reed frowned as he tossed his empty wrapper in the trash. "Are you on an undercover assignment?"

"No, nothing like that. I'll explain later." She crunched on something and then, "We're not telling Parker about Danzig's son, Kaspar, are we?"

"Seeing as how I'm not supposed to be investigating Danzig in the first place, Parker can't know that we're looking at either him or his son. We'll just track Kaspar for now."

"What about Sylvia?"

"Submit the notes from our visit with her to the files but don't send him a notice of the update. For all Parker knows, we're working a Kindred connection for Dontae's death. He's been gathering intel on their routes for me. We're digging into Mookie's story. He's doing the local canvass. He might find something. Who knows how tangled the Kindred really are with this Visage character?" Reed shook his head. "And Sylvia risked her life giving us information. I owe it to her to provide some cover while we still can. All that needs to stay off Parker's radar for now. If it gets dangerous. If he needs to know. We'll read him in."

"He's smarter than he lets on."

"I'm aware. For now, I'll take him with me to talk with the food truck chef. It'll give me a chance to ask him about his research on the Kindred anyway and get a read on where he's at with everything. Plus, he was the one who went over all the surveillance from the houses, et cetera. He could help."

She laughed. "Oh. My. Godiva. He's growing on you."

"He's survived me so far," Reed said. "That's impressive in itself."

Reed finished his call with Nat and then called Parker. They agreed to meet at the station where Parker already was. It took Reed a half hour to get ready and drive over. They met at the coffee cart a block down from the station. Parker was finishing up his coffee when Reed walked up.

"What happened to your face?"

"Oh," Reed felt the split in his lip with his tongue. "Courtesy of our friend Mookie."

"I don't remember you being that banged up," Parker said.

Reed narrowed his gaze. "Do you want a doctor's note?"

"No." Parker frowned. "It's just weird."

"Welcome to my life." He grabbed a fritter and ate it while they walked together toward the parking lot. Before Parker could ask more questions about his face, Reed said, "This food truck chef, the Indian fusion guy, I couldn't get a hold of him. His phone goes to voicemail, which is full. Does he have an alternate number?"

"Same. And no, he doesn't have another number. However, I followed him on social media." Parker held up his phone. "He posted to his followers that he'll be serving breakfast over by Cal Anderson Park this morning."

Reed considered Parker for a moment. "Nice move, man."

"I'm smarter than I look," Parker said with a smirk. "What's your interest in him, anyway?"

"Something he said bugged me." Reed tossed Parker his keys and slipped into the passenger seat. "Unless you have something better to do?"

"Not at the moment," Parker said. "You sure you don't want to drive?"

Reed shook his head, sinking down in the seat. "I have to think."

They found Naveen Garcia parked where East Howell Street and Eleventh Avenue met in the heart of Seattle's, Capitol Hill neighborhood. He'd chosen a spot where the promenade paths crossed and the picnic tables near a fountain invited the early morning dog parents to stop for a bite. The A-frame sign offering free whipped cream puppy cups didn't hurt.

Naveen sold breakfast burritos with kimchi, eggs, and carne asada and Reed wondered why he'd never thought of such a divine combination himself, connoisseur that he was.

They waited in line and when it was their turn, Reed flashed his badge. "Five minutes."

Naveen looked annoyed but nodded. He finished off his line, put up his temporarily closed sign, and then met them at the picnic tables a few minutes later. He was short, tan, had a solid build, and a friendly smile. He looked to be in his late twenties. His apron and hat both had his truck logo of a cartoon chef battling an angry grill.

Naveen nodded at the church building down the block. "I got ten minutes 'til the old ladies get out of their bible study. They're my biggest customers."

"Just a few questions and you're back at your grill," Reed said and opened his leather notebook. He went over the general description that Naveen had given of the jogger he'd seen the morning Dontae's body was discovered. Over six feet, hoodie, sweatpants, lean. Unsure of the ethnicity because of the dim light. The chef confirmed the details. "What about age? How did he move?"

"He didn't move like an old guy. You know, a little hunched over. Those older guys are spry, but they shuffle. This guy didn't. I feel like he was relatively young."

"You told the officer who took your statement at Matthews Beach Park that the jogger ran past you. Do you remember from which direction?"

"Oh, uh, yeah," Naveen rubbed his eyes. "I was one of the first trucks there that morning and I was just getting the grill going when I saw this guy jogging back to the parking lot from the beach. The halogen lights the event staff had set up flickered as he passed, which is what made me look up. We sort of locked eyes and then he slowed. I thought he was coming over but then he just gave me this weird smile, waved, and kept going."

"So, he was definitely coming from the direction of the crime scene?" Parker asked.

"Yeah, I guess he was." Naveen shrugged. "That's all I saw."

"Tell me about his smile," Reed looked at his notes. "What do you mean weird?"

Naveen blinked, his gaze going off in the distance. "I guess what I meant was that the guy's smile wasn't weird so much as it was only half."

"Do you mean he smirked?" Parker asked.

"No, it was more that the right side of his face seemed paralyzed."

"Like from the dentist?" Reed asked. He pulled the side of his mouth down with his fingertips. "Novocain?"

"Yeah, like that," Naveen pointed to Reed. "He wasn't leering or being creepy. He was just paralyzed, I think. Like from a stroke or something."

"But he was jogging?" Reed asked. "You didn't notice a limp or anything like that?"

Naveen thought for a moment. "Not that I can remember. I jog myself, mostly at night, and this guy had good form. He was running at a good clip."

"Other than the smile, was there anything else unique about his appearance?" Parker asked.

"I mean he had an expensive track suit. The shoes alone were more than I make in a week."

"What about his behavior?" Reed leaned forward on the picnic table. "Of all the chef's you're the only one who saw him."

Naveen shrugged. "I told you, it was the flicker that caught my attention. He just happened to be passing by at the time."

"But why did you keep watching?" Reed pushed. "Weren't you on a time crunch, getting your food on, preparing for customers? Why'd you stop and watch this random guy over all the other people milling around?"

"I don't . . ." Naveen stroked his goatee. "You know what? He didn't have a light."

"Like a flashlight?" Parker asked.

"Yeah, yeah." Naveen pointed at Parker. "It was early morning. Still dark enough to trip over stuff. Most of us runners who go out in low light wear a headlamp or something. Reflectors. This guy was head to toe dark. You know, I think that's why I watched him. I was low key worried he'd get hit by a car with all the minivans vying for parking that morning."

Reed flipped his notebook to a page on which he'd drawn a rough sketch of the beach. He pointed to the rectangle marked Dontae with his pen. "The patrolman's notes said the jogger ran past the food truck, but he didn't indicate direction. Can you show me where he went after passing you?"

"He went that way." Naveen ran his finger from the crime scene, past the polar bear people, and along the truck parking area to the parking lot. "Ran right past. Barely stopped."

Reed finished and waited through Parker's follow up questions before they let Naveen get back to his truck and his old lady customers. Reed snapped his notebooks shut. "What do you think?"

Parker shook his head. "If the jogger came from the beach, then he would've run right past Dontae's body. How could he miss it?"

"He didn't," Reed said. "Do we have any video of the parking lot that night?"

"Yeah, in one of those virtual rooms. Detective De La Cruz set it up for me." Parker scratched his temple with his pen. "I looked it over, but nothing stood out, and I didn't specifically search for this jogger guy."

"We should take another look. Maybe a camera caught footage of his face or of him getting into a car."

"You really want to take the time to hunt this guy down?"

"Without a doubt."

"I don't know. I haven't even interviewed the clerk at the gas station where our victim stopped at to fuel his motorcycle." Parker shrugged. "I think if your witness saw something he would've come forward by now."

"That's because he's not a witness," Reed said as they got to the car. "I think he's the killer."

24

Parker drove them to the Technology Tower to pull up the surveillance he'd gathered from his canvass of the neighborhood and the surrounding businesses. While he did that, Reed went up to the materials science lab. He'd sent a copy of the forensic report to the head of the department earlier and he wanted to get her take on the Kraken rounds. He found her in the breakroom, sipping soda through a red licorice straw and chatting with her assistant. They were always young and male and looked as if they'd never survive a harsh Victorian winter.

"I heard peppermint sticks work just as well," Reed said as he walked in. He typed his coffee preference into the serving machine and turned to smile at her while he waited. "Tell me you have something for me."

"Detective Reed," Cravitch said and shrugged in her enormous shawl. "Most disappointingly, I have nothing exciting to report."

"Oh, come on now, Dr. Cravitch, everything you report is riveting." Reed winked at the assistant who rolled his eyes and left. She'd taught an adjunct class at the academy, and he often found her insight helpful. "Please tell me you have something."

"Walk with me," she said and the colorful bangles on her wrist clicked as she motioned for him to follow.

He grabbed his coffee and strode next to her as she spoke.

"Well, the metal used for the Kraken round was neither rare nor expensive. The design is fascinating, don't get me wrong. It's just not made of anything new," Dr. Cravitch said as she pulled off her horn-rimmed glasses and used them to point at him. Her hair was gray and fine, and it flapped in the air stream from the AC as they strolled down the hall to her office. "It's a tool used for death. Fancier, sure, than the standard rounds, but a weapon all the same. Not much there to narrow down the manufacturer."

Reed shook his head. "I may have a bead on the manufacturer. I was wondering more if you learned anything else about it. Something the design itself might suggest."

"Hmm . . . interesting question.," she tapped the glasses on her lips. "It's the scale that's sparks my interest. Small scale is one thing. Shrinking down what is essentially a cruise missile to the size of a marker, well that's something else entirely. It takes skill. Which is expensive. And fabrication. Also, expensive. The cost alone would ensure there aren't a lot of customers who could afford the product. At least not ones with pockets deep enough to afford such a device *and* the free agency to use it."

"Do you think this is some type of military made prototype?" Reed sketched in his leather notepad. "We inquired, but you know the red tape. Back channels are saying no. I tend to believe it. There's evidence that it may be an in-house corporate project."

"I would agree with that. The military has rules of engagement. Largely speaking, of course. This Kraken is judge, jury, and executioner in grand fashion. We like our assassinations much quieter."

"It could be used to mask an attack. To turn a victim into a suicide bomber."

"Then you would be limited to people likely to do that, yes? Or, at the very least you need to get someone close to the target and then hope they are hit lethally." She shook her head. "Entirely too messy. This is a battlefield weapon. Where the fog of war hides evidence and motive. You've scoured the R&D records of companies able to make this and found nothing?"

"We did. It's not a cost-effective endeavor to manufacture or sell these things," Reed tucked his notebook in his suit jacket. "No one on the street would pay tens of thousands of dollars a round, let alone for the unit to operate it. Lots of easier paths to a target. Much cheaper, as well."

Cravitch folded her arms and chewed on the arm of her eyeglasses. "What about people you can't get to easily?"

"You're saying the weapon's necessity points to the target?"

She shrugged. "They'd be under guard protection, isolated, perhaps even a survivor of a previous assassination attempt. I would imagine that includes dignitaries, foreign nationals, possibly dictators or warlords. People of importance and power, but not necessarily beloved."

Like a tech mogul, Reed thought.

"I can check with Threat Assessment, but I haven't heard of any big dignitary, high-value visits. The department gives us a heads up by a least a few months to plan security detail." Reed pulled his notebook back out. "You've worked on the contraband and weapons coming through here. Have you ever seen anything like the Kraken round?"

"Not like this, but other forms of carnage." Cravitch shook her head. "Man creates the most atrocious things to harm one another."

"Or to prevent it." Reed said, remembering Mookie's reasons for getting involved. "A weapon system like this could potentially end a war."

"Sure," Cravitch agreed. "You cut the head off the right snake . . ."

He told her about Visage's phone calls.

"Dr. Cravitch, in your opinion, not as a materials scientist, but as a professor of war. What does this kind of weapon say to you about the user?"

"You always did ask the most intriguing questions." Cravitch slipped her glasses on and looked at Reed with wide, magnified eyes. "It's a show of superiority. Of acumen. To possess this, to have the means to use it, and frankly, pardon my French, the *balls* to use it, is a demonstration of power. Someone is displaying their feathers."

"A show?" Reed took a sip of his coffee. "It's saber rattling."

"Very good, detective. Anything else? Is the tone reminiscent to you of something?"

"It's, uh, he's almost too arrogant." Reed rubbed the scar over his eye as he thought. "He brags, he commands, cajoles, attempts to prove himself before even being challenged. The crime scene was showy."

She nodded. "Look how smart I am. How far ahead of you I am already. Notice me."

"Like those afraid they don't measure up. I've seen it with street gangs. The most dangerous are the ones with something to prove," Reed added. "This guy's definitely not an equal. At least not in his own eyes. Like a prince attempting to topple a king."

"I believe you're correct," Cravitch smiled, a proud teacher. "As usual."

"But what if it was all to draw me in? A deliberate show." Reed shook his head. "So how do I know if I've got the right read on him?"

Cravitch shook her glasses at him. "The killer couldn't help himself. He could have simply stabbed this victim and left a note in his pocket with your name and achieved the same thing. He could have leaked the fact that your name is associated with the victim to the press. But he didn't. He was showing off his shiny new weapon."

"To whom?" Reed tapped the edge of his notebook on his palm. "I've been told that the killer cancelled or sabotaged several sales opportunities. So, who would he be showing it off to if he doesn't want to sell?"

Cravitch shrugged, unconcerned. "That, dear boy, is your department."

Reed left Cravitch and ducked into the stairwell before going to find Parker. He sat in the middle of the flight of stairs and dialed a number he'd gotten from Coyote. Shannae Black. Dontae's mom. She picked up after a few rings.

"Mrs. Black?" Reed asked, listening to a fan rattle in the background.

"I wondered if you were going to call." Her southern accent sounded softer with grief.

"I'm sorry it took me so long," Reed said. "I've been working Dontae's case."

"You mean his murder."

"Yes, ma'am," Reed said.

"I'm getting reports from Fleur's family you don't know anything. Tell me you're not spinning your wheels. Tell me this monster isn't going to get away with this, Morgan!"

"He won't. Not on my watch. And Fleur's family is clueless. They think nothing's happening because I chose not to tell them." Reed rubbed his forehead. "You know her mother and brother, Marcel. They'll cause more trouble than they're worth."

"Yes, that's likely," she said. "Don't keep them in the dark too long, though. They'll get restless and decide to do something stupid to rattle your cage."

Reed remembered spotting their motorcycles following him a couple days before on his way to meet Nat. "I can handle them."

"I suppose you can," she said softly. "You've had to deal with the darkness of the world since a young age. I reckon you've learned how to survive. I just wish Dontae . . ."

He listened to her cry a little. "I'm so sorry. About everything."

"He was getting out. Putting all of it behind him. No more club jobs. He wasn't going to be like his daddy was. He wasn't violent. He loved that girl, and they both love that baby."

"I know, ma'am. In fact, I was hoping you had a moment to help me with some questions that've been bothering me."

"Okay, then," she drawled. "Shoot."

"I've heard from several people that Dontae was working on coming home."

"He was. They have a place near me so I could help with the baby." Shannae sniffled. "You think Fleur will still come?"

"Who paid?"

"Her mama, who else? She ordered a whole bunch of stuff for the nursery. I had boxes coming to my apartment for a couple of weeks. She didn't even ask me before she had them shipped. Then I had to lug them over to their apartment. And you know that woman doesn't spend a red cent unless she's sure she's getting something' for it. Fleur at least was for sure coming soon. And she would never leave Dontae."

"So, it was a sure thing?" Reed jotted down a note to check on Nat's progress on the Spicy Griller angle. "They were definitely intending to come?"

"They gave me a date," Shannae said. "They were due to arrive by

March seventeenth. We were going to have a St. Patty's Day themed fais do-do. They were driving, I think. Dontae hadn't worked that out yet, but he said it was all set. Dontae said he had a payment coming his way before he could leave."

"He said payment?" Reed flipped back in his notebook to his interview with Mookie. Dontae had said something similar to him. That he didn't want to put his payment in jeopardy.

Reed thanked Dontae's mom and promised to update her as soon as he knew anything. He ended the call and then leaned back against the stairwell wall, thinking. Someone paid Dontae with his freedom. Who could do that? Or at the very least fake it?

A text from Parker sent Reed to the Virtual Depot, where they sat through an hour and a half of life-sized door and car dash recordings before they found something. They'd been looking at the first arrivals at the Polar Break Festival, when a man, tall, lithe, dressed in all black, streaked across the screen. He paused, waved at someone off camera, and then kept going.

"There, that's him," Reed said. He leaned in and squinted at the screen. "Play it again."

Parker did, and the man moved like an avid runner. Not breathing hard. Controlled pace. He slowed, waved again, and moved off screen. It was too far and too dark to see the smile.

"We need to get this enhanced," Reed tapped the screen. "They do that here, right?"

"The thing is your partner is one of the best, but she called out sick." Parker sat back and crossed his arms. "Strange, she didn't seem sick yesterday. You wouldn't happen to know anything about that?"

"About her personal health?" Reed raised a brow. "No. If she said she's sick, she's sick."

Parker gave Reed an unconvinced look. "I can go and bug someone at cybercrime and ask them to bump us to the top of their list . . ."

"Don't bother," Reed checked his watch. "I'll call Nat. She might be able to help us cut the line. Can I get a still of that image? I want a print of him waving, one second before, and one the second after. Maybe we can capture the smile."

"You wanted that information on the Kindred's smuggling routes." Parker reached into his messenger bag and handed Reed a manilla folder stuffed with printouts and interview notes. "The search dug up a few more known associates of the motorcycle club in addition to Marcel Benoît, and Dontae Black."

"Do any of the new contacts move weapons?"

Parker shrugged. "Not on paper, but I was going to grab a couple of patrol guys to go turn some stones and ask some follow up questions."

"That's good. Do that," Reed said. "They might give up something useful. Anything else?"

"I'll hit up the gas station clerk too."

"Alright, and I'll see about finding us a tech wizard to help with these images."

Reed stepped into the hallway to call Nat.

"Hey!" she answered. "I was just going to call you. What are you doing?"

He told her about the recording of the jogger. "I'm getting stills. Do you think your hacker friends can enhance it?"

"Get me the recording. That'll work better," Nat said. "I'm sending someone to pick you up. I've found something you're gonna want to see. Go to the North Queen Anne Drive Bridge, and my friend will meet you there."

"When?"

"Like, right now." She smacked some gum. "¡Ándale! Get going! Also, you know me as Cheshire."

"You gave them your cat's name?"

"It's easy to remember," she said with a laugh. "Besides, it's kind of mysterious."

Reed headed for the station's entrance. "What does your friend look like?"

"Don't worry," she said with amusement. "He knows what you look like. Oh, and don't let him know you're a cop. No sudden movements. He's a little twitchy."

"I'm sorry, what?" Reed stopped walking for a moment but could hear that Nat had dropped the call. He set off again, this time in the direction of the parking lot. Reed prided himself on being prepared for the unexpected, but after Nat's last comments, he wondered what he was getting himself into.

25

The North Queen Anne Drive bridge was just up WA-99 along Lake Union. A historical bridge, it was known for its unusually high arch and tulip shaped lighting fixtures on the pier headings, which got it designated as a landmark in the eighties. The bridge arched over an older suburban area with old growth trees that made lush canopies over the streets. The structure's high arches were shrouded with towering White Spruce and Star Magnolias, so much so that you could only see it from the street level. Traffic crossing Queen Anne Drive echoed below, reverberating along the massive steel beams and sloping abutments underneath the bridge.

Marcel stopped below the bridge on the street corner near an old craftsman style house. He backed up the bike, shielding it from view via an overgrown oleander bush near the street and got off. He walked slowly to the bridge, his head turning as he scanned the area. The sky was clear, the air lazy and crisp, with the subtle scent of fireplace smoke. He walked along the road heading underneath the bridge. Passing a guard rail, he peered into the thick bushes growing on the other side. Marcel slowed, something tripping his senses, and he pulled a gun from his waistband, holding it down by his thigh. Underneath the bridge, shrouded in shadows, the sound of a rock pulled his gaze. A mistake he realized too late. Reed lunged out from the bushes, grabbing Marcel into a chokehold, a knife at his throat.

"If you're going to walk up on me with your piece drawn you better make sure I don't see you first," Reed whispered. Marcel tried to yank free, but Reed pressed the blade harder against his neck and he froze. "I clocked you following me all the way from the station. Watched you trying to sneak up on me in broad daylight. What do you want?"

"You owe us answers," Marcel rasped.

Reed let go and shoved Marcel away, making him stumble. He collapsed his blade. "I don't owe you crap."

"Yeah, you do. Why'd you turn on us?"

"What are you talking about?"

"Some nerdy looking detective named Parker has been hassling Kindred members. He's been up at the bar with cops and inspectors, threatening to close it down." Marcel flailed his pudgy arms, angry. "He showed up at people's work and harassed them at their PO's office. Everyone's freaking out. People are leaving town 'cause they all got warrants on them. Come on, man you gotta do something."

"He's doing his job." Reed stepped to Marcel. "And I told you, I'm coming for Dontae's killer. I don't care who they are."

Marcel raised his weapon, his tongue darting between his dry lips. "I should end you right now."

Reed put his hands out at his sides. "Do it."

"What?"

"I said do it!" Reed shouted as he stepped closer, backing Marcel up until he was against the rail and the gun dug into Reed's chest. He glared into Marcel's beady eyes, the anger and dread boiling in his veins. "Do it or don't. Either way your threats end tonight."

"You think you're above—"

Reed stomped on Marcel's hurt toe with his combat boot, deflecting and controlling the gun hand at the same time. The biker doubled over with pain.

"You broke it," Marcel groaned, staggering for the rail for support. He panted, his eyes watering.

"Give me that," Reed growled and yanked the pistol from Marcel. He stepped back, cleared the round from the chamber, rendering it safe before tucking it into the small of his back. "You should get that toe checked out, man. Looks like it might be broken."

"I did! It was!" Marcel shouted angrily. "I think you just broke it again."

Reed grimaced. "Is that all you wanted? An update? You know my phone works, man. I'm supposed to be meeting somebody and you're messing it up."

"I just want to make sure you haven't forgotten what I told you. You find out who the killer is and I'm your first call."

"What you *told* me to do holds about as much weight as wet toilet paper," Reed snapped. "I'm going to do what I do best, and you're going to stay out of my way. Now get out of here. I'm not asking."

"Stop messing with the Kindred," Marcel said with some steel. He hopped on one foot, his face pale.

"Just you," Reed said as he drew Marcel's gun. He pressed the release and dropped the magazine to the ground. After locking the slide back, he tossed the empty gun alongside it. "If I get any more heat from the club, and I mean any, I will come after you personally. You got that?"

He didn't wait for an answer, he just turned and started back down the street leading underneath the bridge. Reed didn't take a breath until he heard the rev of Marcel's engine fade away.

Another twenty or so minutes passed and Reed spent the time sketching the light fixtures and deep recessed rectangles stamped into the cement pillars of the bridge. A distant roar pulled him from his thoughts. The headlights of a car at the far end of the bridge flashed on and off and Reed looked over. Beige and at least ten years old it would be forgotten as soon as it passed. He stepped out from underneath the bridge to meet it. When it stopped, Reed leaned in, and the driver looked at him over hot pink aviator glasses. The kid, couldn't be more than twenty, wore slicked back highlighter-yellow hair, eyebrow piercings, and neck tattoos. He was chewing on a red coffee stirrer as he looked Reed up and down.

"You *gotta* be Yeti" he said with a silver-plated smile.

"Who sent you?" Reed asked.

"Cheshire." The driver flicked his one and only ear, and said, "Name's Taza."

Reed grinned. "Your name's mug?"

"How many handles they got?" Taza asked and his gaze shifted behind Reed. "Don't freak out."

Reed sensed movement behind him and then a black hood swooped down over his head. He put his hands up. "I'm chill. I'm chill."

"Good," Taza said as someone maneuvered Reed into the back seat and closed the door. "I'd hate to waste a tranquilizer dart."

They drove for almost a half hour though Reed suspected half the time was doubling back to confuse him. They hit a bumpy road and the smell of dirt drifted through the hood. Bushes scraped along the side of the car, gravel churned up underneath the chassis and then they stopped. Taza or the other passenger, who smelled like expensive cologne, pulled him out of the car and they flanked him as they made their way along uneven natural terrain. Eucalyptus stung his nose. And the scent of decaying water, specifically rotting pond. Then a squeal of metal and the scent of rust assaulted Reed and they pushed him into a cool, dank space. The door clanged behind him, followed by the rattle of a chain. They led him up several flights of stairs and then another door opened. They walked around for what seemed like five minutes in what felt like a vast, echoing space.

When they stopped. Taza pulled Reed's hood off and smiled. "Welcome to the nineties, my man."

It took a minute for Reed's eyesight to adjust to the meager light streaming in through the skylights overhead. The space was vast, with cracked aqua and hot pink swirl designs peeling from the wall. Storefronts and fast-food joints, dark and caged over, gaped like missing teeth along the wall. Echoes warbled through the dark building. It bounced off the Plexiglass walkway railing and the burned-out neon store signs.

"What is with the cloak and dagger?" Reed rubbed his eyes. "Anyone can tell this is an abandoned mall."

"We were hiding the one remaining entrance not sealed over by the city. No other way into the building." The answer came from behind Reed, and he smiled. He turned to face Nat. Her hair was down with random braids woven through that covered her stitches, and she wore dark cat-eye makeup and a fake nose piercing. She had on a black ripped sweater, black jeans with holes near the thighs, and black combat boots. Burgundy lips rounded out the goth look, and she raised a brow at Reed, daring him to say something. She was standing next to a guy who was bald to the point of the light shining off his head. He had bushy black eyebrows, and a striped sweater. He looked like a kid's puppet show character.

Reed nodded to him. "And this is?"

"Xanadu," the bald guy answered. He nodded to Nat. "Shall we begin?"

"You go ahead, I have business to discuss with him," she said. Nat waited for Xanadu and Taza, to walk away and then she turned to him. "Any problems?"

"No, but the metal mouth kid thinks he's in a sci-fi movie." Reed shoved his hands in his pockets and nodded at her. "What is this? What's going on here? Who are you?"

She looked over her shoulder and then grabbed his elbow, dragging him toward an empty coin fountain filled with trash in the center of the plaza. "Remember when I went to that tech conference in Los Angeles? Cybercrime sent me with Imani?"

"I believe I do," Reed said with a grin. She really did look vicious.

"Okay well that conference wasn't for your average corporate IT geeks. It draws Blackhat hackers, you know, real talent. And people who sell their skills to the highest bidder, including hostile nations. Also, cybersecurity experts and some say, the military. No one uses real names. People don't even bring wallets or phones. All cash. It's supposed to be completely anonymous."

"Sounds totally legit."

Nat rolled her eyes. "Anyway, while there as Cheshire, I made some friends and I'm just, you know, watching where the wind blows."

"That's *literally* the definition of undercover. Guess I'm not the only one with secrets," Reed hissed. "Does Tig know?"

"He's the one who asked me to do it." Nat shifted from foot to foot, her face tense. "The reason I called you here is we can't really explore what we need to via the Virtual Depot, but we have this machine—"

"No good story ever starts that way."

"Just . . . don't judge a book by its cover, okay?"

"Again, not a great beginning."

He followed her toward the far end of the mall where the higher end stores used to be. He could make out the innards of a pet store with the empty reptile tanks still on their stands, though most were cracked or shattered. A security gate was dismantled to form a doorway into one of the huge department stores and they strode past empty chrome clothes racks strewn in pieces across the peeling linoleum. They passed overturned makeup and jewelry counters gone cracked and yellow with age. They walked down a rusted escalator to an underground level and entered what looked like a former high-end salon.

Mirrors from the vanity booths were broken, and long, deadly shards sat in a dusty pile in the corner like someone had swept up one last time and then walked away. A newer snack table in the corner held countless cans of soda, suspicious looking brownies, and every known caffeinated candy known to man. Reed spotted the lollipops Nat always had in her desk. Aqua and pink chairs for drying hair sat pushed up against the far wall and thick black cables snaked out from behind them, up to the ceiling, and across the wall to a bank of display screens and computer consoles. Reed tried to work out what they were displaying. Live streams of some kind of office building, weird blank text windows that kept popping up and disappearing, and some sort of streaming data scrolled sideways in bright pink. It wasn't English.

Nat walked to a makeshift cubicle made out of a manicurist's table and some rescued Formica where she kept her backpack. As she dug through it, she glanced at Taza and Xanadu before settling her dark gaze on Reed. "They think you're a criminal."

"Is that my cover?"

"I said you were a client, but Taza mentioned you had a tussle with someone by the bridge when he made his first pass to pick you up. He said you pulled a knife."

"That was just a squabble with Marcel. He followed me from the station. He wanted an update, as if he's in the loop or something."

"Well, it worked. You're sufficiently sketchy enough to make the cut." Nat pulled out a sheet of anti-nausea patches. She peeled one off and held it out to him. "Stick this behind your ear."

He did and it immediately felt itchy. "Why do they think I'm here?"

"You're a colleague interested in finding some information. I'm getting paid to be your guide and in exchange, you're getting us more equipment."

"Guide?" Reed shook his head. "How am I going to do this, exactly?"

"You're not. I already procured seized equipment through Tig. It's part of your cover. Don't worry. Once we're inside, they can't see what we do, what we say, or who we interact with."

"Inside where?" Reed stepped over a fallen fake streetlamp that had been in the food court. "How are you powering all of this?"

"The task force at cybercrime has it worked out with the city. If this place keeps giving up data, suspects, and results, the city keeps the lights on. Or rather, the authorities pretend they don't realize that the power has been restored here. Patrol steers clear, the 'property owner' requested a wide perimeter. So, we're good. For now, at least."

Reed eyed the two men. They were whispering and Taza glanced over at he and Nat. "Tell me about your two new friends."

"Taza found a way in here, he was couch surfing, mostly homeless after dropping out of university, though he hasn't said which one. He said he was looking for a good place to set up a tent and stumbled onto the entrance. It's a maintenance hatch, really. He pulled power from the street and some water pumps that were still operational to prevent flooding. Once he had enough power to live here and work on his system, he brought in Xanadu, who I think he knows from college. They're mostly data brokers who barter for code and tech for their own use. Not as good as Sylvia, mind you, but not amateurs either." Nat pulled off her sweater and straightened her black tank top.

"And who are you to them?"

"I came in a few months ago after I met them at the conference. I have a lot of connections on the dark web, which they found helpful. I got them code keys to a few data center archives. They made some money selling the personal data recorded by those home help bots and the vacuum ones. Cybercrime had set up the honeypot beforehand. It convinced them of my value." She sat, unlaced her boots, and kicked them off. "I told them Sylvia's stuff was a cache you gave me to use in exchange for what you want. They don't know what's on the data lens and I want to keep it that way. They can make millions selling what she gathered."

Reed took off his trench and draped it over her bag. It was cold enough to see his breath in the air. "She knows a lot of secrets I take it."

"Deadly ones," Nat murmured. "She needs to watch her back."

"And you're just hanging out with them, doing shady computer stuff on your off hours?"

"Hey, Sylvia said it best. How best to steer the ship than to be at the helm? It's a small operation, but we already thwarted an attack on the public transportation system during those torrential rains."

"Oh, this doesn't feel small. This is definitely a lair," Reed whispered to Nat as they walked over to the equipment on the other side of the room. "An evil, digital geek lair."

"Those are the most dangerous kind," Nat said and stopped next to two large round virtual reality platforms each with a stabilization arm rising up from the base. She patted the vest attached to the arm. "This is similar to what you've used in the Virtual Depot rooms, but the vest here gives tactile feedback. It also monitors vitals."

Xanadu sat on the floor with a welding helmet and a portable torch. He was working on what looked like a wet suit with wires running along the neck, arms, torso, and legs.

Reed nodded at him. "What's he doing?"

"He's finishing up your virtual skin," Nat said. "Don't worry about that."

"I don't think that's going to happen." Reed waved his hand to dissipate the smell of the soldering smoke. "What's going on?"

"Sylvia's data lens has already told us a lot." She tapped on a laser light keyboard casting onto the counter and the screens filled with documents. "She's tracked deaths, disappearances, financial transactions. It's all tied somehow, someway to Danzig. I'm pulling together a coherent narrative and we'll go over it with her. Hopefully. It's on you to get her to cooperate."

Reed nodded at Taza and Xanadu. "You trust these guys?"

"I don't trust anybody. Not in this world. I worked on it privately earlier," Nat said as she hit a key to disappear all the documents. She grabbed a smaller suit that was laid out on a plastic table and headed for the restroom. "Suit up. We need to calibrate the sensors to your nerve signals."

Xanadu dragged the other wetsuit over to Reed and placed it gently in his arms like it was a king's robe. "Try not to dislodge any of the wires. It's difficult to repair when you're in it."

It was slick and cool to the touch. Reed walked over to the bathroom, peeled off his suit and shirt and pulled the suit on. It was even colder now that he wore nothing but boxer briefs and a T-shirt. He walked back out to the main salon floor in his socks.

Nat came back from the bathroom in a VR suit and strode over to the platform. Xanadu helped her into the vest attached to the stabilization arm. She looked dangerous in her high tech get up. She held up what looked like a motorcycle helmet with a full-face visor. "This really is the game changer with this system. It has a neural link that helps you manipulate things in the VR world."

"Wait, what?"

"Relax, it's noninvasive. It can track very simple command signals and translate them into rudimentary actions. Picking something up or dropping an object. Like the assist computers for quadriplegics."

"I just think it?" Reed glanced at the equipment with suspicion.

"Not exactly, it's more about action potential," Nat said. She pointed to the other VR platform. "Don't worry about that now. Strap in."

Reed stepped onto the base and Taza buckled him into the tactile vest. He yanked on the straps at Reed's shoulders, and then looked at the monitors. Nothing. He fiddled with the vest controls near the attachment and then something shocked Reed, making him flinch. Taza hit Reed's chest once with his palm. The monitors on the counter went black and then filled with his vitals in bright blue text. Heart rate, respiration, blood pressure, temperature, all of them lit up the display underneath his name, Yeti. A moment later, Nat's readout appeared next to his. Cheshire.

"How many times have you guys used this suit?" Reed asked, rubbing the burned area.

"Don't worry, we have safety measures," Taza said and pointed to an ancient looking fire extinguisher.

Reed's gaze snapped to Nat's who waved her hand dismissively. "It's fine."

"Locked and loaded," Taza said with his metal grin and Reed realized tiny gems were embedded in the silver caps. "Listen, the initial jump is disorienting. Try not to yack on the equipment, okay?"

Xanadu looked up from the control panel. "Try walking around."

Reed took a few steps on the base. It was an omnidirectional treadmill like the virtual reality floor in the viewing arenas at the Technology Tower. The surface was slick with subtle texturing for grip even with his socks. He could run, crouch, walk in a circle and the stabilization arm kept him in the center via the vest.

Taza handed Reed some gloves. "Put these on. You don't need the left and right handed controllers like with video games. We got that integrated last month in the gloves," he tilted his head back and forth. "Most of the time, anyway."

"Do you want to clue me in to what we're doing?" Reed asked and twitched at the onslaught of pins and needles in his arms, torso, and legs. "What was that?"

"Just finding the signals," Xanadu muttered. Red and green lights glowed on his face as he typed. He handed Reed a helmet and motioned for him to put it on. "Activate your heads-up display."

Reed donned the helmet and the face visor lit up like a display screen, but it was transparent. He could still see the room beyond. "It's on."

"The suit has haptic and tactile feedback, hot and cold, even texture at times." Nat slipped her helmet on and snapped the strap closed. She seemed in her element. Excitement lit up her eyes as she adjusted the helmet and then pulled down the face visor. It was mirrored and blue light flooded onto her chest from underneath. In his ear, he heard, "If you take a hit, you feel it in the vest, the suit, the helmet so be sure not to get hit."

"Why does it sound like we're going into a warzone?" Reed asked as he adjusted the vest on his body, shrugging out the discomfort in his hurt shoulder. He glanced at the ankle she'd hurt in the blast. "Are you going to be ok on that left foot?"

"The stabilizing arm takes the pressure off." Nat bounced a little. "See, no pain."

"Get ready to fly, my man," Xanadu said from a control panel held together with duct tape. He moved some levers and gave Nat the thumbs up. "We're jacking in."

"I honestly thought you were going to hand me some actual paper information," Reed muttered.

Nat laughed at that. "When are you gonna learn?"

"You should be honored," Taza said. "This is next generation technology right here. Xanadu wrote the code in college, if you can believe that. And I engineered the suits. We tested it at the conference in LA. No one can touch this setup."

Reed held up his gloves and blue outlines of his palms flashed on his heads-up display as the system calibrated. "This is . . ."

"It's the difference between watching something and being in the middle of it." Taza rapped his knuckles on Reed's helmet. "It's that real, man."

An unsettling vibration moved within Reed's chest. Like a ghost had gone right through him.

"Can you feel that?" Xanadu asked from the console.

Reed nodded and then an ice-cold sensation brushed along his skin. A frigid breeze that felt like snow was coming. He shivered. "That's freezing."

"I have him linked in," Xanadu said to Nat. "We're systems nominal."

A sharp current sizzled along his wrists to his fingertips. He made a fist with the gloves and then, just as suddenly, the sensation of sand slipping between his closed fingers made him check his palms. "What's the plan?"

"We're going on a trip."

"To?" His display darkened, the room disappearing into a sky at dusk with a faint glow on the horizon. Reed put his arms out, confused at the lack of weight. It was as if he was floating in an invisible ocean.

"We're going to The Root."

"The root of what?"

"Of all things." Her voice drifted to him from somewhere in the vast space. "Meet me at the tower."

"How do I find—" A strangled gasp tore out of Reed as he catapulted at breakneck speed through the vastness of the abyss. His arms and legs bent back as the suit simulated heavy inertia. His heart pounded, the wind roaring in his ears. Gridlines raced toward him as a cluster of lights glowed in the deep distance. He couldn't stop, he couldn't breathe, there was only velocity and time and the flow of the lines flying past.

He stopped abruptly and a wave of dizziness washed over him. Panting, he reached out for a handhold, and came back empty.

Nat's voice on the wind, distant and warbling came to him. And then the world exploded with searing light and sound and movement. His feet slammed down onto pavement, the weight of his body crushing. He fell to his knees as he struggled to comprehend what he was seeing. "I can't – This can't be real . . ."

26

An indigo sky bled crimson at the horizon. Vast and all-encompassing the world immediately engulfed him, and he stared with awe at its scope. Sound was muted and Reed worried the speakers inside the helmet weren't working. A low, large moon glowed silver above the brooding metropolis laid out before Reed. Dark, impossible buildings that defied physics pierced the sky and loomed over the neon kissed streets. They bore bright flickering billboards the size of football fields on their facades. Flashes of carnage, cute anime figures, music videos, and other random videos lit up the dark night like lightning. He heard his name again and then the rush of city sounds hit him. He staggered with the wall of noise. Music, the rain pounding the pavement, the splash of the gutters, wind howling between the buildings. Puddles rippled weirdly, in rhythm with a faint pulse of energy.

Static in his helmet and then Xanadu's voice sounded next to his ear. "We're monitoring your vitals. You are go for session."

The rain stopped suddenly.

"Hello?" Reed rose on unsteady feet, his knees weak. No matter the direction he looked, there was always more of the endless, empty city. No cars, no people. It seemed to go on forever into the distance in all directions. He shook his head to clear it, and the weight of the helmet threw off his balance. Reed took a turn. The asphalt felt smooth, like marble, the texture a mere illusion. He caught sight of strange shapes orbiting the overly close moon and realized they were space stations, hundreds of them. Their angular corners stark against the soft curve of the sky.

Towers with rings of fuchsia-lighted windows stood taller than the other buildings. The cluster of cylindrical structures rose in the center of the city. The tallest in their midst, whose floors rotated around an axis like spinning plates, shone the brightest. Its pointed spikes scraped the churning sky and ropes of plasma arched between them. That had to be the tower Nat told him about.

Reed walked toward it, unsteady at first, along the abandoned avenue. The staccato sound of his footsteps rang in his ears. As he went, other structures appeared as if by magic. Each one defied gravity, bending and folding into themselves like mobius strips. Some were bridges, others squat structures with slits of orange light piercing out into the darkness. All of them silent and empty.

And then he saw her. Standing underneath a canopy of cherry blossom trees in a small plaza. They grew right out of the asphalt and their tiny blossoms flickered like pink fireflies.

"What do you think?" Nat asked with a grin as he approached. "Wicked, right?"

"Unbelievable." Reed stared at Nat. She looked so real. Exactly like she had just appeared in the lair minus the tiny mole at her left temple. He would never guess he wasn't looking at, standing next to the same Nat as in real life. A subtle breeze tousled her hair and Reed felt it crawl along his back underneath the suit. It was unnerving and he shivered. When he looked down, he realized he was wearing his black suit and trench coat. Even his combat boots appeared weathered. "Am I recognizable here?"

"No, AI generates a completely fictitious face for you with every interaction. So, you're essentially invisible. No two people see the same face in here ever. You and I are using the same system so we can see each other."

"That sounds sophisticated." Reed touched her shoulder. She felt real inside the gloves. "I heard Xanadu."

"He can send us updates, but he can't hear our conversation unless we toggle over to his channel." She showed him how with her glove.

"What is this place?"

"The Root is essentially the next iteration of the dark web. It's harder to gain access to, you need special equipment, an invitation, et cetera. An anonymous criminal world most people know nothing about. We're going to a place called the Night Market, though it runs twenty-four hours a day."

Reed glanced back down the road and then back at Nat. "Where is it?"

"Here," she said, and waved her hand at the building behind the cherry trees.

The stunning art deco building boasted towering brass arches, vibrant stained-glass doors, and geometric sconces flickering on the walls. "That's beautiful,' Reed muttered. "This is a market?"

"More like a high-end auction house," Nat said, and she pushed through the doors into a marble lobby. Several dozen people filled the area. Many speaking in pairs or cloistered in small groups deep in conversation. If they glanced over, it was with the blank stare of a doll and Reed decided he hated the virtual world.

He and Nat wove around the three-story columns that held up a grand vaulted ceiling. Enormous, it spanned three floors and the center dome gathered around a colossal stained-glass medallion with a purple lily in the center. Where there should be walls, there were instead floor to ceiling views of the ocean floor. Whales swam along the perimeter, jellyfish schools descended lazily along another. Nat walked without her limp, he noticed. Reed followed her, trying not to gawk, but finding it impossible. The market resembled a large museum with branches of hallways leading off the main lobby into different wings.

"The wings are divided into types of products and services offered," Nat explained as they passed. "Everything from pilfered national treasures in private collections, stolen art, exotics, which include animals, identity nulli-fication, washed identities, which are much harder to detect, et cetera."

"A mall of mayhem," Reed muttered. "Where are we going?"

"Data Vault," Nat said and nodded to the far side of the museum.

As they walked, Reed peered inside the different wings. Glass cases housed rotating examples of strange animals, oddly shaped cannisters, enormous jewels, and other valuables. A room down the hallway had a transparent energy field over the entrance.

"What is that?" Reed asked.

"That's people," Nat said, and her voice changed. "We've been trying for eighteen months to get in there. We'll do it."

"Ah hell," Reed muttered. "How does money exchange in here?"

"It doesn't," Nat said as they walked into a posh room filled with long, plush couches. "It's a barter system."

"We have something, right?" Reed asked as a man in a white suit approached them.

His face was pleasant, slightly Nordic, but with the cold eyes of the AI rendering. He wore his snow-white hair in a seventies shag cut and his skin appeared so smooth he looked glossy. Reed had an unsettling uncanny valley moment.

"I'm Mr. October. What does your heart desire?" He asked them with a smile. "Your search is my command."

Nat held out her hand and a holographic rendering of the Kraken round floated over her palm. "I need a net cluster of anything recently connected with this device. I have several link tags I'd like to add."

"That may bump you into a higher offering tier." Mr. October leaned in, regarding the round. He tilted his head. "You're not seeking the sale of this item, merely information regarding its travel through hands, correct?"

"And origin, if possible. As for the sale, due diligence first, then I open my coffers," Nat said, and she tossed the hologram to October where it hovered in front of him. Then she made a gesture and a data lens drifted to him as well. "Here are my offerings."

Reed froze, was she giving away Sylvia's information? Nat's hand slipped to his arm. Trust me.

"This is interesting," October said, perusing the streaming data. "And I think it will suffice. At least for the first round. Shall I lock in your proposal?"

Nat nodded.

"I need the vow," October said.

"I agree to market's rules of sale," Nat said and stepped back. Reed did the same, his gaze locked on October.

"New offering," October said aloud and threw the hologram and data lens into the air.

They disappeared as a wave of energy pulsed through the room. A murmur of voices rose, and Nat turned to Reed. "Anyone who responds must include proof of knowledge. Basically, a piece of information that hints at the authenticity of the offer. If we want to meet with them, their connection is made with us, and we'll hear from them."

"And if we don't get any bites?"

"We leave the offer up and if someone makes an offer after we log out, we'll get an alert on the encrypted account. Then we go back in."

Nothing happened for almost twenty minutes. Reed stared out at the ocean and the whales. He wondered if it was real video or an AI rendering of the undersea world. Nat stood cross-armed next to him, her mind a million miles away even here.

"What are you worried about?" Reed asked.

"The link tags I put in. They were the names of places and people we've come across in our investigation. Dontae, the Kindred, the nickname 'couy-on,' Judge Leone, Tamlin, literally everyone I could think of."

"Makes sense. What's the issue?"

"There's an element of backlash if your real name is mentioned here. I'm worried about exposure." Nat shook her head. "I'm worried about a lot of things with this case."

"What did we offer?"

"A cache of things Cybercrime has taken from seizures. Remember our first case? Prisha? We scrubbed some of her data, I have what's not going to harm anyone, but is intrinsically valuable."

A wave of heat swept through Reed. The suit suddenly hotter than a jacket. Xanadu's voice came through. "*Slight* temperature dysregulation over here. We're working on it."

Reed's gaze shot to Nat. "How long can we stay in this?"

"Not much longer," Nat said. "They're monitoring your vitals. If anything goes wrong, they have extraction protocols. No worries."

He opened his mouth to answer when a series of digital windows snapped into view between them. They were offers. Nat opened them one at a time, perusing the proof. He couldn't make out much. Schematics, project announcements, forum discussions, video renderings, metallurgy reports. She shook her head, discarding one after another. Then she froze.

"Look at this," she said. It was a single message. *Remove your offer. Momčilo "Mookie" Balian is not for sale.* "He was one of the added link tags. That's gotta be authentic, right?"

Something clicked in the back of Reed's mind. Mookie's kin was trying to buy the Kraken from Dontae. His Serbian kin. They'd be looking for their weapon. He moved to stop her, too late. Nat gestured their acceptance and then the world around them pulled to the right, the jarring motion so real it made Reed stumble. No longer in the museum, they stood in a filthy, dark room with boarded up windows and door.

Nat looked at him, terrified. "This isn't supposed to happen."

He tried to reach out to her but couldn't. As if his VR suit had turned to stone, he was immobile, shoulders to toes. "What's going on?"

"I don't know. They're overloading our system, somehow." Nat struggled, angry, seemingly bound by an invisible rope. "I can't connect with Xanadu."

A single line of light traced a long rectangle a few feet from them. As tall as a standing mirror, it revealed a dark, brick room. Piping ran along the walls and a single silhouette stood in the shadows. A man and a rifle.

"Is that a live stream?" Reed asked.

"Yes," Nat said.

The man walked into the meager light of an overhead lamp. His fatigues were black and worn and dusty. Piercing eyes over a full mustache and beard lent a weary, hardened look to him. A soldier of some kind.

"Why do you look for this man, Mookie?" The translation was a half a second delayed. Though the soldier spoke English, the movement of his lips didn't sync up with his words.

"We're not looking for Mookie," Reed said. "We're looking for the man who cheated him and, I'm guessing, you. He said family was involved."

The soldier nodded. "I am Jovan." He folded his arms. "What is this cheater's name?"

"We only know him as Visage." Reed thought he saw the man jerk with surprise. "We don't know his real name."

"That's what the query is for," Nat said. "We believe he is involved in a series of deaths, including the man you were doing business with, Dontae Black."

"Why?" Jovan asked, his gaze narrowing at them. "You are Dontae's family?"

"I was," Reed said. "From our childhood."

The soldier stroked his beard. "So, it is revenge?"

"If possible," Reed said. "If not, then justice."

Jovan laughed, his voice slightly digitized. "You sound better suited to this world than the legal one."

"Oh, crap," Nat said in Reed's helmet. "We're blown."

"How did you know?"

"Who else would you be? The people who knew of this weapon are dead or in jail. And even fewer know of this place. Even less have access. The Kindred, Mookie tells me, has access, but their offerings are not enough to trigger an alert for most. But you . . ." The soldier shook his finger at Nat. "You have just enough, how do you say . . . 'honey in the trap.'" He turned to leave. "You know nothing I need."

"There was never going to be a sale," Reed said quickly. "The whole thing was a ruse to get Dontae close and alone. To drag me into this. Whoever cheated Mookie, jerked you guys around, and killed my friend, did it just to screw over Everett Danzig. He fooled everyone."

Jovan turned, strode back. "No one makes a fool of me."

"This man doesn't even consider you dangerous," Reed snapped back. "Show him you are."

Jovan looked at Reed for a second. "Mookie said Dontae called his partner, Couyon. It was not his real name. More of a nickname, you call it. But it was the one he used with all of us. After this partner cancelled for a second time, I had my men follow Dontae. They set up a final meeting through Mookie, and my man tracked Dontae to the lake the morning we were to meet. We suspected Dontae and his partner were meeting someone else to sell the weapon to, maybe they got a better price and that is why they cancelled. But when my man got there, he heard a blast. I told him to remain and observe, but to hide. He did. Dontae's partner left almost thirty minutes later, Dontae did not."

Dontae's partner had definitely killed him. That much Reed knew for sure. The problem was the only real witness was a shadowy Serbian fighter in a foreign country.

"Did your man see the killer?" Reed asked after a few seconds. "Can he give a description?"

"No. But he took his phone. My man cloned it and sent it to us immediately."

"That's where Dontae's burner went," Reed said, finally understanding why it was missing. "Did you find anything?"

"We have our ways. Revolution breeds the need to learn new avenues of warfighting. It took my men a few days. This man, this ghost, covered his tracks well. But not well enough. We found something. Dontae's partner goes by another name. One we found here, in Serbian intelligence reports. Visage."

Reed looked at him, shocked. "What? How did you get ahold of those?"

"Old buildings have old locks," Jovan said. He held up his hand and a series of files glowed alight between them. "You see what I have here. Now. Your system is locked and cannot log out, download, or take any visual image. I give you twenty minutes."

Nat shook her head. "We need more time."

"And one more thing. You find Mookie."

"What do you mean?" Reed asked, his pulse felt weirdly loud in his ears.

"We sent family to get him from jail. He is missing." Jovan walked over to Reed, stood in front of him, his fake eyes a digital void. "I know who you are, Morgan Reed. You put him there after throwing him from a building. Your payment for what I give you is to find Mookie, safe. Or we will find each other in the real world."

Reed winced as pinpoints of pain flared in his chest beneath the suit. The live stream window collapsed around Jovan, and he was gone leaving them only the files. "Are you okay?" The binding of the suit let up and Reed moved freely. "We have to move fast."

"Yeah, yeah," Nat said already opening the files. "There's twenty. We'll split them." She slid some toward him.

Reed's display screen flashed with images scraped from every wisp of data left unsecure. Concept art of the Kraken from an engineering project three years ago, retired document caches with old emails, and other corporate trash, unsecured update files, dead accounts never closed, hundreds of images. He flipped through them as fast as possible, opening his eyes, letting himself take a mental picture, a trick he'd learned in college. Then he saw the name once, then twice. Visage.

"I found it," Reed said and slid the document to her. "Can you tell me where this is from?" He walked over to her, pointing at the document. "This section, it's not in English."

"Hold on, let me get the translation filter." She gestured with her hand and then the overlay converted the text to English.

Reed squinted. "Does that say Serbia?"

"Yeah," she made the text larger on the digital screen. "Looks like this was found in an archive scheduled for disposal but never was."

Reed checked his watch. "Does this keep the right time in here?"

"We've got five more minutes." She gestured at her files. "I've only gone through three."

"I'm on eight," Reed said and went back to reading. "Let's at least skim as much as we can."

Reed enlarged the view so that the files and data filled his field of vision. He flipped faster and faster through the files, taking in faces, schematics, conversions. The flickering of the shifting images, the video, all of it brewing a headache at his temple.

Xanadu's voice broke into Reed's thoughts. "Just a head's up. I'm getting some elevated readings over here."

Reed ignored him, swiping quicker and quicker through the data. Two more minutes. If he held his thumb on the virtual screen the images moved at double speed. Using all his concentration, Reed scanned as fast as he could. The name Visage was traced by Serbian Ministry of Defense operatives seven years ago to a suspected spy. He was working within the country, but they never found out his identity or which agency he worked for. Then the name went dormant. Almost twelve years later, it resurfaced once, a few months ago, in a transaction with an account named LDLazarus. A transfer confirmation to an offshore bank account previously tagged by the Ministry of Defense as possibly belonging to Visage.

Reed's vision blurred and his pulse roared in his ears. The name meant something. LDLazarus. He knew that name. Knew of it somehow, but he couldn't place it. Death and the cold, dark sea. The spray of waves on weathered boards. The image of paper, tearing, dripping with purple water-color flashed in his mind's eye. A strange smell. Must and decay, like withering flowers filled his head. And then a sudden sense of rising fanned through Reed, his hands twitched, and his eyes rolled back as he gasped for breath. An alarm blared in his helmet.

"Pull him out! Do it now!" Nat reached for him.

He was falling, falling into nothing.

Reed opened his eyes to the chaos of Xanadu, Nat, and Taza leaning over him on the floor of the mall, ripping at his suit. They were shouting, their facies full of fear. He tried to talk but his mouth wouldn't move.

"Would an epi-pen work?" Taza asked. "I got one for my allergies."

"No, he's having a seizure," Nat's voice cracked as she pulled off his helmet and cradled his jaw in her palms. Her eyes held his. "Stay with me! Hey, stay here!"

Reed grabbed her hand. "He's going after—" A dark wave rippled through his head and then all went quiet.

27

When Reed opened his eyes again, he was looking up at Nat. His head lay on her lap on the floor, and she held a cold water bottle to his forehead. She was leaning against a manicure table, her gaze across the way. He was back in the hacker lair or whatever they called it. Xanadu and Taza were nowhere in sight. A headache behind his left eye throbbed and he had the strangest déjà vu feeling. He moved and she looked down at him.

"You tried to die on me, again," she whispered. "Stop doing that."

"There was a name that I . . ." Reed sat up, covered his face with his hands and rocked back and forth, fighting to hold onto a thought that was quickly fading. The last thing he remembered was trying get through all of Jovan's files before the time was up. "What happened?"

"I looked at the vitals data, and I think the neural link in the helmet coupled with the flashing lights of going through the data so fast set off a series of small, focal seizures. You didn't lose complete consciousness. More like fading in and out." She glanced behind him at the doorway. "The guys panicked and left. You've been out for almost ten minutes."

"Thank you for not calling an ambulance," Reed said and looked around the decrepit room. "This would be hard to explain."

"My cousin has seizures," Nat said. "I knew what to do, but you need to see a doctor about this. Has it happened before?"

"Not that I know of." Reed put a hand up at her expression. "You don't know it's because of the MER-C system. This wasn't an intrusive memory."

"Nah, you're right." She made a "whatever" face and handed him the water bottle. "It's just something new that never happened before you injected foreign brain chemistry. Drink."

He finished off the water, fatigue weighing him down. "Do I need to worry about Xanadu and Taza?"

"They'll be quiet. And they'll probably come back. All this equipment is custom." She shook her head, regret on her delicate features. "I'm sorry Reed. I should've anticipated something like this."

"There's no way you could have known. We were running out of time, and I had just found—" Reed sat up straight. "Sylvia's in trouble."

"What?"

"That's what I was trying to say before," Reed got to his feet, the information flooding back. "In the Serbian files, I saw the name Visage associated with LDLazarus." He rubbed his eyes. "I think Visage is going after her." He offered Nat his hand and helped her up.

"I don't understand. What makes you think that code name is hers?"

"Because people are so bad at hiding who they really are. What they're thinking. *Lady Lazarus* is a Sylvia Plath poem and that painting, the one we were talking about in her office, refers to another one, *Point Shirley*. I knew it was familiar. Sylvia was morbidly obsessed with Platt's poetry, it seems. I thought our Sylvia was calling because she was drunk, lonely, but I think . . ." Reed shook his head to clear it. "Those poems are about death and loss and memory."

"You think she's suicidal?" Nat made a face. "I don't know."

"That night, on the phone, she told me that *he knew* that we had met with her."

"You think she was talking about Visage?"

Reed sighed, frustrated with himself. "I think she was saying goodbye because she knew he was coming after her."

"We still don't know who he is for sure."

"Sylvia said she rejected Kaspar's proposal to take down his own father," Reed said. "What if he didn't take that well?"

"But we have eyes on Danzig's son, remember?" Nat walked over to her bag. She grabbed her clothes. The VR suit she was still wearing squeaked as she moved. "Kaspar has been in meetings the past couple of days."

"Someone is in the building with actual eyes on him?"

"No, we're watching his office from the parking lot, following him to lunch and back, like that."

"But he could slip out?"

Nat pressed her lips together and nodded. "Tig only approved a loose net. Oh, man. We just put her name out there in connection with the names Dontae and the Kraken. What if I just put a target on her back?"

"I think he was always going to kill her. Look at what he did to Dontae. And Jovan said Mookie is missing. Visage is tying up loose ends and she's one." Reed strode to the bathroom to grab his clothes. "Call it in. Ask for a welfare check. We need to get to her, now."

Nat called it in as Reed followed her out of the maintenance entrance of the mall. The fatigue and dizziness lessened as they walked, but the heaviness in his chest remained. It was two in the afternoon and a brisk, cold wind erased any warmth the bright sun had to offer. Shadows rippled through the eucalyptus grove. Reed helped Nat limp along a broken path in the tall grass that spilled them out onto the duck pond preserve. Closed to the public, there was a little parking lot for staff where Nat had left her car. She grabbed her tablet and phone from the trunk before they took off. He'd left his own things in his car at the bridge in case Taza frisked him. He'd have to get to them later. Nat handed Reed her tablet.

"There's a file there with everything we've dug up on Kaspar Danzig so far," she said as she pulled out of the parking lot. She got a call, held it up to her ear, and then turned to him. "No answer on Sylvia's phones. Patrol's rolling. They're on their way to her now."

"Where?" Reed asked, trying to read the files as she wove in and out of traffic.

"Her secretary said she was heading home. That was an hour ago, at lunchtime. I've got the address. Here, call her." Nat poked around in her phone and then handed it to him. "That's her private number. Imani got it for us."

Reed held the phone to his ear, willing her to answer. He tried three more times, his gut in a knot. They were only five minutes away. He hung up and told Nat about what he'd seen in Jovan's files.

"So, her name is connected with Visage, for sure?"

"It is."

"Visage must have needed the identity with clearance to gain access to the Root. That's why he used it again."

"Looks like it." Reed peered up ahead. Traffic was backing up. Nat's car was undercover. No lights or sirens. This was going to slow them down. "Serbian officials think Visage was a spy seven years ago there. Given everything he's done, the manipulation, the tactics. I'd say it's a good bet he's the same guy." Reed braced himself against the dash as she veered around a truck. "The file on Kasper says he went to West Point. He has military training. He could easily slip out of his own building if he wanted to."

Nat called in to the follow team assigned to Kaspar. "I need an eyes-on report for our subject. Tell me you have a twenty on him."

Reed held onto the door handle as he read about Kaspar. He went to private schools, did almost nothing in the way of sports or clubs or anything that required leadership. He scraped into college on Danzig's influence and did mostly partying according to disciplinary notes in his university file. Reed wondered how Nat had gotten those.

Kaspar graduated with a degree in sociology and barely that, given his grades. He had some lost years, spent time bumming around Western Europe and Asia seemingly for no reason other than to grow out his hair and beard and take selfies at nightclubs. Reed couldn't quite see his face given the dark room and blurred movement in most of them. Could be deliberate, but Reed didn't know. His travel could mean he was a spy, but he'd be a young one with no ties to that region. He didn't study the language, didn't travel there.

"There's nothing here that would suggest he has the skillset to do this."

"His father was a soldier, right?" Nat asked and ran a red. "He hires ex-military almost exclusively. His Spectre mercenaries are all some kind of special forces if I remember. Couldn't Kaspar have learned in-house? Sylvia said his sister was brutal, too."

"It's possible . . ." Reed's next words died on his lips as they pulled up across the street from a luxury apartment building.

The first responders were there, with ambulance and fire. All milling outside. Given her hurt ankle, Reed didn't wait for Nat to completely stop. He jumped out of the car and hurried across the road. He spotted Parker by a patrol unit, talking to a uniformed sergeant. Reed ran over to him.

"Reed, I heard over the radio," Parker said as he strode up. "This is the Plaques woman you interviewed?"

Reed nodded. "What's going on? Why aren't you up there?"

"It's a secure building. They won't even confirm she lives there." Parker handed Reed a radio com unit. "Their in-house lawyer says we need more than a vague wellness check. We don't even know who called it in."

"I'm not waiting for a warrant," Reed said, pushing through the door. He snapped the com device to his suit collar. "And there is a reason. She's in imminent danger." He flashed his badge at a doorperson sitting behind the reception desk. "Do I need you to get through?" The woman nodded. "Then let's go!"

The doorperson followed Parker and Reed to the stairwell. Her nameplate read Stella and she couldn't be older than twenty-one. She looked at him with confusion as she tried to keep up. "Did you forget something?"

Reed did a double take. "What?"

She used her security card to let them onto the private second floor. "I thought—weren't you just here?"

"What are you talking about?" Parker asked.

Reed motioned for the patrol cops to take the back. "Where are we going, Stella?"

"There's a private elevator." She led them a few yards further down the hall and pointed. "In there." She glanced out of the glass doors at the mass of law enforcement beyond.

"What apartment number?" Reed asked.

Stella looked at him, bewildered. "No, she owns the whole seventh floor, remember? This elevator opens into her apartment."

"What do you mean, remember?" Parker asked, his gaze flitted to Reed, suspicious.

She backed up, licking her lips. "No, I mean, there was a detective here before you guys arrived." Her gaze slid from Reed's frightened. "I think maybe he just *looked* like you?"

"Did he give you a name?" Reed asked. "What did he look like, exactly?"

"He was tall, and I don't know had dark wavy hair, light eyes. He had a suit on, black, I think. He was wearing a medical mask. He said he was sick."

Parker eyed Reed as she rattled off his description. "How long ago?"

"Maybe ten minutes. That wasn't you?" Reed shook his head. Her hands went to her mouth, eyes wide. "He had a badge. I thought he was a real detective."

"Did you see him leave?" Reed asked.

"No, but there's another exit down in the parking garage."

"Stay here," Reed said to her and motioned at one of the patrol guys. "Secure the back exits." Then he pointed at Parker "You're with me."

Nat's voice came over the com. "I'm in the operations van." Sirens and voices came through in the background. "Tell me."

"I've got a possible armed suspect in the building. Tall, male, dark hair, light eyes, black suit and tie." He said as they boarded the elevator. It was small, probably not to regulation, Reed thought, and had no buttons but started to ascend, nonetheless. He pulled his weapon, bootlegging it down at his thigh as he sounded off what he knew into his com. "Witness said he was wearing a medical mask. Possibly impersonating an officer, may have a badge and attempt to breach the perimeter. Check the underground garage exit, Nat, don't let him escape. I'm heading up to her floor."

"They're in the garage now," she came back. "They're moving in."

The elevator stopped. Reed and Parker flattened themselves against opposite sides of the elevator as it opened. White marble flooring, marred with smears of blood and broken glass led into the apartment. Reed stopped the door with his foot, gut tight, weapon coming up.

"Sylvia?" Reed shouted. "This is Detective Reed. Can you hear me?" A thumping sound from further into the apartment sounded. He and Parker flanked the room, Parker going left, Reed going right. The apartment spanned the entire floor, and the open-air plan had little in the way of walls. Instead, massive columns pitched a vaulted ceiling. Overturned chairs, toppled lamps, and other evidence of a struggle lay scattered on the floor.

A noise down the hall, something like metal shifting, pulled him in that direction. He came to a bedroom door and paused. The wood around the lock looked splintered. He pushed it open with his knuckles and found more blood on the camel-colored carpet as he entered. "Sylvia, call out to me."

Further down the hallway, toward the rear of the apartment, a figure slipped past his peripheral heading for the dining area. Reed turned to give chase when a moan came from deeper in the master suite.

He spoke into his com. "Parker, I have a possible suspect at the rear of the house, possibly heading for the garage elevator."

"Copy," Parker came back. "On my way."

Reed pushed into the bedroom, clearing the closets and ensuite bathroom as he went, his gaze traveling the smears on the wall, on the doorway. Broken glass from fallen photos littered the floor. He found her in the walk-in closet. Halfway into a panic room built into the far wall. Marks on the carpet showed she tried to drag herself. He pushed into the panic room. It was ransacked. The killer had been in there.

"Sylvia, no." Reed dropped to his knees next to her. She whimpered, clawing at the carpet, still trying to crawl into the room. "It's me," Reed said, helping her onto her back. "It's Reed."

"R-Reed," she gurgled and pink foam bubbled at the corners of her mouth. Stab wounds, he counted three, upper arm, thigh, mid abdomen. All arterial strikes. Blood soaked her silky white robe.

"Hang on." Reed rasped into his com. "I need paramedics up here right away! Parker, master bedroom." A knife lay on a pile of clothes next to her and he pushed it off to grab a scarf. He tied it around her leg. Slipping off his tie, he knotted it around her arm as tight as he could. The stomach wound, he leaned on it with a sweater, seeing the pain in her eyes as he fought to keep as much pressure as possible. "Who did this?"

"Visage . . ."

"Who is he, Sylvia? Is it Kaspar?"

She rocked her head and tried to speak, gagging as her lips moved silently. Sylvia raised a shaking hand and stroked his cheek, her eyes filling with tears. He caught her hand and held it to his chest, felt her fingers trembling. "Stole them," she rasped. "Ten K-Krakens . . . stop him."

"You stay here and help me take him down," Reed said. The thump of boots coming up the hallway behind him gave him hope. "Help is on the way. You're going to be—"

"N-n . . ." She let out a long rattling breath and then her eyes went blank.

Reed let his head drop down as he released the pressure from Sylvia's stomach. A noise behind him made him turn. Parker stood behind them watching Reed, his gaze resting on the knife.

"Is she gone?" he asked quietly.

Reed sat back on his heels and stared at the still warm blood on his hands. "We were too late. Minutes when seconds counted."

28

Reed stood at the sink of a guest bathroom on the other side of Sylvia's apartment trying to scrub her blood from underneath his fingernails. Steam from the hot water and soap clouded the mirror and when he looked up, he frowned at the crimson staining his white shirt and sleeves. A smear of Sylvia's blood traced along his jawline and bottom lip, and he grabbed a nearby towel, rubbing his skin with piping hot water. His chest tight, Reed stared at the pink water swirling down the drain as the adrenaline making his head pound dissipated into exhaustion. She didn't have to die. He should have seen this coming.

They'd been there for an hour and a half, but it was wrapping up soon. His lieutenant, Tig, arrived with his boss, the chief of detectives. Sylvia was rich and connected and they needed to cover their butts. Word was the media was on their way as well. Reed wanted to wait until they took Sylvia before he left. Back out in the main room, Brandy Zapata, the Critical Incident Supervisor interviewed Reed first, then Parker. They spoke in the corner and kept glancing over. Sanders and his forensic team processed Sylvia's room. Nat's voice floated from the office, and he went that way. She stood at Sylvia's hulking wooden desk, leaning over Imani who sat in the chair, eyes narrowed at a display screen.

Nat pointed to what looked like a directory. "My guess is the overwriting algorithm erased partitions and substituted random data as well as just the multiple passes. Is there anything left?"

Imani shrugged. "I can take this apart back at cybercrime, but the victim hit a kill switch sometime before the attack. This has been going for almost two hours now."

They both looked over when he cleared his throat and Reed nodded for Nat to meet him out on the terrace off the main living area. Sylvia's apartment overlooked a preserve and the scent of wet pine floated to Reed.

"Did you talk to the doorperson, Stella?"

Nat nodded. "She knows it wasn't you but swears it could be your brother. Which tracks given what we saw on Leone's home surveillance."

"What about the guy running out of Sylvia's apartment? No one in the stairwells or the garage?"

"No one saw anyone. We pulled surveillance. Something happened with the system. It shows a guy in a black suit walking into the lobby, flashing his badge, face covered, and then Stella lets him in the secure elevator. All the cameras on both the elevator and Sylvia's floor were down, including emergency stairwells."

Reed caught sight of his own monochrome attire and rubbed his face with both hands. "Perfect."

"We did get one thing. Stella said the fake detective spoke with a muffled sound, and she was pretty sure it wasn't the paper medical mask."

"A speech impediment," Reed scratched at his sideburn. "That could suggest a problem with his lips or mouth."

"Yeah, like partial paralysis that makes you smile weird. That got me thinking. When we dug into Danzig's inner circle, his business advisors, extended family, even his rivals, all we looked at were images. Stills from files. Family Christmas photos, photo ops from events. But other than a promotional video on Danzig, we didn't really take a look at anyone else when they were moving."

Reed snapped his fingers, remembering something. "Jovan's files said they suspected Visage was a spy. He'd have been taught disguise. He could bulk up, change is facial features, hair color."

"Ok, we're looking for a range then?"

"Yes, it's possible he could be wearing lifts or prosthetics. He took the time to dress like me and make sure he was caught on Leone's house surveillance."

"Gotcha. We have to get our hands on candid and unedited footage of Danzig and the people he's met with. We could look for the half-smile the food truck guy mentioned. It's a shot in the dark, but," Nat shrugged. "What do you think?"

"I'm open to anything at this point. If we get some candidates, we could try for a subpoena for medical records and vet for people who've had plastic surgery on their face, maybe received treatment for Bell's Palsy. Whatever the issue it could be recent, even transient." A murmuration of birds undulated in the sky over the trees. Dipping and twisting in unison. Reed thought Sylvia might have found the odd, ominous behavior a proper announcement of her death.

Nat touched his arm, her lips turned down in a frown. "Are you okay? I know you liked her."

"She stood up for herself. I admire that," Reed said. "The way she went out, surrounded by fortifications that did nothing to protect her from Visage. It makes me angry."

"She said he did it?"

Reed nodded, leaning in and recounting Sylvia's last words. "I asked her if Kaspar was Visage, and she shook her head." He scratched his sideburns. "At least I think she did. I can't be certain, but I think so. She said something about the Krakens being stolen and kept whispering, 'stop him.' I would give anything to know what or who she meant."

"I want to show you something," Nat said and led him back into the house. He followed her down a back hallway that led to a supply room. "We processed this room already." Cleaning supplies, bulk dry goods, the detritus of maintaining a residence. Nat walked in and grabbed a ledger that sat wedged between a bottle of bleach and the end of a wire rack. She walked to a folding counter and opened it. "This is a log for what appears to be household supplies."

"Appears to be?"

"Sylvia was the queen of tech. But she runs her house on a paper ledger? Bullshit. That woman didn't buy a cleaning supply in her whole life."

The writing on the pages looked like gibberish to Reed. "Is this coded?"

"That's my bet." Nat pointed to the initials used to indicate each product. "I think she was keeping a secret account, hardcopy only, in case of something like this."

"An account of what?"

Nat shrugged. "Could be anything. Financial information, account names, even people. But I guarantee they're not names of laundry detergent. I'll go back to cybercrime and have the AI, Ada, see what she can do."

"And this?" Reed pointed to the letters VSG in several columns. "Visage?" He pulled out his phone and took a photo of each page. "I'll ask Coyote to take a look. Shady financial dealings are his realm."

Nat looked at him, perplexed. "How could Sylvia be so sloppy? Anyone can figure this out with a little work."

"I think that was the point. Anyone here to rob her would search the office or her safe room. No one would search way back here if she was alive. Who rifles through a locked supply closet during a dinner party?" Reed's gut knotted. "No, this was meant for laypeople to find and decode in case we needed it to solve her murder."

They walked back out to the main room in time to see the elevator doors close on the gurney with the body bag.

"That's so dark. What kind of world did she live in?"

"The kind that titans prowl," Reed said. "Danzig's world."

Reed caught a ride with patrol back to his car at the bridge. He grabbed his phone from the trunk. There were several voicemails. Reed drove home in a daze, listening to Coyote's messages that they had to meet, one from Nat saying she was calling it a night but had confirmed that Mookie was bailed out. The person who paid gave a fake name attached to an untraceable digital transfer card to pay. She was still waiting on some callbacks. The messages ended and he cruised in silence, lost in thought until he pulled into his driveway. Reed was just about to call Coyote back when his phone rang in his hand. The number was blocked, and Reed's pulse roared in his ears. Visage. He answered.

"Enjoy the time you have left because I *will* find you," Reed said evenly.

"I doubt it. Although you did almost catch me back there. You're always two steps behind, aren't you?" Visage asked. "Bad news for our friend, Sylvia. I wondered if you'd leave her there to bleed out to come after me. I guess we know what your weakness is."

Reed gripped the phone, choosing his words carefully. "You should've finished the job because she told me everything before she died. The stolen Krakens, your plot against Danzig. Did you know she kept a ledger? An actual hardcopy, can't be hacked, ledger."

"It's difficult to verify coded information without a witness. From what I hear, dear Ms. Plaques is no longer available."

"So, you knew about it?"

"That's what I was there for. Killing Sylvia was just a bonus. She always was a bit of a harpy."

It was subtle, but there. More so now with the anger coming through in Visage's words. It was the muffled, breathy quality of a damaged palate. He flashed on the blood smeared on his jaw by Sylvia. Right where he would smile.

Reed got out of his car and leaned on his hood. "Tell me something. How did you sweet talk Dontae and Sylvia into telling you anything with that speech impediment?" He baited him. "It's not like you can charm them with that half smile."

Visage was silent for a few moments. "That idiotic food truck chef?"

"Yes, he couldn't forget how creepy it made him feel," Reed lied, pushing Visage. "So how did you do it? How did you convince hardened criminals like Mookie and Dontae to trust you?"

"It never ceases to shock me what people will say to someone they implicitly trust," Visage said. "Of course, it helps that your friend was both greedy and stupid. And Mookie, he is simply salivating to be a real gangster."

Reed gritted his teeth. Keep him talking. "You know what bothered me? Why, if you had connections to Serbia, did you need Dontae's help at all?"

"I wanted his routes through Canada," Visage said. "I had no idea your idiot friend was trying to broker a deal with his criminal partner's family. It was some sort of repayment for protection. I was never going to sell, but after I found out who they were, I had to stall."

"You have plans for those missiles, don't you? Is that why you stole them from Sylvia?"

"Danzig was suing her. He was going to win, and he was going to gut her whole life. She was more than happy to strike a deal with me."

"You double-crossed her, then," Reed said. "Why? You didn't want to share in the victory of defeating Danzig?"

"I don't want to defeat him. She couldn't see past her own trauma to notice that. At least not quickly enough to do anything about it." Visage sighed heavily. "I should have killed her sooner. She was just so . . . fun to play with. Now it seems she has quite literally spilled her guts to you."

Reed's lip curled with disgust. "Sylvia didn't tell me about you. It was Jovan."

"What did you say?" The tension in his voice came through.

"You know Jovan. Passionate guy, intense, armed. He and his Serbian friends are looking for you. He wants the weapons you promised him. How much you want to bet his men are still here in Seattle just waiting for you to make a mistake?"

"I don't make mistakes."

"I wonder if your description would sound familiar to Danzig?" Visage didn't answer. "Your enemies are closing in," Reed said with steel in his voice. "You better hope I don't find you first."

29

After the phone call with Visage, Reed wanted nothing more than a shower, but when he walked through his front door, the scent of cigarette smoke wafted to him. He skirted the kitchen and walked through the condo to the small patch of grass he called a back porch. Coyote sat on a foldable lawn chair staring out at the sunset. Purples and blues bruised the landscape promising a punishingly cold night. Reed walked out, grabbed his spare lawn chair, and sat next to him.

"Do I want to know why you're here?" Reed asked.

"I came to warn you." Coyote had filled a coffee mug with water, and he dropped his cigarette in it. His gaze caught the blood on Reed's shirt and sleeves. "What happened?"

"I lost a witness." Reed looked at his hands. "Visage killed Dontae, Leone, now this incredible woman who dared to fight back. He's a monster."

"Your favorite prey." Coyote nodded out at the horizon. "Unfortunately, you've got more pressing problems. Apparently, the third time is indeed the charm. Marcel and his Kindred brothers are coming after you. Birdie heard them talking down at the hatchet club."

Axe throwing and alcohol really shouldn't mix Reed thought as he rubbed his temples. The headache there throbbed every time he moved his head. Birdie was a travel bartender who frequented various clubs as a fill-in all over town. She had long nursed a crush for Coyote and fed him information on occasion. "How serious are they?"

"She said they were drinking and talking shit, calling you names and razzing Marcel. He lost it and last she heard they'd decided to come and remind you who you're messing with."

"When?"

"Who can tell? They're either gearing up and, on their way, or they're sitting around getting drunker while talking about how they're gonna gear up and head this way."

"Because of Marcel?"

He turned and looked at Reed. "Morgan, you have gotten the better of him three times. He has to save face."

Reed let his head fall against the back of the lawn chair. He stared at the sky, watching the light die. Pulling his phone from his pocket, he handed it to Coyote with the photos of the ledger opened. "Can you tell me what the codes are? Or anything else about it. I need all the help I can get."

Coyote flipped through the photos and his forehead wrinkled between his eyes. "Gonna cost ya a pizza and some beer."

"I'll grab a shower and go get some."

"I'll go." Coyote followed him into the house. He handed Reed back his phone. "I'll need to read a code writer in. There's a woman—"

"Isn't there always," Reed chuckled and walked back inside, down the hall and to his room. He gathered some clean black sweats and a T-shirt and headed to the bathroom, but something caught his eye. "What the hell?"

Blood, a tiny drop, was smeared on the floor near his bed. He bent to look under when a soft scuffling sound in the living room made the hairs on his neck stand. Reed dropped his clothes, palmed his gun from the dresser, and stepped out into the hallway. Weapon down in front of his chest, he peeked around the corner. Coyote knelt on the ground, hands up as Danzig held a silenced pistol to his head. Dressed in a black, long-sleeved shirt and field pants, he looked every bit like the mercenaries he surrounded himself with.

Reed stepped out from behind the kitchen wall, his gun out, aimed at

Danzig's forehead. He glanced at Coyote. His face was bleeding, a ragged tear on his cheek. Pistol whipped. "How many?"

"Just him," Coyote said calmly.

"Stop talking," Danzig shoved the barrel hard against Coyote's ear, making him hiss with pain. To Reed he said. "Drop the gun."

"Never going to happen," Reed said, clearing the beam holding up the kitchen counter. "What do you want?"

Danzig's gaze settled on Reed's bloody shirt, and his face went hard. "Where's my son?"

Reed blinked. "Kaspar?"

"What did you do to him?" Danzig growled.

"Nothing! What are you talking about?"

"You killed Judge Leone and then you went after Kasper to get to me."

"No."

Danzig's face contorted with anger. "You took him. I saw you."

"I was never after Kaspar," Reed said, edging closer. "When I questioned her, Sylvia pointed me toward him, but I think she was afraid to tell me who her real partner was. The one who terrified her. No offense, but I don't believe your son would elicit that from a woman like Sylvia. And I don't think he's sophisticated enough to manipulate you at all."

"No one manipulates me," Danzig said.

"Someone is playing us against each other. A man who calls himself Visage."

Danzig narrowed his gaze at Reed. "What did you say?"

"He tells you I'm working against you, aligning allies, maybe planting evidence. Did he show you evidence I've been tracking you?" Reed reached onto the counter where Nat had left the stack of photos Visage nailed to his walls. He threw them onto the floor in front of Danzig. Images of him meeting with Leone. "He left these to convince me to go and see the judge."

"You could have taken these," Danzig spat. "You were stalking me."

"According to Visage, right?" Reed shot back, watching for doubt, uncertainty. "And he's a helpful friend, too. One who can somehow warn you that something is about to happen, and it does. He seems to have proof of things no one could know. Personal things." A look of recognition crossed Danzig's face. "Sounds familiar, doesn't' it?" Reed edged behind the counter. "He killed Dontae but told me you did it. He sent me after Leone, and then killed him, and he just brutally murdered Sylvia who he was working with against you. You have a traitor in your house. Ask *him* where your son is."

"No, you killed Leone. I saw it. Everyone saw it. Footage of you blowing up his house is all over the newsfeeds."

"What?" Reed glanced at Coyote who looked just as shocked. "I didn't kill him. It was Visage with the Kraken round."

"You were at his cabin, sneaking around, they have you on his surveillance system up there blowing up his propane tank with a charge." Danzig's hard expression wavered a bit. "Who is Dontae?"

"He's the victim on the beach. He was someone I knew."

Danzig shook his head. "I thought it was an unrelated case."

"Visage is setting us up. He told me you killed Dontae for revenge. As punishment for ruining the Ghanzi deal." Reed inched right, aligning the shot. Coyote's gaze tracked him the whole time. Get ready.

"You are not the thorn in my side you believe yourself to be." Danzig shifted behind Coyote, the barrel of his gun moving from his temple to behind his ear. "Stop moving or he loses his face." Reed froze. Danzig tilted his head, his pale gaze unsettling. "Now, who is Visage?"

"I thought he was Kaspar, but I don't think he has the brains or the balls."

"You're correct, he wouldn't dare," Danzig said. "So, you don't know?"

"You do. This is all coming from your world."

Danzig shook his head slowly. "No. No one in my camp—"

"Think!" Reed shouted. "This man is in your midst. Unobtrusive. And closer than you think. He's lying to your face and plotting behind your back."

"Enough!" Danzig snapped. "I want my son."

Reed put his other hand up in a "wait" gesture. "Visage trained as a spy. Worked in Serbia years ago. He can pass for me but there's something wrong with the way he speaks and the way he smiles—"

Though he schooled his expression, the blood drained from Danzig's face.

"You know who it is, don't you?" Reed pressed. "Someone arrogant enough to try to take out the king. Someone good enough to do it. Possibly someone you trained."

Danzig ground his jaw, his temples flexing as he considered what Reed said. "And you think this man has Kaspar?"

"Your son would be your obvious successor," Reed planted his feet, sighting down the barrel of his gun. "How did *you* ascend to power, again?"

Danzig looked at him for a beat, then, "You're viewing the memories, aren't you? Tell me, detective, are you having false memories yet?" His gaze bore into Reed, his tone mocking. "Have the tremors started? How about hallucinations? Are the memories eating up your brain with fever?"

Reed ground his jaw. "Actually, they're telling me about Aurora. Wanna talk about that?"

"I am done with you," Danzig snarled and slammed the handle of the gun down onto Coyote's head, knocking him out before firing at Reed.

Reed dove behind the counter, firing back as a round seared into the meat of his arm. He ducked near the sink, listening. His gun came up when he heard movement over by the hallway.

"This doesn't concern you!" Danzig shouted, all pretense at control gone. "If you get in my way, I will kill you."

"Looks like we both have the same game plan," Reed yelled back. He chanced a peek around the cabinets. Danzig crouched against the wall by the couch. Reed rose to fire, when movement outside the window caught his sight. And then it hit him. Understanding, sure and sudden, skittered up his spine. They were in the same space, he and Danzig. Exactly what Visage needed. "Wait—"

The living room window shattered inward, and a canister tumbled into the house, dispersing orange smoke as it soared into the room. Thick, oily mist choked Reed, making him cough. He knew this weapon. Had encountered it in the field. Reed peeked around the counter; Coyote was still unconscious. He moved to help him when Danzig jumped to his feet, weapon trained on Reed, fury on his face.

"Stop, stop!" Reed shouted. "That's incendiary smoke. You'll light us both up!"

Danzig hesitated. And then a red laser light sliced through the smoke.

"Fire in the hole!" Danzig shouted as a round fired in from the outside.

The oily vapor ignited, and a fireball roared along the ceiling, chewing up the drapes and blankets and couch. The blast threw Reed back and he crawled on his hands and knees in the smoke feeling for Coyote. He dragged him down the hallway by his leather jacket to his bedroom and slammed the door shut, stuffing towels into the crack to keep the smoke out.

Coyote moaned.

"Wake up man," Reed shouted. Ears ringing from the gunfire, he grabbed an open water bottle from his nightstand and poured it on his friend's face.

Coyote sputtered awake, looked at Reed and his eyes went sharp. "What the hell, Morgan, I was only out for a minute!"

"Uh, update, I got shot, my house is on fire, and we have to get out of here." Reed pointed to his window. "We're going out that way."

The heat from the fire burned behind the door. Reed moved to the window on the opposite wall, checked outside and then slid it open. He motioned for Coyote to go first, wondering if Danzig had made it out. Reed remembered the blood on the floor, glanced up at Coyote climbing out of the window, and then looked under his bed. Kaspar Danzig lay blue and cold underneath a bullet hole in between his eyes.

"Nooo," Reed breathed and felt the trap closing in on him.

"Come on, come on," Coyote shouted. He reached for Reed from outside. "Before the cops show up, man!"

Reed took one last look at Danzig's son and then turned and scrambled out the window.

"One second," Reed said once outside, and ran for his back door. He crouched down to peer at his doorknob. Visage had broken the lock to hide the body.

"My bike is behind the condos by the dumpsters," Coyote said.

The wind shifted, blowing the smoke toward them and Reed stumbled with Coyote toward the road running behind the building. The fire was spreading from his home to the adjoining unit. Luckily, his neighbor worked nights and was already gone.

"Take it," Coyote said, when they got to his bike. Hands on his knees, he let out a wracking cough before trying to speak again. "They'll be looking for you in a car. Use my helmet."

"I can't leave you here."

"I'll have someone come get me. Go to Holden House. Lie low. I'm going to see what goes down here for a bit. Any sign of Danzig?"

"I think I hit him, but not bad." A band of steel tightened around Reed's chest. "Nat. He might go after her."

"I'll get her," Coyote tossed Reed his keys. "We'll meet you. Get out of here."

Reed climbed on the motorcycle and pulled the helmet over his head. Coyote's bandanna covered the rest of his face. He drove past the front of the building on the way out, his gut in knots. Flames licked at the trees over the roof and sirens blared in the background. Confused neighbors milled in the yard, hugging each other, crying. Reed's life burned bright against the dark sky, and he soared away from it. Visage was going to pay.

30

Holden House Apartments, South Lake Union
Seattle

Coyote was great at two things, money, and people. He used both to win his Holden House apartments a few years ago in a high-stakes poker game from the owner. Originally meant to ride the wave of gentrification, things took a turn for the investor who had unfortunately decided to build the two story, six-unit apartment complex in an industrial area downtown next to a decommissioned fabrication plant. It was thought that more residential buildings would come, but the wave of popularity shifted, and a storage facility erected on the other side of the apartments sealed the deal. No families. No tourists. Very little foot traffic. Perfect.

Coyote had sweet talked his artist sister, Camile, into creating a hippy-minimalist style aesthetic with tree branch lamps and rattan furniture. A nearby influx of medical buildings and research facilities made it ideal for the clientele Coyote served. Those who wanted to lie low and who needed injuries cared for, but not reported to the police. Plenty of poor interns and technicians were happy to provide medical care and discretion, for a price. But the most important thing about Holden House Apartments was that no one knew anything about anyone there.

Reed had ditched his phone a few miles from his condo and took a winding route, checking for a tail, before heading to the apartments. An hour after he'd arrived, a kid, who didn't look old enough to buy beer, showed up with a medical bag to work on Reed's arm. His name was Klaus and he had freckles on his sunburnt nose. He worked quickly, cleaning and stitching up the bullet wound in less than thirty minutes. When he was finished, he talked Reed through wound care, handed him a bunch of sterile gauze packets, and left. Patting his bandage, Reed flexed his arm. The anesthetic shots Klause gave him helped with the pain.

Now, almost an hour and a half after his life went down in flames, Reed was going stir crazy wondering what was going on. He paced, glad the apartment was larger than the last one he'd stayed in. Coyote hadn't arrived with Nat yet, nor had he called, and Reed couldn't take not knowing if she was safe. Had Danzig sent someone to her home as well? Exhausted, Reed walked over to the sitting area and stared out the window at the falling snow drifting in the glow of the streetlights along the road. It was almost eleven at night and they were somewhere out there.

A burner phone on the end table rang and Reed answered. "Nat?"

"Are you okay?" her voice came through. "Coyote told me everything. You were shot?"

"It's already cleaned and bandaged. It's not bad." Coyote could be heard in the background of the car asserting that he was fine too. "I was getting worried. Did anything happen?"

"I got caught up at cybercrime processing some stuff from Sylvia's home. Then all hell broke loose when your house fire came across the wire. Tig cornered me, asking if I knew anything."

"What did you tell him?"

"Nothing, because I had no idea what was happening. No one called me to tell me my partner wasn't crispy until Coyote texted and asked me to meet him."

"That was my fault. I had to ditch my phone. Did you get in trouble with Tig?"

"No. I'd hitched a ride to the station with Sanders after you left Sylvia's and they could see when my badge entered the building." She hesitated, then. "They revoked my security to enter the Technology Tower and the Cybercrime floor. Temporarily, according to Tig, but I don't know."

"Sorry." Reed squeezed his eyes shut, angry that being near him put her career and life in danger. The sound of traffic floated through the phone between their silence.

"Oh," Nat said, finally. "I got ahold of Xanadu. Well, he contacted me on Cheshire's phone. He and Taza checked the lair, it's ok. So, all our research down there is untouched. But Taza cleared his stuff out. Xanadu said he blew up when they found out from the news that you're a cop."

"And your cover?"

"Blown, but Xanadu doesn't seem to care. I'm not sure why." Nat cleared her throat. "What are we doing, Reed?"

He hesitated for a moment, then, "I need you to make a stop. I need you to go to the warehouse where I hid the metal case."

"Are you out of your mind?" she asked, her voice rising. "You'll cause more damage to your brain, not that it seems to be functioning at the moment."

"I'm lost in the weeds with this. I don't know what's going on. Danzig almost killed me and Coyote in my own home. Then Visage blew it up. I didn't see either of those things coming. What if I miss something else? What if you or Tig or anyone else in my life dies and I could have prevented it? I couldn't live with that." Reed rubbed his eye with the heel of his hand. "I need to view the memory. The one Visage told me to."

"He's done nothing but set traps for you! What makes you think this is any different?"

"I don't think the memory was a trap. I think it was bait or incentive," Reed said. "He told me to view it during one of our first interactions. When he was trying to prove his worth. It would have something on it that would've pushed me toward the judge."

A horn honked in the background and Coyote cursed.

"That doesn't stop what taking the memory does to you," Nat rasped, her voice full of stress. "Did you even read the neurology study I printed out for you?"

"I did and that's why I need you here." Reed held out his hand, it shook, and he shoved it in his pocket. "I need you to bring me back." She didn't answer, but he could hear her breathing on the other end. "Visage has seven more Krakens, Nat. And I just ruined his plan to have Danzig and I kill each other at my condo. Plus, I think Danzig knows who he is now. Visage's well laid plans blew up in his face and he's scrambling. That makes him more dangerous than before."

"So let them kill each other. Do the world a favor."

"He'll sell them, you know that. To get away. Visage will hand those weapons over to anyone who will pay. Think about what someone could do with them."

"I hate this."

"I know. I still need you."

Silence for almost thirty seconds, and then she said, "I have to make two stops."

While he waited, Reed hopped online to see what Danzig had meant about everyone having seen him kill the judge. Social media and local news had picked up the story and video. He watched it for a few minutes and a wave of helplessness slammed down on Reed. He shut it off and went to take a shower. As he passed the bedroom window that looked out onto the walkway, he saw a wiry, pale guy kicking the vending machine with his cast. Reed did a double take but was too tired to care.

As hot as he could take, he let the water pour over his head, washing him of the blood and guilt and anger until he was weak and panting for breath in the steam. Noise outside the bathroom made Reed move and he dried off and put on some adjustable-waist cargo pants and a thick, long-sleeved T-shirt he'd found in the bedroom. Deep navy blue and a little small, they were at the very least, not crusty with blood. Courtesy clothes, Coyote had called them. Better than robes if you need to run. Reed slipped his hip holster onto the waistband of the cargo pants. When he walked out, Coyote was in the kitchen unloading groceries.

He glanced over at Reed. "You good?"

"I'm good. How's the head?"

"Nothing a little ice and some grub can't fix."

"Did I see Mookie outside," Reed asked, grabbing a can of soda from the fridge.

Coyote grinned. "He reached out to me via a Kindred connection and offered to pay for protection. He's been staying here since I bailed him out."

"Tell him I talked to his Serbian kin, Jovan, and they want to hear from him. My life depends on it."

"He'll reach out when this is over. It was my idea to go no contact with everyone."

Reed scanned the room. A pile of equipment sat on the coffee table, the metal case of the MER-C system included. "Where's Nat?"

Coyote motioned down the hallway with the tip of his beer bottle. "She's in the bedroom."

"How is she?"

"Pissed." Coyote took sip and then shrugged. "Scared. Your face is everywhere. Every local news streamer is picking apart rumors of your breakdown after the death of Caitlyn, complete with her police academy photo, and one of you two ice skating or something. They're hashing up the trouble with the Neurogen case. Your leave of absence. That kind of thing. Then they replay your supposed sabotage in slow motion. It's brutal, my friend."

"I saw it." Reed remembered that day and Caitlyn's laughter echoed through his head. He shook it off, pushing down the regret and sorrow of her death.

"Nat got a call on our way here, and it upset her. I don't know what it was about."

Reed went to the bedroom and found her sitting on the edge of the bed fiddling with the display screen on the dresser. She was leaning close, squinting at the video of him supposedly planting C-4 on the propane tank near Judge Leone's cabin. When he walked in, she met his gaze, concerned.

He lifted his bandaged arm. "I'm good. All patched up," he said and nodded at the screen. "What're you doing?"

"They spliced this." She rewound the video released by the mysterious blogger. It had been picked up by several news organizations and there was no stopping it. "There were no cameras at the cabin, I checked." She pointed at the screen. "And this, these powerlines, and trees behind you, they're at Judge Leone's house, not his cabin. Remember he showed us his security system recordings? This is what they spliced together to make it look like you did this."

"Did the blogger tell you anything?" Reed asked, wincing at the pull of stitches.

"She did. She's a mid-level news streamer who mainly does gossip, breaking news, and entertainment. Some collaboration deals, but mostly local. She's got some sway, a decent following, but nothing special. I think Visage picked her randomly." Nat leaned back from the screen and looked at Reed. "Anyway, as soon as the most recent video of you posted, I had Xanadu help me launch an attack on her site. We sent tens of thousands of requests via her subscription link. Her site crashed and her financials *might* have been erroneously frozen for a time. Unfortunately, your story has already been picked up by bigger sites with more reach."

Nothing was going to stop them from dragging him through the mud. Reed already knew that. "Did you find out anything helpful? Does she know Visage?"

"I sent her a message and we talked. This was a couple of hours ago before Coyote picked me up. I told her I'd release my hold on her site as soon as this is over. She admitted the information was sent to her anonymously with a big payment if she posted. She has no idea who sent it to her. She didn't even run it through an AI detector to see if it was altered."

"Coyote said someone called you that upset you."

"That was Parker." Nat frowned, worry in her eyes. "He's been assigned to head up the task force looking for you. I had to check my car for tracking tags, and I shut down my phone after he called."

"You think he's got you under surveillance?"

"If I were trying to track you down, I'd definitely put a tail on me. I was careful, though. I walked to the street behind my house and met Coyote on the corner. No one saw me leave my home."

"There's a whole task force?" Reed shook his head. "What did Parker say?"

"He said he wants to bring you in safely. That he wants to hear your side of the story, blah, blah, blah," she said and chewed on her lip. "Imani said he personally submitted the knife from Sylvia's crime scene to forensics. He walked it downstairs and asked for someone *other* than Sanders to run it."

"Because we're friends," Reed said. "He thinks my prints are on that knife."

"Are they?" Nat asked. "I saw her room. The pile of clothes. In your account you said you moved it."

"I was trying to keep her alive."

"So, you could've touched it." She rubbed her face with both hands, fatigue lining her eyes. "He's trying to nail you for both. If he gets ahold of your phone records. Your late-night chat with Sylvia will bolster the case against you. Especially since you didn't turn in a report on it."

"Unbelievable." Reed shook his head. "Do you think he has my phone records already?"

"I think he has your whole life under a microscope." She looked out the bedroom door at Coyote. "He's convinced you're a bad seed and shouldn't be a cop."

"I don't think he's wrong."

Nat considered him for a moment. "What are you doing? Why're you talking like that?"

"I'm just beat up," Reed said. "Anything else?"

"On the mysterious Spicy Griller seasoning front, I confirmed Fleur's mom owns the online business. You were right. It was a way to send her daughter cash. Nothing there."

"And the data lens Sylvia slipped me?"

"She had hundreds of files on him. Business dealings, personal dealings. His politics, travel including flight plans, and his yacht registration. What he gave to charity, his friends and when he met with them. I don't think the FBI could surveil someone better. Oh, and she had information on his doctors, stolen data from his lawyer's office, likely bought from a paralegal. But get this. She also had lists of random deaths, odd events, and dossiers on a bunch of people I had to look up. The kind of people who pay to remain as anonymous as possible. It's gonna take time to untangle, especially without her help but, it's something." Nat looked down at her hands, picking at the skin of her cuticles with nerves. "We'll get him, Reed. Danzig *will* go down."

"I'm sorry you got dragged into all of this." Reed reached over and squeezed her hands. They were shaking. "I wish Tig had kept you far away from my chaos."

"Kept me from you? I decide what I want, remember? I knew what I was getting into." Nat looked at him and her gaze held his, Reed's chest going tight with understanding. "I saw who you were. I just wish . . . it feels like time is ticking down on . . . everything."

"Nat, I—"

She got up, cutting him off, and shut down the display screen on the dresser. When she looked back at him, it was with a strained smile. "And you know me, the adrenaline rush alone is worth your craziness."

Reed sat on the bed, staring out at her talking with Coyote in the living room. His stomach in knots, he wondered what he was supposed to say. She still thought she could fix things. The problem was no one came back from this kind of attack. No one.

Coyote called Reed over and handed him a stack of papers. They were printouts of the pages in Sylvia's coded ledger that Reed had sent him earlier.

"Now mind you," Coyote said. "it's been mere hours, but my code writer, Kailey is worth every penny. She was able to pull some preliminary findings. He pointed to an entry on Reed's printouts. "The ledger was linked to an account, a secure one, that we traced to somewhere in the Caymans. It'll take some time to get further. The other codes on here are airport codes. La Guardia, Newark, and JFK."

"All in New York," Reed scratched his stubbly chin. "Where was she going?"

"That's where I come in," Nat said. She handed him her tablet. "After her murder, Tig got us subpoenas for her finances. Sylvia flew into La Guardia airport, every few weeks for over year. Stays one night at this hotel in Manhattan, eats at the in-house restaurant, and flies back out in the morning."

"She's meeting someone." Reed flipped through her financials.

"Yeah, but the charges are to her personal accounts. Nothing on the business accounts. So, it has to be personal, this travel." Nat shrugged. "A romantic tryst?"

"Maybe," Reed said, unconvinced. "Could we call and see how much an average meal costs there?"

"I'm looking up the restaurant menu on their website." She skimmed the restaurant info on her phone. "According to these prices, the dinner charge is what you'd expect for one person."

"She ate alone." Reed shook his head. "I don't think this was a rendezvous."

"If she was in town for business then it's likely she met with whoever it was at a different location." Coyote nodded at the tablet. "Away from cameras."

"I think I know where and maybe with whom," Nat said and rose a little on the balls of her feet. "Get this, Helene, Danzig's sister that Sylvia was quick to dismiss, well I dug into her too, but had to go about it in ways that I could get to without a warrant." Nat swiped through to some kind of statement. "She's not in Europe. As of a year ago, she lives in the Lower Hudson Valley now, specifically Westchester."

"That's a commuter town for New Yorkers," Reed said, scanning the document. "These are toll charges?"

"Yeah," Nat said. "Helene has a series of toll charges coming into Manhattan on the same days that Sylvia flew in." She pointed to a line item. "These two charges, going out of Westchester and returning are four hours apart. And this charge, it's a toll road. It's ten minutes after the time stamp on Sylvia's restaurant receipt. "They were in the same area at the same time on the same days."

"Sounds like you found yourselves a conspiracy," Coyote said. "Danzig's own sister and his worst enemy. That's messed up."

"What about Visage?" Nat asked. "Where does he come in? You think they were working with him?"

"He doesn't work with anyone. Not really." The image of Sylvia on the floor flashed in Reed's head. Her frightened eyes boring into him, her mouth moving silently, trying to tell him something. "Sylvia said he stole the Krakens from her."

"You think he double-crossed them both," Coyote said and smiled. "Now that does sound like a spy. And what was she going to do? Kind of hard to report a theft of a weapon that isn't supposed to exist."

"I don't believe that Sylvia knew what Visage was doing to me and Danzig. She seemed genuinely surprised about a lot of what we told her," Reed said to Nat. "And Danzig had no idea who Dontae was. My guess is Visage said he'd work with them to overthrow Danzig, got close enough to take the Krakens, and then betrayed them."

"She knew what his real identity was," Nat said, shaking her head. "Why didn't she tell us? Why throw Kaspar under the bus?"

"Fear," Reed said. "She knew what he was capable of."

"Helene went underground as soon as Sylvia's death made the news. We had someone calling her all night. This morning someone did a wellness check. No one home." Nat looked up at Reed. "Why would Sylvia enter into any kind of deal with someone like Visage? She must have known the risks of it going sideways."

"Because he wanted what she did. For Danzig to die." Reed handed Nat her tablet back, not letting it go until she looked at him. "Nat, we need to get started."

Her lips pressed together, a furrow of worry in her forehead. "On one condition. I decide when to pull you back."

"Nat," Reed began, but saw the look in her eyes. "Give me enough time to find a way to stop him."

The first two times Reed viewed a memory, they'd been unprepared for the fallout. Once in a burning room and the other tied to a chair in one of Coyote's apartments, they'd had to bring him back last time with ice and water and pain. Nat believed she'd come up with a better plan. She laid out all the equipment from the MER-C system case that they needed; the metal containment pod with the memories, and the injector pen to deliver the memory serum into Reed's brain. She left the halo for extraction and the syringe with the augmentation serum in the case.

"Okay," she said and held up a wristband. Not quite a watch, it had unidentifiable components soldered onto it. "My second stop was to get this. It was in my home office. This is a shock bracelet. Think, compact stun gun."

"Oh, this is gonna be so good," Coyote said to Reed. "Hope you didn't make her mad recently."

"Anyway," Nat continued with a shut-up look at Coyote. "It's incremental. I made this so that if your heart rate hit and stayed at a certain point, it would deliver a shock to the underside of your wrist. The intensity will dial up with each time. Hopefully enough to pull you out of the memory. If your heart doesn't slow down or if it stopped, it would dial either me, Coyote, or 911 with your location and an emergency message."

"Dial you?" Reed stepped back. "You thought I would do this without you."

"You have before. Both times," she said. "I wanted to make sure you made it back. Even if I wasn't there."

"I'll make it back," Reed said with a tired smile. "Promise."

Coyote pulled over one of the dining chairs. Wooden with a tall back and sturdy arms, he maneuvered it into the center of the living area. "Who brought the duct tape?"

While Reed taped his legs and right wrist to the chair, Nat used the glass injector pen to extract the memory serum from the containment pod. The translucent purple liquid contained the electrical, chemical, and hormonal signals of a memory belonging to someone that Slater had killed. In it, Reed hoped to find a way to stop Visage and Danzig.

Coyote taped off Reed's left hand as Nat walked over. She held up the injector pen. All three little indicator lights glowed on the shaft.

"Only the one dose, remember?" Reed said, a little nervous.

"I'll make sure." Nat placed her palm on Reed's forehead, her other hand held the needle to his throat. She leaned in, her breath warm at his temple. "Last chance."

"Look what he's taken," Reed said. "We have to stop him."

She straightened up and squared her shoulders. "I'm waking you up the second I think there's trouble."

"I know," Reed said. "I trust you."

Nat took a deep breath and plunged the needle into Reed's artery. "Come back."

Shards of frigid pain rushed through his head as the plunger depressed and the memory surged into his mind. A storm of light and sound and movement whirled around him. Reed gasped for breath and his heart stuttered in his chest. Like an adrenaline shot to his consciousness, his mind exploded, and he knew with certainty that he was in Ezra Tan's mind. And that he was going to die.

31

A hurricane of thoughts and sights and sounds blared through Reed like the rumble of a train. Soft at first until they roared in his head churning through him, pushing him back in time. Laughter and crying. The sound of applause sped up to become rain on a tin roof. Frenetic images of a woman, his . . . Ezra's mom, smiling at him from the counter as she cooked dinner. In his hands, so small to his view, a model of a ship. And Reed felt the surge of pride as he waited to show his father how he'd done it on his own. The table bubbled beneath his arms, vaporizing to nothing as the room turned, spinning away from Ezra's mother, from his home.

Meaning came to him as the memory unfurled, the joy and pride of his accomplishment as Ezra's university arena rose around Reed. The gown and cap, shiny-black under the lights as they called his name. His mother's face in the crowd, the itchiness of his academic stole around his neck as he took his diploma. And then it all shuddered, winking in and out of existence. Reed fell through the darkness, his pulse in his ears as he plummeted into a black, endless void and then he was in the hospital waiting room. Sitting in the hard plastic chairs, nerves slithered in his gut as he read the treatment plan for his mother's cancer. Too much. It was too much money. And then a shadow crossed over what he was reading. Ezra looked up and through his eyes, Reed saw a man that sent the heat of hatred through him. Slater, one of Danzig's Spectre mercenaries stood in front of Ezra, a solution in his hand.

Reed struggled in the memory, trying to move within the thoughts, searching for Danzig or Visage, but it held firm. Stronger than the others. This memory had not been from a dying man. Ezra had been alive and conscious, and Reed's mind fought to accept the vivid scenes. A birthday party grew around him. People materializing as they laughed and clapped. A cake with candles burned warm against Ezra's face and he was smiling, watching the confetti fall into his punch as his family sang. It flashed in and out of existence, bright and then so dim Reed struggled to understand what he was looking at. And then, like a brilliant flash across a still, dark sky, fear and dread cut through Reed's chest . . . Ezra's chest. Something was coming, something he hadn't wanted to remember.

The memory spun, twisting the sky like a carousel and flinging Reed into nothingness. A cacophony of noise crashed into him, and he saw himself through Ezra's eyes in the mirror over the bar. A trendy club strobed into existence around him. Unfamiliar to Ezra. Music thumped, pushing his nerves to the limit as he fiddled with the pill in his pocket, sweating through his polo shirt.

Slater's words echoed in Ezra's head, "She's done it before. She's been caught several times with a fake ID. It's the only way to stop her."

And then Reed knew. He remembered how Slater had told Ezra that it wasn't entrapment, that she drove drunk all the time and this time they'd be ready. She could ruin the judge's reputation if he kept covering for her. Slater had cajoled and threatened Ezra while promising enough money to save his mother. And then Reed understood what they'd done. How they'd drugged her drink and made sure some sympathetic cops were paid and just around the corner.

"Slip it in her drink and call. I'll do the rest," Slater had said. "They'll pull her over and she'll get the help she needs."

Guilt and self-loathing squirmed through Reed as Ezra watched Leone's daughter at the end of the bar with her friends. And then he was moving, choosing a moment they were distracted. No one ever noticed him anyway. Not one, as he reached for a napkin and dropped the pill like he'd practiced. It fell right in, fizzing to nothing in seconds. Ezra hurried away despite Reed's will to stay.

The memory jolted and then Reed was in Ezra's car, behind the wheel, and the smell of old drive through containers assaulted him. Ezra sat watching her pull out of the parking lot. He tried the phone number again. Got the busy signal and panic squeezed the breath out of him. He started the car, hoping if he followed her, he could call the cops himself, but there was something wrong. He got out to look. His tires were slashed. Ezra sprinted in his oxfords to the driveway, missing her as she sped away in a squeal of tires. She didn't get far, he'd seen the emergency lights as he was changing his tire. Revulsion burned through Reed. She'd hit someone and driven away. A man had died, and they covered it up to trap the judge.

A mighty wind flew up around Reed, throwing him forward in time. Ezra stood in his new office, watching the Tamlin woman walk away with her box of things and guilt gripped him. He'd punched the wall, breaking his hand. Time skipped onward, strobing like lightning. Moments flashed in Reed's mind. Dinner with his mother, her proud look ripping through Ezra as he told her of his position as Judge Leone's clerk. Her in the chemotherapy chair, knitting him a scarf for his big trip to the snow. Her skin so thin and pale.

The memory flickered, exploding away like smoke to reveal a frozen forest. A darkening sky over white-capped pine trees. Ezra was in the mountains, nervous, as he sat in a car. Judge Leone's town car, Reed realized and felt the recollection narrowing, focusing. Ezra stepped out and stretched his legs, his stomach still reeling with carsickness. It was late October, after an early storm, and the biting cold of the snowy mountains stung his cheeks. He took a deep breath, and the chill steadied his nerves. Reed tried to look around in the memory, to focus on what Ezra saw that day, but everyone moved with stop motion jerks, like a film being sped up every few seconds.

And then it was later that night. Outside the lodge. Ezra walked back up the snowy trail from the car. Flask in his hand for the judge. He hoped his thought of bringing Leone his favorite drink might help the man's foul mood. On the way he passed a group of men on the sloping lawn. They stood around a fire ring, laughing and drinking. Everything slowed, and the memory changed. The snowflakes drifting down stopped falling and floated mid-air, the flames in the ring snapped and bent as if being broken, and then the brightness dimmed. Like a spotlight focusing on a single corner of the property. Behind a copse of trees in the bright orange glow of a standing warmer, Leone and Danzig stood locked in a heated argument.

Slater's breadcrumb questions pulled Reed to memories he'd wanted from Ezra. "You saw them fighting. You were afraid you'd be seen. What did you hear?"

Reed strained to listen, and then their voices grew louder, their words clearer as Ezra's attention centered on them.

Leone's eyes bugged out. "You're subverting—"

"Enough," Danzig yelled. "Your daughter can get the help she needs, and you rise to the bench as planned or she goes to jail. Whether or not she survives that is anyone's guess."

"I will not be a party to this, Aurora business. It's wrong!" Leone turned to leave, but Danzig lashed out, grabbing the smaller man by the shirt. He punched him viciously in the gut and Leone dropped to the snow, wheezing.

Reed felt the urge to run over, to help, flash through Ezra, but he hadn't. He'd stood frozen in the shadows unsure of what to do.

"You do what you are told." Danzig had leaned over Leone, his movements jerking like stop motion movie. He smiled, a wicked, deadly grin as he held a pistol to the judge's head. "When I have need of you. You will act. Are we clear?"

Leone cowered from the barrel, his breath coming in staccato puffs under the lights. "Please, don't hurt my daughter."

"So, we have an agreement, then, Your Honor?"

Ezra stepped wrong and a twig broke. *Oh, no.*

Danzig's gaze snapped to where he was hiding and then he yelled to the men at the fire ring. "Niklos, uhvati ga!"

Ezra dropped the flask and ran. He stumbled through the snow, his feet sinking in, slowing him. If he could make it to the car. Reed tried to head for the cover of trees, but Ezra wasn't trained. He was in a panic. He scrambled past the firepit, the men lit from underneath by the flames. And in that moment, out of the peripheral of Ezra's vision, Reed's heart stammered. Tall and lithe, a man tracked Ezra's path with a predatory gaze. He shouted at Ezra and though Reed could not understand it, he recognized the breathy quality. The muffled, damaged palate. The man bared his teeth as he threw his drink into the fire. And in the flare, out of the corner of Ezra's eye, Reed saw that only half of the man's mouth moved. Visage.

Turn, Reed's mind screamed in the memory. *Face him!*

He flailed, felt the ties of the chair that bound him tight. He shouted with anger, his voice coming out in a strangled, weak moan. As if in a dream, he was heavy, struggling to move. He needed to see the man's face.

But Ezra had ran blindly. He'd staggered in the deep snow, bumping into trees. Almost to the cars – he yelped when a hand shot out from between the trunks and grabbed him. Slater was there in the dark, a finger over his lips. Hand over Ezra's mouth. Dead eyes, buzz cut, black field fatigues. The green glow of the sky behind Slater washed along the snow.

"What did you see, Ezra?" He whispered, his fist cocking back to punch.

Reed lunged, screaming at the man who'd killed so many innocents for Danzig. He felt his arm come free and then hands on him.

"Reed! Come back!" Nat's voice echoed through the woods. "Reed!"

His mind flew toward it, fighting for consciousness, his chest crushed with pain. A shrill tone sounded in the void. Over and over. Reed couldn't breathe. He couldn't speak as he raced through time and place until he slammed back down into the chair. He gasped for air. Coughing, his free hand clawing at his shirt.

"You're okay," Coyote said.

Reed focused on his face until his vision cleared. The front windows let in bright morning light, and he looked out at the dawn, confused. "How long was I gone?"

"A few hours," Nat said. She stood next to Coyote, her face pale. She had a large icepack in her hands. "The wrist thing didn't work perfectly. It didn't jolt you awake, but you surfaced enough for us to wake you up."

Reed's mind reeled at the lost time. It had seemed mere minutes in the memory. He reached out to her. "I saw him."

"Who?" Nat felt his forehead with the back of her hand. "You're still hot."

"I saw Visage," Reed said. He tore at the duct tape on his other wrist and then his ankles. He made a writing motion over his palm. I need to draw."

"I'll get something." Coyote took off for the kitchen.

Nat looked at him askance. "You're sure, it's him?"

"Yes, but Nat," Reed's gaze flitted to hers, and he held her by the upper arms, adrenaline spiking through him. "We've seen him before."

32

Parker

Detective Reed's condo sat smoldering at Parker's feet. The halogen lamps of the forensic team washed the devastation in harsh light despite the rising dawn. Parker walked, hands on his hips around the charred body. It lay on a yellow tarp and Sanders hovered a camera drone over it, flashing the scorched sinew and clothes in stark flashes. Found by the firefighters, they'd yet to identify the victim. No ID. Nothing but ash and burnt clothes.

"Did anyone see Detective Reed before the fire?" Parker asked the patrol officer working the scene.

Old and a bit out of shape, he didn't look like he much wanted to be there. Parker knew they called him Stucky, but he had no idea why. His name plate read Jones.

"No. Reed's phone went dead about a mile down the road," Stucky said.

"When?" Parker took out his digital tablet and typed out some notes. "What time was this?"

"About the time the hose jockeys were pulling up to fight the fire. Around seven last night."

"So, he was here." The fire crew got the condo under control after a few hours, but the freezing weather had created an ice problem on the scene.

Rather than risk injury in the night, they decided to start early the next day. Now, at five in the morning, hours after the fact, the fire chief finally let Parker on the scene. He scanned the people watching from behind the yellow crime scene tape and spotted a couple men in jeans, flannels, and leather vests. Parker caught Stucky's attention. "Get one of the crime scene guys to take photos of the crowd, will you? Especially those motorcycle guys. They're Kindred."

Stucky left and Parker pulled out his phone. He dialed a number as he wandered up the back embankment to talk in private. She picked up on the first ring.

"I think I've got him," Parker said. "There's a body."

"Who do you think it is?"

"I don't know. I haven't known anything that man is doing since he came on this case. *My* case!" Parker stomped the snow from his shoes with frustration. "Reed leaves nothing but death in his wake."

"Do you think he'll run?"

Parker rubbed his forehead with his palm. Sweat beaded there despite the cold. "Reed was trained by the military to hunt insurgents. He worked undercover for years with the SPD. Criminals count him as their friend. If he wanted to disappear, he could."

"And De La Cruz? Do you think she's helping him?"

Parker stared out at the horizon. "She's fiercely loyal according to her psych profile, but her father was a sheriff, so it's uncertain how far that goes."

"Speaking of her file, De La Cruz has a heck of a lot of shady skills. Disappearing wouldn't be hard for her either."

Parker paced back and forth between the pines. "This is bad. This is so bad."

The caller was silent, her quiet chewing grating on his nerves, then, "You must find him. You've been on the case with him, working with him. Prove that you deserve to lead a task force like this."

Sanders finished with the drone and stood. Parker pulled his jacket closed against the cold wind. "Have you heard anything?"

"I have an alert for anything he or De La Cruz puts through the system. I might expand that, but I'm still debating."

Worry curdled in Parker's gut. "Nothing that traces back to anyone, right?"

"Everything runs through this office. No one will notice if I peek."

"Be careful." Sanders called for Parker, and he put up his hand. Wait a second. "Reed's been keeping me in the dark on purpose. I don't know where he'd go. I'm getting subpoenas for his financials and phone as soon as we can this morning. But he's too smart to use either."

"You know this guy. Do you really think he'll take off and save himself?"

Parker shook his head. "No. He'll run straight into the line of fire."

33
—————

While it was still relatively dark and quiet, Reed and Nat headed back to the evil geek lair. She in her undercover car and Reed on Coyote's loaner motorcycle. It was colder than last time he'd been there, and his breath puffed out in clouds as they walked into the control room, as Nat called it. Reed peeled off the borrowed jacket as he walked in. Xanadu was already there working on the VR platform, wearing the ugliest, purple paisley sweater Reed had ever seen.

He stood when they walked in. "Sorry your house blew up."

"Thanks?" Reed considered Xanadu. "You know I'm a cop, right?"

Xanadu glanced at one of the display screens. It played news coverage of Reed's act of faux sabotage over and over with a photo of him next to it. "I suspect not for long, though."

"Hey!" Nat said. "Not cool."

"Sorry. Either way, your quest to recapture this weapon of destruction while hunting down a soulless tech mogul is a righteous cause. I can get behind that." He held up a finger. "For now."

"Are you good at financials?" Reed asked.

"Yes." Xanadu pushed his glasses up with his index finger. "I'm excellent with numbers."

"That's what I like to hear." Reed handed him some files from Coyote.

The printouts of the ledger they'd found in Sylvia's house. Coyote's code breaker had sent along notes on how to read the entries. "I'm looking for a financial connection between Sylvia and anyone close to Danzig. His sister, his daughter, friends, anyone. The thinnest thread counts. I want to see it."

While Xanadu went through that, Reed and Nat tackled the pile of information they'd amassed on Danzig. She'd managed to offload a lot of files from her police digital tablet before Tig locked her out of the system.

"You're sure you've seen him before?"

Reed nodded, the image of Visage lit by flames burned in his mind. "It was him."

"Where did that sketch go?" Nat held her hand out for what Reed had drawn.

"It's rough. I saw him out of the peripheral vision of a foreign memory. Not exactly an eyewitness account." He ripped his drawing from the apartment notepad.

She looked at it, head tilted while chewing her inner cheek. "I can work with this."

Nat scanned it into the computer and the screen overhead lit up with Reed's sketch, next to an ident-kit shape of a head they used for witness descriptions. She tapped a few keys and then bright blue tracing lines crawled over his drawing measuring contours and slopes, sizing iris and sclera ratio, angling nostril tilt and width. A running stream of photos and videos they'd gathered throughout the investigation flashed underneath. The algorithm highlighted possible matches in red, gave them a probability score, and discarded photos of faces based on the percentage.

"Is this your very own facial recognition program?" Reed stared, mouth open. "How is this legal?"

"It's an open-source AI," Nat said. "You can use it to find out what shirt a celebrity is wearing or locate a chair you saw in a post to buy it. I've just juiced it up a bit with my own augmentations."

"Don't believe her. She literally rewrote most of it," Xanadu said with a click of his tongue. "Woman is a genius."

"How long?" Reed asked as the program ran faster than he could track.

"A few minutes, a few hours," she shrugged. "With ours, Coyote's, and

Sylvia's data, we have a lot to work with but that means we have a lot to go through."

"There's something I'm not seeing," Reed said, holding his head in his palm. "I heard Danzig yell something. A different language. It sounded sharp, like when Jovan talked to us in the VR world."

"Serbian? That makes sense. You said when Visage called you after Sylvia died that he admitted stalling the sale because he didn't want to be recognized. I can take another look into Danzig's dealings in that part of the world, but I didn't find anything the first time." She turned back to the keyboard and started typing. "You said he said something in the memory too?"

"Yes, uh, Danzig yelled when he spotted Ezra eavesdropping on him and Leone." The startled panic of being caught threaded through Reed's mind. His hand trembled and he crossed his arms. But not before Nat saw it.

She didn't mention it and they sat in comfortable silence watching the program run faces against Reed's sketch of Visage. He'd see a face and pause the search, squinting at it, only to discard it. While waiting, Reed spent some time sketching the forest, the lodge, and the swirling patterns of the Northern Lights.

"Oh, the auroras, right?"

Reed looked at Nat. "What did you say?"

"Aurora Borealis," she said. "The Northern Lights?"

"They were in Ezra's memory." Reed traced the word, "aurora," over and over in his book. Flashing on what he'd seen. "They were talking about Aurora like it was a project to be executed. Slater wanted to know what Ezra had seen, but it wasn't much."

"Why do you think Visage told you to view that memory if he was in it?"

"I don't think he knew. Or maybe thought he might be, but it wouldn't matter. The memory pod was full, so no one had seen Ezra's memory. But Visage knew Ezra had been caught spying on Danzig. In the memory, he watched Ezra run away. For all he knew, that was all there was to it. A threat that would convince me to speak to Leone. Slater knew what Ezra had done, too. I just think that at the time that Visage told me to view the memory, he had no idea we'd get as far as we have in identifying him. We have his voice, his description, his connection to Serbia. If I had viewed Ezra's memory in the beginning, when Visage wanted me to, I would never have noticed some unknown goon in the corner of his vision. It wouldn't have meant anything then."

"He screwed up," Nat said and went back to her keyboard. "Which means he might do it again."

"That's what I'm counting on."

After more than an hour and a half, back aching, Reed stood to see if he could get the coffee maker going. He started a pot and then leaned on the table with his hip, watching the news stream. Parker stood in front of the SPD main campus facing a bank of reporters and buzzing camera drones. Just in time for the morning news cycle. He looked wound up.

"We're interested in any information the public can provide about the whereabouts of Detective Morgan Reed," Parker said into the cameras. "He is a suspect in the assassination of federal court judge, Rudolpho Leone, as well as the possible murder of a witness, celebrated tech entrepreneur, Sylvia Plaques. Due to the inconsistencies with his statement and timeline the Seattle Police Department would like to speak with him. The SPD would like to warn the public that he is considered armed and dangerous. Do not engage with this individual. Instead, contact SPD via the hotline or link on your screen. Thank you."

A cacophony of questions and chattering ensued, but Reed had had enough. He turned the screen off. Nat walked over and handed him a printout.

"What's this?"

"Well, when we thought Visage was Kaspar, I did some digging into West Point. He drove the dean around. Brigadier general Charlene Hodges, to be exact. It was a cushy job. No real training. Then he took off to Europe and I don't think he did anything but be rich and obnoxious in several foreign countries."

"He was executed," Reed said quietly. His gaze had drifted to the ident-kit image. The eyebrows and eye shape had been pinned and something about them seemed familiar. "Visage killed Kaspar just to frame me and enrage Danzig."

"This whole twisted game is the work of a psychopath." Nat grabbed a bag of chips off the table and tore into them. "It should be easier to identify these wackadoos."

"They wear their human suits well and blend in," Reed said.

Xanadu stood up from his counterspace and hurried over, papers flying, a look of excitement on his face.

"Behold, progress. I took the code keys your friend Coyote gave us and found this . . ." He put a printed spreadsheet down on the snack table and pointed to a row of codes and numbers. Reed thought some resembled dates but wasn't sure. "Axios Limited. It's owned by a series of shell corporations leading to the numbered account you guys found in the Night Market. The one linked with the name, LDLazarus."

"Sylvia's code name?" Nat asked. "This is her account?"

"Undoubtedly." Xanadu nodded, pushing his glasses back up excitedly. "It's been slowly, over the past year and a half, buying up shares of Sylvia's Interface Solutions stock. I think it's how this Visage character meant to pay for the Kraken rounds." He tapped his pen on a row of numbers. "Look at these deposits. We're talking about millions of dollars going into Sylvia's coffers, but they didn't go into her business or personal accounts. As far as I can tell that money just sat there. There was also another account wiring money to Sylvia's offshore bank. The second one wasn't well hidden. Amateurish, really. It leads back to Helene, Danzig's sister."

"You're telling me that Visage and Helene both stored money with Sylvia by buying her stock? What was Sylvia doing, holding it for safekeeping? A war chest against Danzig?" Reed thought about buying his condo. All the paperwork, the bank stuff. "Like escrow?"

Xanadu nodded. "Sort of, yeah."

"For what? Control of High Rock Holdings?" Nat asked. "Or Danzig's murder?"

"I mean, they'd probably want both, right?" Xanadu asked.

"Either way, that's a conspiracy. What about Kaspar Danzig?" Reed asked Xanadu. "Is he involved in any way?"

"Not that I can surmise, but who knows? All their family assets are hopelessly tangled," he said.

Nat was leaning over the spreadsheet. She looked up at Reed. "Axios's last purchase was the night Dontae died."

"The following business day, the 'escrow' account was drained." Xanadu flipped to the right spreadsheet. "To where, I can't say. But that moola is gone."

"He stole the money *and* the Krakens?" She looked at Reed, perplexed. "I don't get it. How does he get them to trust him? People like Dontae and Sylvia don't trust easily. Neither did Helene . . . how does Visage do that? Why do they think they can just believe him?"

"*It never ceases to shock me what people will say to someone they implicitly trust*," Reed repeated Visage's words. "That's what he said. Who do you trust implicitly?"

"Just automatic, without question?" Xander pursed his lips, thinking. "Doctors?"

"Bank tellers," Nat said, "Uh, psychiatrists"

"Priests!" Xanadu said, pointing at Nat. "Who else?"

"Lawyers," Reed muttered, his mind churning. "The kind who can promise you a way back home."

"Dontae's mystery reason for believing he could move back to Louisiana was a lawyer?" Nat shook her head. "No, we talked to the public defender's office, legal aid places, low-income programs, everywhere. No one's heard of Dontae."

"You know what?" Xander said. "A lawyer could make any kind of legal-sounding crap up and I would believe it. And if you don't have enough money for a second opinion, how're you going to check?"

"You wouldn't. Especially if you were doing something illegal like selling missiles to Serbian fighters." Reed walked the length of the table. "The parole officer had no evidence of a lawyer contacting him about this. Regardless of what Dontae thought, it was never going to happen."

"We should start with Danzig's lawyers," Nat said. "They'd have access to his secrets."

Xander started typing on his laptop. "Do you know how to get into that Westlaw site?"

Nat nudged him out of the way with her hip and took over. "No, you need AttorneyFAQ.law or one of those public records sites. If they filed on behalf of Danzig or his entities, their name would be on it."

The image of Sylvia flashed in Reed's mind. Her frightened eyes boring into his, her hand at his cheek, the blood sticky on his skin. His gaze snapped to the faces flashing on the screen.

"Sylvia tried to tell me. She was saying something that started with an 'n' sound, I think," Reed muttered to himself. And then Ezra's memory blared in Reed's head again. The image of Danzig yelling, ordering them to run after him. *Niklos, uhvati ga!*

Something clicked in Reed's mind. He ran to the counter and pawed through the printed files. He'd had it at the Pioneer Square Café with Nat. When they'd looked at Danzig's inner circle.

"What is it?" Nat asked, hurrying over. "What do you need?"

Reed searched frantically. It couldn't be.

"The picture with the tree. The website one with the blonde—" He found it. The Christmas photo of Danzig flanked by his children. Kaspar and Veronica on one side, Aria and her husband on the other. Nicholas Craig. Niklos. He stared into the camera, a neutral face amid smiles. Cold. Calm. Fading into the background. A snitch. A killer. A thief. "And a spy," Reed breathed.

"Danzig's son-in-law is behind this?" Nat made a face. "He's a finance guy, isn't he? At a hedge fund."

"He's their in-house council," Xanadu said, and a company newsletter flashed onscreen. This is from some awards banquet they gave themselves last year. It's for pro bono work with legal aid. The major firms all do it because they get to claim charity work on their taxes and give themselves trophies." Xanadu looked at Reed. "And get this, my friend is a public defender and she complained once about these kinds of lawyers. She said they hand-pick their cases. You know, to find the ones with maximum sympathy."

"That's how he found Dontae," Reed said. "He pretended to make the move happen. Why wouldn't you believe a big shot lawyer from an expensive firm?"

"And given your past, it wouldn't be hard to find a friend of yours who was in trouble. This Nicholas would have had access to all the research Danzig did on you. It's inevitable he would've found the sealed juvenile file because nothing ever really goes away. Not if you have enough talent and money," Nat said. "Nicolas or Visage or whatever you want to call him went at you through them because he *knew* you wouldn't turn your back on your friends."

"She's right," Xanadu said. "Your service records, psych evals for the military, the police, emails, and texts. Your whole life is out there whether you like it or not."

"That's disturbing," Reed said.

"It's not even that complicated," Xanadu said. "All this guy would have had to do is plug your information into a predictive program and it'll build a decent profile. Broad strokes, mind you, they're consumer grade applications, but still. In the hands of a trained spy, it's a way into your head."

Reed studied his enemy's face. Again, almost part of the background, Nicholas stared out from the photo. "Dontae was telling the truth. He really believed he was going home. This guy used hope as a weapon."

"You didn't know," Nat said. "You can't blame yourself."

"I should have believed him. I should have looked harder for this mystery lawyer." Reed moved the papers around, thinking. "It has to be Nicholas. He would have had access to Danzig. I mean real access, he's family. They ate Thanksgiving dinner together. And Sylvia told us he was an advisor to Danzig, so he'd have run into Slater at some point," Reed said, his mind churning. "He's married to Danzig's daughter. Would have been able to get close to Kaspar. He'd know about Sylvia and her hatred. Helene and her lawsuits. This fits," Reed said, his heart pounding in his ears. "It's him."

"But the man impersonating you—"

"A spy would know how to change his appearance. He's my height and he could bulk up with padding. Throw on a dark wig . . ." Reed nodded at the frozen news stream of him in the judge's surveillance video. "Everything falls into place with this guy." Reed pointed to Xanadu. "What private airstrips are around here?"

"Hold on," Nat said. "What about SEATAC? The public airport is not far."

"Not with his cargo. Money, weapons, possibly multiple passports," Reed said. "He needs a place with little to no security, privacy, somewhere with storage, maybe? Do they do that? Private airports?"

"You think he's hiding the weapons there?" Nat asked. "That's a big risk."

"No, no. Private airport security is as safe as banks," Reed said. "Think about how rich people travel. What they bring with them. And he would want his stash close to his escape route."

Xanadu got back on his computer. "Looks like one private airstrip, Exeter Aviation, offers storage. It's that new one over by the horse track and the old golf course out there by I-5. Exeter is the only airport that is a separate strip and not part of SEATAC so there wouldn't be like, TSA or anything." He pointed to his screen. "And the other place offering storage is a tourist place that offers sea plane rides to the islands. Scarver Sky Harbor. It's over in South Lake Union. Both offer storage with a sterling travel account."

"Wait, hold on," Nat said and scrolled through her tablet. "Sylvia had something about airports in her data lens files. "Let's see . . . travel, flight plans, hotels . . ."

"That's it! Flight plans," Reed said. "Where were they submitted?"

"Uh, here it is. Danzig and High Rock Holdings submitted flight plans at Exeter Aviation. And according to Sylvia's information, his whole family has use of the jets and secure storage."

"What nerve, though," Xanadu mused. "Right under Danzig's nose?"

"Danzig didn't even know his own son-in-law was gunning for him, let alone that he'd stolen a weapon to do it," Reed said. "He wouldn't be looking for danger that close. You should have seen his face when I told him how Visage . . . Nicholas spoke. He turned pale."

"Danzig's got to be looking for him now, though," Xanadu said. "Wouldn't he lay low?"

Reed paced the area by the VR bases, thinking. "By now Nicholas must know that neither Danzig nor I died in the explosion. But he doesn't know if we're hurt or what I told Danzig. The news said evidence of gunfire. Nicholas can't know I spoke to Danzig for any length of time. He may think Danzig doesn't know anything yet and there's time to leave, if he does it now."

"He's got to expect that Danzig is watching his accounts. So, using an existing point of access to jet travel is easier than risking giving out your location via a bank transaction or trying to pay for a jet with cash," Nat said. "You think he'd risk it?"

"I would. It's the only sure way out of here." Reed checked his watch.

"Even if he's not there, the private airport is only twenty minutes away." Xanadu shrugged. "What else are you doing?"

"I like how you think," Reed said as he headed out. To Nat, he asked, "Did Sylvia have tail numbers?"

She limped into his path, stopping him. "Nuh-uh. You can't go out there, everyone and their mothers are looking for you."

"Nicholas has access to unchecked flight out of the country. He has the money he stole from Sylvia and Helene, likely multiple passports if he kept to his spy craft, and a valuable weapon for sale. He might already be gone."

"You don't know that," Nat shot back. "We're essentially guessing."

"The best plan is to move. Get out of Danzig's reach. Nicholas can't hide in a city where Danzig has eyes and loyalists everywhere. And there's likely a price on his head. A guy like him would know that." Reed tried to walk around her, but she blocked him again.

"Hold your hand out," Nat demanded.

"I don't shoot with that one," Reed said and crossed his arms. "I'm left-handed."

She squinted her eyes at him. "Do you hear yourself or is it just dolphin squeaks in there?"

"He's *not* getting away, Nat," Reed shot back. "Not if I can help it."

She shook her head, frustration and fear on her face. "You can't keep doing this."

"I'm trying to stop this all for good!"

"Maybe he's already dead," Xanadu piped up.

They both looked at him.

"If he is, great," Reed said. "I'm going to go and make sure."

"Wait, shouldn't we call the FBI?" Xanadu asked.

"Yes. Do that. Tell them there's a terrorist trying to escape with a weapon and give them the address of the airport." Reed looked down at Nat.

She stood in front of him, arms crossed, face furious. "You're suspended. There's a manhunt for you. What do think is going to happen when everyone pulls up at the airport? You think they're going to thank you and let you go? How're you going to prove your innocence if you add hunting down billionaires to your resume?" Her voice broke. "You're not thinking."

"Nat, call Tig," Reed said, and he maneuvered her out of his way by her shoulders. "Tell him everything. Give him everything."

Nat grasped his jacket. "Don't—"

"I need you to have my back," He reached into his coat, pulled out the burner Coyote had given him, and held it up. "Be my eyes and ears. Help me stop him."

She sighed heavily but nodded. "Don't start a war or anything."

Reed walked backward toward the dark of the decrepit mall, his arms out, an innocent grin on his face. "Don't worry. I'm only going to distract him until the cavalry comes."

34

Parker

Parker's phone buzzed and he reached for it while trying to juggle his breakfast sandwich and paper pocket of hashbrown nuggets in the front seat. He'd just taken his first bite when the call came.

"Parker here."

"He's moving, he's moving!" She sounded frantic, out of breath. "You have to get there first. You have to catch him!"

The frenzy in her voice made him sit up too fast and he dumped his nuggets onto the pedals. "Who? What are you talking about?"

"Detective Reed. Trixie in dispatch said Detective De La Cruz just called in something going down at a private airport. They're sending units."

"What's going on?" Parker checked his radio. It was on. "I haven't heard anything."

"Does it matter? You're the head of the task force. It *has* to be you who arrests him. Otherwise, he'll get away with everything again!"

"Where?" Parker tossed his sandwich on the passenger seat and started the car. He pulled out of the strip mall parking lot. "What's the address?"

35

Exeter Aviation
Seattle

A steel gray sky loomed over the landscape and the muted sun struggled to cast its wan light through the gathering clouds. The air was crisp and dry, and Reed thought he felt snow in his bones as he pulled off the road. Exeter Aviation was off I-5 as Xanadu had said. Reed could smell the horse manure from the racetrack a half a mile down as he rode into the parking lot. The streetside of the building was all glass and would pass for a car dealership if you ignored the giant yellow plane logo over the doors. He chose a place around the side of the building where he could see the tarmac, taxiing road, and airstrip. Beyond that, a grove of trees at the edge of the property blocked out noise for the businesses and manufacturing shops on the other side.

The parking lot itself had a few cars. Reed pulled off his helmet and touched the earpiece connected with his burner phone. "Can you hear me?"

"I have you," Nat said. "I'm at the station. Tig found out about my ankle and told me to stand down. I'm stuck at my desk, but I've got audio and I'm pulling up a map of the place."

"That's perfect." Reed glanced at the airport facilities. "I've got a couple buildings off to the side of the main airport. Is that what I'm looking for?"

"Yeah. The smaller building should be secure storage," she said. "There's a guard just inside the airport building. The website gallery also shows a reception counter, that's it."

Reed looked in the windows as he walked up. The lights seemed low, possibly out. He pushed up his T-shirt and rested his palm on his hip holster. As he reached for the door, a distinct popping sound crackled overhead as a Kraken broke the sound barrier just above the roof. Reed ducked against the wall, his gaze to the sky. It soared away from the building, lights flashing as it began a slow arc.

Reed popped up, swung open the door, and ran inside, looking for cover. "Nat someone set off a Kraken! It's coming from behind the building."

"Oh, no, ok . . . that's the tarmac, the runway."

A security desk sat along the left wall and Reed ran over. He leaned across the counter and caught sight of the security guard. White shirt marred with a single bullet hole to the chest. Reed pulled his weapon and slid around the counter to see. The guard was old, and his rheumy gray eyes stared blankly up at the ceiling, gray hair splattered with red. Reed knelt, felt for a pulse. None. The guard's gun and radio still sat in their belt holsters around his waist. He hadn't had time to react. Across the lobby, the feet of a woman stuck out from behind the ticket counter. One of her pumps was still by the door. The Kraken shrieked back over the roof, returning for a kill.

"Nat, I have multiple gunshot victims—" an explosion rocked the small building shattering the windows in the rear wall. Reed hunched on the ground and a blast of wind blew debris and glass, slicing at his hands. Then everything went quiet, muffled. Alarms blared as if underwater and the fire system engaged. Fire suppressant sprayed down from the ceiling and the flash of the emergency lights lit up the room like lightning. He shook his head, his ears ringing from the blast.

"Buses . . . rolling . . . get out of there," Nat's words cut in and out.

The foam was like Christmas flocking, creating a blizzard of white powder as he ran toward the back door to the tarmac. He clicked his earpiece on and off, trying to hear.

"I don't know if you're getting this," Reed said, stumbling in the broken glass. "I'm okay. I'm going out back to the planes to see if there are any injuries. I think the blast came from there."

He passed a waiting lounge, some tables and chairs surrounding a little coffee kiosk, and a little shop with travel sundries. Reed pressed himself against a far wall near the glass doors. The sound of the klaxon reverberated off the walls of the small lobby. He peered out of the jagged windows. Rows of planes sat parked in the distance, the closest two on fire from the explosion. An autonomous fueling truck, also on fire, made lazy donuts in the nearby grass. A jet parked a few dozen yards away seemed untouched. Reed looked around for victims. But saw no one. With the alarm blaring, he should see people.

Reed crept out the back door of the airport, hugging the wall, weapon held at his chest as he searched for survivors. He walked up on a woman's prone body down a small gap between the buildings. Middle aged, a redhead. She still had valentine stickers on her nametag. Gina. She also hadn't made it.

Reed depressed the ear com. "I've got another victim, deceased out back. I'm heading for the storage building. I see it from here."

Nothing came back. Reed snuck down the length of the airport building, dropping white powder as he went, the fire suppressant itchy on his skin. He moved toward the smaller structure that angled away from the street. The security door sat ajar. Inside, it was long and narrow, and he checked all the aisles of lockers. No one was there. A few of the lockers in front appeared pried at the corners. Papers, coins, and loose bills peppered the cement floor of the narrow walkway. Reed bent to pick one up. A gold Krugerrand. Run money. On the floor, by the leg of a bench, he found blood.

A volley of gunfire boomed outside followed by return fire. Reed ducked, shouting and hoping the earpiece worked. "Shots fired at my location. Be advised active shooter at the rear of the Exeter Airport, back door facing the runway."

He checked the door and looked out. The fire had spread and the black smoke blocked visibility. Chancing it, he slipped from the storage building and ran along the retaining wall to a cement platform holding stacks of supply crates. Someone was dragging themselves across the walkway a few feet away. Reed did a quick visual sweep and then ran for the victim. When he saw who it was, Reed cursed under his breath, grabbed him by the shirt, and dragged him behind the crates.

"What are you doing here?" Reed said to a bloodied Parker as he propped him up. A wound on his right thigh bled through his pants. Not a lot, but enough to worry. "You can't blame me for this one."

Parker laughed, but then hissed with pain as he righted himself against the crates. "I was checking out the storage locker and heard yelling over by that jet. Danzig and some other guy were fighting. Danzig called him Nicholas."

"That's Visage."

"That's him?" Parker blinked with surprise.

"He's Danzig's son-in-law. What were they doing?"

"They were shouting about the Kraken and then one of them pulled a gun. I think I caught a ricochet off that water tank."

"You were stupid to come alone," Reed said.

A tinny voice came from Parker's shirt pocket. "*Is he there? Ben?*"

Reed ground his jaw and grabbed for the phone. "Who are you working with, Parker?"

"Give me that." Parker reached for his phone, but Reed batted his arm away.

"Who is this?" Reed snapped.

"Ben?" the woman cried. "Ben are you okay?"

"That's my wife," Parker said. "She works at the main office. She told me about your call, and I was close, so I got here first, I guess. I was looking for you when I heard the argument."

Reed spotted the tiny camera on Parker's tie clip and yanked it off, holding it up between them. "You're plotting against me with your wife? This isn't the Office of Professional Conduct or Danzig?"

"No! I'm . . . I was trying to do the right thing, ok?" Parker said, defensive. "I didn't know you were telling the truth. What would you think if I told you the guy who invented my phone and my car tried to kill me? I mean, it's Everett Danzig. I thought you were nuts. And then people seem to die around you."

"Yeah, but it's not me killing them!" Reed shook his head. "Do you have your radio?"

"No, I lost it in the blast."

"Where did you see them last?"

"In the hangar." Parker looked at him askance. "Why are you covered in foam?"

Reed ignored the question. "Stay here." He turned to leave, but Parker caught his sleeve.

"He confessed. I got it on the camera. Visage – Nicholas, whatever . . . said he killed Kaspar and Sylvia. He laughed about it."

"Yeah, well," Reed said as he got ready to run for it. "Not for long."

He used the smoke to hide his movement as he flitted from cover to cover toward the hangar. A bank of trash receptacles, stacks of plastic containers, coiled up hoses.

"Nat, can you hear me?" Reed tried. "Officer down. Detective Parker."

Angry voices echoed from inside. The scent of jet fuel and grease hit Reed and then he saw him. Amid a floor strewn with clothes and other travel debris, Danzig lurched toward the far exit of the hangar. It led to the runway where a private jet sat with its hatch up and ladder down. Another figure ran toward it, also struggling to move. Reed ran in, gun drawn.

"Freeze!"

Danzig stopped and then turned, slowly, the gun in his hand. Blood dripped down the length of his cashmere sweater from a gunshot wound to the left flank. He snarled when he spotted Reed. "I told you to stay out of my way!"

"Drop the gun." Reed strode forward, his weapon trained on Danzig's chest.

"He dies at my hand or there will be others," Danzig panted.

Reed shook his head. "Now, Danzig."

"He has Kraken rounds," Danzig wobbled on his feet. "How? Who could make these?"

Reed moved in. "Oh, yeah, Sylvia sends her regards. They're hers."

"That woman," Danzig muttered, to Reed. "He killed my son."

"I'll stop him."

Danzig shook his head. "He's better than you."

"And yet, who's running scared?" Out of the corner of his eye, Nicholas staggered toward the awaiting jet thirty yards away. He carried a fortified case in his hands that was slowing him down. The Kraken rounds. Nicholas started to climb the steps but slipped. "The gun or I shoot," Reed snapped.

"I don't have time for this—" Danzig's gun came up and Reed fired.

The sound was like a thunderclap and Danzig spun, the round hitting him in the shoulder as his weapon clattered. He fell to the ground, grunting with pain. Reed ran past him, grabbing the gun from the ground as he went. He sprinted for the jet, racing to get to the plane as Nicholas fought with the collapsible stairs with his injured arm. Reed got to him and yanked the case from his grasp. He threw it to the ground. Nicholas shouted and kicked him in the chest, sending Reed flying backward off the steps.

Reed hit the cement with a jarring thud, knocking the wind out of him. Overhead, another scream of air and then the pop of the sound barrier as a Kraken shrieked past the jet.

Nicholas reached for the hatch again, trying to pull it up. His gaze locked with Reed and hatred swept across his features. "I should have killed you when I had the chance!"

"You really should have," Reed yelled and leaped for the top of the door. His fingers caught the lip, and he grabbed hold. His body weight pulled the stairs back down and he swung his legs, yanking it open. He clambered up the steps knocking the gun out of Nicholas's hands as they tumbled in a knot back into the cabin of the jet.

"Call off the Kraken!" Reed shouted, shaking the man by his bloodied shirt.

Nicholas broke free and his eyes widened as he rose. Green flashes sliced into the cabin windows. "What?"

"Abort the missile!" Reed yelled, scrambling to his feet between the leather seats.

"I don't have it. Danzig took—" The micro missile soared into the open hatch and slammed into Nicholas. He flew against the bulkhead, and gasped, his mouth opening, eyes desperate as he reached for Reed. "No!"

Reed kicked him in the chest, toppling him into the cockpit, then turned, and ran down the length of the jet. Windows flashed by showing Danzig standing at the mouth of the hangar, the Kraken headset and gun in his hand.

The tail. Get to the tail. The wings have fuel. The body has fuel, Reed's thoughts raced as he sprinted, diving for the galley in the rear of the plane. He ducked behind the metal ovens. One breath. Two.

The explosion hurtled through the plane like a cannon blast. The suppressant on Reed's skin sizzled as the shockwave rocked the jet's nose sideways. The screech of tearing metal roared overhead. Another blast slammed into the side of the fuselage taking the wing with it, spewing fire as it spun. The explosion sent the jet careening over, rolling as Reed tumbled inside. The wall, the ceiling, plates, bottles, and other containers whirled around with him as they toppled. He rammed against the other wall and then everything jolted to a stop.

Reed groaned, and he coughed, his breath knocked out of him. Dirt filled his mouth for some reason. The plane was on its side and Reed stood on the windows trying to catch his breath. He climbed over the seat, pulling his way down the aisle. The front of the jet had broken off and firelight from outside licked through the smoke.

Reed found his way back outside, coughing and retching. His whole body hurt. The plane had rolled onto a grassy area off the tarmac, and he wandered the wreckage, dazed. Scattered fires cast warmth on the desolate scene. Emergency aid robots rolled around the rubble spurting fire retardant foam at the flames. Medic bots scanned the debris for life signs. One came up to Reed, but he pushed it away. Another few rattled along the cement in his direction. He thought he heard gunfire near the hangar, but the smoke obscured the view.

He didn't know how long he walked around. Thoughts muddled, he waded through money, hundreds of loose bills. They blew in the breeze, catching on his shin. Documents, passports, and other items in Nicholas's getaway stash lay strewn around. Singed, and burning pieces of paper floated past Reed as he looked for the Kraken rounds. He found the fortified case on the tarmac and knelt down to open it. The explosion had damaged the lock, but all four that remained sat nestled in the foam, unscathed. As for Nicholas or Visage or whatever else he called himself, if there was any of him left, Reed didn't find it. He did find an odd bag, velvet. It was heavy when he picked it up.

"Freeze!" Parker yelled, his gun up as he half walked half hopped toward Reed.

"Really, man?" Reed slipped the bag into a pocket of his cargo pants before he turned. "You can't think of *anyone* else here you want to arrest more? Where's Danzig? He just blew up a plane with two people in it."

"You look horrible." Parker glanced at the wreckage and his gun hand wavered. "Were you in that thing?"

"He got away, didn't he?" Reed's eye stung and he touched his forehead and came away with blood. His head pounded, but his hearing was getting better. "How?"

"Some mean looking woman and a couple of armed guards pulled into the hangar with machine guns, dragged Danzig out, and took off with him. *Machine guns.* I don't think ten of us would have had enough bullets. I tried but . . ." He gestured around with confusion. "What the hell is going on?"

Reed put his hands to his temple. "Must've been Aria."

"Who?"

"Danzig's daughter." Reed shook his head. "I guess she didn't know either." He handed Parker the case with the Kraken rounds. "Four left."

"I can't believe how close we came to losing this weapon."

"Danzig has the headset."

Parker reached into his jacket pocket and pulled out what was left of the headset. "They ran it over in their rush to grab Danzig."

Reed looked across the street past the field. Patrol lights flashed in the gloom and the sound of sirens floated to him on the icy wind.

"What are you so glum about, man?" Parker asked, following his gaze. "You stopped him. It's over."

Reed let out a breath. "It's never over."

"I have Nicholas's confession on video," Parker said and motioned for Reed. "Come on, you need to get looked at by the paramedics."

"You know I can't do that," Reed said. The sirens, closer now, echoed along the metal buildings. "If you believe me now, then you know everything I said about Danzig is true. Something is in motion. I can't stop."

"You're just so—" Parker licked his lips, then looked back at the airport building. The smoke and fire whorled over the landscape like a battlefield. "You know, it's a shame. I looked for you after the explosion, but you'd disappeared. I think in the confusion, I lost track of you."

"What are you doing?"

"I'm stopping a madman," Parker said and grinned. "By sending one of our own."

"Parker—"

"Get out of here, Reed," Parker said as he turned and limped back to the airport. "Before I change my mind."

A few minutes later, while Parker directed everyone into the warehouse and personnel scurried around shutting the crime scene down, Reed slipped down a dark, back road thinking about fate and fire and how quickly it had all gone down in flames.

36

In the following days, Reed moved from Coyote's place to the control room at the abandoned mall, laying low and trying to figure out his next move. He had no home. Everything he owned had burned to ash. Tig suspended him pending a disciplinary review, though given the choices he'd made, Reed wasn't holding his breath. Nat was cleared, but they transferred her to Organized Crime to work with Parker's new task force there. Temporarily, Tig promised.

Danzig's sister, Helene, surfaced in Switzerland a few days after the incident. She had self-committed to a long-term wellness program and was unavailable. Her lawyers wasted no time in distancing her from the "so-called coup" perpetrated by her, Sylvia, and Nicholas to overthrow her brother. The newly appointed district attorney issued a statement linking Nicholas and Dontae's death to a drug deal gone wrong. To add mud to the water, Danzig's camp spoke on Aria's behalf detailing her husband, Nicholas's, years-long battle with substance abuse stemming from a facial injury he sustained while serving his country. Her decision, after many years of counseling with him, to end their marriage is what pushed him over the edge. They claimed he destroyed the jet in anger and the fire got away from him. He was buried with a closed casket and interred at the Danzig family crypt.

"I'm almost impressed," Nat said, swiping away the story. They sat out in the rotunda of the abandoned mall on the edge of what used to be a reflecting pool. She'd brought gyros and warm cookies from his favorite Greek place, and they ate under the skylight. "Danzig might end up smelling like roses."

"They always do," Reed said and pushed his cookie toward her.

She took it, brought it to her mouth, and frowned. Her dark eyes searched his. "You can stay and fight. Get your job back . . ."

"Even if I'm cleared, and that's a big, 'if,' I will never be a cop again. We both know that," Reed said. "And maybe I should have left after Caitlyn. Maybe you and Dontae and Coyote wouldn't have been in the crosshairs if I'd been gone."

"And maybe we would've died if you *hadn't* been here," she argued, but her heart wasn't in it. She knew he was right. Her shoulders slumped. "This can't be our last meal."

Reed grinned. "It's not. We'll keep in touch. How will I make it out there without my digital warrior?"

"That's goddess," Nat said and forced a smile. "Where will you go?"

"To the beginning," Reed said.

Coyote met Reed on the way out of town. He was smoking near the giant ferns under the bridge where Taza had picked him up. Reed tried to give him the loaner bike back, but Coyote wouldn't have it.

"Meh, you look better on it than I do," Coyote said. "Besides, I got me another."

"How is Fleur?"

"She's better now that you sent her that bag." Coyote flicked his cigarette into the plants. "You're square with Marcel, the Kindred, and his mama. She said you found out who killed her son, and the guy is dead. Case closed. The gold didn't hurt either."

"I was hoping," Reed said. He'd sent along the velvet bag of Nicholas's Krugerrands with a note. *Take Dontae home.*

"I'm a phone call away, brother," Coyote had said, and Reed believed him.

Months later, on a brisk September morning, with the sun barely rising behind him, Reed rode into the parking lot of the motel. The facility was old, utilitarian, with a row of seven motel rooms facing the interstate. Reed parked in the small lot and walked to the office. The neon "open" sign over the door halfway worked, flickering in the window. Blue-green pine trees let off their scent as a slight breeze ruffled the beard Reed had grown during his months on the road.

A young man at the reception desk sat up straighter and adjusted his vest as he watched Reed through the glass door. He pasted on a friendly smile and nodded. "Good morning, what brings you to the Aurora Gables Inn?"

"Just visiting. I'm looking for . . . a friend I believe lives out this way."

The clerk was white, young, and well-groomed, with a trendy haircut that fell in a wave over one eye. "Well, I hope you catch up with him." He slid a brochure across the counter to Reed. "If not, there's plenty to do here this time of year. The northern lights might make an appearance. September through April is the best time to see them and you're right on schedule."

"I'm not here for the lights," Reed said, but took the brochure. He placed a credit card with a fake name on the counter. "Extended stay."

"I'll bet if you told me your interests, I'd be able to help," Jake said with a smile.

Reed glanced out at the horizon. The golden light flickered through the dense trees. He'd been to several towns just like this all over the US since he left Seattle but this one, he was convinced, was the one.

He gathered his things and turned for the door before answering the kid. "I'm here to hunt."

AURORA FRAGMENT
A MEMORY BANK THRILLER
by Brian Shea and Raquel Byrnes

Plagued by the intrusive memories of a dead killer, Detective Morgan
Reed is drawn to a remote and troubled Alaskan town.

Fixated on his relentless hunt for Danzig and guided by the fragmented
memories of another, Reed is compelled to the mysterious town of Aurora,
Alaska. His search intersects with the case of Hazel Hill, a missing intern
from the local paper, who vanished while investigating her best friend's
suspicious death. Caught trespassing by the local sheriff, Reed is coerced
into a deal: help the sheriff solve Hazel's disappearance...or face charges for
breaking and entering.

Joining forces once again with Detective Natalie De La Cruz, Reed's case
sweeps them across a landscape shrouded in snow and secrets. Aurora,
with its cursed history and sudden prosperity from Aurora hybrid apples,
holds more than meets the eye. Relentlessly pursuing the town's closely
held secrets, Reed and De La Cruz encounter the covert operations of the
Malum Genetix facility under the aegis of the Rexford dynasty, and the
spectral tale of the Sirak, a legend as mysterious as Aurora itself.

Their quest for justice uncovers a deep vein of deceit, linking Hazel's tena-
cious reporting, a recent rash of unexplained fatalities, and the insidious
spread of corporate avarice that threatens to tear the town apart.

In *Aurora Fragment*, the riveting third installment in The Memory Bank
series, Brian Shea and Raquel Byrnes masterfully combine near-future
tech with ancient mythology to create a techno-thriller where memories
fragment, realities blur, and the truth is as elusive as the aurora itself.

Get your copy today at
severnriverbooks.com

ABOUT BRIAN SHEA

Brian Shea has spent most of his adult life in service to his country and local community. He honorably served as an officer in the U.S. Navy. In his civilian life, he reached the rank of Detective and accrued over eleven years of law enforcement experience between Texas and Connecticut. Somewhere in the mix he spent five years as a fifth-grade school teacher. Brian's myriad of life experience is woven into the tapestry of each character's design. He resides in New England and is blessed with an amazing wife and three beautiful daughters.

Sign up for the reader list at
severnriverbooks.com

ABOUT RAQUEL BYRNES

Raquel is the author of critically acclaimed suspense series, The Shades of Hope trilogy, Gothic duology, The Noble Island Mysteries, and epic Sci-Fi Steampunk series, The Blackburn Chronicles. She strives to bring intelligent characters with diverse backgrounds to the forefront of her stories.

When she's not writing, she can be seen geeking out over sci-fi movies, reading anything she can get her hands on, and having arguments about the television series Firefly in coffee shops. She lives in Southern California with her husband, six kids, and beloved Huskies.

Sign up for the reader list at
severnriverbooks.com

Printed in the United States
by Baker & Taylor Publisher Services